D0970424

DEO

Deon, Michel.

Where are you dying
tonight?

C1

DATE

DISCARDED

© THE BAKER & TAYLOR CO.

WHERE ARE YOU DYING TONIGHT?

WHERE ARE YOU DYING TONIGHT?

~~~

MICHEL DÉON

~~~

Translated from the French
by Julian Evans

THE ATLANTIC MONTHLY PRESS
NEW YORK

♦

The translator gratefully acknowledges the invaluable help of Lisa
Evans and Hannah Longrigg in preparing the manuscript.

First published in 1981 in France as *Un déjeuner de soleil*.
Published in Great Britain in 1983 by Hamish Hamilton Ltd.

First Atlantic Monthly Press edition, July 1989

Library of Congress Cataloging-in-Publication Data

Déon, Michel.
  [Déjeuner de soleil. English]
  Where are you dying tonight? / Michel Déon ; translated from the
French by Julian Evans.
  Translation of: Un déjeuner de soleil.
  ISBN 0-87113-321-0
  I. Title.
PQ2607.E525D3513   1989   843'.914—dc 19   89-119

Printed in the United States of America

The Atlantic Monthly Press
19 Union Square West
New York, NY 10003

First printing

WHERE ARE YOU DYING TONIGHT ?

His first appearance dates back to 1925, in the fourth form at Janson-de-Sailly. One morning in February the master on duty came in followed by a tall boy who looked about sixteen or seventeen, with blond hair falling onto his shoulders like a young girl's and blue eyes enjoying the curiosity aroused by his dress: bare feet in rope sandals, brown corduroy trousers, motley woollen shirt and tight-fitting waistcoat in reversed sheepskin. I remind the reader that this is 1925 and that this mode of dress, which today is so common because it has been universally adopted by the chain stores, would have created a stir at the time; it certainly seemed singularly unsuitable for the clientèle of a rather snobbish *lycée*, children of middle-class families who had made money from the war and young Russian émigrés whose fathers, all colonels and princes, had been re-cast as cab-drivers in Passy or fiddle-players in the night-clubs of Montmartre.

The master on duty exchanged a few murmured words with the French master and pointed out a seat at the back of the class. For thanks the boy nodded his head. He had no exercise book, no textbook, not even a penholder; he sat down quietly, his arms folded on the desk. The master took up his lesson where he had broken off. André Garrett, my father, who has related the story of Stanislas' entry in his diaries, remembered that the lesson was on *La Farce de Maître Pathelin* which the master read out in the gravelly accent he always used for old French. We found out the Christian name of the 'new boy' the next day, from the class register: Stanislas. But his patronymic, made up of paired consonants only just separated by a single vowel, remained unpronounceable. Faced with the protests of the masters who refused to wrestle with such a jaw-breaking name, the powers that be in the school decided to simplify these barbarous sounds by eliminating four consonants and adding a vowel, from which came Beren, Stanislas Beren, a style which the newcomer accepted without flinching and kept for the rest of his life.

A more model pupil would be hard to imagine: he was always on time, without an exercise book or textbook, his arms folded on his desk, a smile spreading across his rather solid features whenever the master regaled the class with a joke he had been trotting out for years. It was supposed that it was because of his total ignorance of French that he had been put in the fourth form, despite his height and his age. At the first break, his new classmates had surrounded him to try and draw a few words from him. In this mixed milieu, where many of the pupils had a second language – English or German or Russian or Spanish – Stanislas showed his incomprehension by an odd movement of his head, either raising his chin or simply his eyebrows. Now and again he would utter a short string of strange words in a sweet voice. When the masters were consulted, some recognized Greek roots, while others were adamant that they were dealing with a Slav dialect. Interest, lively to start with, soon faded. One single pupil endeavoured to keep some contact with this friendly boy who smiled easily. He was my father, André Garrett. In a class photo taken just before the end of the school year they can be seen, side by side, in the back row. They used to communicate by gestures and small gifts. The gifts – bars of chocolate, photographs of actresses – never came from Stanislas. Quite obviously his parents, if he had any, never gave him a single penny in pocket money. He used to come on foot from some unknown *quartier* of the sixteenth arrondissement, always wearing the same rope sandals. If it was raining, he would come across the rue de la Pompe bare-footed, his sandals tied around his neck by their laces. He seemed to possess only one pair of trousers, one shirt and his sheepskin waistcoat. In a *lycée* with fairly strict discipline, where the pupils were punctilious on points of dress, he was strangely at variance; but an invisible authority protected him. One day a new junior master who was supervising the pupils at the rue de Longchamp entrance saw him arriving barefoot. He seized him by the arm to stop him coming in and was on the point of throwing him out into the street when some of the boys intervened:

'Sir, it's Stanislas Beren. He's in 4A.'

Stanislas made no protest and stood outside the door, looking indifferent. My father ran to fetch the master on duty who arrived in person to tell the over-zealous junior master that this boy was indeed a *lycée* pupil.

'A special pupil, I grant you. He is here to learn French.'

The new master, trying to make amends, brought Stanislas in with a pat on the back. Once he was under cover of the quad, he put on his sandals and joined the line of boys waiting for the English master to arrive. There must have been an order given that none of the masters was to question him. They were to content themselves with the fact that this polite boy who said nothing was paying attention. In June there were the yearly examinations, at least for those who had not reached the required standard. Stanislas, of course, was exempted. He appeared to have made no progress in French, although he could answer yes or no, and knew how to say hello and goodbye, occasionally thank you. What was going to happen to him during the holiday? My father unburdened himself to his father, who went to the *lycée* where he had a long conversation with the master. The secret was well-guarded; but the result was that, on the thirteenth of July, Stanislas arrived at avenue Mozart shortly before the family's departure, which had been set for that afternoon to avoid the congestion on the roads. André's mother had a slight crisis at this point. Generous in a rather old-fashioned way, she liked to take an interest in the private lives of her servants, occasionally to take an immigrant family under her wing or to assist in the works of a ladies' committee at the Church of the Annunciation. The apparition of this unkempt beggar with his long, girlish hair, his awkward features, his clothes which she immediately condemned as clownish, discomposed her so much that she could barely manage to smile at him. On the instant, she decided to change it all: his hair, his clothes, his caked fingernails.

Let me reassure the reader: this is not to be just one more story of a bourgeois family – my family – which I intend to recount here, but that of Stanislas Beren and, for his part in it, that of my father, who was his first and possibly sole friend. With one or two exceptions, my grandparents' only appearance will be in the story of that summer. I hardly knew my grandfather, because he died in 1939, at the beginning of the war, when he was seventy years old and I was not quite four. One image of him has remained with me by one of those tricks of memory which, without any apparent reason, records a silhouette or a scene, isolated from their vanished context. I see him again forty years later – I have no idea what time of year, or what time of day, the morning probably – in vest and long woollen pants, a thick, rolled-up towel around his neck: red in the face, his beard dripping with sweat. The scene has engraved itself on my memory by its absurdity. In fact my grandfather used to cycle in a bathroom with white tiled walls but, for a child, there was a kind of madness in his exercising. Where did he think he was going on a bicycle with no wheels? Six months later, he died of a cerebral haemorrhage on learning that war had been declared. In the Museum of Modern Art at Beaubourg there is a full-length portrait of him by Kees van Dongen, against the background of a racecourse (either Longchamp or Deauville). In the photos I have kept, he appears in many different guises: in his pink coat for a stag-hunt in the forest at Compiègne, in a bathing costume with shoulder-straps on the beach at Deauville, as a racing driver aboard a 1907 Christie V4, as a pilot in a 1912 Farman, and lastly seated next to his chauffeur in a forty-horsepower Renault coupé, the same one which, fresh from the factory, took Stanislas and my father on holiday in the summer of 1925. It is not difficult to guess that he was a true enthusiast of new inventions and things mechanical – which perhaps explains the violence with which his son, my father, reacted against them and why, until the war of 1939, he always went about Paris by bicycle, never boarded an aeroplane, only took trains with the greatest reluctance, and always refused to have motors on the succession of sailing-boats which were his sole sporting aspiration.

My grandfather was what is commonly known as a tycoon, with fingers in many pies. He liked to buy up failing companies and factories on the point of bankruptcy (after minutely detailed inquiries), put them back on their feet with the help of avant-garde methods and brand new processes, and then re-sell them. In the interests of truth it must be said that not every inspired idea was blessed with success. He passed through many crises and ended up more or less ruined, first by the depression of 1930, and then by the Popular Front in 1936 and the war in 1939 just as he was about to launch an 'organized tours' travel agency, a new idea which was to be developed on a large scale twenty years later. One cannot be an innovator with impunity. He would certainly have been astonished if anyone had predicted that the only business of his which would survive the vicissitudes of a period as calamitous as it was flourishing would be the publishing house he had bought from a fellow Oratorian, Jérôme Quintin: a house specializing in poetry, Editions Saeta. In 1930, crushed by debts, abandoned by his wife, and seeing the threat of prison looming large, Quintin made the rounds of his friends and very quickly gauged how little interest his beloved authors aroused in the circles in which he had been brought up. By one of those contradictions with which he was familiar in himself, and also out of natural generosity, my grandfather (whose knowledge of poetry did not go beyond Sully Prudhomme, André Theuriet or *Le monologue des bouffons* by Miguel Zamacoïs) opened his wallet, paid the debts, gave the defenceless dreamer Quintin a roof over his head for the six months he had left to live . . . and put the key under the mat at Editions Saeta, little imagining that by doing so he was preparing the futures of his son André, of Stanislas Beren, and of myself.

I suppose that the personality of Stanislas Beren interested my grandfather in much the same way as a business facing ruin: in five months Stanislas seemed to have learnt only ten words of French and had stayed exactly the same as he was at the time of his somewhat outlandish arrival in the fourth form. My grandmother immediately christened him 'the Danube peasant', an ethnic approximation which subsequently turned out to be quite false.

The forty-horsepower Renault – whose star soon faded, for, after 1927, my grandfather became passionately keen on the front-wheel drive cars engineered by Grégoire and bought a Tracta and a Cord which he kept until 1939, when my father, at the front, sold them for a song to finance his purchase of the complete works of Samuel Bernstein in the edition which came out in June 1940 and was immediately pulped because it was on the German blacklist; but who still remembers the lugubrious prosifying of Samuel Bernstein, whereas Tractas and Cords have found places in automobile museums and inspired all the cars of the future – the forty-horsepower Renault, I was saying, took them off to Deauville, to the family property which today has disappeared, carved up and sold off by the developers. My grandmother feared the sun as much as the rain and lived confined to the drawing-room or her bedroom, while her husband showed himself off on the beach, at the turf or around the green baize of the casino. Yet of course one could not have imagined a more faithful and devoted couple.

It was in this summer of 1925 that my grandfather must be credited with one of his best hunches, and his best investment. Hardly had he arrived at Deauville than Stanislas began to speak, not just a few words, but an excellent French, albeit still a little slow.

'It's the Normandy air!' asserted my grandmother.

Whatever it was, it was certainly surprising. In two or three months, without taking a single note, without giving anyone the slightest clue, he had learnt French and could speak it almost without accent. The only sign that might have made one suspect he was foreign, and the thing which differentiated him from his classmates, came from a slight affectation, a hint of over-refinement. He talked like his literature master. All through his life, Stanislas recoiled from common abbreviations: always took the 'underground railway', went to a 'moving picture', drove in an 'automobile' and dictated his letters

9

to a 'stenographer'. Later, in the eyes of the critics, his work sometimes suffered from this affectation, which was first of all involuntary, then quite definitely intentional and even cultivated; but this is to anticipate: in 1925, Stanislas Beren's work does not exist. There is only a tall, skinny boy; his hair is too long, his awkward features have an underfed look, and his clothes are threadbare and quite unsuitable for a walk on the *planches* at Deauville in the company of his friend André Garrett.

My grandmother remedied all this. However little I have said about her until now, I reproach myself for having perhaps ridiculed her unjustly. She was not ridiculous, but because of a moral rigour and a deeply-felt reaction against the brilliant and dissipated life of her sister Félicité, she bent her character to the rules of an outdated era, refusing to see that the first world war had ruined the conventions, the ideas, the relations between human beings, a way of living and even a way of thinking which had been hers before the great upheaval. The name of Félicité is out. The reader will find it recurring again and again in this book. Félicité was fifteen years younger than her sister – my grandmother – who had brought her up; that is to say that in 1925 she was thirty years old, had been widowed three times and was now living with a dadaist. My grandmother loved her too much to judge her; besides, she had brought up this much younger sister as her own child, with all the spoils of indulgence, and she preferred to reproach herself for being unable to inspire her with any principles. Was it for this reason that she was so uncompromising with my father, her only son? Was this why – in vain – she wrapped him in a cocoon and only let him out with the greatest caution, trying to inspire in him a dread of bad weather and – so much did she fear extremes of heat and cold above all else – to inculcate in him the habit of wearing long underpants and knitted vests? Yet she did not end up demoralized by her total failure. Once he had taken his *baccalauréat* (at the same time as Stanislas), my father burned his woollen underwear, bought himself a Star which he anchored at Cap-Ferrat and went down to as often as he could to go sailing on his own, and apart from the Midi reserved his affections entirely for Paris. The day that he shook himself free of her burdensome guardianship, grandmother Garrett simply sighed resignedly, as she had done at the news of each of Félicité's marriages. She had lost her sister and now she was losing her son. Having said that, she was a cultured woman who read endlessly and a musician who could have become a concert violinist had it not been for her family who held the opinion that the artist's life is the source of all vice. Despite her gentleness, however, she was occasionally inflexible. So, scarcely had she arrived at Deauville than she dragged Stanislas to the barber and made him have his hair cut short, then to the tailor where she ordered white flannel trousers, a blue blazer and, for the autumn, two English-cut tweed suits with gusseted pockets. Footwear was a more difficult matter. He detested shoes, would only wear rope sandals, and the only way she could overcome his loathing was to buy him shoes which were a size too big for him. This is very much in evidence in the photo taken that same year of Stanislas and my father at a tennis match they were watching: Stanislas, with a touch of ill grace, is sticking out an enormous foot. André, expecting a rebellion from his friend, was amazed to see him accept this external transformation with such relative willingness. To tell the truth, he was even disappointed by it for a short time, until he realized that Stanislas had conceived a boundless admiration for this woman who, before she was forty-five, was dressing like a woman of sixty and who, in the age of jazz and surrealism, of the first supercharged cars and Lindbergh's transatlantic flight, was living in the times of the comtesse de Ségur. And this admiration, which he retained for the rest of his life, is the key to the character of Anne de Beautremont in his first novel, *The Secret Life of an Orgasm*.[1] Several times Stanislas said to me, 'You will not know anything if you aren't born in the country, even if you don't stay there. You will not have any personality unless there has been the authority of a grandmother in the family, a strong and crushing authority which you learn to rebel against. All the other rebellions, afterwards, seem derisory.'

Up until then, the friendship of the two Janson boys had been founded on unspoken agreements. Speech transformed it. In reality Stanislas had learned French very quickly, thanks to the gift for languages which he subsequently developed, like a game, to amuse himself.

'Well then, why didn't you say anything to me?' asked André. 'Why didn't you join in the classes?'

'Because, my friend, I wanted to give myself a holiday. It's very pleasant to sit and listen to the music of the words. I enjoyed it infinitely. You've been hearing it since you were a child, so you've no idea of the secret grace, the almost invisible, inaudible grace of the French language. Its contours are soft, polished with use and the centuries. Even when a foreigner doesn't understand it – as I didn't at

[1] *La Vie secrète d'un orgasme*, Editions Saeta, 1932.

the beginning – he can quite easily imagine the sense of a sentence. And anyway, I liked watching you all in class, observing you, comparing you to the children I've known in my own country, giving you marks, imagining your parents and how you live in your families, everything which differentiated you from me.'

André – I shall stop calling him my father, which is a slightly absurd title for a man who, by dying on the twelfth of May 1940, has stayed younger than me – André kept a diary which I have in front of me: a dozen spiral-bound exercise books with yellow covers. He noted down everything with a schoolboy's meticulousness; but from that summer of 1925 onwards the diary changes in tone, as if to register a transition in his adolescent life, a prelude to his adult one. The majority of his conversations with Stanislas are reported in them. The notebooks are all the same type and when one counts the pages it becomes obvious that some of the pages – occasionally two or three, in others nearly half – have been torn out, as if André had wanted to erase what there was of himself in these notes and keep only the parts which concern Stanislas. Together with their correspondence which I have in my possession, and the first notes passed under their desks in the fifth and sixth form and the philosophy year, there is no more reliable source of information; and yet one finds virtually no clues to the origins of this peculiar boy who materialized one morning in 1925 at Janson, where the arrival of a Hottentot could not have created more of a stir. Despite the richness of the notebooks and the hundreds of letters, the reasons behind his coming to France remain a mystery. Stanislas and André have consistently left the question unanswered, feigning to disregard it, to consider it utterly unimportant from the moment when Stanislas, having adopted the French language, made it clear that he would adopt French citizenship too. One thing alone is certain: he had come with a Nansen passport. He was only naturalized in 1936.

We have to feel our way in this business of Stanislas' origins. He wanted there to be a mystery and he would have kept it that way if the first thesis which appeared on his work, in the United States,[1] had not claimed that Stanislas was the illegitimate son of Ferdinand of Saxe-Coburg, tsar of Bulgaria in 1908. I do not know where this tall story sprang from. It is possible that Stanislas himself was its author, amusing himself by weaving one of those mysteries which he would either simply forget, or be astonished when, later, people took them

---

[1] First published by the Hoover Foundation (1955); subsequently by Simon and Schuster (1957).

seriously. The author of the thesis, Charles B. Walker, had come to meet him on two occasions: once in Paris, then again in Venice in 1953 where they had conversed at length for almost a week. This so-called 'revelation' had annoyed Stanislas sufficiently for him to hark back to it in one of our conversations in 1960.

'The whole story is ridiculous. The Saxe-Coburgs supplied Europe with enough kings for us not to need to saddle them with natural children as well, and you'd have to be out of your mind to imagine that a Saxe-Coburg could give birth to a writer or an artist. No, I am not Germanic, Bulgarian or any combination of the two, I can assure you. It's much more complicated than that.'

He took down a review from the bookcase. It had an orange cover, like the short-lived periodicals of which so many appeared between 1925 and 1939. I have checked in the archives of Editions Saeta and at the Bibliothèque Nationale: *Passwords* was only published in three issues.[2]

'Here, have this copy. It's a relic. Nobody knows how to read these things. Perhaps you will.'

There is nothing more paralyzing than a compliment like that. All I could see first of all was a poem by Stanislas in which one finds two of the themes of his work, the resigned nostalgia for his lost country, and his confidence in his adopted language; but I was conscious that I had to look for a more obvious key – one which was as clear as day when I had discovered it, but which might remain invisible to those insensible to a poem's puzzles – and as I copied out the lines I unearthed their acrostic. I have reproduced it here, such as it is, although it is certainly no masterpiece. Stanislas was twenty-four years old when he published it; he had just been through a surrealist phase after his encounter with the poetry of Apollinaire and he was trying to listen to his own voice:

> *P*ardon me, my country, I have forgotten you,
> *L*et the curtain fall on your existence disdained.
> *A*lone, I was born, one day, somewhere else,
> *V*oice come to another language, another land,
> *N*either *heimatlos*, nor from the Black Mountain.
> *I*n the centuries since, I have wept.
> *C*ome now to an end, my tears run dry. My eyes
> *A*t first light have seen the invisible.

[2] *Mots de passe*: 3 issues, February, April, June 1932. Editor André Garrett (the author's father). Address as Editions Saeta. Poem quoted from issue No. 1.

It would have taken a long time to discover the meaning of the word Plavnica had there not been another clue which identified it more closely. The Black Mountain could stand for Monte Negro. Another key left no doubt. In his second novel *The Countdown*[1] the hero's name is Jezero Skadarsko. In Serbian, 'jezero' means 'lake', and Skadarsko is quite simply the Yugoslavian name for Lake Scutari on whose shore Plavnica lies. Is that where he was born? I am inclined to think so, despite his denying it when I questioned him; but what he denied was no more obviously true than what he confirmed and his desire to throw all investigations off the scent was always, even with me, stronger than his taste for simple truths.

'Georges,' he said to me, 'I came into the world one morning in February at Janson-de-Sailly when the master on duty handed me over to the French master. Before that I was in my mother's womb. God bless that saintly woman! I should not have ventured out, but once I'd poked my rather long nose outside, there was no going back. You're never better off than when you're in your mother's womb and it's madness to come out just for the sake of running after adventure; but men are mad, as we all know. I have often hoped I was the son of a bishop. Like Apollinaire.[2] Alas, it seems I shall have to renounce that dream, although there is quite definitely something unctuous about my person . . .'

No, there was nothing unctuous about his person. The word was a quote from André Thérive who was unmerciful with him on the publication of *The Countdown* and who later, after the war, went back on his critical stance and devoted long, hagiographic articles to Stanislas. Really I have no memory of any unctuousness whatsoever in Stanislas' behaviour, unless one was deceived by his courtesy, which enveloped and caressed until suddenly a lightning dart of sarcasm remedied the first sugary impression.

I can only add one last clue to the chapter of his well-concealed birth: his reaction one day when I mentioned Alphonse Daudet's

---

[1] *Le Compte à rebours*, Editions Saeta, 1936.
[2] At the time of this conversation (1960), Pierre Marcel Adéma's biography *Guillaume Apollinaire* (La Table Ronde, 1968) had not yet appeared. This work claimed that the known facts made it reasonable to conclude that the poet was the son not of a bishop, but of an Italian aristocrat, Francesco Flugi d'Aspermont, with whom Angélique de Kostrowitzky had fled Rome in 1875 when she was barely seventeen years old. Stanislas Beren was aware of this too (although I don't know his sources), but it amused him to believe in a legend that Apollinaire would neither confirm nor deny; just as he liked to hear himself referred to as 'the son of a king' in the true sense of the term or in the figurative sense.

Tartarin de Tarascon. This, it will be remembered, is about a so-called prince of Montenegro who swindles the poor Tartarin out of everything he owns.

'It's an unspeakable book,' Stanislas snapped. 'A cruel and vicious book, as bad as *Don Quixote.* Daudet and Cervantes both make far too easy game of the fool. What are they making fun of? Courage and a man's dreams. There's nothing more cowardly. In any case, who is the cheat who makes off with Tartarin's purse while the poor man thinks he's killing a real wild beast and is only dispatching a lion that's deaf and blind? Who is this unscrupulous character? Why dress him up in an assumed country's name? Did you know, Georges, that after his *Tartarin* Daudet was never able to set foot in Tarascon again . . . If I had had anything to do with it he wouldn't have been any better advised to present himself at Montenegro.'

*

Let us not try to make out that we are dealing with irrefutable facts, but rather with circumstantial evidence. In 1961 I tried to get to Plavnica. International worksites had attracted thousands of young people who were building a motorway which was to span the country from north to south. Superb straight lines would suddenly peter out and vague sign-boards would indicate diversions across fields. Torrential rain had turned one of these fields into a swamp and I had to abandon my car, stuck in the mud up to its bonnet, unsalvageable. In 1962, I renewed the attempt; I was arrested at Kragujevac and spent a week in prison for having paid for my petrol in dollars, because there were no exchange offices open. Once I was freed I was given twelve hours to leave Yugoslavia. In 1963 I tried my luck once more and, coming from Greece, stopped for the night at Skopje which, apart from its Moslem quarter, is – or rather was – a queer place with no charm at all. At about two in the morning, an earthquake reduced Skopje to a pile of rubble. My room on the first floor of the hotel collapsed into the cellar and I emerged, unscathed, through a ventilator shaft. My car, flat as a pancake, had travelled its last mile. On the journey home, I stopped off in Venice and went to stay with Stanislas for a few days. I related the string of misfortunes I had suffered.

'In your position, my boy, I would not push my luck. Plavnica is not on your road. The fourth time you won't save your skin. I've done with Plavnica: it doesn't exist any more.'

He did not want to talk about it. The only person who could have revealed to us where Stanislas was born was aunt Félicité. Their marriage licence must necessarily have included his place of birth. But she would say nothing on the subject; in fact I suspect that she has always given their marriage a false date to mislead people. One would have to go through the Seine archives to get any clue – but does one have the right to exhume what has been buried with so much care? If it was Stanislas' wish not to be born of anybody, is that not strictly his right in the eyes of literary history, that part of history to which he belongs? Besides, in what respect can the name of his father, the name of his mother, or the place where he was born, explain the spontaneous generation of his talent, the birth and life of his work? We must, out of respect for the man, stop where our suppositions stop; what we can infer hangs on the little-known history of Montenegro, a Balkan principality under the Berlin treaty of 1878, then a kingdom in 1910, then incorporated into Yugoslavia in 1918. For some years there was an underground movement of Montenegrin separatists. We can presume that if there are any left today, they are using their rifles as crutches. Our imagined story goes like this: Stanislas Beren is the son of one of those deposed princes who refused to bow to the rule symbolized by the Karageorgevitches. Might this prince have entrusted his son to France so that he could be educated and, one day, sent back to his country to take his place at the head of the revolt? It is possible. Until he finished his degree, Stanislas' education was paid for unofficially by the French government. The contributions were miserly, it is true, as if France felt guilty about encouraging a scheme against her ally Alexander the First, but on the quai d'Orsay there is always some civil servant nourishing shadowy schemes which will be brutally consigned to the archives department when his successor arrives. In 1931 the subsidies stopped without explanation. Stanislas' invisible protector had reached retirement age.

In Paris Stanislas lived with an uncle of some kind who scraped a living from an oriental spice business in an alley by la Muette. My father only caught sight of this relation once and described him in his personal diary: a yellow, dried-up old man sitting at the back of his shop in an armchair which was disgorging its stuffing, smoking his hookah. Customers were more frequent than might be imagined; this middle-class French quarter was peopled with countless Russian and Balkan émigrés. All the same the business could not have been a thriving one and this uncle, as I shall reveal later, had a small sideline. It would be wrong to imagine that Stanislas concealed his only relation. It was the uncle who hid himself away, an eastern mummy indifferent to everything but the hookah which he smoked from morning till night. Did they talk to each other? Beyond what was unavoidable, even that is not certain. Stanislas shed no tears on his uncle's death in 1930, any more than he had ever admitted having a father or mother. He had had the good fortune to be thrust into a new world where he had suddenly been born at the age of seventeen, one morning at Janson-de-Sailly. So what use are references? The title of his first long poem, *My Spontaneous Generation*,[1] clearly shows the idea he had formed of himself.

The summer of 1925 is crucial to Stanislas Beren's life. In a few weeks he discovered almost everything which was to illuminate his life: a violent love of the French language; literature, through the first books his friend lent him; and the social life of the bourgeoisie, which meant, at least at this period in history, a bourgeoisie that, beneath its appearances of frivolity, had preserved a style and a taste for patronage. Stanislas also discovered . . . aunt Félicité, who swept in one afternoon with three trunks and ten hatboxes. She was thirty years old, as I have said already, and the moral and physical opposite of my grandmother, her sister. Aggressively, she sacrificed herself to fashion: short hair, eyes of royal blue outrageously made up, rouged cheeks. Was she beautiful? Definitely not, but she had one of those faces which radiate character by virtue of a forceful nose or mouth, or a long neck. Those who knew her during this period say that her fascination lay more than anywhere else in her voice, which was husky, almost masculine. The best portrait of her at the time is the one painted by Kisling, for whom she seems to me to have been the perfect model, to the point where all Kisling's other portraits of women resemble her, and as if there were only one single mould to inspire the painters and writers of the roaring twenties. In her wake there followed a small but constantly changing court of admirers: composers, musicians, stage designers, poets and theatre people who danced to the tune she called, and whom she summoned or dismissed with absolute authority. When she died in the spring of 1968, nine years before he did, Stanislas showed me an envelope containing a few notes written in a hasty and clumsy hand.

'No woman,' he said to me, 'has had more influence on the writers, musicians and painters of her time, and look what she has left: notes for her laundress and her maid, an itinerary for a visit to Apulia, a transfer form which she forgot to send to her bank in London, a rough

[1] *Nouvelle Revue Française*, issue of April 1933. The poem has an introduction by Jean Paulhan: 'A poet fallen from the skies.'

draft of a will for her lawyer. I have looked among her belongings for letters from Chirico, Picasso, Reverdy, Stravinsky, Diaghilev, Bakst. Nothing. It all went in the wastepaper basket. One day when I saw her throwing away a letter from Drieu la Rochelle and tried to stop her, she replied, "There's no point in keeping anything. The earth will grow cold. There'll be no more men and our vanities will be dead and gone." What could I have said that would have made any sense?'

Thanks to Félicité, Stanislas and André were introduced to the fringe world of literature and poetry, André because he had immediately shown her his first poems, Stanislas because the 'Danube peasant' presented one of those odd cases for which she often had a passing fancy. As is now well known, this was no passing fancy, but a great love which lasted forty-three years.

In 1925 my grandfather was passionately interested in photography. He was continually buying new cameras which he ordered from Leipzig. He discarded cameras with plates and bellows for portable cameras which were easier to handle. The Garrett family albums are particularly rich up to 1930: the time when my grandfather became passionately interested in what was still known then as wireless telegraphy. Photographs of Félicité and her friends abound in the summer of 1925; André and Stanislas can be recognized among them, both still timid and schoolboyish although the latter looks much more of a man than his seventeen years. For me, who only really knew Stanislas and Félicité from 1946 onwards, on their return from the United States when I was ten years old, it is difficult to recognize in this young woman, with her boyish hairstyle, her skirt which did not reach her knee and her loose V-necked sweater revealing her long neck adorned with several rows of pearls, the woman of fifty who disembarked from the liner at Cherbourg on Stanislas' arm; he was discreetly supporting her because she was already unsteady on her feet, a victim of that creeping sickness which slowly, with an occasional reprieve, paralyzed her to the point that she spent the last ten years of her life bed-ridden. The contrast with my grandmother is staggering. Their appearances could not have been more different. The one was set stiffly in the fashions of 1910: long dresses, hair scraped into a bun, a choker which earned her the name Madame de Grandair; the other not in fashion, but ahead of it like someone scarcely taking the time to breathe the air of her time and already preceding it. As I said, Félicité had been married three times: the first time in 1914, to a banker who died three months later during the counter-offensive on the Marne; the second time in 1918, to a young American officer killed by a bullet between the eyes on the eve of the armistice; the third time in 1920, to the painter Italo della Croce, who had little talent, but such a strong and generous personality that Félicité's entourage forgave him his mundane and uninspired art. Croce had died in 1924 from an attack of uraemia, and she had inherited an impressive fortune, as she had done from her two preceding husbands, as well as the house at Cap-Ferrat; for this conventional artist, this manufacturer of elegant portraits and official frescoes for the League of Nations and the banks, had converted the fruit of his daubing into pictures by Braque, Juan Gris, Derain, Dunoyer de Segonzac, Vlaminck, Friesz and de Pisis, painters whom he liked and whose innovative paths he knew it would have been pointless for him to try and follow.

Thus Félicité, in 1925, found herself quite by accident in possession of an enormous fortune (quite how enormous she neither knew nor cared) which, in this mad postwar era giddy with inventions and the pleasure of being able to live again, earned her the fascination of the literary and artistic circles. An easily consoled widow, she had been living for the last months with Béla Zukor – or to give him his real, less resonant name, Jean Poilé – a dadaist poet of academic tediousness, but who probably aroused in her other emotions than poetic ones and paid himself out of slim volumes published at the author's, or rather Félicité's, expense. She came to Deauville without him, conscious that he would not fit in, that at the Garretts' her poet would only be capable of pathetic scandal-mongering at the expense of the middle class. Béla Zukor was foolish to let himself be put on one side for a month. He lost his footing and because of it conceived a sourness which remained with him, unabated, for the rest of his life.

It was not, as one might imagine, one of those situations of love at first sight when Stanislas and Félicité first met. Félicité was returning to her family crowned with the halo of celebrity. People were talking about her brilliant and unfortunate marriages, her friends in Paris, London, Rome and New York. On her property at Cap-Ferrat she had been visited by Freud, Marinetti, Valery Larbaud, Isadora and Raymond Duncan, Pavlova, Bakst, Nijinsky and Georges Carpentier; and yet she had found time to devote to her sister, who was at the opposite end of the spectrum to that world, to her brother-in-law whom she loved for his enthusiasm for living in the modern age – even if that age were purely mechanical – and to André, my father, whom she loved like a son. Why should she have been interested in this unknown friend of his, Stanislas, with his borrowed graces in his new suits, who walked uncomfortably in shoes which were too large for him? However remarkable his sudden mastery of the French language, Stanislas was still very timid. One day he said to André, who noted it in his yellow exercise book, 'It is terrifying to know nothing of a country, of its literature, its painting, its history. You cannot have any idea of how much I have to catch up on. Your aunt mentions a name, Proust. I go straight to the bookshop, and there are ten volumes to read. It is ludicrous.'

He devoured everything, but more than anything else he listened. His almost magical gift for assimilating what he heard, the excellence of his memory, the liveliness of his intelligence and his curiosity quickly put him level with André. My grandfather, a great reader of scientific reviews and company reports, respected the passions of others. For these young boys, to whom he would have preferred to be giving golf lessons, or swimming or tennis coaching, but who professed a total lack of interest in all sports, he opened an account in a bookshop. I have discovered a note which describes the resolutions made by the two boys:

We have six years to assimilate the essentials of:
a) French culture: two years
b) English culture: one year
c) German culture: six months
d) American culture: six months
e) Russian culture: six months
f) Spanish culture: six months
g) Portuguese culture: six months;
given that we will be able to gather the pearls of the Greek and Latin authors within the school curriculum, and that our year of philosophy will be devoted to German philosophy because there is no other kind.

Thirty years later, when I came upon this naive and ambitious memorandum and showed it to Stanislas, he spoke unironically about their categorical programme.

'We fulfilled our obligations. It was intoxicating. In fact to begin with we understood nothing, but all the same something stuck, that background of emotions, of feelings, of experiences which gave us the impression of having lived so many different lives in such a short space of time that when the day came for us to shut our books, we should die, to be reborn straight away as infant prodigies.'

*

At the beginning of the new term, in October 1925, Stanislas astounded the new masters in the fifth form. They had been warned and were expecting to see some sort of half-wit vegetating at the back of the class, an exotic barbarian who for some obscure reason was being protected by a higher authority. In the French composition which opened the term's examinations, André came first and Stanislas second. The master, a cynical young man, explained to his pupils.

'Beren, your essay is by far the best; it demonstrates that you possess a superior intelligence. But I have placed you second for two unjust and wholly legitimate reasons. Your writing is almost totally illegible: deciphering what you have written is an imposition for which I intend to make you pay. In addition you have a very approximate idea of spelling. You will say to me . . . no, you won't say anything to me, you are, with no good reason, well brought up, because of some kind of charm which you haven't had to learn. . . . Perhaps I imagine that privately you will say to yourself, "Spelling is for idiots." But you will be wrong. You love the French language. You have yet to learn that it is through its orthography, often obsolete, and through its rules of grammar, often cumbersome, that you will discover the aesthetic qualities which are its glory. As for you, André Garrett, the breadth of your knowledge is surprising for someone of your age; but you are carried away by everything, you don't know how to be selective. You will have to learn to choose. That is essential. The boy who has come third in this composition is way behind both of you. Having said that, it is my pleasure to inform you other gentlemen of the fifth form of your crass ignorance. You express yourselves in pidgin French and think about nothing. Your culture stops at your comic books. I have too much respect for manual labour to recommend that you abandon your studies and take up joinery or plumbing. No, gentlemen, you are definitely ripe for the universities.'

In 1931, when Stanislas and André decided to reopen Editions Saeta, their first aim being to publish *The Secret Life of an Orgasm*, they remembered their fifth-form master, whose offhand manner and the sarcastic remarks he made about the son of a senior civil servant had got him relegated to a provincial *lycée*. They offered him the job of being their first reader, and Georges Dupuy gave up teaching to devote himself to publishing books with the two pupils he had won over, at that memorable beginning of term in October 1925, by his generosity and his lucid cynicism. With unshakeable modesty, he played the thankless role of literary adviser until he was called up in 1939, when his talents were put to use running a clothing store for the army. Who would imagine that the Germans would want to take a quartermaster prisoner? When Dupuy returned after the war with tuberculosis, he still found the strength to work for the next fourteen years until his death in 1959; it seemed as if he had survived only long enough for me to come of age, so that he could hand over to me the running of the publishing house in which he had never wanted to be more than an unobtrusive worker. A proud and private man, he had chosen the humblest office in the building and kept himself to himself, receiving only those authors that he liked, and calling the others, the ones from whom the house earned its livelihood, 'suppliers', whose manuscripts he happily hacked at with his judicious red pencil and who contributed greatly to the style of the 'Everyman' collection (which was imitated so often that we eventually abandoned it). To listen to Georges Dupuy one might have thought that he detested literature, but his cutting remarks bore witness only to an obsessive love for something he could never forgive for disappointing him. Two years after his death, when I was going through the archives at Saeta, I discovered his reading reports; I was sufficiently impressed by them to compile a collection whose publication would, I hoped, pay some tribute to this noble and uncompromising servant of literature.[1] Despite Stanislas' preface the book enjoyed no success at all, which must have made our friend smile in his grave. He had, at the beginning, decided once and for all that his own literary activities would never amount to anything, but that with a word he could awaken in a writer's heart the self-confidence he lacked. It is certain that he had a very strong influence on Stanislas, as we shall see later; there is no doubt that if Stanislas, at least two or three times in his life, resisted the temptations of fashion it was because he could imagine the mocking smile of Georges Dupuy.

During the school year of 1925–6 the master established some order in the impassioned minds of his two pupils, selected their reading matter, and on Thursdays took them to museums, moderating their breathless enthusiasms. Later, the theatre, cinema and lectures alternated with visits to the old parts of Paris or the châteaux of the Ile-de-France. Although he himself was incapable of straddling a bicycle or kicking a football, Georges Dupuy pleaded the cause of sport to my grandfather, so Stanislas and André received their coaching in tennis, swimming, golf, boxing and fencing.

---

[1] *Une littérature prénatale* by Georges Dupuy, with a preface by Stanislas Beren, Editions Saeta, 1961.

'You're a pair of bookworms,' he said. 'I'm going to expose you to fresh air, in fact make you everything I didn't know how to be. And don't worry: when the time comes, when you feel like it, you'll drop me.'

They did not drop him. Several times, especially after the war, Georges Dupuy displayed feelings of bitterness about this to Stanislas.

'You're disappointing me by not forgetting me. You're turning all my ideas upside down. I implore you not to let me believe in gratitude or loyalty; both are false ideas which can only bring down misfortune on a man's head.'

★

From the Deauville summer of 1925 onwards my grandmother had taken on another task, that of civilizing Stanislas. With that abruptness which protected her from the immense reserves of her kind heart, she taught him how to eat properly, how to dress properly, how to talk to women. It was to her that he owed his worldly ease, unexpected in a boy who had spent his childhood in crumbling huts or even more likely in the sparsely forested mountains around what is now Tito-grad. The most remarkable thing was that, instead of rejecting this authority as his forceful personality might have inclined him to do, Stanislas also knew how to listen. He had soon measured the extent of his ignorance and now perhaps he was motivated by a secret wish to erase his childhood. Never did a young man show so much keenness to emerge into the world. I have kept a few lines taken down in haste after a dinner one evening in Venice (1972):

Janson represents three incredible years. Your father and I planted trees, impatient to see the results, but conscious that we would have to wait. I was surrounded by kindness, by generosity, by delicate attentions which all contributed to making me fall in love with life. On that point I have to disagree with Monsieur Dupuy,[1] who considered that to cherish a child was poor preparation for life. Your father was my brother, your grandmother my mother, your grandfather my patron – and Félicité my mistress. *That* I wanted to shout from the rooftops, but I had to stay silent for obvious reasons

[1] Their formal relationship remained unchanged right up to Georges Dupuy's death, as if the distribution of roles had taken place once and for all at Janson-de-Sailly. The French master was always Monsieur to Stanislas, and Stanislas was always Beren to the master. Eventually, of course, it became something of a private game.

of propriety. Only your family knew, and as they worshipped Félicité they protected our still clandestine affair.

How and when this came about is difficult to say. Neither he nor she would tell. Apart from them, André alone knew the truth; however, there are always clues in Beren's work, even if several of them are wilfully misleading. Can we assume that the story related by Timothy Jantzenovitch in the second chapter of *Salvation and Death of a Hero*[1] is more or less true? The novel is not Stanislas' best, but there are some chillingly frightening pages on Amsterdam at night and the desperate loneliness of a man who has lost everything. In his empty Binnenkant apartment his last remaining possession is a mirror into which he stares, scrutinizing his face where every incident of his life is marked by a wrinkle or a scar or a carious tooth; one night Stanislas introduces a young man with long blond hair, wearing rope sandals and laced up tight in a sheepskin waistcoat. The anonymous young man puts down a parcel tied with string in the middle of the bare room and is about to go when Timothy stops him with a beseeching gesture:

'Stay,' he said to him. 'I want to tell a story that my mirror refuses to hear because it finds me too old and too ugly. If I try to make it understand that it definitely did happen to me, it refuses to believe me and emphasizes that refusal cruelly by reflecting a single image, that of the old man of today. Yet I was once a young man who would have looked like you, and one evening when I had been talking too much, in the throes of excitement and pleasure produced by Debussy being played by a white-faced virtuoso, I turned to my neighbour. I took her hand. She responded to the pressure of my fingers, we waited until the end of the concert, I went home with her and we have never been parted since. How many women are capable of such absolute certainty? I will tell you straight away: very few. Thus, having possessed certainty, I have to proclaim out loud that I am a happy man. You see, young man, I live with her in this room; I have taken out all the furniture so that she no longer bumps into it, for she is unsteady on her feet. She likes to stand by the window and contemplate the canal and the Gothic houses opposite. When she stands like that for a long time, her forehead pressed against the window pane, a patch of vapour appears where her lips are, and I press my own to it to taste her breath, the fruit of her

---

[1] *Salut et mort du héros*, novel by Stanislas Beren, Éditions Saeta, 1969.

24

mouth. Thus I come to know the eternity in which nothing can separate us. Young man, you see before you a very happy man, and I do not know what is holding me back from returning your parcel to you and showing you out and asking you never to set foot here again, because you are upsetting me; and my wife, who sets great store by appearances, is there in her corner, motionless, so as not to suffer from your pity.'

The young man goes out of the room, leaving Timothy alone with the parcel in front of him; after a long monologue, he makes the decision to untie the string. Inside, in a silver frame, there is a photograph of a woman of whom Stanislas gives such a minute description that one recognizes the thirty-year-old Félicité. This short passage in the novel seems ambiguous, incomplete; but the author wished it so: a melancholy, concealed confession of a man who sees death on the prowl and no longer knows whether the reaper has already done his work or is yet to come. The previous year – 1968 – Félicité had passed away in Venice.

Leafing through my father's notebooks, I have found under the date of 17 February 1928 (they were both in their philosophy year) a few lines which shed some light on the scene in the novel. Did Timothy Jantzenovitch live it, or dream it? André has noted:

Yesterday evening Mother and I were supposed to go to a concert. The programme was Debussy who I am not excessively fond of, but Mother likes it and I suppose that's good enough. At six o'clock I come down with a diabolical fever, so Mother calls the doctor who stethoscopes me and takes no risks with his reputation, sticking me straight into bed with infusions of vervain and some thermogene wool. Mother refuses to leave me and telephones Félicité to offer her our two seats. Félicité doesn't want to go on her own, so Mother suggests that she take Stanislas. I'm better this afternoon although I've still to keep to my bed. Stanislas came by for five minutes, tired and distant.

'I can't stay long,' he said, 'I've got some philosophy prep to hand in tomorrow.'

I had the odd impression that he wasn't the same as usual, and he didn't say a single word to thank Mother for the concert. It's not like him at all.

The intrigue could not stay secret for long. André was the first to know (19 February 1928):

Stanislas, who is incapable of hiding anything from me for more than forty-eight hours, has just told me a jolly good item. Sensational! In the space of an evening, after the concert, he has become aunt Félicité's lover. He is behaving like a man in a trance or drunk, in a complete daze. I must admit that my first feeling was one of anxiety: won't our friendship suffer, and will we still be able to follow our plan to acquire a universal culture to the letter?

It seems, according to other notes from the diary, that in fact there was some uncertainty to start with, then life organized itself around Félicité. My grandmother learnt the whole story from her younger sister. She was outraged for five minutes, for form's sake, but preached no sermons. Her morality applied only to herself: she would have considered it a sign of the very worst upbringing to importune her loved ones with it. My grandfather found the affair 'amusing' and was delighted by it. All in all the union between the young 'Danube peasant' and Félicité was blessed from the start, however unusual it appeared to be. In addition, Félicité immediately stopped running after what she had been seeking in vain until then. The only person who had any real complaints was Béla Zukor, the dadaist poet with the flamboyant pseudonym. He woke up to find himself in the street with a trunkful of his unsold and unsaleable volumes of verse. This misadventure filled him with an implacable hatred of Stanislas, whom he pursued for the rest of his life with malignant gossip and inflammatory articles, pouring scorn on his work with a dogged venom which would have seemed comic had the victim not occasionally been deeply wounded; a number of these poisoned darts reached his most sensitive points, just where he himself had doubts. When the Berens returned from the United States where they had spent the five war years, Félicité's ex-lover, who had just discovered patriotism and was brandishing it with as much fanaticism as he had spat upon it before the war, greeted them with an article virulent in its indignation. . . . This vermin, who had never, within living memory, offered a fellow human being a glass of water, who crawled around his painter friends and begged them to add a drawing or a dedication to rare editions which he immediately resold (swearing, when these indelicacies were unmasked, that he had been robbed); this vermin, a literary has-been only glorious for a few months because of a poem – if one can call it that – dated 1930 in which he exhorted the 'Stalin the genius' (sic) to launch his troops in an assault on the Vatican and sodomise the pope, that great enemy of the proletariat; this vermin – Félicité's one error – had set himself up since the Liberation as the Fouquier-Tinville of a tribunal which condemned to silence the writers that he, as an utter mediocrity, hated. Having published books during the Occupation, they were judged guilty of high treason and collusion with the enemy, which evidently struck from the roll of literary history everyone who counted apart from Jean Poilé, alias Béla Zukor. Giono he accused of being a German spy, Montherlant of procuring for the Kommandantur; Jouhandeau was responsible for Dachau, Chardonne had been Hitler's *éminence grise*, Drieu la Rochelle was Himmler's mastermind. Then, like a louse laying nits, he produced an article which accused the Berens of growing rich in America while the French were suffering beneath the yoke. None of it stood up, but the era drew from this kind of poison the power to forget the abjurations and cowardice of its own recent past. Stanislas did not stoop to defend himself against such absurd allegations. Actual charges can be denied, but rumours cannot. The article was remembered by many, and since journalists steal from each other unscrupulously, it was repeated – deformed from year to year – in newspapers and magazines to the point where Stanislas and Félicité, disheartened, began to live abroad more and more.

*

A photograph of Félicité, taken during the summer of 1928, shows her as love had transformed her in the space of a few months: she had let her hair grow, dropped her hemline and discarded the cigarette-holder she used for the cigarillos which she smoked frantically until her dying breath and which accentuated the huskiness of her voice. She was now dissatisfied with her large apartment on the boulevard Malesherbes and she sold off its furniture (not to be regretted, because its style was modern and frightful) and moved to a suite at the Ritz. Like André, Stanislas was still at the *lycée*. After class he would arrive at the hotel, his school books jammed into a carpet-bag, settle down at a table by a window overlooking the old courtyard, and do his homework, while she stretched out on her bed and read before taking him to dine at Prunier's, Larue's or Lucas-Carton's – whose doormen slowly got used to him handing over his carpet-bag full of textbooks and exercise books, then going to sit at the table reserved for Madame della Croce. Stanislas began to put on weight, but as soon as my

27

grandmother mentioned this fact to Félicité, she had dietetic meals brought up to her bedroom and only went out to Maxim's on Sunday evenings (which necessitated the acquisition of a dinner jacket that the future poet and writer accepted blithely from his mistress). He became slim again. He was made for the good life, but in small doses.

In another photograph taken the same year, shortly after André and he had passed their *baccalauréat* – perhaps not brilliantly because they scorned the exact sciences, but at least satisfactorily since they were both equally aware that these conventions had to be disposed of in order to be able to start living – Stanislas appears already grown-up, a man, while beside him my father is still a bean-pole who has grown too quickly and is uncertain whether he should have rebelled quite so suddenly against long pants and woollen vests, whether he might not catch cold as his mother predicted. This photograph was taken at Cap-Ferrat shortly after the examinations. Stanislas is not at his best. Something, some incident or reflection, has annoyed him and his face reflects the irritation which he knows he has a duty to conceal but which is all the more evident, almost exaggerated, because it seems that no one has yet noticed. There is no doubt that at the beginning Félicité was quick to belittle him in public and only little by little did she stop being defensive towards him. With an unerring instinct she detected in this gauche young man something more powerful than the lush appeal of youth: the first fruits of a resolute spirit, a character which the years would etch on Stanislas' face in lines so distinct that when he was in his forties no one who met him doubted that this was a man of high intelligence and, more than that, an artist.

And Félicité needed just as much strength of character to confront a jealous and censorious society with such a young lover. Because of the high standards she applied more to herself than to others, she did not show herself in public alone with Stanislas during their first summer. André played the part of chaperon. What could be more natural than for a nephew to spend the holiday at his aunt's house with a school friend who, more than likely intimidated by luxury and the strangers he was meeting, listened rather than spoke? Thus Stanislas learned that if someone said 'Jean' they meant Jean Cocteau, that 'poor Raymond' was Raymond Radiguet who had died at twenty, that 'Paul' was Paul Morand, and that when a bewhiskered old gentleman spoke of 'young Marcel' he was referring to Proust. The two friends plunged themselves into the books of these heroes who seemed so familiar and accessible to them, and whose presence – whether actual or ghostly – made their work so familiar that they imagined they could hear the authors' voices as they read. Stanislas was the more assiduous in these bouts of avid reading; André was already spending part of the day sailing in his Star around the bay of Villefranche. That this summer of 1928 should be important in the work of Stanislas Beren is evident. The house and garden by the sea appear almost immediately in *The Secret Life of an Orgasm* and Cap-Ferrat plays the leading part in the novella he published thirty years later under the title *A Peninsula*.[1] If one is to believe the reports in André's diary of what Stanislas confided to him at the time, the curious liaison between him and Félicité carried none of the brimming sensuality that one might expect between a young man of twenty and a woman of thirty-three. Certainly they would sometimes stay together at night and Stanislas would get back to the room he shared with his friend at dawn, but Félicité was not a woman of the bedroom. Only once in her life had she let herself be carried away to sexual excesses, by a sex-maniac called Béla Zukor, and now that she had freed herself of him, she retained a feeling of having been degraded which reinforced her modesty. Her relationship with Stanislas progressed as if their union could only be secured by being maintained at the high level which she had determined to impose on them, even if it meant Stanislas taking his pleasure elsewhere and keeping him by more durable bonds than physical love – which she would tire of before he did by virtue of the difference in their ages. Did Stanislas understand this straight away? He may well not have done. He was consumed by what Retz calls 'the fires of the senses' which take themselves for love, and it infuriated him to be kept at a distance by her in this unprecedented chapter of his life. One day when she had shut her door to him he flared up.

'She despises me,' he let fly at André. 'She plays with me. I can only go into her room if she decides to let me. One evening she will throw me out and I shall not be able to say a word. Nothing, do you hear! I shall go back to my little hole at la Muette, back to uncle Dimitri who hardly ever speaks, back to my hovel and that smell of spices which is so intolerable, where the only conversation in the evenings is the gurgling of his hookah.'

In his exercise book on the same page, André has glued in the margin a sheet of writing-paper with Félicité's letter-head: La Désirade, Saint-Jean-Cap-Ferrat, Alpes-Maritimes. On it there is a short poem written in André's own hand, but there is no doubt that he copied it out to salvage it as one of Stanislas' first attempts. In each

[1] *Une presqu'île*, Editions Saeta, 1958.

verse anguish and sadness well up, a tribute paid to happiness by an unquiet spirit:

> Oh this sea that breaks
> and these endless skies
> with my fists to my eyes
> I weep for their sakes
>
> I see you, it takes
> me to our tenderness lost
> to our bodies tossed
> light that dusts and cakes
>
> Death's cold resort
> where your footstep forsakes
> your picture still partakes
> along the small port
> of forever as it awakes.

I quote this forgotten poem by Stanislas not because it is remarkable, but because it is one of the first, if not the first, and it already demonstrates that style which was his own, the concision and restrained passion. It must have been written after a passing estrangement, of which there were several that summer as Félicité defended herself with that brutality that women possess when they are faced with an unpalatable truth. Was this the first time for Stanislas? No. But it was love for the first time. His previous adventures? Horseplay. André has noted one day when they were in the sixth form: 'Stanislas is f. . . the maids'.[1] Without further comment. Félicité was indeed his first love.

*

'I have never loved another woman,' Stanislas said to me as we returned from Félicité's lugubrious funeral at San Michele in 1968.

He had forgotten Audrey, he had forgotten the others, the ones that she had served up on a plate to distract the anguished and melancholic soul of the man who was thirteen years her junior; and he had forgotten the ones he had quietly treated himself to, thankfully without her knowing, because she would have suffered, regarding

---

[1] Dated 17 March 1927, in André's exercise book; but what discretion there is. Today a student of his age would write the word out in full and do away with the dots.

each one as a betrayal of their pact. But, as someone once said, memory is oblivion, and when it is time to settle accounts, all that still exists is the memory which we slowly shape and perfect within ourselves. Félicité watched over him to save him from the sufferings of clandestine affairs. She also watched over his first writings, notably his poetry which, to a great extent because of her, has remained dispersed and fragmentary. Stanislas was perhaps not a poet in the strict sense of the word. Félicité, with her demanding nature and her unfailing instinct, did not allow him to be. As if she were accountable for what was to 'remain', from 1928 onwards she tore up and threw away every one of his faltering verses and unconscious imitations. On the one hand she seemed to love her life of ease, and on the other, more privately and hidden even from the majority of her friends, this frivolity was rigour itself. Although Stanislas, youthful and impulsive, at first rebelled against this censorship, he eventually accepted it and admitted that Félicité was never wrong, or very rarely. She would not let anything mediocre pass. André has recorded the categorical verdict she delivered one day on a fashionable novelist:

Naturally it's not good and nor is it bad, not even very bad which might give us hope that his talent will return. It's simply mediocre, by which I mean to say it's irremediable.

There is no doubt that Stanislas was rather unhappy in that fine summer of 1928, unhappy in the way a man can be when a woman who is important to him holds him at arm's length, reassuring herself of his sacrifice without relinquishing any part of herself. Wounded in his self-respect, Stanislas struggled proudly and alone. André was of little help to him, spending almost all day on his boat. One may imagine the thoughts of this exile cast into an unknown world and discovering its multiple complexions. Every day there were ten people to lunch and as many to dinner, and Félicité always put Stanislas at the bottom of the table. Guests thought it proper to address him in polite banalities like, 'Is this your first time at Cap-Ferrat?' or, 'Are you staying here for long?': harmless questions more often than not – though not always – which he received with growing annoyance, convinced that this collection of snobs and artists, multi-millionaires and spongers, were taken aback to find a 'Danube peasant' in this paradise ruled by such a woman, and were reminding him not to outstay his welcome.

I am aware that in trying to convey the right key to the relation-ship between Stanislas and Félicité I seem not to be particularly generous towards her, but I remain convinced that she was violently at odds with herself and that contrary to appearances a great passion, the passion of her life, had been kindled within her. She found it hard to come to terms with, and once she had, did not mean to spoil it by hurling herself recklessly into it. A romantic soul may well scorn these misgivings but at thirty-three, after three marriages and an affair she wanted to blot out of her memory, Félicité was definite-ly not a romantic soul. Her world, which she loved and which loved her in return, would not have forgiven her if she had gone and hidden herself away on a desert island with Stanislas.

Georges Kapsalis, the gallicized Greek who was her intimate friend and probably her sole confidant after André's death, told me forty years later, in 1968, shortly after we had accompanied her to her final resting-place in the cemetery of San Michele, that he had guessed everything from the very first day.

'We were both completely frank with each other. I'll confess that, to start with, I used to tease her gently, until I realised that for Stanislas she was nursing the first great love of her life. At the beginning, she used to cry in desperation about it. Yes, in front of me, believe it or not. . . .'

As he talked, in the neighbouring room of the palazzetto, the one whose windows overlook the Largo Fortunio, Stanislas, alone, was pacing up and down, and we heard his heavy step measuring the beat of his grief, as if the imaginary distance he was travelling between two walls in the sepia light of the day's end was taking him away from the dark reality of the coffin being lowered into the double grave which was waiting for him. The stone had not only covered Félicité, it had covered a part of himself which was finished and would never be revived, and like every man who loses a part of his life's breath, he asked himself why fate was so cruel as to leave him alone and vulnerable, like a child. I would have liked to be close to him, even though no words would be exchanged, believing that simply holding his hand would, however slightly, absorb his shock. Georges Kapsalis guessed what I was thinking.

'Leave him,' he said. 'For him, this is the time when there is nobody but her, and I can promise you that he sincerely believes there never was anybody but her – as he will no doubt feel the need to tell you. Your presence or mine will only bring back tactless memories of things we all witnessed. Let today go. This evening we shall take him out to dine with us, to stop him from going through Félicité's things, stroking her dresses and crying over her useless jewels, scraping at the bottoms of drawers and finding photographs which will tear his heart in two.'

★

Had I ever looked at Georges Kapsalis properly? He was part of the scenery, a permanent guest everywhere on condition that he was sent a ticket for the train or aeroplane. In Venice I perceived the extent to which he was a cornerstone of that edifice constructed by Stanislas and Félicité. He had been their confidant, their friend, the peacemaker of their stormy hours. In short, this casual and slightly cynical Greek had given them his life. He had ruined himself gambling without really minding, and after the war he lived in an attic room in Cannes, accepting people's hospitality without needing to go cap in hand because he was so well-loved and they were always repaid by his ready wit.

'There's one thing I have never told you,' he said to me on that mournful Venetian day when we felt so close. 'The man we're listening to walking up and down in the next room, who is my friend, who has replaced your father for you, and who is one of the great French writers, showed me one day that he could have changed my life if I had wanted it. That expression of his, sometimes distant, sometimes polite – imprinted with the condescending attention that he gives to people and things alike – has not always been his expression. There's been another which he concealed and repressed when he became conscious of the danger. And he deserves credit for that, I can tell you. It was at Deauville in 1930. We were in the paddock. I'd had an extremely bad week . . . I'm sure you know what I mean. Of course I wasn't ruined, as I've been for the last thirty years, but . . . well, I hadn't had any luck. I was almost depressed! Despite your grandfather's forced good humour. We were watching the horses walk around the paddock and, although I'm not bad as students of form go, I just couldn't make up my mind; then Stanislas leant over and murmured very softly in my ear, without the slightest conviction, "Number 2." I hadn't overlooked number 2, a young grey, a bit too handsome to inspire much confidence, but in the end, for fun, for the sake of the challenge, I put my money on him. And I won. Three more times, Stanislas suggested a number to me and each time I won. I know you don't like betting, and that horses bore you, and you imagine quite simply that Stanislas knew his way around better than I did. But no, my young friend, Stanislas knew nothing, or next to nothing. He *saw*. This experience repeated four times might have convinced me, but I am naturally sceptical. I needed more proof. I bet on his numbers for a month. Except for one occasion when the jockey fell, he didn't make a single mistake. From that moment on I began to observe his expression. It was no longer the expression that we know. Impossible to describe and, even today, I ask myself whether he mesmerized the horses or whether he was obeying some internal vision. I can assure you that it was almost frightening. You know me well enough: I am, well . . . I've been a gambler, but even though a gambler bets to win, he can't tolerate the idea that he's submitting to a higher force than chance. So for two months Stanislas helped me and I had a golden run of winning which very quickly terrified me. I felt I was committing blasphemy. . . . Yes, I even thought I'd made a pact with the devil or some other obscure force. We'd said practically nothing to each other, Stanislas and I, by the end of the racing season, when I told him I wanted to share my winnings with him. If you'd seen his expression! I thought he was going to kill me. "No," he said, "it's impossible. *I've no right.*" We talked the whole of that evening and then I ventured to make this mad plea, that he should never use his gift, not for me, not for anybody else – whoever it might be. You see, I persuaded him that we were running a terrible risk. I told him he was never to touch a pack of cards or to bet – even if I did the actual placing of the bet – on the horses. I know that you're completely wrapped up in the rationalism of your youth and that you're thinking I'm an old dotard talking drivel, but just remember: I'm a Greek, I believe in the evil eye, in the omens of destiny and nature, and perhaps Stanislas and I are more closely related than we thought. We're both men of the Near East with an alarming conjunction in our blood: because we are the sons of the gods, but also the sons of the heroes, in other words the worst rabble in mythology. . . .'

Georges Kapsalis had never said as much to me as on that afternoon in 1968 while we listened to Stanislas' footsteps in his big study next door. Three or four times Stanislas stopped pacing and Georges fell silent, waiting for the door to open, but it remained obstinately shut. The noise would begin again and Georges would make another observation.

'The reason he stopped just now was to take a book off the shelf. It's always been his habit when work refuses to progress. Generally, he chooses a poet and recites a few verses under his breath – perhaps you can hear him, your ear is better than mine – then he takes heart again and carries on walking. Have you noticed the carpet? At both ends there's a spot where the wool is worn and flattened. That's where he performs his perfectly precise about-turn. Reading, always reading. That man has devoured mountains of books since he came to France. A terrible hunger, as if he wanted to make up not just for his own lost time but his ancestors' as well, those people of his that we can easily imagine as petty warlords or brigand kings. In 1928 when I saw him at Félicité's table, intimidated by the idiotic questions which were being fired at him and answering in monosyllables, I asked myself what extreme passion was at work inside this muscular youth. We didn't know at first, but when his first novel was published I understood. Félicité's friends no longer looked at him in the same light then, and I must say that his outward behaviour changed completely and utterly as if, with this book of his, he had paid his entrance fee into this demanding set of people who were so easily moved to scorn. All the same, occasionally one saw an unmistakable smile appear on those serious features. This young man was already brimming with assurance and he was enjoying our ignorance of him and of his great ambitions.'

'But Félicité's friends suspected something, didn't they?'

'Yes, of course, despite his being so uncommonly discreet. One day at Cap-Ferrat, as we moved out onto the terrace after spending longer than usual over luncheon – which must have annoyed him, having that athletic frame and being so strong and energetic – he simply leapt over the edge. Oh, it wasn't a great height, twelve feet or so, but it was rather impressive because suddenly we saw him disappear like a devil vanishing into his cave; perhaps he had crashed down on to the rocks bordering the parapet walk. Félicité let out a yell and rushed to the railings to see him standing there, smiling and waving, before running off at the double towards the village of Saint-Jean. Reverdy expressed everyone's surprise, rolling the r with his thick, earthy accent: "Built like a gun, but what a strrrange gun," and Gaby Deslys added, "A proper six-shooter," which annoyed Félicité so much that it took her a year to forgive her. I repeated all this to Stanislas a long time afterwards, and he hooted with laughter: "A six-shooter? It has happened, but not with her. She was so uninterested in sex. With one . . . two others. . . ." Have you noticed how his eyes glaze over when a chance remark reminds him of a woman, or a friend? Suddenly he feels so close and conspiratorial towards that memory that everything around him pales into insignificance. He's still there in body, but his memory sails off somewhere else. You expect to see him disappear over the balustrade, leaving behind him just a small pile of unnecessary clothes.'

*

At eight o'clock in the evening, we heard the sound of footsteps approaching and, after a pause, as if he had hesitated briefly, Stanislas opened the door. He stood for a few seconds in the doorway and smiled at us.

'What about dining at Simonetti's? You must be dying of hunger.'

I had always been fond of Georges Kapsalis, but until that lugubrious Venetian afternoon which followed Félicité's funeral in 1968, I had not realized that this slight man, who was so careless about himself, concealed a great understanding of life beneath an air of benevolence which irritated me sometimes because he seemed to lack discernment and be benevolent towards anyone and everyone. In truth, Stanislas and Félicité had probably never had a more attentive friend. He had watched over them, and their relationship in which nothing could be taken for granted. With an elegance unaltered by the wear and tear of those all too brief years towards the end, he had come to terms with his impoverishment and accepted his parasitism as a sovereign irony; he made a brilliant virtue of a sad necessity in accepting the charity of train and 'plane tickets, of the small cheque from one person or another to settle his tailor's bill or his slate at the Carlton bar, and of the last-minute invitations to bridge or to dinner because the hostess had discovered, panic-stricken, that there were thirteen people at the table.

Why hadn't I questioned him before? After Venice I saw him once more, in Paris. Already his thoughts were far away as if he had a premonition that death was very shortly to snatch him away from the world of pleasure and friendship that he loved so much. He spoke of the letters that Stanislas had written him in 1930 at the time of his first flight. They were, he insisted, documents of considerable importance. He would give them to me on condition that I promised not to use them without Stanislas' consent. Georges went back to Cannes and died the following day. With some revolting excuse about unpaid rent, his landlady wrote me that she had seized his worn-out clothes to sell them to a second-hand dealer. All the rest – his keepsakes and his letters – had gone in the dustbin. Or at least that was what this obnoxious woman claimed; three months later I found ten letters from Stanislas to his Greek friend in a print and autograph dealer's.

Georges Kapsalis and I would have been in each other's confidence earlier, had I been able to forget a bad childhood memory, one of those secret, nagging shames that one finds it so hard to rid oneself of even when one confesses them – as I did to Stanislas who laughed about it and ridiculed me but nevertheless filed it away in a corner of his memory to transform it later, as he always did.

The result was a short story published in the *New Yorker*[1] in 1970, a year after Georges' death. The original, in French, was lost by Stanislas. As happened with Stendhal, whose articles in the *New Monthly Magazine* had to be reproduced very tentatively, in the hope that the first transition of our language into English had not falsified him too much,[2] I have tried, though without really succeeding, to capture Stanislas' tone in this extract from *Paradise of a Gambler*. The story is about a gambler who has always laughed off his defeats and who has just lost his last franc. He borrows enough for a ticket from the doorman at the club and takes the métro – forgive me Stanislas! – the underground railway to a jeweller who will buy his tiepin, the only valuable object he has left. It is this pin, set with a decent diamond, which will allow Dimitri Papanou to make a dignified exit. He feels a genuine joy at the idea of putting an end to his gambling, and his life; he looks forty years younger. The world seems to him full of charms which it will be sublime to leave. He is even oblivious to the silent disapproval of the travellers around him, who are irritated by his antiquated elegance. Dandies are out of place in 1970; but Dimitri, who has always perfected his own grooming with more than a hint of disdain for anyone who dresses sloppily, does not care. He will not fail to play his part as the curtain comes down. Then, at the rue de la Pompe stop, a group of schoolboys, who have been let out early, get on. Individually, they are no worse than any others, but being in a gang grants them a kind of immunity. They are laughing and kicking up a din, jostling around him when Dimitri recognizes the young Jean among them, son of one of his best friends, a child he has known from birth and often bounced on his knee. He wants to make some kind of friendly sign to him, shake hands or kiss his cheek, but Jean hides behind his friends and there is another outburst of sarcastic remarks and crude jibes which amuses the other passengers no end. Everyone is laughing at Dimitri, at his Borsalino, his stiff collar, his spotted tie,

---

[1] *New Yorker*, 1 April 1970: *Paradise of a Gambler*.

[2] Stendhal wrote in English in the *New Monthly Magazine*. This must have produced some stylistic difficulties when his articles came to be translated back into his mother tongue.

his perfumed silk handkerchief, his cream kid gloves, his grey suit (from Johnson's at 3 Savile Row), his beige spats, his silver-topped cane, his fine, white palikar's moustache:

Dimitri Papanou suffered like an arrow the revelation that he was an affront to this world, sick, weary, jaundiced and bad-tempered as a chained dog is bad-tempered. Because little Jean did not dare acknowledge him, Dimitri detested himself. He had never loved himself passionately in any case, and to tell the truth he had sometimes come to despise himself secretly, but for such derision to be poured on his head suddenly made him loathsome in his own eyes. He felt a wave of nausea so violent that his free hand clenched the handrail in rage. His eyes closed, he suppressed a sob of rage and despair. What rhyme or reason was there to his perfect suicide, his beautiful dream of throwing himself into the sea from the gardens high up on the cliffs of Monaco? How deeply he had felt that this volplane over the flowers and the exotic plants and the dive into the intensely blue waters would impart some meaning to his sordid existence! If Jean did not come over to him within the next minute, his endurance would snap. The next station came and Jean made no move. Other travellers got on, jostling Dimitri who, in the harsh glare of the neon, looked like a wax figure with its eyes closed. A violent blow bruised him in the small of his back, perhaps from the toolbox of a plumber whose filthy odours he perceived as a further challenge. The underground train moved off. Dimitri opened his eyes again. The children were uncontrollable now, mocking him all the more rudely because they felt the tacit encouragement of the adults delighted at the persecution of this ageing exquisite. Dimitri raised his hat to beg a lady to excuse him, went up to the sliding doors, wrenched them apart with a furious energy and let himself fall beneath the wheels.

Imagination has the sacred right of embellishing love and dramatizing death. My own story in the underground with Georges Kapsalis – alias Dimitri Papanou – only served as a starting-point. It is quite true that one day, as I came out of school with a group of schoolmates, I recognized our Greek friend in a second-class carriage where his slightly over-smart dress clashed with that of the other travellers. One should not try to mingle with the six o'clock crowds when one has decided, from an early age, to dress like a dandy. I think I had an immediate foreboding that something unpleasant was going to happen and that I should hide myself from him. Did he see me, recognize me among those scruffy boys, so noisy and jeering? I never found out, but when my school friends began to taunt him with their heavy sarcasm and call him a gay dog, I saw him stiffen and restrain himself from lashing out with his cane. Insensitive to his dignity they continued, making fun of his dashing moustache and the smell of his perfume, which he exuded in waves and which struggled vainly against the underground smells of dust and sweat and burnt electricity. After three stops, he decided it would be preferable to get off. He stayed standing on the platform, bewildered and deeply wounded by the grimacing faces which were still jeering at him, their noses squashed against the glass. I never found out whether he had picked me out from the others, and for a long time afterwards I felt horribly ashamed. If I had gone up to him my friends would have kept quiet. Possibly they would have taken it out on me at the next morning's break, but I would have protected the man whom I knew to be Stanislas' and Félicité's best friend; I would have saved him from that cruel attack. For years I avoided him and he must have thought me hostile or indifferent. It was only on the afternoon of the funeral in Venice that we talked openly to each other, and then again one last time in Paris.

It was a great shame. He knew so many things, and I think that, despite his discretion, he would have talked freely to me, notably on the subject of Stanislas' first flight in 1930.

*

But let us not get too far ahead. Our chronology has only taken us as far as 1928 when, after the *baccalauréat*, Stanislas and his friend André matriculated at the literature faculty. In his diary my father has noted:

Classes start tomorrow. We have already spotted a table on the terrace outside the d'Harcourt from where, sitting in comfort and drinking *cafés crème*, we can follow the comings and goings at the Sorbonne. It will be a most instructive spectacle. Men of our age who have gained a cultural gloss and some taste for literature will penetrate the temple of knowledge; later, they will emerge, before our very eyes, stupefyingly ignorant, emptied of all their passion, already old men, prepared to crucify innocent schoolboys. We shall not follow their example. We are poets and we intend to save our genius from the dictatorship of dull archivists and tutors.

We can recognize, even in the terms he uses, the influence of Georges Dupuy, their master at Janson who, despite being posted to the provinces, continued to influence his two young pupils. Thanks to his having undergone the experience himself, they did not fall into the glaring trap of university study. But was Dupuy right to smother André's nascent talent at birth? I have discovered a letter from him addressed to my father and dated January 1929: 'Dear Garrett, I want to do you a small favour: don't take yourself for a poet. Best wishes. G. D.' André, having cheerfully torn everything up, wrote in his notebook:

Freedom at last! M. Dupuy has liberated me, I am no longer a hostage to poetry. Have joyfully sacrificed a few hundred execrable verses. I shall now devote my life to the literature of others. What a relief! And with what enthusiasm I can envisage the future! Must speak to Father tomorrow about doing something with his investment in Editions Saeta which has been gathering dust ever since he bought it.

At this time there is still no question of considering Stanislas as a great poet or a future novelist. Shortly after Georges Dupuy's peremptory verdict, we find in André's diary this note of commiseration:

Stanislas continues to scribble. What courage! It's true that Monsieur Dupuy has not clipped his wings as he did mine. In fact, I shouldn't be surprised if he's secretly urging him on to work.

No bitterness, as one can see. Friendship overrode everything else. Even if they did not reserve a permanent table on the terrace of the Café d'Harcourt it is, on the other hand, certain that they did not set foot in the faculty and that they even absented themselves from the examinations. What could be simpler? They both claimed that they had passed their first certificate and went down to Cap-Ferrat for the vacation, assured that neither my grandparents nor Félicité would bother to check and that the civil servant on the quai d'Orsay who continued to send Stanislas a meagre allowance had other fish to fry.

Acting out their wild deception to the end, in June 1931 they gaily returned home one morning, Bachelors of Arts. Stanislas was applauded much more loudly than my father. How energetically had he overcome his handicap, mastered French and made up for the time he had lost during the three months of his disappearance! There is, in the biographical notes of the numerous articles published after his death, frequent mention of this degree that he never took and never boasted about after the day that he claimed to have received it. Perhaps Félicité, during the course of that summer, made some small show in front of her friends of the merits of this 'Danube peasant' that she had decided to marry. The cause had by now been given a long time to mature. She loved him and he loved her – which is not the same thing as saying that they loved each other. Félicité wanted the marriage. She got it. It confirmed a bond which had been shaken by the famous disappearance. Félicité had no alternative but to admit that she had trembled and suffered with an excessive desire for possession, which the journey to the town hall put an end to. Georges Kapsalis had a very clear memory of the ceremony which took place before a few close friends at Cap-Ferrat.

'In the course of the luncheon that followed,' he said to me, 'we saw before us a radical change take place in her. Her anxiety, which was gnawing at her more than we would have believed possible, magically disappeared. One cannot pretend that she blossomed, because she was not the kind of woman to blossom, but we knew that some internal tension had disappeared. Now that Stanislas was her husband, she would no longer suffer from any liberties he decided to take. He could go away for six months, a year, she would always find him again in the end. She lived in the peaceful certainty that they would never part. As regards him, I believe that his feelings were, if not similar, at least related: his new ties with Félicité put an end to an irritating situation and offered him a refuge from which nobody would be able to dislodge him on those days when he was weary and embittered; then Félicité would soothe his soul and guide him back to the work he had forsaken through doubt or the heat of one of those passions which he never denied himself, not for the sake of kudos or because he was weak, but because he felt a vital need of them to nourish his work which was his reason for living. Yet one thing prickled him for a long time: Félicité was still called Madame della Croce. Everyone who knew her called her by that name. It seemed to be difficult to go against this habit and for her to become, overnight, Madame Beren. The success he had with *The Secret Life of an Orgasm* a few months later and the warm reception it got among her friends did not substantially alter the situation. One day some thoughtless woman – either as a joke or out of sheer malice – introduced Stanislas to an utterly idiotic Russian princess as Monsieur della Croce; he went so pale that I thought he was about to slap her. All through the luncheon I waited for a scene, but it was evident that he had calmed himself and was contemplating a practical joke rather than revenge. When we got up from the table, the guests started laughing: Stanislas had pulled out a shirt-tail and it was sticking up proudly between two of his fly-buttons. The funniest part was the desperate efforts of one or two people to draw Stanislas' attention to his indecency – nudging him, murmuring things in his ear – and his feigned incomprehension. When at last he was no longer able to ignore the whispering, he put his shirt-tail back inside his fly without the slightest embarrassment and continued to perorate with such perfect ease that people laughed all the louder.'

★

In 1930, before the marriage, Stanislas had already moved in with Félicité. In Paris he had a room adjoining hers at the Ritz, and during the vacations, in the summer, at Christmas and Easter he followed her to Cap-Ferrat or Deauville. Meanwhile he had not forgotten his uncle Dimitri in his store in Passy and he visited him at least twice a week, a duty that he respected faithfully, as if through this last link he were trying not to cut himself off entirely from his secret past. One morning in March 1930 he found the store closed and was only able to get in with the aid of a locksmith and a policeman. Uncle Dimitri had died in his armchair, holding the stem of his hookah in his hand. The locksmith and the policeman are no longer available to testify to the truth of the scene described, seven years later, in *Cryptogram*, where the hero, S., discovers his father dead in the same circumstances as uncle Dimitri:

Contrary to what one is in the habit of believing in such cases, he did not appear to be sleeping at all. Indeed, he was very much awake, his eyes wide open (albeit slightly glaucous, with the pupils dilated as if to see better into the void), his head tipped against the back of the armchair; and as the masseter and the temporalis had suddenly relaxed in death and then set stiff with rigor mortis, his mouth yawned open, revealing a horse's teeth, long, yellow and regular, so that the locksmith (whose father had been a carter and who still knew a reasonable amount about the care of horses) instinctively bent over this purplish chasm to determine the age of the old man. He was about to pull back the right cheek to examine the molars when three flies, which were laying their eggs on the curled-up tongue, flew out in fright and buzzed frantically about the shabby room, lit by a yellow forty-watt bulb swinging on its wire in a current of air. S. realised that his father was dead and he was happy for the old man, who had found by himself the best possible solution to his vegetative life, suspended by the single thread of the gurgling and the cold smoke of the hookah. If there were a world beyond, his father had entered it without making any concessions, just as life had mummified him in these final years, in the middle of a hypnagogic dream where he could hear, coming from far away on the steppes but getting nearer day by day, the thudding hooves of the hordes of knights standing up in their stirrups, preceded by the reek of leather and wool grease. Only one thing troubled this inexpressible peace: the frantic reproductive activity of the flies which, to an ignorant observer, seemed somehow unbecoming. Thankfully S. was a cultivated man. He had read Lucian of Samosata, who concurs with Plato in affirming that the soul of the fly is immortal, insofar as it is nourished by mortals.

These lines shed no light on the personality of uncle Dimitri. Who are these hordes of knights galloping across the steppe? Is it just an image born from an access of lyricism, or an allusion to the Cossack origins of the old grocer? On two occasions I heard Stanislas claim that he had Cossack blood in his veins. The most difficult thing to explain is how the exiled uncle made a living from a store which was visited by no more than ten customers a day. One begins to wonder what he lived on, apart from memories brooded over in his armchair. He must have had some other means, a hidden hoard even, whose whereabouts were known to Stanislas. It is not, for the moment, possible for me to give my sources, but I think I can state positively that it was thanks to these funds that Stanislas was able to disappear a few days after the funeral, to vanish into thin air, leaving only a letter for André:

I have gone to get some fresh air. Do not worry. I shall be back. Calm Félicité for me. I shall have no other secrets from you in the future, but this time I must.

André has written in his diary:

Stanislas has obeyed an order. Or a summons. One or the other, sparked off by the death of his uncle Dimitri. He has gone back to see his mountains, his parents if he still has any. It seems to me that he'll come back, but I wouldn't bet on it for certain. We must be brave and, like aunt Félicité, not display our vulnerability.

When he came back three months later, shortly before his final exams, Stanislas was lean and tanned. In truth, he was not exactly tanned, but his normally pale features had acquired a bronzed, weather-beaten look. In what circumstances, he would not say. A few days after his return, Félicité telephoned André to ask him to try and find out how Stanislas had come by the two scars on his arm. Their regularity and symmetry indicated that they were either inflicted with his consent or that he had been held down by force. There were two crosses drawn on the outer side of his arm: two crosses with members of equal length, orthodox crosses, perhaps the sign of some sect, an indelible brand which would forever remind him of his origins. André came up against a wall of silence. Stanislas refused point-blank to talk about the scars. Life continued as before, with the exception that, as I said, Félicité cemented their match with a bond that only death could sever.

Stanislas and André were hardly ever apart. I was about to say that they were writing *The Secret Life of an Orgasm*, but that would be ambiguous because not a single line of it was my father's; he only appointed himself the guardian of the work and talked about it in his personal notebooks with a lyricism which would sound naive today. Indeed, the germ of nearly all of Stanislas' work is present in this book, together with some awkwardness which will soon disappear. In a first novel a writer sows his wild oats, and the cost is borne by his publisher because only on the day that the writer has a finished copy in his hand will he be in a position to distinguish what should have been ruthlessly thrown out and what, for him, is an enduring truth.

This first essay is crammed with Stanislas' hesitations; one imagines that it is written by a man who, with teeth clenched, is so obsessed by the idea of revealing the secret of his being that, in order to conceal himself better, he adds mask upon mask in the vain hope of deceiving his reader. Would the press have taken any notice of it if Stanislas had not been Félicité's husband? The question is a difficult one to answer, because the critics who discussed him were so independent and so much less anxious than they are today to frogmarch a young writer into a category. Even had she wanted to, Félicité would have been incapable of soliciting anyone, but ultimately the reports of her dinners and the prestige of the artists who surrounded her made it inevitable that Stanislas should attract attention. Later, when, after the war, she grew weary of receiving guests and her illness gradually reduced her activity, it was Stanislas who became the centre of interest in Paris when they passed through, in Venice, and for the two or three months of the year that they spent in the pretty house in Chelsea where he ended his life.

The Secret Life of an Orgasm is the fruit of an internal battle which lasted two years, a battle with words, with the flood of ideas, images and grandiose visions which those words brought into the open and tarnished pitilessly. Through it Stanislas learnt how physically painful, insulting, indecent and naive it is to write a novel. There were, naturally, some high-minded newspapers ready to brand the book as obscene, to denounce it as scandal for scandal's sake, some even suggesting its seizure. If these pious people, so hyper-anxious about public morals, had taken the trouble to open the novel and read it carefully, they would have looked in vain for a risqué scene. There are none. The title is merely a provocative spoof invented by André who wanted to celebrate the re-opening of Editions Saeta with a bang. He could have confounded the moralists; he chose not to. Its aura of scandal served the book well with a small section of the public and did it no harm at all among the wide audience that Stanislas would enjoy with his second novel, *The Countdown*. The one passage that might have been cut by a strict censor preoccupied with making the whole world asexual, is the completely decent and proper allusion in the first paragraph to the chance sexual encounter between a deserter and a large peasant woman with very solid ankles who is bathing naked in the river. The deserter kneels down on the steep bank to drink and suddenly sees, mingled with his own reflection, the milky-white reflection of the woman. He grasps her hand, pulls her onto the bank and takes her there and then, without her saying a word. She seems almost indifferent to what is going on and when he rolls off her, she stays spread out in the cool damp grass of the meadow, not even turning her head to watch the man go as he makes his way towards a clump of trees where he plans to hide until nightfall. The constables on his trail catch sight of him, block his escape route and shoot him down. Hearing the gunshots, the woman experiences a spasm of pleasure. The boy born from this union becomes a soldier at fifteen, a general at twenty, emperor at twenty-five and god of his people at thirty. The day he is proclaimed a god, he commits suicide in order to secure for himself the only immortality which is worth having. The sceptre is taken up by Anne de Beautremont, an authoritarian woman who has been the mistress of the palace. It is she who has procured for the solitary emperor the women he has needed, taking care, each time she sees him ready to form an attachment, to banish these utilitarian creatures and ensure that the hero devotes his energy exclusively to his people. When the emperor-god dies she assumes power, and in order to cool the overheated imaginations of the people, she demobilizes the army and sends the soldiers back to work in their fields and their market stalls. A terrorised Cabinet votes in a series of laws which, on the face of it, are rather odd: the wearing of long underpants becomes compulsory, as do lenitive infusions after dinner; mothers must nurse their own babies; and engaged couples must wait three years before they marry. Anyone who wants to carry on with the grand, heroic dream is mercilessly executed or sent to the salt mines, and Anne de Beautremont explains to her ministers (on their knees) that history cannot be repeated and that after their days of Glory the people can have no salvation unless they forget their god and put on carpet slippers.

*

The reader was justifiably surprised. Swept along on an epic adventure, he suddenly saw the author burst out laughing and hold that same adventure up to ridicule. The closing pages gave him the impression that he had been made fun of, that a trick had been played on his naivety. In reality it was not the reader that Stanislas Beren was making fun of, but himself, as if, suddenly conscious that he had let his imagination become inflamed, he had come back down to earth. The ending was badly received by the few critics who liked the book. They had let themselves be taken in and then the author had laughed in their faces; but Léon Daudet, Emmanuel Berl and André Bellessort defended Stanislas. They were the only three to notice his writing, his imagination, his sensibility curbed by sarcasm. 'In short,' wrote Bellessort, 'Monsieur Beren has everything going for him. He has yet to become a writer – which, with his gifts, he undoubtedly will be – but he must not continue to jeer at us. That would be too puerile for a man of his quality.' Jean Cocteau, interviewed on the young writers he had read over the winter, said, 'I see only one who is clothing himself while all the others are frantically stripping off: Stanislas Beren, a discreet writer in an age of indiscretions.'

The phrase raised some smiles. People saw in it one of those brilliant paradoxes with which Cocteau always wound up. But he was quite right. Stanislas was and remained a discreet writer.

In *The Secret Life of an Orgasm* there is no allusion to the fugue of 1930. The action takes place in an imaginary country where a chain of mountains borders a coastline left ragged by a tideless sea. On the valley floors men work at a brisk pace, but as soon as a certain altitude is reached life slows down and sometimes even stops. A population of shepherds lives a life of contemplation: indeed, some are considered to be saints because they become so static in their contemplation that they waste away on their stone seats, clutching their crooks. They become mummified by the wind and birds of prey peck their orbits clean. The people call them the guardians of Olympus. Although I have never been able to have it positively confirmed, it seems that this is a Serbian legend. Did Stanislas go back to his mountains when he disappeared? I am inclined to think so. If he did, it was not out of nostalgia but because he wanted to make his final farewell. Life had summoned him elsewhere – and it cannot be denied that this elsewhere was more pleasant, especially in the summer of 1932 at Cap-Ferrat. In one sense the novel's publication justified Félicité, even in the eyes of those who had not read it. As for André, he could be satisfied: the first book published by his publishing house had been noticed; the result of him pointing this out to his father was that the latter generously advanced more capital, thanks to which they were able to buy the rights to a number of foreign novels, pay the translators, give themselves some publicity and look to the future. Editions Saeta was run on a skeleton staff: Georges Dupuy who read and copy-edited the manuscripts, and one secretary, Emeline Aureo, a charming spinster tortured by cystitis who worshipped Stanislas. The two friends used to arrive before everyone else, sweep the offices, package up the parcels of books and take turns to go down to the telephone in the café on the corner, since it was six months before Editions Saeta was given a line. The comparative success of *The Secret Life of an Orgasm* allowed them to close the offices for two months. Future projects would ripen in the sun, at the water's edge or out in the boat.

Here I have to place an event which has perhaps more importance for me than for Stanislas' biography, although it sheds light on his behaviour too, and on what some have called his 'taste for mystification' but which I want to try to analyse more closely. The novelist at his blank page is an omnipotent creator. He distributes the roles, separates, unites, condemns to death, plays with chance and most importantly breathes love into a look, an encounter, a secret affinity which delivers his characters from their solitude or indifference. Once his book is finished, he is like a king without a throne, returning to the masks and mediocrities of life, helplessness he can do nothing to remedy, events over which he has no hold. This moment, before the trigger which sets off a new book in him, is a time of pain and frustration. He is like one of those mothers of large families who, between births, complains that she is no longer fulfilling her task of procreation and waits impatiently for the next round of suffering to begin.

During the summer of 1931 Stanislas, who had been forbidden by Georges Dupuy to write a word while he was on holiday, measured the extent of his fall from grace. He was living among characters in a novel, without any power over them. Among these characters was one for whom he had a particular affection and with whom he talked long and passionately in the evenings, but who during the day retreated onto his small yacht with the sky-blue hull which he had re-christened *Saeta*. Stanislas was infuriated by the ease with which André slipped from his grasp and suddenly disappeared off to his boat to spend the greater part of the day sailing out beyond the headland. Stanislas discerned a flaw in their friendship, almost a betrayal, and accused him of robbing both their lives of valuable time. Had they not got a vast programme to carry out? When by chance the *Saeta*, with its light Marconi sails, became becalmed out past Saint-Hospice Point, Stanislas would get out the binoculars and spy on André, who was capable of staying in the same position for hours, ensconced in the bottom of the cockpit, one arm resting nonchalantly on the boom, the other on the deck, his hand within reach of the jib-sheet. When Stanislas had had enough of this inactivity, he would jump into the villa's outboard and go alongside.

'Shall I give you a tow?'

'Oh no, I'm fine.'

'But you'll be stuck there for a week!'

'There'll be a breeze at sunset. I can wait till then. Who's coming to dinner?'

'Albert Einstein, the President of the Republic and the Pope.'

'In that case, there's no rush. They can wait. Offer them a drink.'

And Stanislas would depart, furious, brooding on some way to upset André's serenity. Eventually he succeeded, in the happiest and most unlikely way, by inventing a girl that he claimed to have met on the road which went round the headland. He described her out walking, always alone, her hair blown by the wind. Her eyes were of a blue so pale that had it not been for the certainty of her step you would have thought she was blind. Each time he related the story Stanislas embroidered on this apparition: she was the beginning of a novel, the incarnation of grace on earth. Nothing less would have sufficed to jolt

André out of his nautical dreams. Then one day, Félicité invited some neighbours, the Dumonts, to lunch. They came with their daughter.

'Is that her?' André asked Stanislas.

'Yes.'

'She hasn't got blue eyes, she's got green eyes.'

'I must have made a mistake.'

'She hasn't got long hair.'

'She cut it off yesterday.'

Reality was joining forces with fictional invention in the most simple and convincing way. By the time lunch was over Stanislas had realized, to his amazement, that he had won. André did not slip off back to his boat as he usually did. Equally, he did not say a word to the girl that day, but there was no mistaking that he had seen her and that she had seen him. They were not going to spoil everything with the small talk of two people indifferent to each other. They had better things to confide as soon as the noise of voices ceased, a noise that did not interest them, a noise that separated them. Of them one can say that they loved each other, and for both it really was the first time. They married the following year and I was born in 1936, killing my mother. Of course, André had not been fooled for long by Stanislas' story, but he admitted in his diary on the eve of the wedding:

> Would I have paid her the same attention, with the same promptness, if Stanislas had not embellished her image and prepared the feast for the eyes that was her first appearance? I'll be asking myself for a long time. I'll never know and it hardly matters. I am marrying Marie-Claire tomorrow. Stanislas invented us to each other. I saw through his tricks a long time ago.[1]

Swiftly and intuitively, Stanislas sensed that the secret powers of the imaginary world were to be treated with respect. When I had recounted the reasons for my uneasiness with Georges Kapsalis to him, he immediately conceived the short story that I have quoted above, but he took care not to write it before our friend had passed away from a natural death, if death can be natural.

'It is not that he would have read it,' he said to me in 1971. 'It only ever appeared in the *New Yorker* and he did not speak English; but one does not use words to gamble with the lives of one's close friends. In

October 1932.

1937 I wrote a story from day to day, as I was living it,[1] and then one evening the woman who had inspired it was with a man I did not know, and she made a friendly gesture, entirely innocent – placed a hand on his arm to underline a word she was repeating to him – and although I felt no jealousy at all, not even a twinge, I resolved to finish this book, which was weighing on me, by flinging my mistress into the arms of a complete idiot. And that was exactly what happened six months later, and not because she had read the book – which stayed in a drawer for a year before I made the decision to publish it – but because I had written it. When the novel came out, she sent me a sarcastic little note, telling me how little imagination I had. I would have had to serve a writ on her to prove that it was not I who had copied her, but she who had copied my novel. It was she who owed *me* money for the copyright. We must be on our guard: we walk on thin ice, and our existence is so fragile that the least sentiment out of place will alter its course. If, in your secret nights, you should amuse yourself by writing a novel, and if I should feature in this novel in a recognizable guise, I beseech you here and now not to make me die a violent death. I cannot bear the idea.'

'I shan't be writing any more novels!'[2]

'Tut-tut . . . we all say that!'

It would have been more honest of me to confess to him that although I was not writing a novel I was, on the other hand, preparing an essay on him and that I was taking notes on each of our interviews. But perhaps he knew it, and perhaps the only reason that I am able to penetrate further into the life of Stanislas Beren than anyone else today is because he wanted it that way, relinquishing to me, in our conversations of those final years, all the things he was willing to make known one day, and keeping to himself everything that he wanted to bury in the past.

★

[1] The book in question is, of course, *Cryptogram* (Editions Saeta, 1938), which I shall talk about on the subject of 'the woman who had inspired it'. Stanislas affected, out of courtesy, to assume that one had not read his books and he never quoted their titles, just the publication date, as if to consign them to the indifference of the past. With me, this courtesy verged on the coy.

[2] This promise was kept. Certainly I had, at twenty, written and published a novel which had poor reviews from the few critics who took any notice. Pascal Pia said succinctly, 'This is the poor man's Beren.' Thanks to which, Béla Zukor woke up to the idea of getting at Stanislas and immediately added in an article in *Lettres Françaises*, 'Pia has made a mistake. It is better than he says. Georges Garrett is the rich man's Beren.' Far better to bring the curtain down straight away after such a brilliant début.

On that evening in 1970, two years after Félicité's death, when he spoke to me in veiled terms about *Cryptogram* and the woman who had inspired it, we were in London, in the house in Chelsea where he preferred to live more and more, Venice only summoning him because he hoped to rediscover the life which had been breathed into it for so long by Félicité's presence and which, since her death, had deserted it. He would begin a book in Paris or London, but he could only continue it and finish it in Venice. In the afternoon we had walked along the Embankment from Westminster as far as the statue of Thomas More.

'He does not look happy,' Stanislas had said. 'Not happy at all, but one can understand why. Being decapitated cannot be much fun, especially when one does not know that one will be canonized in four hundred years' time. That long-delayed recognition might have reconciled him with humanity had it not been for me giving vent to a certain minor chaos in that telephone box next to him, and sometimes doing it in an extremely loud voice. I have telephoned a great deal from here – you see, it could not really be done in the house with Félicité there, especially the last few years when her bed was next to the only telephone – a great deal, to a person towards whom I had friendly feelings and who had even friendlier feelings towards me. One day I shall tell you about it, if you promise not to pass on her name and not to reveal what I owe her.'

We had been walking for a good two hours, meeting only joggers in their tracksuits who ran past us along this little-frequented stretch of the river.

'Paris is the most beautiful capital city in the world,' he said. 'More beautiful than Rome, though Rome is still beautiful; but there are degrees of beauty, and I have always felt that a town's beauty is determined by the river which flows through it. You see the Thames very rarely here. It makes you think these Londoners are hiding it. The Manzanares in Madrid is a pure accident. The Tajo at Lisbon is already the sea, or at any rate, they call it the sea. The Hudson in New York is just a trading route, and the Tiber only emerges with any tragic grandeur at the Castel Sant' Angelo. Whereas the Seine is part and parcel of Paris: from Bercy to Saint-Cloud it is an endless spectacle. Nothing hides it. Everything shows it off. However, having said that, I prefer London for almost indefinable reasons: perhaps because I can walk for hours without meeting a familiar face, without feeling crushed by the buildings and monuments. The monuments here are laughable, you cannot take them seriously. They are nearly all from the last century. Why in London can I walk for hours without meeting a familiar face, and why in Paris can I not turn a corner without bumping into someone I've already seen? I know just as many people in London as in Paris. I like being alone, more and more. I think I shall finish up like a stylite in the desert, like Simeon, I mean the first one, the one from Antioch, because the second was utterly dull and I shouldn't have anything to do with him, nor the third who was such a bad example, struck down by lightning in Cilicia. You have to be careful in your choice of saints. Let us go back now, can we? I am tired.'

We drank some tea by the bow-window which looks out onto the garden where Félicité had planted some thornless rose bushes – a miraculous plant brought over from Assisi. A year later the bushes had flowered, but grown thorns at the same time. 'We shall have to resign ourselves to the fact that we are not saints,' Félicité had said.

I never knew whether Stanislas liked talking about himself, or hated it. Probably both at once, as he feigned forgetfulness about his own life and only preserved memories of those times which had nourished his books. He would say nothing on the other times. Nothing on his childhood, nothing on his fugue in 1930; and nothing on the never-ending adventures which he filed away under the heading of bodily hygiene. But he liked to talk about my father, who had never been portrayed, even in silhouette, in any of his books.

'André was my only friend. Although he was younger than me at a time when that mattered, I may say that I respected him. He possessed that straightforwardness and reserve which their intuition somehow dictates to young men destined to die young. The only time we were not quite so close was between 1932 and 1936. Marie-Claire did not drive any wedge between us, but she existed and that made André less available. It is difficult to forgive one's friends for getting married. By marrying Félicité I had come closer to your father. When he married Marie-Claire, he seemed to me to have betrayed the clan, which was a completely false impression: in fact, Marie-Claire united us. Even so, I found it hard to accept her and to treat her like a younger sister, despite the fact that her angelic nature delighted me. On the subject of that angelic nature I have a secret to share with you. At the end of 1935, Marie-Claire was pregnant: to begin with, they hid it from me, but obviously I had to find out. In my heart-felt fury, I had to come to terms with something that they scarcely showed – he was as prim as she was demure: that not only did they love each other, but they made love as well. Do not get the wrong idea: I never had those sort of tastes, even if my brand of friendship was aloof, tyrannical and fundamentally egotistical. But I could not get used to the idea that André could be like me, that he needed love in order to live. If he had had a few flings I should have applauded enthusiastically. We should have confided in each other. Marriage needs secrecy. I was excluded from that secrecy. You were born, and Marie-Claire died because of a stupid mistake, a moment's negligence on the part of a nurse, and I experienced a terrible loss. Fate had struck André and so it was striking me too, by condemning to inconsolable grief the first person to hold out a hand to me when I was only a "Danube peasant", in the words of your dear grandmother who was always last in geography and first in generosity. The most curious thing is that André's death did not hurt me as much. After the armistice we had had no news of him and for some unfathomable reason nobody was really alarmed. We all assumed that he had been taken prisoner and would send out some news through the Red Cross. Félicité wanted to leave for America. Our journey was absurd, it was awful. I still feel ashamed about it, as fugitives do. In New York in October we heard that André had died. Honestly, we did not even cry. We were beyond tears. Félicité even smiled when she said, "Now I know for sure: it was written in his way of living and being." That morning I walked from our apartment on Fifth Avenue as far as the Battery, a long walk by anyone's standards, between high walls like geometrical honeycombs. I had the impression I was going along a tunnel, deafened by the clamour of Wall Street, stifled by the smoke from the docks on the Hudson. When I emerged from the tunnel I finally saw the Battery, where the first Dutchmen landed, a naked and exposed expanse like a hand extended towards Europe. The horizon was wide open. I could see the Statue of Liberty, which has ended up by being beautiful because of its ugliness, and then I kept saying to myself that if I stood up on the tips of my toes, instead of the flat and circular horizon, my eyes would be able to distinguish the chaos of Europe, its mountain ranges, its ragged coastlines, its graves. André was there, asleep in his uniform, and I should never see him again. From now on it fell to me alone to keep the promises which we had made to each other and to accomplish the ambitious programme we had laid out in our youth – which, in the end, was not as childish as it had seemed. And then I thought of you, four years old and without father, mother or grandfather. Literally surrounded by a hecatomb. How would you manage while I was away? Your grandmother would do a marvellous job with your health. But what about your inquisitiveness? It seems to me now that in fact it did not go off too badly and that there was no need to worry.'

It was dark outside. The Chelsea garden had disappeared and Stanislas stood up to draw the curtains. He served the tea himself with the ceremonial gestures which he always observed for the good things of life: whenever he served a wine, carved a roast, prepared a cocktail, or opened a precious book; even when he addressed his first words to an attractive woman to whom he was introduced – and whom he captivated in seconds but would not pursue if he detected the slightest vanity in her. The day before we had been to Fortnum and Mason's to choose a new blend of China tea, and I had been amused by his suspicions, his doubts, his scepticism. There was an aspect of play-acting in his behaviour and, at the same time, since Félicité had gone, a desire to please at all costs. This was the tea we were drinking, and after a few sips he judged it too smoked. Tomorrow he would go and see his salesman and ask for a milder blend.

'That is fashion for you. You launch the fashion for smoked food, and willy-nilly people start smoking everything: cold meats, entrées, fish, tea. It must be resisted. I am shocked at how little discernment people have, people who claim to know about eating and drinking. They will gulp down anything. And you notice that it is the same thing with literature: immediately there is a school, everyone rushes to the pupils' grubby copybooks. I am not saying that everyone reads them, but they certainly buy them. When I came back from the United States in 1946 – I was not as old as all that, thirty-eight – anyhow, I had been reasonably successful before the war, published three books, people had talked about me, and I had two manuscripts in my luggage. The choice of publisher posed no problem since Monsieur Dupuy was back from his prison camp in Silesia and had re-opened Saeta; better still, he had found out that, by one of those strokes of luck which he was unable to account for, some obscure American whose first detective novel we – your father and I – had published in 1939 had become the darling of the intellectuals and the public's golden boy. Jean-Paul Sartre was reading him openly in the Flore and the Coupole – which was the equivalent of taking full-page advertisements in the national papers – and Simone de Beauvoir was confessing to the women's magazines that every morning she read him avidly in the lavatory and that thanks to these long sessions, enthroned and enthralled, she no longer suffered from either boredom or constipation. In short, our author was selling in the hundreds of thousands and every book was being made into a film. Editions Saeta was in very good shape, and in addition, Félicité had decided to give it some help so that when you reached your majority you would find a publishing house which was thriving and a tradition to be continued. Monsieur Dupuy published the first of my American manuscripts[1] which had sunk without trace when Doubleday had issued it in a translation – which, I might add, was execrable and should not have been accepted: nor would it have been, had I had slightly more self-respect. So the French edition came out later, which has a way of infuriating our supercilious and nationalistic critics. I was punished: not a single line appeared in the press. I had not been ignored, I had been struck off the literary map. Existentialism was the fashion and it was the poor man's Sartres and the worthless copies of de Beauvoir who were claiming everyone's attention. It was they who represented fashion, the fashion that turned its back on the past and finally discovered the truth to which, henceforth, we all had to conform. For ever. Béla Zukor had already published his venomous article in *Les Lettres françaises*. Cynically, I wished that he would give a repeat performance for the sake of the book, which might possibly have sparked off some controversy or aroused some vague curiosity. But the unspeakable man kept quiet. I think Saeta's sold three hundred copies of that novel, and those three hundred copies were probably stolen from the booksellers who, of course, subsequently had to pay the publisher for them. One small sign comforted me: there were thirty copies printed on some of that scrappy esparto paper which was so difficult to find in the post-war years. One morning a bookseller came to buy these thirty originals that no one wanted. I asked to see him. We became great friends. He taught me to love beautiful books, which was something new to me, and he taught me to take care of the books that I had previously discarded once I had read them, ignorant of the feverish emotion they might be charged with when one picked them up again ten years later. You see . . . I owe a great deal to everybody.'

*

But who does not owe something to someone? I often found myself deploring in Stanislas a humility and a modesty which I am not certain were absolutely sincere, despite the fact that if one affects those feelings for long enough, one ends up not duped by them, but

[1] Once more, Stanislas disdained any mention of the title of this novel. Called *Trust Me* in America (Doubleday, 1943), it was published in France under the title *Crois-moi* (Saeta, 1947).

honestly believing in them. The only thing that can be said with certainty is that right up until his last writings he doubted himself with a kind of ill-concealed masochism. The indifference with which *Trust Me* was greeted would not have wounded him had it not been for an additional incident which he took rather badly. In New York, during the war, he had met André Breton fairly regularly. I shall not pretend that they were ideally suited to each other, but in the end, the remoteness of France, the small circle of émigrés in which they moved, and the sincere admiration that Stanislas felt for some of Breton's writings, notably *Nadja*, facilitated their contact and opened the way to a sort of friendship, inasmuch as friendship had any meaning for Breton, who only ever demanded servility from his entourage and whose only companion at the end of his life was the inane Benjamin Péret who simply parroted all his proclamations. In *Trust Me*, on page 124, there is a quotation from Rimbaud:

I conclude by finding the confusion of my spirit sacred. I was idle, prey to a weighty fever; I envied the beasts their bliss – the caterpillars which represent the innocence of limbo, the slumber of virginity.

Two words have been omitted. The passage should read '. . . the innocence of limbo, the moles, the slumber of virginity'. Because of those missing moles, forgotten perhaps by Stanislas, perhaps by the type-setter and proof-reader, Breton flew into a blazing rage – not in the press where he wrote very little, but in a letter of four pages of lacerating invective, asking Stanislas to address no further word to him, and to avoid even looking in his direction unless he wished to be chastised in public. Breton levelled his usual subsidiary charges too, that Stanislas was a pederast and an instrument of the Vatican. Obviously, the omission was culpable, but mistakes of this sort do appear in books, escaping all proof-reading, and only striking the eye once the book is published and distributed to the bookshops. In fact, it *was* rather hard to see how caterpillars represented 'the slumber of virginity' in any way, but Breton's ragings bore the signs of a paranoia bordering on the grotesque, and were utterly disproportionate to the outrage committed on Rimbaud. In the first place, Stanislas had never been counted among the number of Breton's 'disciples' and his excommunication from the surrealist clique was equivalent to excommunicating an unbeliever. And in any case, between two writers, all that would have been necessary was a friendly letter pointing out the misprint, which could then have been corrected in later editions. But by violating Rimbaud, Stanislas had violated Breton in person. A worthy classical essayist and an uninspired poet, condemned to his 'automatic writing', Breton identified himself with his gods and could hardly bear others to touch them. Rimbaud belonged to him.

'I have kept the letter,' Stanislas told me that evening in London in 1970. 'It is here with some other papers which you will be able to read one day, should you decide you want to. And should you not want to, you have my permission to tear them up. They are here, in the safe in this room. . . . No, it is not visible, I have taken one or two precautions: when all is said and done, I live in these houses fairly sporadically and they are easy game for thieves. But let me say that I am not afraid of being robbed. It has happened to me and the thing I hated most was not the loss of any object of value, but the mess, the pointless damage, the destruction for its own sake. There are stupid thieves who will break in without any finesse and I try to tempt them as little as possible. Imagine them coming here, well informed: they know that there is a safe let into the wall. With a little expertise they will realize that the safe is behind one of the pictures. It will take them less than five minutes to lift down that attractive Hockney drawing and find it. They will break it open, take what they want, and leave. There is a combination lock: remember it, eight letters, Félicité. The day that I leave you, a solicitor will be instructed to leave you alone in this room for five minutes, which will be just long enough for you to take away the papers that I intend you to have: a few unfinished pages, Breton's missive, some letters I have kept as memories of past loves, a list of people to be told, including one or two women who will have collections of letters from me which you will be able to use with their permission. . . .'

In 1977, when Stanislas died, I was summoned by the solicitor and events took place according to the wish expressed seven years earlier; but Breton's letter was not in the safe. In its place I discovered a small piece of paper: 'Finally I decided to tear up the volley of insults: it condemned a serious negligence on my part, but more important it made Breton look ridiculous. Peace be with the ashes of the sergeant of Rimbaud's bodyguard.'

The other papers were of enough consequence for me to postpone discussing them for a time, except that there were some which have a bearing on Stanislas' peculiar gift for 'writing the future'. Just as he had foreseen in *Cryptogram* the end of an affair which, by a peculiar trick, had conformed to his own novelistic invention, Stanislas had amused himself – though can one say 'amused', despite the lightness of tone and the irony which jeered at all melancholy? – by writing a short biography of half a dozen pages of a character who is so much like himself that there is no room for doubt. People who are curious about his birth are discouraged: he dodges the question with a curt 'what interest does it have?'; but otherwise the character's life had substantial parallels with his own. And his death occupies, proportionally, the largest part of this synopsis of an autobiography, as if Stanislas, more and more convinced of his super-lucidity, had wanted to settle the details of his own death so that nothing was left to chance. In the twilight of a life devoted to architecture, the hero, who has no name – let us call him S. – decides to construct a scale model of an ideal city in the open desert. The city must be self-sufficient. The moment one leaves, one is swallowed up by the sands; but behind the high walls which protect the inhabitants, luxuriant vegetation flourishes thanks to a geyser which supplies the city with water. S. has thought of everything: the inhabitants – even down to their physique – their houses, the traffic, sports grounds and the places to which men retreat from the promiscuities of marriage: cafés, restaurants, clubs, gaming rooms, brothels. Once his ideal city is finished, S. perceives sadly that he himself cannot be integrated into it, that the model is too small and that really he ought to have constructed it to life-size and taken refuge in it to escape his own disillusionment. He has installed a sort of platform, a control tower, in the hangar where his papier mâché constructions stand, and with the aid of his control panel, he rules the lives of his automata. In the beginning the game fascinates him, then he gradually loses interest until it bores him completely, to the point where one evening he falls asleep, and as his head slumps onto the keyboard, panic breaks out in the city. S. does not care. He is dreaming. In fact he is dreaming that he is making love to one of his creations, a woman with steely grey eyes, and his pleasure is such that an embolus dispatches him without his being aware even for a moment of his own death. Under the weight of his body the control panel collapses and the automata are immobilised. Gradually they will turn to dust like the body of S. himself.

After the word 'finis', Stanislas had written, 'Slightly cowardly, isn't it, as a "happy ending"? Dying without suffering, without knowing it! Very hedonistic. Yet would anyone refuse such a pleasant way out if he were given the choice between violent death, a long drawn-out, painful death, and a clean, instantaneous death? We must be honest.'

I shall not labour the point about the symbolism of this sketch discovered after his death. It is too conspicuous as it is. A novelist is an artist and, within the hierarchy of art, he is probably the greatest of creators, the closest to God, and at the same time doctor to his own mind; but his work and his characters are threatened by the encroaching sands of neglect. When he dies, the illusory movements which signalled a life being lived are turned to stone. His creation is frozen for eternity. Yet all this is simple; what is important lies elsewhere. Stanislas wished himself a merciful death. He almost had it, in circumstances which I shall recount later. His power to 'write the future' stopped at himself. When he guessed, by some inexplicable intuition, which horses would win, he could only pass on the names or numbers to Georges Kapsalis: making any personal gain from them was not even conceivable.

On the evening of that long conversation, which penetrated the sequence of his life in a very random way but touched on all the things he liked to evoke both directly and enigmatically, we went out to dine at Wheeler's, five minutes' walk away. They always kept the same table for him in the basement, where he liked to sit with his back to the panelling, facing the curve of the spiral staircase; and he claimed that he had had dozens of ideas for novels while he watched the legs of the couples stepping down it, legs betraying indecision or fear or assurance. He could identify adulterers, newly-weds, actions for divorce, simply from the way those feet were placed on the steps. In *Where Are You Dining Tonight?*[1] there is a brilliant dissertation in the same style on couples at a concert, when the hero, Maximilian von Arelle, discovers that the woman he loves has fallen in love with her husband for the second time simply from the way she listens to Markevitch conducting Stravinsky's *Firebird*.

We dined on sole meunière which he ate with that slight and refined greediness which hostesses would watch out for with a hint of anxiety, because he manifested both pleasure and displeasure with equal promptness. In one of these moments of contentment it was possible to ask questions which were not always greeted with an evasive answer. I ventured to ask him, 'Who was the lady you telephoned so often from the box next to Thomas More?'

He raised his head, took off his glasses and smiled. 'You really are very inquisitive. What do you think of this chablis?'

'Decent enough.'

[1] *Where Are You Dining Tonight?*, Editions Saeta, 1960.

'You are right. No more than decent. The lady whom I telephoned so often has her name written on a large envelope in my safe which contains the only three letters she was able to write me. You can read them when the time comes. They are of absolutely no interest and you will be good enough to give them back to her in exchange for the hundred or so letters I must have sent her. I think I probably made some slight, but reasonably flattering, observations about her figure and the desire which she inspired in me. And what is left? Nothing to be compared with the pleasure this sole is giving me. . . .'

Four years separated the publication of *The Secret Life of an Orgasm* from that of *The Countdown*, which is a long time when one imagines the impatience of a young writer who has seen his first book generally well-received despite one or two sharp reactions, and who is certainly fired by the desire to return to the fray against the critics, who were much more influential then than they are today. Stanislas was already aware that his second book would be a formidable test. The first offender may be granted a reprieve, but the press will come down heavily on him should he repeat his mistakes. Yet it was not this fear which held him back, but Félicité. It is more than likely that she advised him to give up the idea of dashing off a novel in the pleasurable circumstances in which he found himself in the winter of 1932–1933. Two pieces of evidence, one tenuous, one not so, support this proposition. The first is an interview in *Nouvelles littéraires*[1] at the time of publication of *The Countdown*:

Question: You appear very calm, which I find slightly strange. I would have imagined you more anxious by nature.
Answer: Habits are formed very quickly. With the third book. . . .
Q: You mean the second. Unless something has escaped me.
A: I loathe the number two. Allow me to leave it out.
Q: So you will skip the twenty-second as well?
A: No, I shall stop at the twenty-first. One always writes too much. . . .

The curious thing is that if one takes a bibliography of the works of Stanislas Beren, it stops at the twenty-first entry; but it is evident that he had given himself away. In André Garrett's diaries there is a note for 15 June 1933 which is unequivocal:

[1] *Nouvelles littéraires*, 16 May 1936.

Arrived at the offices this morning to find Stanislas squatting in front of the fireplace, burning paper, an entire manuscript crisping and curling in the flames.

I: What on earth are you doing?

He: I am doing justice to myself.

I: You're no judge of that.

He: Félicité can judge for me.

I: Doesn't it upset you?

He: On the contrary. I feel a kind of joy, an unexpected pleasure. . . .

And that is how it ended up, a novel for which we had found a rather nice title: *Where Are You Dining Tonight?*

André was right: the title was a good one. In fact, it has already been mentioned as the title of a novel he published in 1960. About this second *Where Are You Dining Tonight?* I shall have more to say later.

*

Félicité used to read over his shoulder. Until she died there was nothing, with the exception of one novel (*The Countdown*), which he published without her having read it through first – although it would be going too far to imagine that she approved of everything. The important question is, how did she endure his more transparent pages? For fear of betraying the essence of the woman sharing his life, or possibly as a result of an unspoken pact between them, he took great care not to evoke Félicité in any of his novels; but he made liberal use of their circle of friends and later of the one or two women – I suppose I should say 'many' – who passed in and out of his life. *Salvation and Death of a Hero*, published a year after Félicité's death, is the only book where one comes across an allusion to her, notably in the passage quoted above in which Timothy recalls the Debussy concert which unites them for ever. There will be people who will judge him by his frequent infidelities and say that he could not have respected her, but that would be a superficial way of looking at their relationship. If there was only one person in his life whom he respected, she was that person: in one of the letters I was able to save from the estate of Georges Kapsalis, Stanislas had written to his friend:

Félicité is frightfully worn down by her struggle with pain. Merely crossing her room, leaning on my arm, is a torture to her. She walks bent over double, and yesterday I caught myself walking bent double with her, in an attack of mimesis which was simply a cry of tenderness and compassion, an attempt to alleviate some of her suffering. I need hardly tell you that I was no good at it, and that she burst out laughing and kissed me, saying how sorry she was for me. In the single being that we have created from our two bodies and two minds, she has been the skeleton without which my flaccid flesh would have lost all its form, like those melting watches of Dali's which have always fascinated me. Imagine the physical effect that her decline is having on me.[1]

The novel he had burned in the fireplace at Editions Saeta could only have been about Félicité, inspired by her and her life and her friends. When she read it, she had only one desire: to tear it up, to erase what he had written. At least, that is what one imagines. For all her fashionable and aristocratic airs, and her absurd fortune, she had remained the most discreet person in the world. In this she resembled her sister, my grandmother, to whom the slightest exchange of tittle-tattle was a sign of incredible ill-breeding. In company, Félicité was always ready with a contemptuous remark to crush anyone who disclosed a secret intimacy, and she would take it almost as a personal insult if the homosexuality or dissolute habits of a friend were revealed. With Béla Zukor, she had all but fallen in with these 'Parisian ways', and she was slow to forgive herself. It was perfectly all right to say in front of her that Stravinsky had no talent whatsoever, even though she might have an abiding admiration for him, but she would fly into a terrible rage if anyone were to tell the story of how the aforesaid Stravinsky had, on leaving a ball at Coco Chanel's, vomited in his top hat, to the great disgust of José-Maria and Misia Sert who were taking him home in their car. Stanislas, on the other hand, was fascinated by these idle and malicious remarks; he discovered life within these stores of gossip aired in Félicité's absence. He had characters laid bare before him, of whom all he had previously seen was their dullness and their conventional side. 'It was,' he admitted,

wonderfully amusing, and more revealing than one might imagine. Life was not that surface over which, until then, I had been sliding without managing to get a grip. I discovered the immense hypocrisy

[1] Letter dated 20 November 1967, slightly less than a year before Félicité's death in Venice.

of those who gossiped and of those who were being gossiped about. In many respects that might seem base, but a young man's education commands a certain price.[1]

Félicité's verdict, condemning his second book to an auto-da-fé and denying us all knowledge of it, opened Stanislas' eyes. She had prevented him from publishing an imperfect novel, but much more than that, she had taught him an exactingness which was to be his *modus vivendi* from then on. Reality exceeds everything that the imagination can create, so one has to imagine the imaginary, to go one better than the fantastic, in order to avoid emotion becoming fatally bogged down and embalmed in platitudes. He had worked this out instinctively in his first novel, but his relative success and the new circles, intellectual and abrasively witty, which he moved in had led him astray. He would not return to them.

*

In the first years of his life with Félicité he spoke little, much preferring to listen. This reserve earned him a number of nicknames whose echoes – when they reached him – amused him enormously. Several letters to André Garrett are signed 'Boz', 'L'Iroquois',[2] 'Le Poldève',[3] and 'Le Persan'.[4]

Béla Zukor, who was still pursuing him with unabated loathing, sketched him in *Bonsoir* as a pastiche of Boileau and, in memory of Valentin Conrart, called him 'frequently thick and wisely silent'. Stanislas had kept the article and he showed it to me that evening in 1970 in London when we were searching in his papers for anything which might be useful to an English student writing a thesis on intuition in his work.[5] It was dark outside, and we had sat down on the hearth rug with a wood fire burning in the grate: everything which

---

[1] *Revue de la Table Ronde*, October 1951: 'Good education in a man of letters.'

[2] *Iroquois*: an expression for badly spoken or unintelligible French: *Ce n'est pas du français, c'est de l'iroquois.*

[3] *Poldève*: the name given to a native of Poldevia, a non-existent territory (supposedly in Africa) invented by Parisian students in the 1920s. The French Government was hoaxed into promising Poldevia relief from colonial oppression as a result of their demonstrations.

[4] *Persan*: a reference to Montesquieu's *Lettres persanes*, published anonymously in Amsterdam in 1721.

[5] *Intuition in the works of Stanislas Beren* by Conrad Vet, Oxford University Press, 1972.

seemed to be of any interest went into the wide mouth of a huge envelope, the rest Stanislas tossed into the fireplace. In the jumble of loose notes and ragged cuttings, an envelope containing some photographs fell open.

'Oh,' he said. 'I thought I had lost these.'

The photographs were of no great quality, but they had resisted the passage of time and were neither yellowed nor torn, protected by transparent paper. The first was a three-quarter view of a car, but this was no ordinary car, as Stanislas pointed out.

'A Duesenberg Model S, 1933. Vladimir had just done 125 miles an hour on the motor-racing track at Montlhéry.'

Vladimir? I could have played ignorant, but Georges Kapsalis had told me about Vladimir and Nathalie, neighbours from Cap-Ferrat of whom Félicité had said on one of her rare days of intimacy, 'Nobody else came as near as those two to taking Stanislas from me.'

The second photograph showed a young man leaning against the bonnet of the Duesenberg, smiling, in white trousers and a dark short-sleeved shirt. A leather helmet and goggles with large smoked lenses were hanging from his hand. In the third picture he was at the wheel, with the windshield down. Sitting beside him was a girl, or woman, who had her arm raised as if the car were about to leave and she were waving goodbye. Her features were easy to distinguish: a round face framed by short hair cut in the 'windswept' style which was in fashion that year. Inside this enormous car, with its spoked wheels and its four chromed exhaust pipes emerging from the bonnet to join up beneath the chassis, Vladimir and Nathalie looked like children who had been given a toy which was too big for them. The following photograph had been taken on the Moyenne Corniche, very probably up by Eze-Village, before the sharp bend which is swallowed up by a tunnel. The camera must have been badly focussed and the blurred picture gave an impression of great speed. Nathalie was driving, bare-headed, wearing her brother's bulbous goggles. Her eyes hardly reached the top of the steering wheel and she could only have seen the road a long way in front of her.

'We called this spot the tunnel of death,' said Stanislas. 'One turned the bend, dazzled by the sun, and then suddenly one was blinded by the darkness, five or six seconds in the pitch dark. They loved to scare themselves.'

The fifth photograph showed Nathalie sitting on a stone wall overlooking the sea, in a swimsuit. With her hands resting on the edge, her straight arms raised her shoulders and hunched her up, hiding her slender and attractive neck. She looked embarrassed at her own amusement, at the mischievous expression she knew was in her eyes, an expression which was not to be found in the last three snaps: once between Stanislas and Vladimir, her arms through theirs, then alone with Stanislas at a garden table, a dachshund on her lap, and, probably the same day, the very next moment, still at the table, lifting her head towards Vladimir who is standing behind her chair.

Stanislas put the envelope away and leaned forward to open the last drawer of the chest, which was full of albums. He went straight to the one which contained two portraits of Vladimir and Nathalie. Vladimir – his hair plastered down, his eyes too bright for the sepia print, almost the look of a blind man, his face rendered insipid by the retoucher; and Nathalie – her shoulders bare, a sash of gauze veiling her breasts, her eyes too bright for the photograph too, her mouth accentuated by the darkroom artist, her hair short but frothy.

'The young, the beautiful, the rich!' said Stanislas, in English.

It was true that they resembled the imaginary heroes of Fitzgerald, the sexless demigods who suddenly ruled the twenties. One imagined them wearing white caps or headbands and sweaters too large for them, and holding tennis racquets or golf clubs. These portraits – the work of a famous photographer, Madame Albin-Guyot – had captured them at their happiest and most superficial: an attitude they were not above putting on for ordinary people's sake. Their expressions, so similar – Nathalie's perhaps had a hint more melancholy – had something puerile about them, a shade of impudent bravado, and the portraitist – by the kind of lighting which had made her reputation – had accentuated exactly this aspect of their characters without realizing that, at the same time, she was also doing justice to the solitude into which they had fallen, grievously wounded when there were no spectators left. Yet, lightweight and transparent, they still aroused love, as if these photographs had, once and for all, immortalized the youthfulness which would desert them only when they were confronting death and succumbing to its irresistible charms.

*

Stanislas picked up the file we had been looking at again and took out a whole page of a newspaper, *L'Excelsior*, dated 20 September 1933. This particular page was always given over to photographs of current events, and on that day the entire page was devoted to the accident which had cost Vladimir and Nathalie their lives. There was a picture of the marvellous Duesenberg with its nose rammed into a tree, its bonnet buckled and lifted off, its front tyres burst, a door swinging open. The caption stated that this was indeed a 1933 Model S, similar to the one in which Prince Nicolas of Romania had recently contested the Le Mans 24 Hours Race. The other, smaller, photographs showed two bodies lying together on the grass verge, covered by a blanket. However, the reporter had taken advantage of a brief moment when none of the policemen was looking, to uncover Nathalie's face. Her hair, sticky with blood and earth, clung to her forehead, but her features had kept their child-like purity and her lips were parted in a last smile.

'I do not think she can even have been scared,' said Stanislas. 'It did not occur to her.'

The caption stated that Vladimir's face was no longer photographable and that those who had known him would want to remember him as he had been at the Comte de Beaumont's recent ball, in the company of his sister, he as Watteau's Gilles, she as Raphael's Joan of Aragon.

'The quality of the newspaper photograph is very bad. I did have the original, but their brother Serge begged me to let him have it. They were a little prince and princess holding hands.'

There were two more photographs in *L'Excelsior*: Nathalie with her husband, the Swedish multi-millionaire Dagmar Olsen, and Vladimir with his American wife Eva Blessington, heiress to the stores of the same name. Nathalie had stayed married for a week, Vladimir a month. Elsewhere in the report readers were informed that 'the unfortunate victims of a second's foolhardiness were the children of a Caucasian prince' and that they had 'met a death which was worthy of their fabulous existence'.

Stanislas put away the cutting and the photographs.

'One day you will be able to make use of that. Ten years after they died I put them in a novel, the only one which had any success in the United States,[1] but . . . I don't know, perhaps because of Félicité who did not like them. . . . What I felt for them, a grieving tenderness, an admiration for their aristocratic behaviour, I expressed badly. . . . You know, people thought they were rich because they never paid for anything. In fact, I think it would be nearer the truth to say they were not poor – I suppose even that is quite unusual. After the accident,

---

[1] *Singtime!*, Doubleday, 1944; published in France as *Les Temps heureux*, Editions Saeta, 1948.

Serge, their elder brother, who happened to be in France and was about to go back to Brazil, arrived, and I spent some time with him putting what they had left behind in some kind of order. Their deaths had brought their paralyzed creditors back to life. Do not imagine, though, that we saw a horde of rats descend. Despite their anxiety, they were held in check by their respect for Vladimir and Nathalie, as if they believed them capable of miming death as a final trick on all of us. The two prodigal children had done a disappearing act. They were bound to reappear, more beautiful and more seductive than ever, spend insane amounts of money, throw parties, and buy another Duesenberg or a Rolls. Serge was forty years old, perhaps ten years older than Vladimir, fifteen more than Nathalie. I do not know what he did in Brazil: he was married, having cashed in on his title and his charm. The high life no longer amused him. He talked about his wife Rosalinha, and his children, and the *fazenda* where he lived in the *sertão*, and I sensed how painful it was for him to come back to Europe and rediscover the flavour of a life which he had possibly once led just as wildly as his brother and sister, but which he wanted to forget, to sweep into the ashes of his extinguished past. I even had the impression that he grew his beard, and trimmed it *à la* Nicholas II, to look older; but beneath the tight curls the family looks, the sensual mouth and the round, dimpled chin, were clearly visible. And his eyes! They were the eyes of Vladimir and Nathalie. Even with that beard, even with his waistline beginning to thicken and his hair to thin, he remained their brother, affecting an air of carelessness and indifference towards everything until, a moment later, I would find him sobbing uncontrollably on his sister's bed; seeing me, he would be furious and hurl abuse, only to beg me to excuse him immediately. Wandering through that empty house where the servants hid themselves as if they were afraid of us, we came up against the presence of Vladimir and Nathalie everywhere. They had gone, leaving signs to reassure us; they were coming back any minute: they were testing the new carburettors on the Duesenberg, and we had only to drink a cocktail while we were waiting for them, one of those excellent Manhattans Vladimir gave all his friends the recipe for. One had only to ring and the boy would bring in ice and shaker; suddenly Nathalie would appear in the doorway, her back to the setting sun which outlined her slim and carefree body, like a puppet in a shadow-theatre, while Vladimir was putting the car back in the garage. Everywhere – in drawers, on a large silver dish in the hall, in an old and utterly worn out leather saddlebag which had probably crossed Russia at the time of the epic flight, in the pockets of a jacket thrown down on an armchair – we found envelopes, none of which Vladimir had ever opened: a fabulous sum owing for champagne, gin and whisky to a grocer in Nice, a tailor's bill, a dressmaker's bill, one from a bootmaker, one from a garage at Beaulieu which had been supplying them with petrol for over a year. The total was frightening. Serge would put his head in his hands: "But how, how could they have done it?" He cursed the trusting souls who had made such an existence possible. We ransacked the house to try and find any sign of rational behaviour. Suits by Chanel and extravagant creations by Schiaparelli overflowed Nathalie's wardrobes; apart from one or two summer evenings, I had never seen her dressed other than in straight skirts and her brother's sweaters. Vladimir had two hundred ties. He never wore ties – apart from a black one with his dinner jacket. In the drawer of the bedside table we found a cheque book which had hardly been used, and what stubs there were had been left blank. By telephone the bank reassured us. The account was neither in debit nor in credit. Folded carelessly behind the cheque book were two cheques, one in dollars signed by Eva Blessington, the other in Swiss francs signed by Dagmar Olsen, which had been waiting to be paid in for six months. Serge breathed again: these two cheques would amply dispose of the mountain of bills. I myself gave hardly a thought to this vulgar detail because it didn't concern me, and in any case I should have found it more magical for them to vanish through a trap-door just as their creditors were rousing themselves. For Nathalie's ex-husband and Vladimir's ex-wife to have continued to support them spoiled the utter beauty of the thing. I suppose the two sprites remained oblivious to it all, as the cheques gathered dust in the bedside table, unused, and even ridiculous. But since Serge had arrived, since we had been searching through the deserted house, one thought had worried me to the point of making me feel ill; remember, when loved ones die, it is first and foremost ourselves that we see, that we feel sorry for. Yes, I confess I was searching for a sign from Nathalie, anything which would drive away a little of my grief . . . just a little . . . I never expected more than that. Then in the end I was relieved of a great deal of my grief. I received a message which was like an arrow in my heart because it was a message from the dead. I had written to Nathalie, you see. I know you have already guessed as much. . . . It is my besetting sin. If a woman stirs my emotions I do not say so to her face, I write to her. Yes, I had written to Nathalie. Three times. An irrepressible need which, when I thought about Félicité, I felt as much more of a betrayal, that first time and all the other times, than the fact of desiring somebody else's body. I had scribbled these letters in the early hours of the morning, after one of those mad evenings from which we came back exhausted and stupidly happy, although for me it was a torment to let them go and to hear their Duesenberg drive off as I closed the gates. They left me, abandoned me when all I wanted was to stay with them for ever; but how could they possibly have known? They continued the party, just the two of them, without it giving way to any pangs of loneliness; they carried on laughing, perhaps drinking a last glass of liqueur before keeling over into bed, sometimes not even bothering to undress. Oh! do not go imagining things. I never believed in any incestuous relationship and, if it did happen, it was purely by chance, two or three times, with no forethought, no thought at all, and the next day they probably did not even remember it. No, you must understand, these two human beings possessed a secret and utterly terrifying key to life: they enjoyed themselves. I could join in with their pleasures but, deep down, I believe they had no need of me at all, although they loved me in their own way, like one of those toys which sparks off a brief burst of enthusiasm without our foreseeing that in fact we shall soon tire of this toy in favour of another one. We were still in the first flush of enthusiasm and the idea of any disenchantment was as far from their minds as it was from mine. But had I disappeared from one day to the next their existence would have carried on at the same hectic pace. Naturally I loved Nathalie without a second thought for the fact that I stood little chance of being loved by her and, worse, that by setting myself between them I ran the risk of seeing happiness go up in smoke the day that Nathalie and I locked ourselves in a bedroom and made love, excluding Vladimir from our pleasure. . . . You are wondering if I found my three letters. Well, the answer is yes. . . . But I did not lay my hands on them immediately, because they were hidden. Remember that there is a difference between Nathalie's carelessness with all the notes and invitations which she hardly ever opened and left scattered all over the villa, and those three letters: by some inexplicable intuition, my hand touched upon them in a drawerful of underwear, which I had opened because I wanted to run my hand over the white silk slips and knickers which Nathalie had once worn, the stockings in which I imagined her young body, so gay and now cold, with an uneasy pleasure. I was thunderstruck by the revelation. Nathalie had had a secret from her brother. Vladimir had not known about those three letters. There was a flaw in the love between this mad couple, a very tiny flaw it is true, but had destiny not intervened, perhaps I should have taken Nathalie away, perhaps I should have unbound her from her brother. There is no way of telling whether they could have lived without each other and whether the inevitable estrangement of Vladimir would not have been intolerable, both to her and to me. . . . But to return to the letters, when I grasped them, with the fear that one feels face to face with desecration, my first thought was that they were still sealed. Nathalie had opened them perfectly cleanly with a very sharp pocket-knife. I could see her, biting her lower lip, attentive, the girl who was always on the verge of giggling suddenly serious, reading those lines as I re-read them in turn, sitting on her bed, as she must have done herself: the room wreathed in her perfume, the window open on the garden and the sea, the warm onshore breeze lifting the curtains of white tulle. I re-read myself because letters like those, which I must say have often seemed to me like messages in bottles, are forgotten by the writer as soon as they are sent. I did not remember having said any of those things to her and I must confess, casting all modesty aside, that I had forgotten, despite writing them only a short time before, what was in those letters and that it was beautiful.'

'Have you still got them?'

'No, I tore them up with the feeling that it was imperative I forget the whole mad adventure. It was inconclusive, and yet there could be no conclusion now that Nathalie was dead. But there was an answer . . . or, to be more precise, she had thought about an answer and she lacked only the means to express herself with the slightest seriousness. On a sheet of blue Ingres paper I could decipher several words, pencilled in red and slipped into the envelope of the third letter: a few disconnected words, a few haphazard strokes, and the only thing which was important to me: "I love you." I was filled with an appalling feeling: suddenly I was wildly grateful to the destiny which had claimed her life with Vladimir's, Vladimir whom I loved as much as her and whom I did not have time, thank God, to betray.'

*

This long monologue has not been re-invented. For several weeks, I had been taking notes while we talked. Stanislas took no notice. He told these stories for his own benefit as much as mine. Not once did he ask to look through what I used to type out the following day. Each moment belongs only to itself and already the only truth which mattered to him was his own. What others thought was true seemed derisory and meaningless to him. However close we were, through the memory of my father and the friendship he had shown me from the day I had been old enough to understand him, what I might be thinking was of no interest to him. Thus, as he delivered his long monologue on Vladimir and Nathalie, I had the impression that he was talking to an audience inside his head. I could almost have left the room without his noticing; and he made only one reference to the novel which his two friends inspired ten years later and which was, as I have said, a creditable success in the United States and a flop in France the year it appeared (1948), before, thanks to the magic word of mouth, *Singtime!* or *Les Temps heureux* established a wide audience for itself, becoming 'a password'[1] to some and later remembered by many as a successful film in 1972.

Writers obviously have the unchallengeable right to embellish life in their work (or to blacken it), but one consequence of this is that Stanislas, faced with such a ready listener, may have found himself sorely tempted to confuse hard facts with facts modified by his imagination; in which case it might seem rather pointless to compare the account of the deaths of Vladimir and Nathalie as they were sketched by Stanislas Beren one evening in London, with the book which fictionalized the story.

Singtime! recreates the couple in nearly all their physical characteristics, except that Nathalie, as far as I can judge from the photographs, was less beautiful in real life than Stanislas wanted it to be believed in his portrayal of her in a novel. Her true face, round and sparkling, could not be lent to the woman of the novel without risking incredulity, for her beauty had to be one which distilled a fatal perfume from her very first appearance. Nathalie had a full and firm body, bubbling with life. In the novel she gains height and loses her delightful bosom. Vladimir, on the other hand, is perfectly recognizable, just as he is in the photographs, with his mocking smile and athletic shoulders. As for the narrator, although he seems to be almost invisible because of his excessive shyness, he nevertheless plays a leading role, since he is the cause of Vladimir's and Nathalie's suicides. This is where the novel parts company with the true story. In *Singtime!* Vladimir discovers that Nathalie is in love with Charles (the name

[1] The expression is Roger Nimier's, from an article in *Liberté de l'esprit* in June 1952, where, alongside *Les Temps heureux*, he quotes Alexandre Vialatte's novel *Les Fruits du Congo* (NRF, 1951). Nimier, whose knowledge was encyclopaedic, knew of the existence of the three issues of the episodic review which, under that title, had sunk without trace in 1932, so his remark was doubly tongue in cheek.

under which Stanislas depicts himself). Up until now Vladimir has lived a privileged and protracted childhood, despite his brief marriage to Barbara E. (in reality Eva Blessington). Blinkers have concealed life from him. He has never counted the cost of anything, nor has he counted the women he has seduced. Suddenly, he is brought up brutally short, as he discovers that it is intolerable to him to think of the pleasure which Nathalie is giving to this interloper, this Charles. She has betrayed him in the lowest, most vulgar sense of the word. The intruder has brought them both down to earth, and now their insouciance is no more than a mask, a poor, punctured paper moon. At the bottom of an abyss Vladimir, who has not made a single gesture which might reveal his despair, envisages an existence without Nathalie. Impossible. Nor can he imagine that Nathalie could live without him; and in order to grant his sister a peace that he is incapable of finding within himself, he decides to arrange her 'suicide'. The accident is prepared in the minutest detail, at the same spot on the Moyenne Corniche where, some years before, Isadora Duncan had been killed, strangled by her scarf caught in one of the wheels of her Bugatti. At Cap-Ferrat, lunch invitations are specially sent out. The interval before this lunch, set in the large drawing room whose bays overlook the garden and the sea, is the bravura piece of the book. Here is a whole parade of what comprised the population of the Côte d'Azur at the time: spongers, free spirits, cynics, idlers, even artists, who, barely knowing each other and unable to understand why they find themselves in the same room, devote their time to catty attacks on their neighbours. They have no wish to shock one another – indeed, they are a remarkably insipid bunch – but simply to be daring, to give themselves a reputation for outspokenness and establish their right to be invited to lunch by this couple about whom they know almost nothing at all, but whom legend has already taken hold of, even before a death staged with a touch of grandeur. Faintly worried, to begin with , by the non-appearance of Vladimir and Nathalie, and suspecting some sort of practical joke, they begin to lose their composure but are reassured when one of them opens the door to the dining room and sees the table laid for thirteen people. Then they are seized by another kind of panic. Either one of them will have to leave, or Nathalie and Vladimir will have to invite a fourteenth guest. The valet replenishes the cocktails; finally, at two o'clock, drunk and ravenous, they sit down to lunch and consume the meal in absolute chaos, each guest delivering his own monologue and paying not the slightest attention to his neighbour. The lunch looks like turning into a battle worthy of the

Marx brothers until Charles – the lover – appears and announces that Vladimir and Nathalie are dead. The guests fall silent, stunned by the news. Two of them have sufficient presence of mind to stuff their pockets with *petits fours*, another finishes the champagne and passes out, and a woman who has a fit of hysterics is taken advantage of by a man who slips ice cubes down the front of her dress to discover that she has false breasts.

Kléber Haedens, reviewing *Singtime!*,[1] rightly observed that this scene was also a piece of theatre, if not a full three acts then at least a curtain-raiser, and he encouraged its author to write for the theatre. Some years later I re-discovered this article and wrote to Stanislas suggesting that, in fact, this was a good idea and that he had been wrong not to try it. He wrote back:[2]

I have never written for the theatre. That is the authorized version of the truth. But if you want to know the other version, here it is: I have written two plays which are in a drawer somewhere (I honestly have no idea where). Perhaps I am too arrogant to put up with knocking on doors and meeting directors who do not read the manuscripts which are submitted to them and are only looking for an author who has written the play that they did not know how to write themselves. Anyway, there is another overriding objection: I am no good as an actor. Shakespeare, Molière and Guitry were good actors. Today Roussin, Billetdoux and Dubillard are excellent actors. I should not even know how to read my play to the players, as Ionesco, Anouilh and Marceau do so well. It is a gift which I do not possess. To have a play at the Comédie Française you have to be able to read your play to the players. I respect them too much, I like them too much to want to make them sit through two hours of monotonous stammering.

After the ludicrous failed lunch, the novel continues with the arrival of the brother Basile, in other words the man we know as Serge. Basile is in his forties. He brought up Nathalie and Vladimir before marrying a rich South American who has just borne him his sixth child. Frantic at the discovery of how his brother and sister have been living, he searches everywhere, in this house which calls them to mind so clearly, for whatever mysterious fever has possessed them. Every-

[1] *Samedi-soir*, 12 April 1948.
[2] Letter dated London, 15 December 1970.

thing seems to lay the blame at his door. For the sake of security and because of a kind of weariness with life, he has abandoned two children who were dearer to him than his own. The stories he hears told about them, the parties they gave and the parties they went to, the reckless, squandered pleasure-seeking, bring home to him the extent of his desertion. The idea of going back to Brazil soon becomes intolerable and, so that he may join his brother and sister in spirit, he throws his own great party at the villa, barely a week after the funeral. The evening is a sinister one. Only busybodies and voyeurs turn up. When the last guest leaves, Basile attaches a stone to a rope around his neck and drowns himself in the pool. Charles, having been unable to bear the idea of going to the party, arrives at first light when the music has fallen silent. He smokes a cigarette at the poolside and leaves before the servants and police arrive.

★

The novel finishes without our discovering where Charles goes. Stanislas openly admitted that it was far too easy to put an end to a story with a suicide. He saw it as a weakness of the novelist who wants to make life 'heroic' at all costs. In reality, the double deaths of Vladimir and Nathalie had poisoned their elder brother's existence and shattered the happiness that he had carved out for himself. He never got over it, and when he went back to Brazil, it was to die there two years later, gored by a bull.

★

In the wake of the shock that Stanislas suffered from the death of the couple who had crossed his path at such breakneck speed, Félicité realized that unless she took control of the situation, she would lose her husband. She closed the house at Cap-Ferrat and took him to Paris. Very quickly she discovered that Stanislas would only be able to forget if they went far away, if they put thousands of miles between themselves and France, on a steamer heading for the Far East. Georges Kapsalis accompanied them, factotum, friend and court jester, indispensable and exasperating because whenever he was needed, he was glued to a gaming table. He was nearly left behind in Macao and Hong Kong, and Félicité made him swear that he would not touch another card until they returned to Europe. Georges was one of those people who desperately want to have things forbidden them. It so rarely happened to him. But he soon spotted a loophole and, taking Félicité at her word, continued to play backgammon and roulette, diversions to which she resignedly agreed. It was from him that I discovered that for the first thirty days of the outward voyage – as far as Colombo – Stanislas seemed so indifferent to both the ports they called at and life on board that he might just as well have stayed at home. All his days were spent reading on a chaise-longue at Félicité's side. It was during this period that Stanislas discovered Conrad, whom he thereafter placed on a par with the few others he truly admired. André Garrett, whose passion for Conrad knew no bounds, had unearthed the complete works for him, but unlike his friend – who had been drawn to Conrad by his own love of the sea – Stanislas, who had no time for boats and thought the sea too big, did not read Conrad to quench his thirst for storms and adventure. What obsessed him was the shadows in which Conrad's characters moved, and the writing, tight and so pure, which plunges into 'the heart of darkness' and brings back, as he put it, 'the rags of dreams, incomplete as the destinies of men'. It was undoubtedly to Conrad that he owed, albeit in a quite different register, his taste for the hero cast out by life, whose soul is insidiously parted from his body. *Lord Jim*, which he confessed to having read probably a dozen times, seemed to him one of the greatest novels of all time:

The initial error, the one which destroys an existence, can perhaps explain everything. The story of Eve, the apple and the serpent is really too far-fetched, but there must be, somewhere in the history of man, an original sin, less simple and more awful, which is still poisoning us and for which we will never forgive ourselves. In a sense it is rather reassuring: we have a conscience. There are days when we doubt this. And even days when we lose all memory of it. But a conscience there assuredly is, that makes man an utterly different being from the animals. To take it one step further – a risky step – I would say that it is perhaps the least bad proof of the existence of God.[1]

The steamer called at Piraeus, Port Saïd and Aden. Stanislas did not even go ashore. He sent André a series of telegrams: SUPERB STOP ENTHUSIASM STOP I MISS YOU STOP THE EARTH IS

[1] From *Things I read . . .* , a posthumous anthology of articles, Editions Saeta, 1978.

ROUND STOP HAVE PROOF OF IT STOP. Since one had to be somewhere, he was just as well off on the deck of this ship as anywhere else. Perhaps he was even better off there, sheltered from the fragments of their lives that Vladimir and Nathalie had scattered on their way. Both Georges and Félicité were careful not to mention their names. Félicité, with more wisdom than she had shown up until then, was counting on the healing properties of distance as well as time. In the past she might have seemed frivolous and capricious, becoming the mistress of this man thirteen years her junior without considering the consequences; but she had not married him without reflection. And now she loved him. He was a part of her life for ever, and she had realized that her future role would be to protect him, from himself and from others. In this she did not fail and, already, lying out in his deck-chair by her side, Stanislas knew that Félicité was there to cure him, even though he still cherished the sundering of his being, the two friends from whom he had been amputated but who still hovered on the rim of his memory, whose presence became suffocating, almost palpable, on the sleepless nights when he saw them in his mind's eye and stopped them just as they were about to crash into a tree. One night he must have moved and moaned, either from fear or anguish; very softly, from the next bunk, came Félicité's murmur, 'I'm here.'

The rest was just a silent documentary film on the Near and Middle East. He watched the images glide by: the wide red caiques at the entrance to Piraeus, the boys diving for pennies at Port Saïd, the feluccas at Alexandria, the sackalevers on the Red Sea. During the hours when the screen was blank, Stanislas read Conrad and lunched and dined in the company of Georges and Félicité, more often than not at the captain's table. Fortunately his cabin was a long way from the saloon where, every evening, an orchestra in grey dinner jackets and pink bow ties played the popular tunes of the year for the enraptured couples on the dance floor. . . . These melodies – nearly all English numbers: *Red Sails in the Sunset*; *Smoke Gets in Your Eyes*; *A Little White Gardenia*; *Capri* – these melodies had made Nathalie melt every time she heard them: she had hummed them during the day, and in the night clubs she had begged the musicians to play them. Obviously, tunes like these were unlikely to transport the soul to sublime heights and Nathalie would certainly have acquired a greater mystique had it been a Schubert sonata or a Mozart concerto which unfailingly brought her to mind; but ultimately it was Nathalie one was dealing with and, however high her death had exalted her, she was not naturally ethereal. She had not even been naturally romantic. She had simply been joy. Stanislas had kept in his pocket the piece of blue Ingres paper with the fatal words inscribed in thick red pencil: 'I love you.' Fatal because they had stopped there. There had been neither 'very much' nor 'a little' nor 'not at all'. Just 'I love you' frozen in mid-flight and forever indelible.

*

When I asked him – this was the same confessional evening in London in 1970 – if he had ever thought of committing suicide, Stanislas fetched a copy of *Where Are You Dining Tonight?* (the second novel he had written under this title) from one of his bookshelves and opened it without hesitation at the page where a woman announces to Maximilian von Arelle that she is leaving him and asks him whether he will kill himself. He says nonchalantly:

'I am not against suicide, but I do not admire it either. The temptation has never crossed my mind. Let's be crude about it, and say that it is all contrived. From the moment one is persuaded of that, suicide can only have one positive value, which is to imperil the equilibrium of the loved one who never imagined that you would be capable of it. A way of punishing the defaulting partner. One cannot deny that this is rather shabby behaviour. While we're snug and warm in our coffin, the people we leave behind reel at our accusations with no chance of proving us wrong. The idea itself is quite an amusing one really, although one does pay dearly for it.'

'You make me go quite cold.'

'Oh, don't catch cold. Run off back to your husband. He'll warm you up.'[1]

*

After Aden, the steamer headed into the Indian Ocean and the cruise began an entirely new phase. Hitherto, the passengers had amused themselves with what they had been able to see from the deck-rail: Piraeus, the Dodecanese, the coastline of Egypt, the Suez Canal gliding slowly by, the ochrous shores of the Red Sea. Suddenly, they were thrust back into austerity, to a journey without scenery: two thousand five hundred nautical miles to Colombo, thirteen days of sky

[1] *Op. cit.*, p. 120 (1960 ed.).

and Indian Ocean blues. A sudden storm as they left Aden marked
the transition, then there was flat calm and a sticky heat which on the
first-class deck produced a procession of shorts and short-sleeved
shirts revealing the shortcomings of the gentlemen and, among the
ladies, a lesser youthfulness than they had been able to claim each
evening in their long dresses and make-up which resisted the glare of
the ballroom lights. Stanislas and André corresponded by telegram.
Stanislas entrusted the telegraph operator with a quatrain by Levet:

> The *Armand Behic* (of the shipping line)
> Goes at fourteen knots on the Indian Ocean . . .
> The sun goes down on the highways of crime,
> In a sea pressed flat and empty of motion

André replied with a poem by Larbaud on the station at Cahors:

> Traveller! Oh, cosmopolitan! suddenly
> Deconsecrated, crumbling, despised by here and now,
> Standing slightly back from the line,
> Old and pink among the miracles of morning,
> With your useless awning,
> To the sun on the hills you stretch your empty platform . . .

Stanislas immediately sent back three lines from Supervielle's
Landing Stages:

> Behind the dull sky and the grey sea
> where the ship's prow carves a modest furrow,
> beyond the closed horizon . . .

André replied with a stream of abuse:

Damned half-scholar! Why don't you quote the last line – 'There
lies Brazil with all her palms.' Will you ever learn any geography?
You're going to Ceylon, which is nowhere near Brazil.

In the radio room, where they were more used to sending messages
along the lines of 'Angèle and the puppies are very well', or instructions to the Stock Exchange, the operators enjoyed themselves huge-
ly. Who were these two madmen spending a fortune on sending poems
to each other? Delivered from his landbound oppression, Stanislas
already felt better. In a small notebook he composed sketches of
passengers he had noticed on deck or in the dining room:

Monsieur van Badaboom is on his third voyage to the Tropics. He wears a white pith helmet on his morning walk in case the captain should invite him onto the poop-deck. This has not yet happened. M. van Badaboom is disappointed. He is getting neurotic. Might there be enemies of Flemish Belgium on board? Or might some indiscreet person have noticed that he wears a truss?

Madame Ozovair has certain problems, implied by her name. She is in her cups, having drunk them to the dregs. How is she to bear her menopause and her washerwoman's cheeks? Madame Ozovair has many crosses to bear. She would gladly go for long and energetic walks along the deck (the upper one) if a corn on her left little toe did not torture her so. One's state of health is never what it should be.

Mademoiselle Cunégonde has no shadow. In the Tropics this is normal, but in everyday life it is rather tedious. The explanation? Mlle Cunégonde is herself a shadow, the shadow of her parents who protect her from the sun and the sex-maniacs. One on either side, she confronts with downcast eyes the covetousness of the males lounging on their chaises-longues. Who will be the first to penetrate this deathless demoiselle? A young ensign has danced a *paso doble* with her (one ought to say a passion *doble*) and assures us that she is hot but does not wash her pussy. Scandal-mongering or truth? Find out for yourself.

Major Littleprick has re-enlisted. He was getting bored with the white skins, organdie dresses and Sunday hats in his Yorkshire village. Life isn't over when you're sixty, dammit! And in India there are still some fine people who aren't put off even by bow legs. On the contrary! He is returning to look after the Maharani of Hiwilfukmi who is bored with paying her lovers cash on the nail. In his suitcase the major has courses of vitamin injections to cure princesses in the doldrums.

Monsieur Gaston is the inevitable cashier who has done a bunk and is treating himself to a suicide cruise. Out of the corner of his eye he scrutinizes his fellow diners to find out how to eat asparagus and snails and oysters. He is a little at a loss with all these dishes, but he is happy despite being cross with himself at not having taken his time and bought some new suits before his departure. Fortunately, we have on board the Right Hon. Wickpick who has a private income of a million a year as well as out-at-elbow jackets, socks full of holes and flapping shoes. M. Gaston finds him a man of question-able respectability, suspecting him vaguely of being a cashier on the run from his bank. They might have a great deal in common. Alas, Wickpick speaks nothing but English and his English is incomprehensible. M. Gaston is reduced to answering, 'Yess' or 'Sanke you'.[1]

He was not quite back on his old form after the shock of the burned novel, the summer months spent going to parties, and the fear of the void following his friends' deaths, but he was discovering that words were a first-rate medicine. Once again he wanted to play with them, to assemble them as a child is absorbed by assembling his bricks and forming unexpected shapes. Between Aden and Colombo he composed fifty short comic poems, resonant with puns and spoonerisms. He posted them in Colombo, but the envelope never reached André. All that was saved was a number of rough drafts in the notebook where he had recorded his sketches. He probably corrected and improved them when he came to write them out again, but even as they stand they bear witness to how much he enjoyed playing with assonances:

> *La Double Méprise*
>
> *'Quelle vie!'*
> *s'écrie la pie.*
> *Le corbeau qui*
> *pisse sur un puits*
> *se méprend sur le mot*
> *et se croit monté comme un barbot.*
> *La pie pieuse*
> *se voile les yeuses*
> *et clairement épelle: v, i, e.*
> *'Pas si vieux!'*
> *dit le corbeau encore beau*
> *mais faible en ortho.*
>
> *Inscription sur un mur d'Ur*
>
> *'Je ne sais pas ou elle habite,'*
> *dit la jolie Hittite.*
> *Au mot bite le Moabite*
> *sourit finement et vite*
> *souleva sa lévite.*

[1] Published in *L'Ingénu* (a quarterly review of arts and letters), no. 2, March 1979, these sketches are to be included in the Pléiade edition of the complete works of Stanislas Beren to be published in 1985.

'Oh, vous vous méprites,'
dit la jolie Hittite,
'je parlais d'une amie petite!'
'De petite,' dit le Moabite,
'point ne débite. . . .'
Et, désolé, la remit au gîte.

Histoire Sentie
La maîtresse du vizir
à l'épileur exprime son désir:
'Ma Vénus est un vrai hallier,
je voudrais que vous la débroussailliez.'
'Façon tirelire?'
risque l'homme de l'art. Et de rire.
'Oui, pour des billets, pas de pièces,'
précise-t-elle en liesse.
Il s'y met sans attendre
et lui épile le tendre
mais, bientôt suffoqué, apres avoir éternué,
renonce à continuer.
La dame, vexée, dit:
'Pourtant vous aviez consenti.'[1]

When he entrusted me with the small notebook containing the portraits and I discovered the rough drafts of some of the lost poems, I

---

[1] As it is impossible to render even half the puns in these short, scabrous poems, they have been left in the French. A close translation will give enough vocabulary to enjoy them: *The Twofold Mistake*: 'What a life!' / cries the magpie's wife./ The crow who is pissing down a well / mistakes the word / and thinks she is referring to the size of his sexual organ./ The pious magpie / averts her eyes / and clearly spells out the word./ 'Not as old as all that!' (again, he hears the wrong word)/ crows the crow, a handsome bird / but weak at spelling.

Inscription on a wall at Ur: 'I do not know where she lives,' / said the pretty Hittite girl./ At the word 'prick' (*bite* referring back to *habite*), the Moabite/ smiled sweetly and quickly / lifted up his robe./ 'You are mistaken,' / said the pretty Hittite,/'I was talking about a little friend!' / 'Little, hum?' said the Moabite, 'well, I can't make it any smaller.'/ And, sadly, he put it away for another day.

Heartfelt Story (as usual, one French word means many things: the title plays on two meanings of *sentir*, 'to feel' and 'to smell'): The vizir's mistress / expresses her wishes to the depilator:/ 'My Venus is an absolute tangle,/ I should like you to clear away the undergrowth.'/ 'Money-box style?' ventures the artist and wit./ 'Yes, but notes only, no coins,'/ she states gaily./ He sets about it without further ado / and removes the hair from her soft spot,/ but, soon suffocated and sneezing,/ declares he cannot go on./ The lady, thoroughly cross, says:/ 'But you consented'. (The reader may draw his own conclusions about the pun of the last line.)

sent him a photocopy of what I had found. He wrote to me from Venice:

'Good grief! I had forgotten. Not exactly creations of genius. I was just enjoying myself . . . and yet, can one ever tell! Everything else I have written will be as old hat as Paul Bourget, relegated to out-of-print catalogues; and the smart teachers of the new wave, forsaking the dictation of Mérimée or *The Cicada and the Ant*, will make their little pupils recite *Inscription on a wall at Ur*. Anything is possible. It was a shame that the envelope intended for your father got lost. Now I remember: besides the dirty poems, which are the only survivors, there were one or two neat games with words, obviously without the grace of a Tristan Derême, whom I admired greatly at the time – have you read *The Orange-coloured Onager*, no of course not, you are an unbridled ass – and without the spotless candour of a Jean Tardieu ten years later. Having said that, this avalanche of puns, an aspect of the French language I had paid little attention to until then, augured well: I was in much better health than I looked, and all that was preventing me from showing this to Georges and Félicité was that I did not want to get well too quickly. My image of myself as the hero with a ravaged heart had, at least at the beginning, so satisfied me that I was loath to change it, even though doing so would have put an end to Félicité's worries. Basically I wanted somebody to pander to my vague yearnings; I liked the idea of somebody being concerned about me. Remember, I was twenty-five but I had only *really* been born in 1925, the day I came to Janson-de-Sailly. What happened *before*, I discount completely. In the space of eight years I had emerged from limbo, and embarked on manhood. Today I think this is what is called 'accelerated training', and what is common practice for plumbers, electricians and boilermakers ought to be possible for the happy few. By the time we called at Colombo I was cured, or almost, but I did not want to show it. So I did not go ashore with Georges and Félicité, who hired a car and came back three hours later, disappointed and bad-tempered. Georges was furious that he had not observed any bare-breasted women. He had got Ceylon and Bali mixed up in his mind. While I was waiting for them I stayed on the deck overlooking the gangway where the new passengers were coming aboard. Between Ceylon and Singapore we would be performing a new play with new actors, against the same backcloth of promenade deck, bar, dining room and ballroom. On the gang-ladder I was struck by an ash-blonde head which reminded me of Nathalie. Leaning on my elbows on the deck-rail, I could see a mop of hair and two shoulders in a blue surah dress. In the evening I found the ash-blonde lady in the bar. She was English. I do not know if you are like me, but I have lost count of the number of disappointments I have had in my life from following a blonde head which turned out to have an unlovely face. Well, for once that colour and style of hair belonged to a woman whose beauty was worthy of them. I must have a photograph of her somewhere, I cannot think where. I shall find it for you if you are keen to see her, although it is not important since nothing happened between us. Well, to say 'nothing' is perhaps to be a little cynical, as if an emotion – to say nothing of feelings – only materializes after the bed business. Which did not take place. She was going to join her husband at Singapore, and she held fast to her principles. Her head was stuffed with received ideas, including a rather scornful attitude towards the French. I had seven days to persuade her, not to sleep with me – which would have been rather tasteless with Félicité there – but that we were made for each other, in short, that a wild passion held us in its thrall. I think I pulled it off too: it seemed to me that she left the ship at Singapore feeling deeply tragic, convinced of her own heroism in willing Destiny to pass her by. Do not think this was all a callous game on my part. From her adventure that woman gained such a high idea of herself that her life was transformed by it; while I forgot her the minute she disappeared into the crowd. She wrote to me for a long time afterwards, ardent, passionate letters written in an unbearably silly tone. I could have done without her generosity: all I had wanted was her help in getting even, in winning the battle to struggle out of the shell of my self-indulgence. She had done that for me. I had schemed well and sharpened up new weapons against the day, not very far off, when vanity would point out to me a woman to be conquered, or when love threatened to paralyze me. The woman was called Maureen; she was unimportant.[1]

*

From Singapore they set sail almost immediately for Macao and Hong Kong where Georges Kapsalis, despite his promises, was swallowed

[1] Letter from Venice, 12 November 1970.

up by the illicit gaming houses. After a three-day search Félicité finally laid hands on him. Needless to say, he was absolutely cleaned out, and he had even lost his signet-ring with the Kapsalis motto: *Doxa to theo*. Crestfallen and bitter with himself for breaking his word of honour, he acquiesced in being dragged onto another steamer which took them to New Zealand, then from Auckland to the Society Islands and Tahiti, where he was hoping to meet up with one of his friends, a former ambassador and great poker player. The reader will already have realized that Georges, through not paying attention, was about to let himself down again and that, just as in Ceylon he had failed to see the naked breasts of the Balinese women, so now in Tahiti he would not meet his old friend – who had retired to Haiti. Stanislas, aware of the misapprehension since the beginning of the voyage, had maliciously kept it alive, and it was not until they had been staying in Papeete for two or three days that he disabused him. In the second *Where Are You Dining Tonight?* Maximilian von Arelle has a brother Wilhelm who admires him to the point of wanting to do everything that he does, even picking up his mistresses as each is discarded in turn. Wilhelm persuades Maximilian's most recent victim, the beautiful Aida, to spend a few days with him at the Levant Hotel in Tripoli; but when he arrives in Tripoli, in the Lebanon, there is no Levant Hotel, and he is advised to go to Libya, where he goes half-mad on learning that there is no Levant Hotel there either. He is told to try his luck at Tripoli in the Peloponnese where, of course, when he arrives, at a filthy hovel reeking of goatskin and wool fat, he is given a letter. Aida reproaches him for having abused her trust in arranging a meeting to which he never came, thereby plunging her into the blackest, most gloomy thoughts and making her feel utterly suicidal. Wilhelm, who is not completely naive, swears that he will no longer be duped into desiring his brother's cast-off mistresses. 'There are advantages to be gained from knowing one's geography, the geography of the heart as well as that of the *genii loci*,' wrote Stanislas in epitaph to the chapter. Who could he have been thinking of, if not of Georges Kapsalis and his unsuccessful meanderings in the Pacific?

With his stiff collar, spotted tie, spats and ivory-handled cane, Georges was not exactly made for Polynesia, any more than Félicité had been intended by nature for these islands. She had made up her mind to set up residence there for a few weeks, possibly as long as two or three months if Stanislas took to the place and forgot what he had left behind him in Europe. It is easy to imagine the extent of the sacrifice she was making for her husband: finding herself twenty thousand kilometres from home, in the middle of the Pacific on an island with the most rudimentary of creature comforts, and with a tea chest of books to read but only Georges Kapsalis to talk to, was a severe trial. She rented two large *farés* at Paea and had very little to occupy her time besides bathing and reading. Her neighbour and friend from Cap-Ferrat, Somerset Maugham, had lived very nearby in 1916 and had discovered in the debris of Gauguin's former *faré* a glass door with a painting of a tall *vahiné*, naked to the waist and holding a grapefruit in her hand. The door had been brought back to France where Félicité had often admired it. Now the days of making such discoveries were gone, and in addition Tahiti was going through the most unrewarding period of its chequered history. The anarchical development of Papeete, the unwieldy bulk of an administration which received its orders from Paris, and a puritanical church which was stricter than ever, seemed to have killed the zest for life so often celebrated by the first visitors. Félicité could not understand her servants at all. They looked after her but stole from her shamelessly. With no memory for faces, she failed to realize that the *vahinés* and *tanés* who were so solicitous in their attentions were always changing, and hardly stayed longer than a week after they had pilfered enough – usually a very modest amount – to allow them to survive without working for a time. Stanislas, aware that Félicité would not put up for much longer with a situation to which he found he had adapted very well, had the good fortune, when he was out trying to catch flying fish one day, to meet James Norman Hall and Charles Nordhoff, who had settled on the island and married two Tahitian beauties. They had just published their trilogy on the mutiny on the *Bounty* and were writing *Hurricane*, which was to be their greatest success. Félicité became friendly with them and visited their house at Arue almost daily. They had distinguished themselves in action in France during the Great War and now lived by their writing, mining the rich and inexhaustible seams of Polynesian folklore. When Stanislas saw that Félicité was in sufficiently interesting company, he joined a schooner which plied the archipelago of the Tuamotu islands and came back with cargoes of copra. He did not return until two months later, the day before Félicité was due to leave. Suddenly she had been there too long: having exhausted the charms of an exotic existence, and weary of mosquitoes and floury food, she had packed her trunks and booked a passage on a ship bound for France via Panama. Georges Kapsalis fully expected a stormy scene. It did not come. Was Félicité disarmed by Stanislas' new demeanour? He had returned bronzed by the sun and the sea, apparently happy and, as usual, tight-lipped about his absence. However, the evidence seems to indicate that he did not live a completely hermit-like existence and that he even spent several happy days on Bora Bora in the company of one particularly attractive *vahiné*, who appears in a minor role twenty-seven years later in *Where Are you Dining Tonight?*, under the name of Moetia (the name of one of the daughters of the chieftainess Arii Taimai Salmon). If she knew – or guessed – this, Félicité can only have been pleased about it. Her sister, grandmother Garrett, unabashed by common proverbs, had a habit of saying that, in love, 'one devil drives out another'. The only encounters Stanislas himself mentioned are, first of all, his meeting with Alain Gerbault who had just arrived in Polynesia for the second time on his new cutter, the *Alain-Gerbault*, and had dropped anchor in the lagoon of Ahe atoll. Had they got on well together? In theory, it was doubtful. Their characters were too dissimilar. Gerbault had quit Europe, which he could no longer tolerate, and he would never go back. He was going to live the life of an ascetic and devote himself to the study of Polynesian history and customs. As for Stanislas, he was there only by accident, and for a reason which, in truth, was pretty trivial: to forget a woman. Yet despite Gerbault's suspicious nature, Stanislas must have passed the test. They joined forces and lived together for ten days on the atoll, then sailed on the *Alain-Gerbault* to Rangiroa, another atoll further south. There they parted company, losing sight of each other for good; but Gerbault remained in Stanislas' memory as an itching presence. If a man is over-sensitive, why should he not make his escape? In the lagoon at Rangiroa there was a fine black-hulled schooner lying at anchor, whose owner was known to Gerbault as a result of a call he had once made at Papeete: this was the Count von Lückner, a former officer of the German navy who, during the Great War, had gone in for piracy in the Pacific aboard the *See Adler* and had even attacked Papeete where he had intended to take on fresh supplies of coal and would have done so, had the port authorities not scuttled the *Zélée* in the channel between the coral reefs. Von Lückner, aloof and arrogant, was a man of great charisma: there was, on first contact, an iciness in his manner and he held the same fascination, Stanislas said, as the sight of a beautiful woman on a mortuary slab; but once the *See Teufel* had put to sea, the portrait of Hitler hanging in the mess would be turned to the wall, von Lückner would open the first bottle of champagne and his iciness would vanish. Behind the pose there was a man and a remarkable sailor. Gerbault behaved as if he appreciated only the sailor in von Lückner and pretended to be oblivious to his posturing. But he knew what was going on: on the pretext of a millionaire's whim, von Lückner was in Polynesia with an eye on the next war, scouting out the possibility of new offensives with his German pirate-cruiser. Stanislas got on well with him and accompanied him as far as Hiva-Oa in the Marquesas Islands, whence he returned, as I said, just in time to set out again for Europe. It was from von Lückner that he borrowed the physical appearance, the cynical conversation and the charm of an erudition that knew how to touch lightly upon its subject which he later used to sketch the memorable portrait of the father of Maximilian and Wilhelm von Arelle.

Stanislas did not produce any book from these three-month-long wanderings in Tahiti, the Marquesas and the Tuamotu archipelago. Nevertheless, there are traces of them here and there, notably in the opening sentence of *The Countdown*: 'It is the time of day when, in the narrows of Tiputa, on Rangiroa, the divers Matoi and Toi feed muraenas to the sharks.' The subsequent events have nothing to do with this opening, and once he had finished the novel Stanislas could just as easily have cut out this strange way of establishing the time of an action which unfolds in Europe. When I asked him what lay behind his use of this sentence, so remote from the spirit of the narrative that followed, he confessed to me that it had been suggested to him one day by Chardonne (in front of Cocteau who related it in *Portraits-souvenirs*): 'Start a novel any way you like, even something along the lines of "One beautiful summer's night . . .", and the rest will follow.' Likewise his experience of the extraordinary fauna of the Pacific often prompted reminiscences which were inexplicable unless one knew that, during his three-month disappearance, he had dived and fished with the islanders wherever he went. Thus, in *The Bee*,[1] when Roger Sanpeur is invited to the fancy dress ball given by the Sansovinos in Rome, he arrives disguised as a 'greater spotted Baliste', and when Albina asks him what his spots and orange nose are meant to signify, he answers, 'Marine biologists call me the *Baliste niger*,[2] but to my friends I'm known as the polka-dot fish.'

In *Three is a Crowd*[3] Abraham Siniaski, the financier who has fallen in love with Margot Dupuy, settles himself in her drawing room on a sofa upholstered in a gaudy baroque design, whose colours he takes on

[1] *L'Abeille*, novel, Editions Saeta, 1963.
[2] A variety of trigger-fish found in the South Pacific.
[3] *Vivre à trois*, novel, Editions Saeta, 1967.

in a matter of minutes like the '*synanceia verrucosa*, a genuine wart-covered stone-fish whose venom is deadly if one is clumsy enough to let a vein anywhere near its sting. Fortunately for her preservation, Margot has few veins and much luck, and Abraham Siniaski will never be able to paralyze her with his venom.'

Equally impressed by the flora, Stanislas now conceived a lifelong love of the scent of *tiare*, that smooth and sweet perfume of Tahitian skin and hair. In *Where Are You Dining Tonight?* Maximilian cruelly bites Moetia's shoulder with its sugared and intoxicating tang of *tiare*. Attempts to make it grow in the garden at Cap-Ferrat were fruitless. One frangipani sapling did survive for a number of years, but it died in the first winter of the war. From 1947 onwards, when the first airliners established a regular link between Tahiti and Europe, Stanislas often had himself sent a handful of the white *tiare* flowers, which arrived wrapped in a damp banana leaf. Arranged with a little water in a dish, they would open and envelop the room he was working in with their fragrance. Jean Dubouchez, the father of 'the woman who inspired' *Cryptogram* – one of those episodic characters with which Stanislas liked to sprinkle his narratives like an engraver who etches marginal figures around his central motif – Jean Dubouchez, approaching his sixtieth birthday, discovers, with a child-like sense of wonder, that he has a weakness for sailors. We see him wandering unsuccessfully back and forth in front of the ministry on the place de la Concorde, making eyes at the sentries; then one day he hears that 'in the Botanical Gardens you can see as many sailors' pom-poms as you like'. He rushes to the spot and, seeing only mothers out walking their children along the avenues, asks one of the park-keepers who, with the contempt which a little learning has for illiteracy, points out some shrubs with orange-coloured flowers in a greenhouse: 'Your "sailor's pom-poms", as people vulgarly call them, are in fact *Calliandra surinamensis*.'[1] Harrison Willard Smith had presented Félicité with a bouquet of these delicate flowers when they visited his botanical garden at Papeari.

The informed eye would have no difficulty in detecting the references to Stanislas' Polynesian journey of the winter of 1933–4 in the twenty or so novels which came after it. He was continually mindful of what had dazzled him, but despite the temptation, he always denied himself the opportunity of going back, probably for fear that the second encounter with those skies and that ocean would disappoint

---

[1] Also known as redhead powderpuffs.

him and destroy the picture he had kept of them. He had many such quirks of caution. And in any case the consequences of the 1939–45 war convinced him that Europe was well able to contain his ambitions. After going to New York in 1946, he never stepped beyond its frontiers again, apart from an occasional trip to Morocco. But Polynesia continued to live in his imagination. In London, in the house in Chelsea, several shelves of his library were occupied by travelogues, photograph albums and studies of the flora and fauna and peoples of the Pacific; and the photograph of himself which, with a hint of self-satisfaction, he used as his publicity photograph, shows him during the course of that winter in the Pacific, emerging from the water, a pareo around his waist, brandishing a blue caranx (*c. melanpygus* is written in his hand on the back of my copy) on the point of a harpoon.

A good many years afterwards – it was in 1967 when Stanislas published *Three is a Crowd* – Pierre Dumayet,[1] taking as examples two of those sentences which, scattered throughout the novel, brought the reader up short, asked him if he had not occasionally experienced a struggle within himself against a certain affectation of pedantry. I made a brief note of his answer:

The creation of a novel is a kind of alchemy. One never knows what one will find in the last retort flask; it could be gold, it could be mud. The reason being that the materials one uses have sometimes been collected a very long time before, and it is quite possible for them to degenerate in the meantime. However, many are not biodegradable and they come to light again from one's memory, young, new, and so precise that the temptation to use them in their integrity is very strong. So, what better integrity could one wish for than that theoretical one created by botanists and marine biologists?

The return journey via Panama was uneventful. In Paris, in early spring, André was waiting for them impatiently, exhausted from bearing singlehanded the responsibility for Editions Saeta. The company was in a bad way. Since *The Secret Life of an Orgasm* Saeta had published nothing successful enough to put it on a sound footing. It was imperative that they come up with some authors and ideas for new series. André remarked in his notebook at the time (April 1934):

[1] 17 November 1967, a broadcast entitled *Books for All* by Pierre Dumayet and Pierre Desgraupes.

Stanislas has grasped the problem at once. No authors? he said. We shall have to invent some. . . . Fine by me, but how?

Two days later he writes:

Stanislas has come back with a solution. We leave for Deauville tomorrow. The entire Normandy Hotel awaits us. Father has telephoned. We have ten days' free bed and board to see our plan through.

These few sibylline phrases shed the only light on a mystery which the two friends did their best to befog even further in order to throw the critics off the scent; but what everything points to is that while they were shut away in a room in the Normandy Hotel they were writing, as a team, taking it in turns, the first volume of a collection of detective novels which, because of their novelty, their so-called 'American' style, would become immensely successful. This first volume was entitled *Death of a Foal in its Mother's Arms*,[1] followed by a second, put together at Cap-Ferrat two months later: *AC/DC*.[2] Who did the writing, who dictated, who corrected? It is impossible to know for certain, although we would probably be right in supposing that it was André, the great lover of cheap American gangster novels, who imposed the style while Stanislas invented the plots. In October they shut themselves away once again at the Trianon in Versailles, and came back with *The Derelict*.[3] All three were written by someone called Fred Ginger. Where had he sprung from? André, who adored cinema musicals, had simply combined the names of his two favourite stars, Fred Astaire and Ginger Rogers. In the mass of American popular novels, André had no difficulty in locating a half-dozen authors who had the required style. The series swiftly found its market, overwhelming its first two authors. Fred Ginger published another three volumes. The publisher's blurb stated that he lived in Chicago, was a mulatto, married to a blonde Swede, and had spent five years of his life in Sing Sing for armed robbery. The American authorities persistently refused him an exit visa, so he was unable to come to Paris to be interviewed on the radio or answer journalists' questions. In 1938 Editions Saeta announced the death of Fred Ginger, shot through the

[1] Editions Saeta, in the *Crime Pays* series, 1935.
[2] Do., 1935.
[3] Do., 1936.

neck by a single bullet from a rival gang. The series was established and no longer had any need of him. Who could imagine a better way of getting rid of him than by liquidating him with as few scruples as he had shown in his own lifetime?

Obviously there is no question of formally attributing Fred Ginger's books to Stanislas. One cannot recognize anything of him or his manner in them. When I questioned him about it, some years later, he said, 'Oh that! Nothing very wonderful there. Although I must say we had some fun doing it, your father and I. Like a stylistic exercise. I have good memories of the ten days in Deauville. In the mornings we warmed up with a run, three or four times up and down the deserted beach. We were befriended by an Alsatian. He used to come up and bark at us until we threw a stick into the waves for him. Then he would spring after it into the foam and fish it out, snapping it into small pieces before coming back to yap around our feet. Your father used to collect those shells called razor-shells, with so little idea of what he intended to do with them that when we returned to Paris he left ten kilos of the things in our room. We lunched on pancakes and cider in a small restaurant by the station and we dined on hot prawns at the Regency in Trouville. Odd memories, do you not think? Why did that dog stay in my mind? Why the collecting of razor-shells, and why the buckwheat pancakes and the hot prawns? Actually, if I think carefully, I can find other things: I remember a dish of sea-food that we had the greatest difficulty in finishing, and your father kitting himself out in a chandler's, with a blue oilskin and a fisherman's cap which he used to wear pushed back on his head with its peak up, as they do in Honfleur. We were on our own, with all of Deauville to ourselves. The air was so quick, so fresh and so good that our cheeks were bright red by the time we went back to the room to fill it with smoke and work. Our Fred Ginger died four years afterwards . . . it was about time: we had run out of ideas and would have felt uncomfortable repeating ourselves. In any case, I was working on *The Countdown* by then. Deauville is a good memory, and I can tell you why: it was exactly as if your father and I were back at the *lycée* preparing for an examination, copying from each other and correcting each other. The women were in Paris. We were free, *free* . . . which is all very childish, I know. Of course we should not have revelled in that freedom so greedily and so pleasurably had we not known that once the novel was finished we should return to the very agreeable and reassuring fetters which bound us to Marie-Claire and Félicité. Evidently.'

This manufacturing of American-style detective novels is replayed in *The Bee.* Roger Sanpeur, of the *'Baliste niger'* disguise at the ball given by Mario and Albina Sansovino in Rome, is generally assumed to be one of the idle rich. In reality he owes his lifestyle to a secret existence of forced labour. One month in two, he disappears. For the publishing equivalent of a slave-trader he turns out detective novels in which the whisky flows and the women smoulder, all of them blonde, poured into satin dresses and wearing mules with pink pom-poms. The men kill, torture, steal, and abandon intoxicating creatures who swoon after they have been made love to. The funny thing is that Roger Sanpeur, a gentle soul, timorous by nature, could not hurt a fly. The first-fruits of love render him unbelievably clumsy with women. When Albina, who devours his novels under the dryer at the hair-dresser's or at night to help her get to sleep, discovers that Roger is her favourite author, she throws herself into his arms with such sudden-ness that he becomes impotent. She then kicks him out of her life, upon which he attempts to commit suicide, but since he has no idea of how to use a pistol, the bullet meant for his heart ends up lodged in his shoulder. (Stanislas, very skilful with guns, liked to make fun of clumsy people.)

Félicité was able to set her mind at ease. Her patience and under-standing had helped to exorcise the ghosts of Vladimir and Nathalie as much as the long voyage and his subsequent frantic labours with André. Stanislas had learned, too, that one forgets even the most harrowing grief, and when he wrote *Singtime!* in New York in 1942, he actually derived an unexpected pleasure from it. Despite its tragic ending – the deaths of the hero and heroine and their brother's suicide – it is a sparkling book whose characters have a great appetite for life.

In 1934 Stanislas Beren was twenty-six years old. He had lost much of his awkwardness and looked more like a tennis star than what we normally call an intellectual. He was not handsome in the strict sense of the word: his nose was too long, his eyes were set deep in their sockets, his mouth was a little too greedy-looking, and he was known to be abrupt when he was intimidated. People who knew him in the mid-thirties remember a young man of few words who always seemed to be waiting, visibly impatient, for Félicité's friends to leave. In his diary[1] André Garrett notes:

> Stanislas did not utter a single word during the entire dinner. At one point he scribbled something on a page from his notebook and passed it to me quite openly: 'What a bore! When are they going to bugger off? I want to be alone with you and F. What will they do if I unbutton my fly, get my prick out and dip it in the mayonnaise? After the gasps of horror have subsided I can see Oswald Winterthur murmuring to his dreamy wife, "Darling, that is what I call an asset." I swear I shall do it if you raise your little finger . . .' I did not raise my little finger, Stanislas did not get his prick out, and we missed a marvellous opportunity to rid aunt Félicité of some society bores – for whom, despite her intelligence and her sense of humour and good taste, she sometimes has an inexplicable weakness.

He had made a start on *The Countdown* and was petrified by the fear that Félicité would advise him once again to burn everything, so he was only writing on one corner of a desk at Editions Saeta, where he spent his mornings with André. When she consigned the manuscript of the first *Where Are You Dining Tonight?* to the flames Félicité ran a risk. Let us say that it was a calculated risk, and that Stanislas' apparent

---

[1] 12 December 1934.

inactivity did not worry her. It is, in fact, quite probable that André lost no time in betraying his friend and telling Félicité that Stanislas was secretly and secretively writing something that between themselves they were calling an 'effort'.

The Countdown is a novel entirely apart from the mainstream of Stanislas Beren's work. We have seen that the hero, Jezero Skadarsko, takes his name from a Serbian lake on whose shore Stanislas very likely spent the first seventeen years of his life. This Jezero, whom the author presents as 'a man of less than average height, with black hair cut very short because no comb had ever been able to discipline it,' is a mild-mannered intellectual from some Balkan state or other. He takes refuge in France and teaches in a ghostly university, where the students occasionally turn up at classes and examinations if the weather is not too fine in the Luxembourg gardens. Jezero often finds himself confronted by an empty lecture theatre; occasionally the concierge's ginger cat comes and sits on a bench in front of him and watches him with her grey eyes whose pupils contract when the sun filters into the room through the rose-window overlooking the lectern. Shortly afterwards, the cat goes to sleep and her purring reverberates around the lecture theatre. Should Jezero, as a mark of reprobation, stop in the middle of a sentence, the ginger cat wakes up and stares fixedly at him with her grey eyes until he begins again. Come the spring, the days are so fine and warm that the students are all in the gardens, and Jezero becomes used to being alone in front of the two hundred empty seats. The ginger cat remains faithful to him; sometimes she arrives after he has started, sometimes she is already there when he walks in. She settles down on her bench with a knowing air, although Jezero, in a deliberate act of insubordination to the scheduled syllabus, has decided to initiate a series of lectures on the close relationship between death and time. The ginger cat's interest is nevertheless undiminished. Every time the words 'death' and 'time' are mentioned in the lectures, which is frequently, she opens her eyes, even sneezes, but she never moves. One day Jezero stops in mid-sentence, because he has suddenly seen the ginger cat arch her back. An invisible hand is stroking her. She stretches herself from head to tail and rolls over as if she were entwining herself around someone's leg. Jezero develops the certitude that there is an invisible being present at his lecture, who strokes the animal's fur when he gets bored. In this improvised lecture on an abstract theme, the authoritative judgment of the lecturer is found wanting. He is unable to produce the original thoughts he is seeking. Consequently he finds that he is often handing out banal remarks just to give himself some breathing space. Soon, holding the ginger cat's interest becomes so essential to him that each day Jezero goes home and prepares the next lecture with a rigour of which he had never imagined himself capable. One day he speaks with so much conviction that he experiences a need to close his eyes as if he is reciting to himself. When he opens them again, an oldish man – possibly in his seventies – is sitting in the front row with the ginger cat on his lap. He is a man that Jezero is certain he has met before. He is the same height as Jezero himself, in other words fairly short. He has come to the university in blue drill trousers and a white sweater of coarse wool, which even the most informal students would not dare to do, and is apt to light cigarettes on which he hardly puffs at all before grinding them out with his heel. The casual attitude of this character towards his lecturer is so pronounced that Jezero eventually decides to say something to him.

'Carry on!' the man simply answers, stroking the ginger cat absent-mindedly.

The voice is familiar. Sonorous, and assured at the same time as possessing an ironic and scornful note, it evokes something that Jezero knows very well: this is how, in his attic room where he prepares his masterly classes for the following day, he tries to pitch his voice, without ever succeeding. To start with, he refuses to believe what is happening; despite the truth becoming increasingly obvious, he summons up all his will-power to ignore it. But the old man, initially reserved, eventually intervenes in a lecture where Jezero, his inspiration gone, is floundering in a comparison introduced in defiance of common sense.

'What you mean, in essence, is that time can be called a provisional death and that death itself is pure time, infinite and absolute. So enunciate it clearly, I beg you, without periphrasis. We are not children, the ginger cat and I. We have no difficulty keeping up with you. This idea – which is not new – has never been expressed with enough simplicity. Your merit – if you achieve it – will be to have been the first to express a prime truth, without taking refuge in the usual logomachy. A little fortitude, Monsieur, we are a few years apart – forty-five, if I am correct – and you'll see, we'll be in complete agreement. Συμφωνία, as they say in Greek, hmm?'

Dumbfounded, Jezero leaves his lectern and steps down from the platform to approach the unknown speaker, who suddenly stiffens and goes waxy like a corpse, to turn in the space of a few seconds into a skeleton whose bones immediately crumble to dust. The ginger cat springs onto the lecturer's shoulder and purrs happily. Jezero, choked and speechless, cannot go on with his lecture. This is the moment chosen by the vice-chancellor and the education minister for their solemn tour of inspection. Jezero is justifiably censured for 'playing with a cat – not even a pedigree animal, but a ginger alley cat – instead of instructing his students in the elementary rules of logic'. He is not dismissed, but he offers his resignation. Nobody believes in his story of a seventy-year-old student, and now he is the one wandering in the Luxembourg gardens until nightfall, up and down the boulevard Saint-Michel until the early hours, then around Les Halles where, quite suddenly, at Le Pied de Cochon, he sees the unknown man, who, sitting at a table with a young, ginger-haired woman, is blowing on a spoonful of stringy onion soup. The man has seen him but makes no move to beckon him closer. It is the young, ginger-haired woman who gets up and comes towards him, smiling.

'Don't you recognize me?' she asks.
'Yes . . . I think I do.'
'You're lying! I've caught you out. You've never met me. Well, come now . . . don't get cross, come and join us. The professor will be delighted to see you.'
'What professor?'
'Jezero Skadarsko.'
'I'm Jezero Skadarsko.'
'We'll see.'

Although he is generally impervious to the charms of ginger-haired women, Jezero finds it difficult to take his eyes off this particular woman, with her luxuriant hair and a black dress cut so low that it almost exposes her generous breasts. Before he has even had time to make a gesture – the gesture naturally being to plunge his hand into her bodice and reassure himself that her breasts are free, in other words that they belong to the first person who takes a fancy to them – the young woman gently wags her index finger at him.

'No, not here! And not now! Jezero has something to say to you.'

He sits down at the table facing the professor who also claims to be called Jezero Skadarsko and who, for the moment, is entirely preoccupied with finishing his onion soup, however hot it might be. When the last spoonful has passed his lips, he calls the waiter and very courteously asks him to convey his compliments to the chef. The waiter listens respectfully and disappears smartly in the direction of the kitchens. Then the seventy-year-old man turns towards Jezero and looks him in the eye with such intensity that the young lecturer experiences an acute discomfort which he describes as 'a sudden withering of my skin and my skeleton, a weakness in my arms and legs, and a mental block which concealed from me the name of the old man'. When he apologizes and asks the man his name a second time, he hears 'Jezero Skadarsko', but this time is not remotely surprised because he has forgotten his own name. As for the young woman, she maintains that her name is Redja Matchka, which is not really surprising in the circumstances.[1] Around them is all the bustle of Les Halles as it existed before being transferred to Rungis: greengrocers in clogs and blue aprons, butchers in white splashed with red, fishmongers in yellow oilskins, night-birds come in from the darkness, their chins blue with stubble, and their scantily-clad female companions shivering with cold. Jezero the Younger is stunned. The unfamiliarity of his surroundings disturbs him and he decides to leave, but Redja Matchka takes hold of his arm and restrains him. Jezero the Elder is talking. The first words have been drowned by the noise of the restaurant and Jezero the Younger catches only the end of a sentence which seems to have nothing to do with what follows, it:

'. . . transcendent in the sense in which Montaigne used it when he took fright at the "transcendental humours" which dissociate themselves from the body. You are I and I am you. There is one moment in life, just at the halfway point, where we shall meet one another face to face again, like today. For the present, your eyes question me and mine remember. Do not forget: the day that you see me again, you will know from then on that you have passed that halfway point. Until that moment, I can advise you, at least if you have the humility to ask my advice, and then you will watch the way I live and learn from my mistakes. We shall always be on the same slope; you will be walking down to the peace of the valleys, I shall be climbing up to the heights obscured by clouds. Your progress is the

[1] *Redja Matchka*, in Serbo-Croat, means 'ginger cat'.

right one, mine is against nature – and on that point I ask you not to consult the moralists, who like nothing so much as platitudes and continually side-step the paradoxes of life. Now, dear Jezero, I have talked too much. Let us shake hands and say not adieu, but until the next time. I leave you in the company of Redja Matchka who has two or three essential things to teach you.'

Jezero the Elder stands and makes his way towards the far end of the counter, where the enormous barmaid looks at him with an expression of wonder and admiration which must delight the heart of any man, even coming from a barge of a woman whose bosom fills her black satin bodice to bursting. She hands Jezero the Elder a bill which he signs without giving it a second glance, and he goes out to be swallowed up by the crowd milling around the greengrocers' stalls. Redja Matchka gently takes the hand of Jezero the Younger, henceforth plain Jezero, and he realizes that without this unknown woman whose heady perfume only just covers the pungent smell of burnt fat lying heavily on the bar-room of Le Pied de Cochon, the loneliness, the clamour, the departure of his namesake, the misery of the dawn so agonizing for those who have had no sleep, would be unbearable. Even the prospect of soon finding himself in bed for the first time with an unknown woman – who will have to teach him everything because this philosopher is barely aware of the facts of life – would be unbearable were the unknown woman any other than she.

They leave the café by the same route as the old man. The barmaid has resumed her crabby expression and does not even give them a smile. A moment before a fascinating person, in the form of Jezero the Elder, had passed through her rude mammalian existence, and she is ruminating on an old dream of what her life could have been with such a 'gentleman of quality' had she not sacrificed herself to her children. Conscious of their insignificance, Redja Matchka and Jezero slink by, ashamed. Redja Matchka has put on a light cape which floats around her and does little to hide her bust, leaving the swell of her breasts uncovered. They are like . . . like . . . Jezero is incapable, despite a superhuman effort, of finding the *mot juste* to qualify the woman's breasts. The immediate simile that springs to his mind is marble, but that would be premature because he has had no chance to verify their firmness, and to call them 'milk-white' would bring the barmaid's bosom too much to mind. Yet there is absolutely no doubt that what he is dealing with here are very beautiful breasts, breasts that have never nursed a child and whose coral-pink nipples are prominent enough for him to disregard their pallor. But what use are words when a great event is imminent? Jezero is already cursing himself for his clumsy behaviour. He feels so awkward, so incapable of talking about anything other than the subject of his next lecture ('Are the moral sciences moral?') that he is on the point of giving up; just then Redja Matchka puts a hand on his shoulder, wheels him round to face her, laces an arm around his neck and kisses him on the lips. There on the pavement, among the crowds of people streaming past who, unexpectedly and charmingly respectful, neither jostle them nor make offensive remarks, he discovers that the physical love which he has dreaded for so long is going to be a pleasure.

But where? He is quite sure that this young woman, so delicately made-up, not a hair out of place, her only adornment a gold bracelet and brooch, will be unimpressed by the garret where he lives, its creaking mattress, the dubious sheets, the bedspread full of holes, the sink with the morning's coffee cup still unwashed in it. And how will she manage to wash herself when he will have to fill a pitcher from the tap on the landing and pour its contents into a cracked enamel bowl for her? It seems that Redja Matchka has preternatural powers and that she has already guessed the cause of his discomfort.

'Let's go to my place!' she says, and a carriage stops beside them. A chauffeur in a grey uniform, with jodhpurs and black leggings, gets down, doffs his cap and opens the door for them. The interior is so incredibly luxurious that Jezero scarcely dares sit down. The young woman takes his hand and the carriage sweeps them across Paris to a beautiful forest, within which an avenue of oaks leads to a Louis XIIIth manor house whose windows reflect the golden-red rays of the sun with an almost blinding brilliance. The door opens by itself and Redja Matchka, having let her cape slip to the ground, walks up the stone staircase leading to the first floor. Jezero follows her as a dog does a bitch, for she has raised her skirts to uncover her ankles. Beneath the stocking, a tiny gold chain can be seen around one of these ankles, and Jezero is deeply troubled by the sight. The books he has read, and the Japanese engravings shown him by a colleague, have imbued him with a rather radical kind of erotic sense which excludes every poetical approach to sensuality. This ankle encircled with gold throws him into confusion and has such an immediate and potent effect on him that he asks himself desperately whether he is not about to experience the heights of pleasure there on the staircase, without having even caressed Redja. Worse is to come. Having been dragged into a sumptuous bed-chamber where a canopied bed awaits them, and the walls are damasked in red and silver, with Venetian mirrors and a carved wooden lectern carrying a book open at a drawing of extreme suggestiveness, Jezero's raging desire suddenly vanishes and when the young woman clasps him to her, she is immediately aware of his lack of passion.

'I know what the matter is!' says Redja Matchka and, grabbing his hand, she dashes down the stairs into the basement of the house to the kitchen. In the centre of this vast room is an equally vast table, which is still cluttered with plates and dishes containing the remains of a meal. With an energetic backhand Redja sweeps the dirty crockery onto the tiled floor where most of it is shattered, then she stretches out full length on the scrubbed wood. Jezero is once again consumed by a mad desire which she slowly guides inside her. After this, they have sex repeatedly: in the wash-house with its faint smell of laundry singed by the iron, in the servants' quarters where Redja dresses up in the apron, lace cap and black stockings of a lady's maid, and finally in the luxurious, damask-clad bed-chamber where, thanks to his recent experiences, Jezero's inhibitions dissolve. Exhausted, he falls asleep with one hand resting on his mistress's breast. Awaking several hours later, he finds himself alone in the bed. Without the canopy, the furniture, the ornaments and the lectern, he might have thought it was all a dream. He leaps out of bed, plants himself in front of the full-length mirror and sees himself, naked, with grey hair at his temples and on his chest; his legs are spindly, his face wrinkled. Frantic at the idea that he has been asleep for so many years, he looks down and cradles his penis in his hand, and perceives that the pathetic image offered by the mirror is no real reflection of a perfectly healthy organ ready for further service. Then he inspects the rest of himself and finds he has no grey hair and his face is still that of a young man. The image in the mirror is not his reflection, but another appearance of Jezero the Elder who smiles at his dazed expression and says very slowly, articulating each word,

'I warned you that we should be meeting often. Redja Matchka has taught you many things. It is up to you to make your own use of them. Now put your clothes on and go back to your university.'

Jezero the Elder disappears and Jezero the Younger, with great relief, sees himself in the mirror. He feels rather ridiculous in his nakedness and gets dressed, retrieving his scattered clothes from the various rooms where he has made love with Redja Matchka. The house is deserted and he wonders how he will find his way back through the forest. When he opens the door, he is astounded to step into a street where a bus and several taxis are passing. Night is falling and the street lamps are coming on. Outside a pork-butcher's there is a queue of people. Children with satchels under their arms are coming out of a primary school on whose pediment are the words, 'The future belongs to all men', attributed to Edouard Herriot. Jezero does not recognize this part of the city and decides to go against the current of the passers-by who must logically be heading for the outskirts where they live, after their day's work. Within a few minutes he arrives at the place de la Concorde and has only to follow the Seine in order to get back to the Latin quarter where, perpetual student that he is, fearful of venturing elsewhere in the great city, he has chosen to live. He is overcome by a new feeling: he is going to shake himself out of his Peter Pan state and become a man. Already he no longer looks at women the way he used to. It seems that at his lecture the following day, the students, who have come in large numbers, have been alerted to his new incarnation. They listen to him enthralled. The vice-chancellor, who has hidden himself in the room, comes to congratulate him and begs him to forgive his outburst of bad temper two days earlier. Jezero the Younger sees the gates of glory open wide before him. He is confident: Jezero the Elder will watch over him and counsel him. And far from disappearing, Redja Matchka is passing the time enjoyably by scattering herself among the women he meets: one has her thighs, another her voice, a third her grey eyes, and another is a nymphomaniac. Fascinated by the way Jezero thinks and uses words, the women students satiate him with their charms. His reputation grows, thanks principally to his female admirers, and so much so that his former country summons him back. He returns in triumph. There the head of state, Kralj, wants to make him prime minister, but Jezero, on the advice of the old man, declines the post because it is too much in the public eye and he runs the risk of assassination as much as being riddled with bullets by a firing-squad. He will be Kralj's Père Joseph, his grey eminence, benefitting from the advantages attached to anonymity as well as to the exercise of real power. Power to judge what can be done for and against men's stupidity, and anonymity for the joyous pursuit of a lifetime's debauchery. At the halfway point he meets his namesake. They now resemble each other in every respect. No one can tell them apart, and they have to be given numbers: Jezero I and Jezero II. Their experience of life is such that the world would belong to Jezero I if he did not disdain power. The two men go their separate ways: they are both without illusions now – an infirmity which, when all is said and done, is perfectly bearable – and they have nothing more to teach one another. We see them still addressing friendly signs to each other as they draw further and further apart, right up to the moment when Jezero I discovers the valley of the dead as Jezero II accedes to the mysteries of limbo.

*

There is no doubt that the end is rather perfunctory. At one time Stanislas thought of writing a second volume which would recount, in detail, the life of Jezero Skadarsko as the power behind the throne of the sovereign Kralj. But he gave up the idea and condensed the final episodes into a few pages. André has this to say in his notebook:[1]

> Laziness on Stanislas' part? Or perhaps he had just wearied of the fantastic? We were envisaging a great series of novels, something to bear comparison with *Men of Good Will*, but wild and raving. Jules Romains can sleep in peace. Stanislas has got an idea for another novel which will be very different. He even has a title for it: *Cryptogram.*

The same fate awaited several of Stanislas' books. The last fifty pages overwhelmed him with boredom: he would already be dreaming of another novel, even though he knew it would be at least a year before he started writing it. He was in Venice in 1969 when I sent him a list of questions to which he replied piecemeal over several months. I made a point of asking him what had led him to give up the story of Jezero Skadarsko's political life. This was his answer in full:[2]

> Unlike you, politics has never interested me. All the same I realized that it was talked about a great deal from day to day, and when I started writing *The Countdown* it was my intention to dismantle the whole comical mechanism of authority and power. Alas, as soon as I had come to grips with this thorny problem, I perceived that I did not believe in the task I had set myself, any more than did my hero. Think about it: Jezero is a philosopher, or perhaps more a moralist. As an intellectual, he has performed his meditations on the subject of power. The day that he has the chance to exercise it, it occurs to

[1] May 1935.
[2] Letter dated Venice, 10 November 1969.

him that political action implies a renunciation of the grand business of Knowledge. That he cannot do. Otherwise his whole life as a young man will have been a nonsense. So he resigns himself to playing the unobtrusive role of Kralj's grey eminence and while he continues his quest for pure knowledge, the sovereign is left to dirty his hands and take the responsibility for the policies he, Jezero, has inspired. Critics might point out that this moralist Jezero would do better to lead a different kind of life, and that the women and wine for which he has such an immoderate liking are difficult to harmonize with his own precepts; but an anthology of Jewish sayings by Georges Levitte offers an answer: 'In orgy itself, as in imbecility, there is a certain wisdom.'

So I gave up the idea of developing the theme of the conflict between Knowledge and Power in a second volume. It was not really my cup of tea. I was twenty-six and only interested in poets. The day that Jezero cast off his inhibitions and his timidity and his scruples, I lost interest in him. One should know when to stop. While I was writing that novel I enjoyed myself thoroughly. Your letter drove me to re-read some passages from it and I confess immodestly that I enjoyed enormously the sixty pages which tell the story of Jezero's exploits with the pretty redhead with the grey eyes. What a scandal that was! I was called a pornographer, a polluter of society. There was a precedent, with *The Secret Life of an Orgasm*, because of the people who had not read it and assumed it was a piece of erotica. That was how the reputation started. All things considered, I found it rather flattering. The funniest thing is that I knew less than anybody on the subject of eroticism and that it was all from my imagination. Apart from . . . well, to be honest I copied the hero pretty extensively, and a real Redja Matchka did turn up to suggest *Cyptogram* to me. That was another of those encounters between the real and the imaginary which I find endlessly fascinating.

Having said that, if you want a laugh, you should try to find the article laid by the squawking Béla Zukor a few days after the book appeared. Quite funny. A pastiche of me which he signed, 'certified true copy, B. Z'. In each paragraph I was made to repeat, '*J'ai zéro, j'ai zéro*.' My sworn enemy was quite witty in those days.[1] More thoughtful and not so funny was the article by Roger Caillois which opened my eyes. This was André Bretonising with a difference: intelligent and subtle, it made one aware of his imminent disagree-

[1] I have searched in vain for this article in the newspapers in which Béla Zukor wrote. Might Stanislas have invented it? It is not impossible.

ment with the Surrealists, which showed itself markedly in his first book, *Le Mythe et l'Homme*,[1] which came out two years after mine. Caillois considered that I had walked a precarious path, but that I had mixed the fantastic and the supernatural very originally. In some ways that is the direction I have taken in my writing since, as those who read me must have noticed. . . . I shall be expecting you next week. You will have to bring chest waders if you want to get across Saint Mark's. I have been punished by having to make do with Quadri's and Florian's for the past two days. All this water makes me think of the shipwreck of my life since Félicité has gone.

The shipwreck was not final. A woman came into his life two years later and I believe that, despite the tragic ending to the affair, it was one of the happiest episodes in Stanislas' life. Was he taken in by himself when he talked about 'the shipwreck of my life'? I think he was. The sentiment which united Stanislas and Félicité has no name. One can talk about friendship, complicity, tenderness without any of those words containing *everything* that bound them. I would add humour, and Félicité quoting an aphorism coined by her friend Jean Rostand: 'Love can never be mediocre, and to use it for basely conjugal ends is to degrade it.' To which Stanislas had immediately replied, quoting Rostand back at her: 'Love will not fail to suffer for the acts of cowardice which it suggests. Its only chance of enduring in marriage is if both are to each other as if they did not love each other.' And Stanislas also pointed out that Jean Rostand was, in his private life, the best of spouses.

Yet storms did threaten their secret understanding several times. It is certain – Georges Kapsalis confirmed it to me – that after the voyage to Polynesia, when Stanislas started to write *The Countdown*, they went through a crisis which all but separated them. Its origins did not lie in one of those adventures of Stanislas' which he was unwilling to deny himself and which Félicité accepted in any case, but rather in the kind of suspicion he no longer bothered to conceal from the implacable judge with whom he shared his life. In a letter to André Garrett in 1935, Stanislas sets this out clearly:[2]

I am unable to make Félicité understand that I am at a period of my life where I have greater need of loving understanding than of

[1] Gallimard ('Les Essais'), 1938.
[2] Letter dated Saint-Jean-Cap-Ferrat, May 1935.

critical lucidity. I am constantly aware of her severity, since I do not write a line without thinking of her judgment upon it, but I will not have her, *in addition*, saying to me in her motherly voice that my book is a failure. So I write in secret, which is the height of absurdity. I ask her to talk to me and then if she points out an inappropriate word or a repetition or a common epithet I get furious with her and accuse her of reducing me to impotence. When she says nothing I find myself so lonely that it is intolerable, and I imagine that I mean nothing to her, the worst thing of all. Her calmness exasperates me. My state of nerves inspires pity in her. As the wireless enthusiasts say: we are no longer on the same wavelength. And all this just at the moment when I am feeling a wave of enthusiasm for this *Countdown* book which, once I have finished it, will probably only be fit for the wastepaper bin. Without you, old friend, I would be lost for good. Shut up shop, bring Marie-Claire, and fly to my side.

The book appeared without Félicité having read it. André took her the first copy, and when he found out, Stanislas disappeared for a week. When he came back – very much the worse for wear, I think he had been drinking, but where? – when he came back she welcomed him with such gentleness and simple kindness that he realized she had liked *The Countdown*. The cloud had passed. Stanislas confided in André:[1]

I should not have forgiven her if she had continued to love me and my book had been truly bad. In any case, she is incapable of such a thing. Everything is arranged very tightly in her little head. Have you noticed how her brain is held in place by a narrow forehead and concave temples? The only access to it is by the eyes, which are like two glazed doors of such a bright and light brown that one would almost think it a watercolour brown. When there is an outburst of temper that brown iris shoots fire. When all is calm, it has a slight transparency, just enough for my piercing gaze to distinguish through those glazed doors a piece of machinery in impeccable order – albeit fragile – whose workings we must be careful not to upset. Perhaps it is the perfection of the mechanism which paralyzes the speaker – when he is sensitive to it. In other words, Félicité is someone it is not possible to shock. Dali tried it the first time, and

[1] Letter dated London, 10 May 1936.

it fell so flat and he read such pity in her pursed lips that it was the last time he tried to fob her off with surrealism on the cheap; she can flatter herself that in her presence the notary's son from Figueras stops talking rot and becomes what he really is: a man of rare intelligence and an intuition that borders on genius.

So all goes well and we return in a week's time for the EVENT. I hope you have prepared yourself, and that your father and mother have told you how babies are born and that you will not be too surprised. They will be there by your side, with the odd restorative to boost your morale. I must ask you to note down all your anxieties and your most minute thoughts so that we can decide which is the more painful, having a child or producing a book. I have indicated my wishes to Marie-Claire – a girl – and I hope she has understood me. She knows I shall not tolerate a boy. And take note: on her eighteenth birthday, I demand to be allowed to take her to dinner for *two* at Maxim's.

They came back the day I was born. André needed them badly. The hoped-for child was a boy – me – and Marie-Claire was dying. I have never heard Stanislas talk about this time without a terrible emotion. Fate had struck a blow at the only friend he would ever have; and it is possible that even André's own death was less heart-breaking for him. Straight away, the fact that I was a boy receded into the background. I imagine that I was taken on as a bad job to be made the best of by my grandmother, while Félicité, Stanislas and André left for Venice. On their return two months later, they learnt that *The Countdown* had reached its first thirty thousand copies, which was an unhoped-for success in times as difficult as these (June 1936). The printers' and paper mills' strikes restricted the print runs, but they still passed the hundred thousand mark by the end of the year. The book had found its public, articles both sour and complimentary were being written about it, and the word was being passed along: 'You must read pages 40 to 90.' With *Ulysses* (all other things being equal, I hasten to add, for Stanislas considered that not only was the latter a work of genius, but also that the contemporary novel in its entirety sprang from it), with *Ulysses*, Joyce had been the victim of the same misapprehension: the only pages people read were those where Mrs Bloom talks to herself while she is being made love to. In *The Countdown*, the pages on the gymnastic exercises performed by Jezero Skadarsko and the beautiful Redja Matchka found so much favour with the public that the rest of the novel went unnoticed. In October, André had the clever (commercial) idea of producing a special edition of these pages illustrated with etchings by Hans Bellmer. The two hundred numbered copies disappeared in days. Stanislas discovered to his surprise that even the most enthusiastic readers can read an entirely different book to the book one has written. He soon decided where he stood, and years later, I saw him still keeping his temper, on this occasion with a would-be blue-stocking who was saying to him, 'I read an article of yours in a magazine. Excellent. Very funny.'

'Which article was that, *madame*?' (With that courtesy which was like a slap in the face.)

'Last month, yes, last month . . . very funny.'

'In the *Paris Review*?'

'Yes, that's right, in the *Paris Review*.'

'*Madame*, I never thought that in writing an article about death I should amuse you. I am delighted, as you can see!'

'Good heavens, what an idiot I am!'

'No, no, not at all, not at all.'

With *The Countdown* he had said goodbye to the loneliness and timidity of his youth and renounced, in advance, the idea of 'power' and 'honours'. But there were few people to perceive this, and the majority of readers wallowed in the steamy depths of the redhead with the grey eyes whom Jezero was pumping up on the kitchen table of the sumptuous manor house deep in the forest. Editions Saeta owed a debt of gratitude to those frustrated people for whom Jezero had provided these unsuspected pleasures. Saeta's name was launched and its finances were thriving. The person most delighted by the misapprehension of the book was M. Dupuy. It justified all his cynical views. He remarked in a letter to Stanislas – then in Venice – that it was the best thing that could have happened:[1]

You are famous and misunderstood. People read you because of a few blue passages and ignore the rest, which will be discovered later on. You haven't exhausted the entire interest of today's reader in one book. In twenty, thirty or fifty years' time people will pick up *The Countdown* again; then nobody will be shocked by your eroticism and it will stop casting its shadow on what you wanted to say, which was so fundamental and so *right* that I felt a kind of pride in it – it was, after all, I who discovered you in the fifth form. Dear

[1] Dupuy never dated his letters, but by cross-checking one can locate this one around the beginning of June 1936.

Beren, look after yourself, look around you and rest assured that you are a writer. One single word of warning from your old beak: never write the same book twice.

The 'beak' had nothing to fear. Beren would never write the same book twice. When he got this letter, he was discovering Venice, which was to be the great revelation of his life. He was staying in an hotel facing Santa Maria della Salute with André and Félicité. A year later he said in an interview with the weekly *Marianne*:[1] 'Venice makes me hungry. When I am in this city I am seized by an enormous appetite. I cannot stay in one place, nor can I sleep. All the time I want to rush to the window so as not to miss a second of the life of the Grand Canal and the lagoon.' The word hunger well describes the greedy way he threw himself at, and into, Venice. André followed him. His diary entries for this period are silent about himself, and remain silent up to his death in May 1940. His own concerns were henceforth utterly unimportant. My name – the same of his son – does not once figure in the notebook. Nothing of that nature counted any longer in relation to the publishing programme, Stanislas' work and, obviously, his days out sailing (at Bénodet now, since he had decided never to go back to Saint-Jean-Cap-Ferrat where he had met Marie-Claire). So in Venice he was content to follow Stanislas; although I doubt that he took the same, almost childish, pleasure in discovering the city. In *Where Are You Dining Tonight?* Maximilian von Arelle gets up from his bed at night while his mistress is asleep and stares fixedly out at the lagoon: long, black, ghostly shapes slip through the buoy-dotted channel with their decklights winking, bringing to Venice their cargoes of shining faces, lovers transfigured by the city of the doges; and Maximilian wonders if love can survive between those who do not have the *right* to stay in Venice, but are condemned by fate to leave her magic circle.

One day shortly before Félicité's death we were bathing on the Lido – remarkably beautiful once one has turned one's back on the grand hotels, the villas of the well-to-do, and the multi-coloured lines of tents erected on the sand – and as Stanislas emerged from the water after a long swim, he gestured to the Adriatic.

'*C'est ma mer!*' he said. 'Write it as you like. *Mer* or *mère*, it is mine.'

Was he imagining the jagged Dalmatian coast beyond the horizon, and Lake Scutari (Jezero Skadarsko), and the Komovi mountain

[1] 12 June 1937.

range so densely ringed with giant pines that the Olympian solitude of its bare summits seems utterly unapproachable? I can only repeat the vow he made to himself never to tell the story of his past; but he may be forgiven for voicing these thoughts as the memory of his wandering childhood among the Montenegrin *maquis* dogged him still. The Adriatic would remind him of it, and to the signs which it addressed to him he replied several times with short poems, which he mentioned without showing to me and which I was unable to find among his papers. In his eyes Venice was the custodian of the Adriatic and this was not the least of her offices. She had ruled over these waters by force, and now she ruled by courtesy, with a grace defeated and decaying but unutterably beautiful.

By one of those instincts which emerged so strongly in her that they were immediately translated into action, Félicité realized that Stanislas would not live without Venice now. For want of a romantic role which the difference in their ages now forbade her, and perhaps because of the ease with which Stanislas could slip through her fingers, Félicité decided to link their lives to Venice, with the feeling that the beauty of the surroundings, appropriate to their strange love, could rekindle its flame which that year was dim indeed. She rented a large flat on the rio del Veste, next to the Fondamente della Fenice, until after the war, when they left its dark and damp interior, and its over-steep staircase which exhausted Félicité, for the red palazzetto on the Largo Fortunio. So from 1936 onwards, Stanislas revelled in the idea of no longer being a stranger in Venice. He had the time – a whole lifetime – to get to know this city which had invaded his senses from the moment of their first meeting and in which he claimed to find himself 'not as the result of some vulgar process of metempsychosis, but by an *organic* affinity'. Taking as his example Arcimboldo, who used to compose the most repulsive faces out of elegant arrangements of fruit and vegetables, Stanislas was very fond of the idea that his soul – in other words, the hidden spirit, imagination in its raw state before the written and spoken language has endowed it with a form – was in Venice's image: baroque and stagnating, salvaged from the waters, and gaudy, riddled with an infinite number of canals frequented by an infinite number of characters who played comedy one day, tragedy the next, always on stage, always in a hurry, appearing three-dimensionally in broad daylight, or disappearing like ghosts down narrow alleyways, leaving no trace but the echo of their footsteps. His identification with Venice was so great that, as with everything which *really* touched him – in other words, with the certitude that it would remain with him until he died – he wrote little about the city, contenting himself with a discreet allusion here and there, or an evocation of colour. In *Three Card Trick*, published in 1957, Jerome Grant goes to Venice with his best friend's wife, Elvira. Arriving at night, they emerge from the station to find the rain beating down, so instead of taking the traditional lovers' gondola, they climb aboard a vaporetto which drops them at their hotel, the Danieli. They have seen nothing of the Grand Canal and they stumble hastily inside through the revolving doors. Soaked through, they go up to their room to change. Then they find themselves marooned. The riva degli Schiavoni is flooded and can only be negotiated by walking on flimsy duckboards. Forced to dine in the dining room of the Danieli which looks like the dining room of any other European luxury hotel, they begin to feel they have missed their entrance into Venice and both drink too much chianti – the author specifies that it is an Antinori because that particular wine comes from a Tuscan farm once owned by Machiavelli and Jerome Grant thinks himself a Machiavelli of love. They retire to bed and, making love with Jerome for the first time, Elvira lets an obscene word escape her lips. Her lover, shocked, reproaches her with a vehemence intensified by his drinking too much chianti, and the gentle Elvira reveals herself to be so excitable that they come to blows. Regaining their composure, they decide to leave Venice by the first train, at six o'clock. From the icy vaporetto, they can just make out, through the dark sheets of rain, the blurred outlines of the palaces. That is all they see of Venice, and love does not survive the journey. When Jerome Grant goes back some years later with another woman about whom he knows almost nothing, Venice's welcome on a fine autumn afternoon is so conspiratorial that he knows, in the last lines of the book, that this time love is to be vouchsafed him.

*

In *L for London*, which is not a novel, despite his giving just as free a rein to his imagination in it, but more of a collection in the style of Thackeray visiting Paris or Stevenson wandering through the Cévennes, he has painted a series of portraits of eccentrics, who are legion in that city and all quite mad – though not raving mad as is more often the case in France where conduct which deviates from the norm gets you put away immediately. No, these are mad eccentrics in a thoroughly

English style[1] whose circle of acquaintances, in strict adherence to the sacrosanct 'no personal remarks', leaves them free to carry their fantasies and paranoia to extremes. Among these eccentrics one stands out, a certain John Mine, a banker by profession, married, father of three children, who for thirty years, as punctually as Phileas Fogg, has been leaving his home at eight-thirty in the morning to travel to the City where he has made his way up the ladder rung by rung ultimately to become, at the age of fifty, director of a small private bank. At the weekends, from Friday evening to Monday morning, he hangs up his bowler hat and umbrella and takes his family to Portslade in Sussex where he has a pretty house by the sea. For two days he mows the lawn, prunes the rose bushes, chops wood for the sitting-room fire, listens to music and even exchanges the odd non-controversial remark with his wife and children. By the time he retires his existence will, within this careful lifestyle, have achieved perfection. But this is to reckon without Mrs Mine who, one day, on the occasion of their twenty-fifth wedding anniversary and in an outburst of romanticism which is definitely at odds with her physical appearance, slips the word 'Venice' into the conversation. At first, Mr Mine is so surprised by this that he is lost for a reply, but after all, he is not made of stone and between Earls Court and Bank in the morning and Bank and Earls Court in the evening, he ruminates on this idea of Venice. A business deal happily concluded with an Italian arrives at exactly the right time to persuade him that when all is said and done, the Venetians are not all savages and that if Mrs Mine, who has been an ideal companion for a quarter of a century, desires it, then there is every good reason to satisfy her, if only because in the years that still remain to them she will better appreciate the charms of Portslade and the comfort of their seaside retreat with its beautiful view of the beach and cliffs. So that September they fly off to Venice, and begin their visit according to the very precise map and timetable prepared by the travel agency; but after three days of exhausting walks around the city Mrs Mine's totally unsuitable shoes are pinching her feet badly and she is, though uncomplaining, in great pain. Thus she greets with delight the news that the fourth morning, from nine o'clock to one o'clock, will be devoted to visiting the museum of the Accademia. His guidebook in hand, Mr Mine provides a commentary on the pictures,

---

[1] Stanislas was convinced that there was an interesting study to be done on the connection between nationality and derangement and once suggested it to a young psychiatrist who was looking for a subject for his thesis.

giving the name of the artist, his period and the subject treated. The couple's assiduity and respect are exemplary. They are not the kind of art-lovers to disparage the opinions of the little book (another fifteen hundred lira!) purchased on the way in. Mr Mine admires Veronese and Tintoretto, Mrs Mine prefers the pretty scenes by Canaletto and Guardi. This mild disagreement delights them, giving them the impression simultaneously of having personal tastes and a critical sense. Everything changes, however, when they find themselves in a small room off to one side, rather like a treasure chamber, where the smaller canvases are hung. Among them is Giorgione's *The Tempest*. John Mine suddenly feels his heart pounding like a hammer. When his wife, after a quick glance, moves on to Mantegna, Bellini, Piero della Francesca, John stays frozen in front of the Giorgione of Giorgiones. He is struck by a lightning-flash of intuition which tells him that, up to this minute, his life has had no meaning, that in staying riveted to his desk all week and mowing the lawn at Portslade at the weekend, he has quite simply *not lived*. He feels reborn and, like a baby, he chokes, his face goes blue, he wants to shout and weep and, in a desperate gesture, fighting for breath, he tears his shirt collar open. 'In short,' writes Stanislas at this point, 'John Mine is struck by what those penny-a-line novels call "love at first sight".' The reader will have guessed that this is the moment Mrs Mine chooses to return to her husband's side and tell him very contritely that really, her feet are hurting her more than ever and she would like to go back to the hotel. Looking up (she is five foot three to his six foot three), she sees the collar askew, the tie-knot loosened, and her husband's haggard expression; convinced that he has suffered some kind of attack, she shouts for help. An attendant rushes up and, seeing him, John Mine comes to, turns his back on *The Tempest* and suggests to his wife that they leave. 'Your feet are hurting and it would be quite inhuman of me to inflict any more of these pictures on you; in any case, they all look alike.' ('Except one!' he thinks.) Touched by his concern and quickly forgetting her anxiety, Mrs Mine trots off to find her way out, thinking only about sewing the button back on her husband's shirt. They stop at the postcard counter and she chooses one or two reproductions, to which he casually adds the Giorgione painting, not without a certain feeling of guilt. While they are walking towards the traghetto which is to take them to the other side of the Grand Canal, he analyses his remorse with the lucidity gained from long years of monetary dealings. Mr Mine sees clearly that he has committed a mental infidelity, that a woman has entered his life and shattered at a stroke twenty-five years of conjugal happiness firmly founded on mutual respect, that is to say, mutual ignorance. From now on there will be things he will have to conceal; he may even have to lie. He shivers at the thought, and his wife thinks he is cold, despite the mildness of the September weather. Every morning, in the days left before their return to London, John Mine has to invent a pretext to disappear for an hour and hurry to the Accademia. It is not so much the painting as a whole that stirs such passion in him – his ideas on painting are very general ones – but the woman offering her breast. His experience of the female body is of the most limited. In fact, when he got married at the age of twenty-five, he was a virgin and it was only thanks to a college friend with whom he had had several lessons of comparative anatomy – dear Henry! – that he had any knowledge of sex at all. Unveiling herself on their wedding night, Mrs Mine had taught him in the space of a few minutes all he knew about the shape of the female breast, the triangular geometry of the female sex and the *odor di femina*, a smell he was not sure was any more pleasant than that of an underground station. After bearing three children, Mrs Mine was no longer what could be called a great passion and, in order to make certain that there would be no further offspring, they had stopped making love without feeling the lack of it. The encounter with Giorgione's woman has rekindled a quenched fire, opened new horizons. This beautiful woman with her domelike stomach who looks as if she has only one breast, and who turns her head to the voyeur summoned by Giorgione, is a dream suddenly formulated and suddenly made flesh, lucid and perfect. If one looks at her from a short distance, she would seem to be turning her head towards the spectator, but with a magnifying-glass one can more easily distinguish an expression which is – alas! or perhaps all the better – absent, not to say vacant, unless it is preoccupied by the invisible. Mr Mine finds a great elegance in the bare feet, as he does in the hand placed on the bended knee. Mrs Mine has not accustomed him to such refinements and her hairstyle – permed in silvery-grey curls – cannot compete with the attraction of the Venetian blonde hair of Giorgione's woman which falls down either side of her face in two finely wound plaits. The scope of his inspection of the painting, repeated each morning, widens. Mr Mine is irritated by the bush which masks, like a metal grid, a part of the loved one's body, then he muses that in the end it is better that the Accademia's visitors do not see the sandy-coloured shadow below the stomach of this woman whose immodesty is entirely ingenuous. He feels the same about the veil covering her shoulders. Attention is concentrated on the movement of the child who is half-opening his lips to grasp the nipple. The appeal is so direct, the image so sharp that John Mine immediately feels its effect and quickly closes the front of his mackintosh so that no one can see the lump outlining itself in his left trouser leg. Blushing, and convinced that the crowd milling around the small room full of masterpieces can only be staring at his own, inopportune display, he endeavours to calm himself by examining the rest of the painting. He is troubled by the man standing on the left, in profile and therefore watching the nude woman who, indifferent to his presence, sits on the bank and suckles her child. Is he the father or, if not the father, is he planning to violate her in this remote place? Should the woman cry out, no one will hear her. Lightning streaks the sky, thunder rolls down the narrow valley, and the houses in the village have closed all their doors and windows. Mr Mine wants to warn her of the danger, to entreat her to return to her cottage instead of staying there by a tree which might be struck by lightning. The character on the edge of the painting really is very disturbing. One has only to notice the insolent way he carries his head. The museum catalogue states that he is a soldier, although even with him leaning on a spear stuck in the ground, he does not look like one. Is it in fact a spear? And if it is a shepherd's crook, why is it so long and why is there no flock behind the shepherd? In fact, the costume is not a soldier's, nor is it a shepherd's. It is much too becoming in its studied casualness. The breeches are embroidered, the puff-sleeved shirt spotless and the red bolero much too expensive-looking for a peasant. Mr Mine is perplexed. If he had the nerve he would get some scissors and cut this careless character from the canvas, keeping only the admirable landscape background, the river flowing beneath the narrow wooden bridge, the sky streaked with lightning that bursts over the houses with its unreal light. Unfortunately he must return to London, to the house in Kensington and the office in the City. He now feels the awful wrench of honouring his duty and meeting his obligations. He buys a rather poor-quality print of *The Tempest* and a number of slides, with the intention of getting hold of a projector and screen. Once he is back home, he sets aside a room to which he has the only key. Mrs Mine begins to worry, but he reassures her with the news that he intends to study the history of art, a pastime which will occupy his idle days when he retires. In fact, Mr Mine's only interest is in Giorgione whose output is far from prolific and about whom more has been written in conjecture than in certainty. In the evenings he locks himself in his study and projects the slides which show both the whole and details of the painting. His love has by now passed all bounds; he is so overcome by it that he gives up his weekends at Portslade where there is nowhere to build a secret room for his daily assignation with the naked woman of *The Tempest*. Eventually he conquers his shyness and places an order for the shepherd-soldier's embroidered breeches, hose, shirt and bolero from a costumier in Covent Garden. He keeps them locked in a drawer and in the evenings, alone in his study, he dresses up to spend a pleasant hour in front of the image projected on the screen, filled with the ineffable feeling of being closer at last to his loved one whose wearied gaze avoids him (this he considers a charming feminine wile). Of course eventually he shows himself to Mrs Mine and his children in this outfit, but their surprise is moderated by their expectation of some-thing of this sort ever since he shaved off his moustache and let his hair grow. The last hurdle is cleared when he ventures into the street one Saturday, but South Kensington has seen plenty of others like him and he goes almost unnoticed, only just attracting the attention of a group of Japanese tourists who immediately brandish their cameras at him and shoot him in a hail of flashguns. Mr Mine poses obligingly. It seems to him that the whole world acknowledges his love. And when retirement comes, he settles into his character and lives with his wife whom he continually praises to all their friends for her kind, accom-modating nature. Not once does the idea occur to him to return to Italy to see the original.

*

Of all the portraits which make up *L for London*, that of John Mine is one of the most successful. One can detect its sources in Stanislas' own passion not only for *The Tempest* but for all of Giorgione's paintings. Every time I went to Venice, Stanislas would drag me off to some new discovery and we would often finish with a brief look in at the Accademia: first, the Carpaccios which give such an exact idea of Venetian procession-days in the fifteenth and sixteenth centuries, then a short detour to the treasure chamber where *The Tempest* reduces its audience to silence with its mystery and its inexplicable depth. I remember him saying, almost every time, 'Nobody will ever know what Giorgione wanted his paintings to signify. That is the privilege of pure art. He freed Italian painting from its conventions by evoking a vision whose only loyalty is to beauty.'

The reason I have summarized this story is to show how, in

Stanislas Beren's work, fictions were born from encounters with an object, a landscape, even a simple look. In short, he was Mr Mine, fascinated by Venice, fascinated by Giorgione. To this revelation his talent added a fictional dimension whose origins were not always understood by the critics. It is important to notice that Stanislas says very little about Venice itself in the story of Mr and Mrs Mine and gives only the briefest description of their visit. Always the same worry of his words not doing justice to the spectacle of Venice.

In 1957 when he was invited to write a preface to an album of photographs devoted to Venice, he declined on the grounds that he was not competent: 'I cannot do it. Cocteau will do it much better. He came twice and he saw everything.'

Cocteau wrote the preface[1] and Stanislas was so impressed by it that he asked a copyist to transcribe onto parchment the poem with which he concludes. The parchment was framed and placed in a prominent position on one of his library shelves. Occasionally we used to recite a few lines:

> Where can I see dancers on the tips of old brown leaves,
> So many lions sleeping on thresholds under eaves,
> So many wooden needles, iron fine as finest hair,
> Marble fine as lace-work and horses in the air . . .
> So many pigeons walking up and down
> In tailcoats with hands behind their backs? . . .
> Where can I see golden sea-horses harnessed?

The portrait of Stanislas painted by de Pisis in 1947 is hardly a portrait at all. One can recognize his face by its hollow cheeks, its sensual lips, and the forcefulness of the forehead, but the eyes are lagoon-coloured, the prows of two gondolas emerge from his temples, and the background is a scene of frenzy in a bloody and chaotic palace sinking into watery depths. De Pisis had grasped, in an instant, that painting Stanislas meant revealing the Venice which was in him. Likewise, it is important to record Stanislas' mistrust of the artists who 'dared' – his word – to paint Venice. He excepted François Salvat whom he saw, one day on the terrace outside Florian's, indifferent to the friends who surrounded him, take a small sketchbook from his pocket and dash off a water-colour which was so perfect that he could not help telling him so. A friendship was born and Stanislas bought

[1] *Venise que j'aime*, Editions Sun, Paris 1957.

several of Salvat's Venetian canvases; by one of those quirks in his nature, he did not keep them in Venice, but hung them in his study in London instead. Did the same quirk pursue Félicité in her furnishing and decorating of the palazzetto on the Largo Fortunio? Although the furniture was Italian, bought in Florence or in Venice itself, the walls were covered in modern paintings as remote from the spirit of Venice as it was possible to be. Here we have to pay tribute to one of the few influences Félicité came under: as soon as they had settled in, she formed a friendship with Peggy Guggenheim which lasted the rest of her life. It was through Peggy Guggenheim that Balthus, Max Ernst, Staël, Tanguy, Brauner, Giacometti, Mucha, Chirico, Chapelain-Midy and André Beaurepaire, whose first painting she bought in 1946, came to dominate the walls of the palazzetto. They rampaged through a house whose atmosphere bordered on the melancholy, and where their presence was felt as a provocation to begin with, it gradually became a great sign of life and vigour revived. Having said that, Félicité was not prepared to admit just anybody to her walls. She never bought a Picasso, claiming that the finest were already in museums or private collections and that now the Malagueño was wandering pitifully off course, going over old ground where his genius was being drained by exercises in sensationalism. What about Miró? 'He costs too much. If I really wanted one I could do just as well myself, then at least I could use the colours I liked.' Magritte? 'The resident surrealist copycat. He paints like an undertaker.' Stanislas did not go along with all Félicité's judgments, but through her, and through Peggy Guggenheim, he learnt that the love of art is a choice as much as anything, and sometimes it has to be a cruel choice too, unfair and biased if it wants to be a living choice. After Félicité's death not one new canvas was added either to the palazzetto or to the house in Chelsea, as if, once she was gone, he was no longer sure of his own taste.

Several times in the course of 1969, I spent whole weeks with him, particularly in Venice; there, in a desperate attempt to give his suddenly deserted life a justification which it did not need, he made himself go for walks and adopt a routine which would give his working hours a framework. Rising late, he would read what he had written the day before and answer the morning's post, then leave the house at midday for Saint Mark's Square where the ritual varied according to the seasons. In winter, when the sun paled, he would install himself on the terrace at Quadri's until one o'clock, then lunch in a trattoria and come back to Saint Mark's where, the sun having moved around, he would sit on the terrace at Florian's until three. In summer, on the other hand, he shunned the blinding sunlight and reversed his visits to Florian's and Quadri's (where, so many times, I found him reading the paper at arm's length because he hated being seen wearing glasses). If it was raining we would sit at a table inside Florian's. The waiters always contrived to reserve the table 'under the Chinaman' which had been the favourite table of Henri de Régnier, Emile Henriot and Jean-Louis Vaudoyer among others.

'He is a very timid Chinaman,' Stanislas used to say to me. 'Look how his head is bowed. Embarrassed? Yes, probably by the painter who has asked him to pose with his beloved just as she is clinging to him. Which would seem to prove, moreover, that a fine green and red coat and long moustaches suffice to make a seducer. And have you noticed her? She is a mouse, all pink and white. Looks utterly unreliable to me. In Quadri's, across the square, the frescoes move me less since I have been alone here, but I did love them very much once, because what they represent – Venice on holiday – is absolutely what I experienced here at the beginning.'

Several times too, I discovered him gone for a few days to Torcello, where he had his room at Cipriani's Locanda and took his lunch in the garden with the pomegranate trees.

'Why is the weather always so marvellous when I retreat here? The light on this island is stronger than anywhere else. There are ochres and greens which will never fade. In the evening, when the last tourist has departed, one can hear only oneself. I work very well in my bedroom. It has no table, but I put a board across my knees. I leave the window open, and in come the geckos who have been sleeping in the ampelopsis all day. They scuttle up to the ceiling and stay there for hours, observing me. . . .'

*

I quote these points of reference and these reflections so that the reader can see properly what kind of place Venice had in the life of this man, even though it appears rarely in his books. When I made a remark about this one morning, as we were crossing Saint Mark's Square, he feigned astonishment.

'Good grief, yes, quite true! I had not thought about it . . . there must be a reason for it.'

And a few minutes afterwards, as we were sitting on the terrace at Florian's, he said, 'The reason, I think, is this: do you betray the person who has made you his or her confidant? You don't, do you? Therefore I shall repeat nothing of what this city has murmured to me. But believe me when I tell you that, despite the festivals and despite the masques, this is a sorrowful city. Perhaps the most sorrowful in the world: an ageing beauty tragically surrounded by looking-glasses which all send back the same decrepit image.'

A surprise awaited Stanislas and André on their return from Venice in 1936: a man was camping on the doormat outside the offices at Editions Saeta. Curled up in the angle of the doorway, legs hunched up against his chest, he was asleep with his head on his knees. When André's hand was placed on his shoulder, the man awoke without starting and looked up out of a gaunt face overrun by a several day-old beard. His black-ringed eyes were bright with fever. Emeline Aureo, the secretary, came running up the stairs, brandishing her handbag, lamenting that she had not been there for Stanislas' and André's arrival.

'He's mad!' she cried from the landing below. 'Mad! Don't take any notice of him.'

She was so out of breath that the words came out in hiccups. 'He's been here a week!'

Without moving from his crouching position, the man screwed a monocle into his right eye and asked in a hollow voice, 'You are Stanislas Beren?'

'Yes. And you?'

'I am Jezero Skadarsko.'

Almost speechless with indignation, Emeline Aureo raised her handbag, ready to strike the profaner. 'He is not! He's Belgian.'

The false Jezero (or true Belgian) straightened up, stiff from his uncomfortable position. What might have been a tramp turned out to be a man dressed in a brick-coloured English tweed suit which, though crumpled by the nights of vigil, splashed with mud on the trouser bottoms and spotted with grease on the lapels, suggested an elegance not long gone.

'I have been waiting for you,' he said. 'I have had enough of my life of debauchery. I have quit Kralj and the temptations of kingmaking to return to my garret in the Latin quarter and my lectures, my students, my poverty too – my delicious, intoxicating poverty! But there is a detail missing from my past: where did I live? This is one of the gaps in your novel: with the typical offhandedness of those writers who tell a story without giving either the location or the period in which it takes place, you do not bother to say exactly where it is that I live. So, Monsieur Beren, I beg you to tell me in which street, at which number and on which floor my dear little room is to be found. The belated student, the lecturer drowned in his own verbal diarrhoea, wishes to go home. I should like to point out – in order to lead you no further astray – that, contrary to what you have been told by this white-hot virgin, I am not Belgian.'

'But it was you who told me so!' cried Emeline Aureo indignantly.

'That, my dear lady, is no reason at all.'

Solemn to the point of buffoonery, he had already won over Stanislas and André who, at his urgent request, took him down to the Rendez-vous des Amis for breakfast – that bistro on the rue des Saints-Pères which, in all innocence, played a considerable part in literary life between 1933 and 1970, the year when its *patron*, Petrus Saint (a joke of his father's, that name, which dogged him from his first schooldays to his death-bed, when the parish priest ventured one last reference to it) retired, his fortune made, to Romanèche-Thorins to tend a vineyard which produced the one bad wine he served. There was a colourful and continuous stream of thirsting writers to his counter, come to empty half-bottles of beaujolais and jugs of mâcon blanc which renewed the vigour of discussions begun in the nearby offices of Grasset, Stock, Saeta or Gallimard. The day that Petrus Saint's successor modernized the Rendez-vous des Amis, installing neon lights, a new formica bar-top and pretentious chairs around ridiculous tables, the regulars abandoned it, and a year later the new place was closed and sold to a boutique owner eager to display his shelves of tight-fitting jeans and aggressive-looking motorcyclists' jackets. It is true that the old bistro was squalid, smoky and noisy, that the glasses were not washed properly and that the smell in the Turkish-style lavatories was enough to make you pass out (although, to judge by the graffiti, André Gide, Paul Valéry, Mallarmé and Marcel Proust had all derived great pleasure from relieving themselves there). Petrus Saint, who complained continuously about these reprobates scrawling all over his walls, tried to identify them among his regulars. The 'Aren't you Marcel Proust?' that he directed at Desnos one day has not been forgotten. Desnos of course said no, to which Petrus Saint replied, 'And a good thing too, he's a bloody disgrace! Suppose children read those things, eh!' But there were no children at the Rendez-vous des Amis, just a small company recharging its energies in discussion or acid exchanges. In various guises Petrus Saint makes appearances in the novels of André de Richaud, Albéric Varenne, Marcel Aymé, Antoine Blondin, Kléber Haedens, Roger Nimier, Michel Braspart, Jacques Laurent, France Norrit and Michel Férou among others. He can always be recognized by the thick, unbroken bar of his eyebrows and his wart-covered hands. Literature took possession of him without his ever being aware of it, or curious enough to open the books written by these unemployed drinkers who hung around his bistro at the most irregular hours. His barking voice, his monumental stupidity, his avarice (never in the memory of any customer had he offered a drink on the house), his irritation when anybody called him Amphitryon, created a character tailor-made for his regulars; they, committed like so many writers and poets to bitter sarcasm, carped continually at this troglodyte barkeeper and saw in him the image of virtue prospering by their vices: Petrus drank little, ate cheaply, went to bed only with his wife (an appalling old hag who spent her time concocting evil-smelling stews in the back kitchen) and refrained – for fear of being asked for a rise in wages – from fondling the backsides of his skinny waitresses while they were washing the glasses (so badly!) with their chapped hands: 'Cold water only!' he would shout. 'It washes better and doesn't cost a penny!' But the wines were good, notably a sauvignon from Saint-Bris and a red vézelay which could not be found anywhere else.

All of which is to say that the arrival in this exalted forum of letters of Stanislas and André, escorting a young man wearing a monocle and a crumpled suit, came as no surprise to Petrus Saint; he served croissants and *cafés filtre*, shortly followed by *jambon d'Auvergne*, and a *rosette de Lyon* to partner a Clos de la Cure which had come up from Saint-Amour in the barrel. On the stroke of twelve, as an end to the conversation was nowhere in sight, the pastis appeared. The stranger was in full flow, and the story of his life with Kralj was told with a luxury of detail, all the more surprising as this last part of Stanislas' novel had been more or less glossed over, leaving his readers' hunger unsatisfied. Now, quite suddenly, here was *The Countdown* being extended by a previously unpublished chapter, here was the imaginary Jezero Skadarsko, in the shadow of the petty tyrant Kralj, hatching international intrigues, crushing the enemies of the régime, taming the state mafia, organizing the happiness of the people in spite of themselves, and meting out popular leadership and repressive treatment with diabolical skill. On the subject of Jezero's secret debauches the stranger supplied precise details which were all the more crude for being proffered in a cold and indifferent voice.

A novelist may be inspired by a real person, but it is altogether less common for a real person to be inspired by a paper character and to say, 'I am he!' then ask the author for his address which he had neglected to indicate, and deliver an epilogue. All the more so since Stanislas had been inspired by no one in creating Jezero Skadarsko unless one accepted, as one might at a pinch, that Jezero is a projection of Stanislas, an amusing caricature of what would have awaited him had the Garretts not taken him in in the summer of 1925 at Deauville, and had Félicité not civilized a coarse young man come down in rope sandals from his mountain home. In which case, if one were to accept this last proposition, the stranger with the monocle was therefore Stanislas, who could now contemplate in him a tolerably well-fitting double. The man's real name matters little. He was to disappear three months afterwards in the grip of chronic alcoholism, having played a dual role. He had taught Stanislas that novels have two secret lives: at the moment of their creation they have a brief and obedient life in the author's mind, then another life, subjective and unruly, in the reader's mind. And the stranger with the monocle was also responsible for introducing Stanislas to Elise – his sister – the woman who inspired *Cryptogram*.

The way *Cryptogram* is constructed is entirely different from the two earlier novels. The character who calls himself 'I' and is denoted only by an initial, S., keeps a diary. The confusion is sufficiently well maintained for the reader to believe that what he is reading is a true story, even though the word 'novel' appears beneath the title on the jacket. Years later, I may say that Stanislas invented more in this book than people believed he did. He did keep a diary, and when the adventure with Elise came to an end, he closed his notebook for six months. Then, on André's insistence, he reopened it and realized that he was holding a novel in his hands, provided, of course, that he rewrote it, changed the names and altered certain facts to avoid compromising 'the woman who had inspired it'. Thus the stranger with the monocle is introduced by the name of Oscar Dubouchez, the only name we shall refer to him by. Dubouchez, the reader may remember, is also the name of the middle-aged man who develops a taste for sailors and rushes to the Botanical Gardens in the hope of encountering some 'sailors' pom-poms'. This Jean Dubouchez, a late-comer to homosexuality, is the father of Oscar and Elise.

In *Cryptogram* the meeting with Oscar is described much as I have just described it, with little embellishment, except that the three men are supposed to have broken up the party only the following morning, after an heroic, twenty-four-hour long tour of the bars of Montparnasse; in fact, Stanislas and André abandoned Oscar at the Rendezvous des Amis on the stroke of one in the afternoon, asleep with his head resting on his arms on the table where all their empty glasses had accumulated. Oscar Dubouchez was a poet who was never able to write any poetry and who, aware of this sterility, soon destroyed himself. In today's language this son of an industrialist would be called a drop-out: a drop-out who thought he could exploit society by leaving unpaid slates everywhere and never dreamt that his sister would trail behind him and settle them all. His financial immunity had contributed in no small degree to his present high idea of himself and it was probably this idea which had led him to take himself for Jezero Skadarsko. Aided by his alcoholic delirium, the identification had become an obsession. Stanislas and André took an interest in Oscar Dubouchez, an interest I have no wish to qualify with easy epithets. Let us say that he amused them in the way that an unusual object discovered on the doormat might. He roused the indignation of the faithful Emeline Aureo, who could not bear to see a stranger appropriate one of Stanislas' characters. Had she not ended up believing in Jezero just as much as Dubouchez had? During the twenty years of fanatical devotion which she gave to Editions Saeta she was, by turns, loved, jilted, taken up again, left panting on a bed, betrayed, taken up again, as happy and as desperate as the women who appeared in Stanislas' novels. This is not the last time we shall encounter this identification of the reader with one of the novelist's characters: Mimi Bower, who appeared later in Stanislas' life, believed that she was Nathalie and the resemblance was so perfect that two hours after the first look she exchanged with Stanislas, she was in his bed, rounding off a novel that the author thought he had already finished. Just as Oscar Dubouchez, in committing suicide by overdrinking, invented a quite new ending to *The Countdown*. As for Emeline Aureo, she had given herself to Jezero Skadarsko in her dreams and was in no mood to tolerate him appearing at the door of Editions Saeta in the person of an unshaven drunkard who had spent the night there. When Oscar died, she did not conceal her relief. One is justified in wondering whether this identification is more of a disappointment than a tribute to a writer: he believes he is creating, then the characters in his novel overtake him, escape him and then, with a sudden loss of heart, make their way back to him.

Elise makes an early appearance in *Cryptogram* when she comes to fetch her brother (and pay the bill) at the Rendez-vous des Amis. Because Petrus Saint is rougher than he need be in helping her to manhandle Oscar into the waiting car, she gets angry and reminds him that children and poets are not to be maltreated. S., who has been standing by with an indifference excused by his twenty-four hours of non-stop drinking, enjoys this remark and introduces himself. Elise is much too agitated to pay attention to her interlocutor's name and, with that lack of discrimination peculiar to her, judging S. by appearances, she bids him sit next to Oscar on the back seat and keep him reasonably upright.

She takes them to her flat, at 145 boulevard Saint-Germain (this time the exact address is given to forestall the reproaches of any future Oscar Dubouchez), and S. and Elise are obliged to carry the barely conscious man, his monocle still in position, upstairs. They undress him and put him to bed after forcing him to swallow some Eno's salts to ward off his hangover. Hardly has he been laid down than Oscar falls asleep. Elise is sharp and disagreeable towards S., who has recovered his spirits. She reproaches him for having egged her brother on to drink. Her insincerity is so obvious that S. bursts out laughing. Nobody needs to egg Oscar on to drink. The difficult thing is keeping up with him. As Elise asks him his name a second time, he admits that he is the author of *The Countdown*.

'But why,' she asks, 'why didn't you give Jezero's precise address in your book? Really, I don't understand. What harm could it have done you?'

S., taken aback, declares that it is precisely because he does not want strange readers going and knocking on the door of some poor professor who has nothing to do with Jezero's story. Elise, annoyed with herself, then offers him the use of Oscar's bathroom if he wishes to shave, which he does straight away, before joining her below in her three-roomed flat whose windows look out onto the church of Saint-Germain-des-Prés. Elise, at first sight, has a most ordinary face: grey eyes, short, dull blonde hair, a mouth which her lipstick has squashed into a clumsy cupid's bow; but her body seems promising enough, despite being hidden by an ill-fitting dress which, funnily enough, comes from one of the great couturiers. It does not take S. long to decide that a man of taste owes it to himself to teach this dogmatic young middle-class woman how to make herself up and do her hair, how to dress decently, and how to make love. He will take care not to shock her, going about it gently, and to begin with he pretends to listen to her with an attentiveness which is so over-courteous that anyone but she would see it as insulting; but Elise is impervious to such subtleties at this stage and, faced with this man whom she thinks must be intelligent because he is a writer (naive apriorism: such preconceptions still abound in middle-class families), she delivers summary, damning and authoritarian verdicts on all topics in order to impress him and to mask her panic at the blunder she has just committed in taking him for one of her brother's parasitic friends. In fact, not all her opinions are completely ridiculous, and S. says to himself that there is something to be made of her, that in violating her – morally speaking, because he is already convinced that she will surrender the rest any time he chooses – he will change the life of this woman who, with a raving alcoholic brother and – as he soon learns – a father obsessed by sailors, is at the end of her tether. He is also aware that she is not a woman to let herself be rushed and that, intelligent in a very mediocre way, she will rebel if he does not tread carefully.

One unkind critic, who shall remain nameless, took issue with Stanislas for giving his readers only the kind of women who look as if they have just emerged from a beauty clinic or the hairdresser's. Such women do people his books, and how could it be otherwise when a novelist has shown, with a rare constancy spanning more than forty years, considerable discernment where women are concerned. One surmises that even if it is unfair to those who do not possess 'perfect figures' and whatever their moral qualities might be, a man who likes women will always have an initial preference for those whose faces and bodies seduce him. Certainly, there are a good many womanly bodies in Stanislas' novels, but there is nothing stereotyped about them, and in the first three novels they make no more than anecdotal appearances. The solid and appetizing peasant woman who arouses the deserter's lust by bathing naked in the river in *The Secret Life of an Orgasm* has nothing refined about her. Then a sequence of dolls pass in and out of the life of the general-emperor-god who is the issue of that union. Anne de Beautremont ensures that they do not linger. Certainly, in *The Countdown* there is the ginger cat, Redja Matchka, but she is gone before Jezero wakes up and, in truth, after his initiation, Jezero prefers first drab women students because he enjoys the challenge of releasing their sexuality, and later, as the power behind the all-powerful Kralj, whores who confirm him in the belief that physical love is the most necessary and most vengeful of human activities. In *Cryptogram* Elise Dubouchez, as she is painted (and as she was in reality), is utterly unremarkable, and it is by way of a game to prove his own power that S. metamorphoses her without her being aware of it. In short, the author was reversing his own situation since it was a woman – Félicité – who had brought him to maturity. We may speak freely about Elise Dubouchez, the one who survived, that is; the other, real one was so far metamorphosed that she can no longer be recognized except by those who are in the know.

The conversation they have on the afternoon of their first meeting reaches almost theatrical heights of misunderstanding and borders continuously on the ludicrous. When S. advances the opinion that Stendhal's best novel, had he finished it, would have been *Le Rose et le Vert*, Elise sniggers.

'You mean *Le Rouge et le Noir*. . . . You've obviously only read the first volume. . . . There are two. . . .'

This cast-iron proof of her ignorance leaves him enraptured. The luck of it! A would-be bluestocking who thinks herself knowledgeable and knows nothing: he will have to teach her everything. He cannot imagine a more heady situation. Now S. is confronted by a problem of geometry. Two parallel lives cannot meet unless a tendentious assumption is made, that the parallels are magnetized; then, if the attraction is strong enough, at a given moment, they will defy the original postulate and touch. All it needs is diligent cunning from him and a moment of weakness from her.

Cryptogram is a novel about seduction which appears cynical if all one sees in it is calculation, but behind the calculation is a tale of a man whose spirit is troubled and who seeks to restore his faith in himself. It cannot be denied that S. deserves little of our sympathy. He is too keen to try out his tricks and schemes at the expense of a woman's heart and sensitivity. Elise, one tells oneself, is what she is. Why interfere with the satisfaction she feels about the way she lives, why destroy the illusions she cherishes about her intelligence? Her figure, at least at first, before the transformation, is dull and scarcely desirable. So S.'s only redeeming feature is that he is going to perform his experiment on the most difficult of models, the one least likely to inspire enthusiasm.

In reality Elise was neither stupid nor unattractive. Félicité confirmed this one day when she saw me reading *Cryptogram*.

'Don't take everything you read in there as gospel truth,' she said. 'Stanislas made himself out to be much worse than he was in the character of S. and the woman he calls Elise was much less mediocre than he pretended she was afterwards. And you know, it wasn't Stanislas who taught her to make herself up and dress properly. I did it. But novelists have all sorts of rights, including the right of the author of *Cryptogram* to conceal the fact that he brought Elise to luncheon and dinner at the house when he was afraid that he might be too bored with her *en tête à tête*. I accepted her, just as I also accepted many others, and I found it made very little difference to me. To begin with, Elise tried to impress me, but between women those hostilities don't last. I warned her to stop saying the things she was saying, and after a while she kept her bitchy remarks to herself: things like, "Our age difference doesn't count. I've always wanted a big sister like you so that I could have someone to confide in." I can tell you, too, Elise was desirable. It was just that her bad taste, her awful dresses and suits, hid a nice body which she failed to appreciate, not out of modesty or shame but because she had no spirit whatsoever. Stanislas does not confide in me about these things, but I guarantee you that he had his pleasure with her.'

*

I have not forgotten that conversation. It was 1956 and we were in Deauville for Easter, sitting at the Café du Soleil while Stanislas and Georges Kapsalis were spending a day at the races. Félicité was finding it increasingly difficult to walk, and whenever she found a reasonably soft and comfortable chair she would sit down and feign a sudden dreaminess, looking out vacantly over the sea and waving vaguely at the friends who walked by, naming them for me because she thought it her duty to teach me the who's who of the world into which, at the age of twenty, I was emerging. I can see again the profile I saw then: hooked nose, thin mouth, sharp chin, a heavily rouged cheek under the cloche hat she was now never without; drinking her tea cold through a straw from a tall glass.

'I thought what Stanislas did was quite amusing,' she said to me; 'drawing up a handbook of seduction without appearing to do any such thing, and making another person divert from the course of her life completely. The funny thing is, he thought he was handling a puppet, but the puppet turned out to be a jack-in-the-box. One day, Elise just packed her bags and left him. *That* he did not seem to expect. This was his little Laclos period. It didn't last.'

'Should we reprint the book? You know Monsieur Dupuy has told Stanislas he thinks we should.'

'Dear Monsieur Dupuy . . . Stanislas is his property. I should envy him. He knows him better than I do. Reprint it? Yes, but I think with a preface to explain that it's a book which has to be read in the light of the time it was written, 1937–8. What was daring then hardly seems daring at all now, does it. . . .'

★

I immersed myself in *Cryptogram* once more. The hero – this transparent S. – has instantly grasped how necessary it is to flatter Elise-the-bluestocking, so instead of taking her to Maxim's in order to be seen with him – and thus compromised, he judges vainly – he arranges to meet her in a gallery showing an exhibition of Braque's latest work. In his eyes Braque is a test. The world is divided into two camps: those who love Braque, and those who hate him or know nothing about him. Elise has been expecting a more conventional onslaught for which she has prepared her usual defences. Taken by surprise, she has to pretend to 'know'. She knows Braque's name and she has seen one or two reproductions of his paintings, which is enough for her to believe she 'knows' about Braque and can judge his work. In answer to S.'s invitation she pouts doubtfully: has he really nothing better to offer her? Braque, she assures him, is on the way out, Picasso is the man everyone is talking about! S. says what he thinks of Picasso as if it is evident that she thinks the same. Miserably, Elise immediately concurs with him and sacrifices her platitudes on the altar of the intelligentsia. Their meeting at the gallery is one of the great chapters of the book. It possesses a sly comic quality which will reappear in his subsequent works in a less overt form, without that over-obvious scornfulness which detracts from *Cryptogram* as a whole and occasionally leaves the impression that the novel is the revenge of a man betrayed.

In the embarrassing situation in which her absurd remarks have put her, Elise has already lost her footing and, to cap it all, she mishears one of S.'s observations on Braque's use of grey and confuses it with Juan Gris. S. corrects her, pretending to think that she is comparing the two painters. Elise immediately agrees. The reader will have guessed that she is by now at a serious disadvantage. The next day, when he takes her to the cinema to see *The Battleship Potemkin* by Sergei Eisenstein, S. humiliates her once and for all by not even smiling when she makes it obvious that she thinks the Soviet director is also the inventor of the formula $E=mc^2$. The realization of her blunder is one of the most desperate moments of her life.

His campaign to convince her that she is an idiot is by no means over when, one evening after the theatre, he leaves her standing at the door just as she has invited him upstairs for a glass of champagne. Elise melts. She is quite positive that in this respectful and erudite man she has discovered absolute love. It only remains for S. to introduce her to a slightly older lady friend of his (Félicité in fact, but the S. of the novel is unmarried) who will teach the girl that she can choose how she wishes to look. Very soon Elise is lightening her drab hair, making up her eyes, and no longer dressing like a frigid suffragette. Her final defences crumble. At the mercy of the man who has made her aware of the extent of her pretentiousness and ignorance, she prepares to surrender to him. At precisely that moment he disappears for a fortnight without a word. Elise's anger is such that she regains her perspective, realizing that she has been tricked. Which is exactly the reaction S. has hoped for, and when he reappears and telephones her, he is delighted to be welcomed in tones of assumed indifference. The second conquest begins and this time S. goes about things in a completely different manner. He no longer humiliates the poor girl; on the contrary, he puts her on a pedestal and makes the most insignificant of her remarks spell-binding. Should she claim that the Eiffel tower is an insult to the beauty of Paris or that Céline writes bad French, he supports her wholeheartedly. Knowing that she carries a secret torch for her brother Oscar, he asks to see him with her more often, and he even manages to stop the boy's drinking. By now, Elise is utterly baffled. S. has been unwilling to say where he has been for the last fortnight and she suspects him of having mistresses everywhere. She develops the most absurd theories about him and even goes so far as to question a friend (in reality, André Garrett): is S. a homosexual? The friend laughs in her face and points out that S. is one of the most sought-after men in Paris, although for a month (here Elise quickly calculates that this corresponds to the date of their meeting) he has not really been himself, behaving in a distracted manner, concealing some of his appointments, working frantically. When S. hears via his friend that Elise is making enquiries into his morals, he feigns indignation and disappears once more, this time for a week. Elise, however, is less miserable on her own account than she is at the sudden and unexpected despair of her brother. Ever since S. has been taking an interest in him, Oscar has been attempting the impossible task of drying himself out. Of course, no one is under any illusions: Oscar had reached the point of no return several years previously. When he is sober he is pitiful, and all his wit and imagination waste away as if they have been imprisoned. One glass of alcohol is enough to revive them and Oscar happily accedes to their needs. He has been through his 'Jezero Skadarsko' period, which was given way to a 'Nathanael, throw this book away . . .' period skilfully suggested by S. one evening when he reads him some extracts from *Les Nourritures terrestres*. Straight away, Oscar goes on a tour of the bookshops and, taking Gide's work from the shelves, tosses the books into the mouths of the drains. Elise has to run after him and pay for the damage, but one bookseller nevertheless calls the police and without Jean Dubouchez, who has well-placed friends (and not only in the navy), Oscar would have found himself in prison.

★

In *Cryptogram* the picture is so black – the stupidity of the young woman, the cynical machinations of her seducer – that Oscar emerges as the only truly sympathetic character. In fact, Stanislas did feel genuine brotherly affection for him. In his diary André Garrett confessed that he had never met a man so mad and so touching at the same time:[1]

Dined yesterday evening at the Coupole with Stanislas and the couple he calls Elise and Oscar. Elise I find tedious, always out to impress, although she has improved since she has had a vague idea of her inadequacy. Oscar is irresistible, and he is quite wrong to take himself for the hero of the novels he reads, because he is so much better being himself, being the original hero of a novel who needs no author's imagination to exist. He recites entire pages of Stanislas and Gide and Aragon. If the surrealists were to meet him, they would have to raise a monument to him, but then they are only interested in politics these days, all dreaming of becoming councillors under the banner of the Popular Front. Desnos – the most intelligent and the most honest of all of them, the only one who has any taste for freedom – bumped into Oscar at Petrus Saint's bar and they had the most bizarre conversation about the *Raft of Medusa*. They claimed to have met each other on it and to have eaten, *flambées* in Armagnac, the private parts of the drowned man that Géricault painted in the foreground, naked but for his socks. Around midnight, Oscar keeled over, utterly exhausted. This happens every time; he falls asleep on a café table, a bench at the Dôme or, as we found him one morning, on a doormat on the landing. The odd

[1] 15 September 1936.

thing is that, almost everywhere Oscar goes in the otherwise vicious, sniggering and bitching world in which he acts out his particular eccentricity, he encounters indulgence more gentle than amused. They don't throw him into the street when the bar he has fallen asleep in finally closes. He gets put in a cab, his address is given to the driver and all in all there is a series of good-natured deeds which get him as far as his bed where his sister tucks him in. The one time he had his wallet stolen, it wasn't really stolen: the thief, who knew him well, gave it back to him the next day. He goes through life like a child, protected by his weakness. Yesterday, at the Coupole, I heard somebody at another table asking the head waiter who the chap with the monocle was. 'He's a poet,' was the answer he got. A poet with no poems, a man who would rather put poetry in his life than on paper. The waiter was right.

Elise is beaten. That we are aware of already. The important thing is to find out what shape her fall will take – if one can talk of a fall where a woman in such a hurry to consent is concerned. Perhaps even more importantly, we need to find out the circumstances of her fall, for both her pride and her initiative have been lost from the start. She knows that there is no escaping it, but she is no longer in a position even to decide whether it should be at night or during the daytime. Let us also reveal that it will not be the first time, but the second. The first time was a disappointment, a single experiment, the memory of which still mortifies her, and she has come through her ordeal frustrated; it has taught her nothing about pleasure and left her with an animal distrust of men's behaviour towards women. Now, by a commonplace kind of inevitability, she has found herself involved once again with a man whom she is perceptive enough to include in the category she detests. None the less, she feels confident that this seducer, for all his endless ruses, will at least know how to share his thrills of pleasure with her. Every woman in pursuit of love is a sister of Emma Bovary. While Elise is dreaming of sublime embraces on the moonlit beach of one of those Polynesian atolls which S. has described to her at length, or in a Scottish inn on the edge of a furiously melancholy loch, her seducer is meditating a lesson in love in a place where his victim will be unable to dream, where the surroundings will be so ghastly that she will shut her eyes and concentrate her thoughts on him in order to blot them out. He may not quite be envisaging a coal cellar, a potato shed or the front seat of a car (with horn disconnected), but he is sure that she will be forever crushed by the ugliness and promiscuity of his chosen venue.

When Elise, her defences gone, is at last capable of abandoning her dreams and receiving him – alone – he takes her to a house of assignation in Montparnasse. But for its closed shutters the house, in a tidy, quiet, residential street, is hardly distinguishable from the others. Entering by a modern wrought-iron gate, they go into a small lounge where the telephonist at the reception desk collects the money, hands over a key with a number corresponding to the floor and presses a buzzer to warn the chambermaid. The lift is out of order, and on the stairs they meet a couple coming down, a whore and a fat man as crimson-faced as if he were coming out of a free-thinkers' banquet on Good Friday. Elise bows her head and tries to keep her heaving stomach in check as the chambermaid greets them on the landing with a toothless smile, two towels and a bar of soap. The room itself is infinitely depressing, with its curtains drawn and the smell of air freshener failing to mask the musty smell of the previous couple's sweat. There is a hideous mirrored wardrobe, a double bed of dark wood with its fresh sheets turned down, a hand-basin and an obscene bidet. At the head of the bed, a large mirror reflects the battleground and above it, built into the ceiling, another mirror dominates the scene. By now Elise is in tears. She is a long way from her sandy beach and coconut trees, from romantic walks in the forest and a night on board a boat on a moonlit lake in Scotland or Italy. In fact, she does not understand what he wants nor why he is inflicting this torment upon her. When S. undresses her, she stands passively, her arms hanging limp, her face blank. He is surprised to discover a delightful, girlish body with small, soft breasts and long, slim legs. Her sex is discreet, a light shadow between her thighs, without that predatory and fuzzy appearance which is distasteful to him. He is moved and a vague feeling of remorse stirs in him, which he rather enjoys; then, congratulating himself on his power over this woman, he caresses her standing up, held against him, more to allay her legitimate fears and her understandable shame than to see her sink into his arms. Elise does not open her eyes once during the two hours they spend together and when he orders her to get dressed she does so mechanically, turning her back to the mirror. She stumbles out, ignoring the couple they meet on the stairs: a woman of about sixty, her face over-rouged, accompanied by a young man with permed hair. In the car she refuses to say a word until he puts her down at her front door. She shakes her head dumbly as he makes a move to follow her, then mumbles, 'Thank you.'

'Until tomorrow, at the same time,' he replies.

The next day he takes her to the house again. The receptionist is expecting them and graciously hands them a special key to the room adjoining the one they had the day before. The room is plunged in darkness and the chambermaid leads them to a couch. They sit facing a wall which stays dark for a few minutes. Suddenly a rectangle lights up, framing part of the neighbouring room. Elise recognizes the awful furnishings, the bed, the wardrobe, the pink and blue wallpaper, and realizes that she and S. are behind a two-way mirror. A couple has just entered the other room, unaware of the voyeurs. Elise suppresses a shiver and makes to clasp her lover's hand; he firmly, though not unkindly, pushes her away because he wants her to go through with the spectacle on her own. As it happens, the opening moments are quite comical. The woman is pretty in a provincial sort of way. She has succumbed to her first adventure with a man who, though only slightly older than she is, would like to appear sure of himself, but all he can do is shake like a leaf. The young woman has sat down on a chair, her knees tightly together, her handbag clenched in her lap to defend herself. The man takes off her beret for her (held on by a hatpin) and gently unbuttons her blouse. From time to time, he takes off an article of his own clothing – jacket, waistcoat, tie, braces, shoes, trousers – and is eventually left in his long underpants and sock-suspenders. Her breasts are bared. They are not very attractive breasts. At last she lets him push her bag to one side, lift up her skirt and remove her stockings. She is simultaneously consenting and paralyzed. He completes the business of undressing her without her letting go of her handbag. Through the smoked glass of the two-way mirror it is difficult to make out the colouring of their faces, but the man looks as if he must be crimson, the young woman very pale. He eventually succeeds in standing her up and propelling her towards the bed; she falls onto it and turns over, offering her loins and her artless buttocks to him, the sudden sight of which raises a smug smile on his face as complacency overrules desire. Their coupling is depressing and painful to watch, so much do they give the impression of mimicking love, offering a poor and counterfeit version of it. The man takes off his long underpants, but keeps his sock-suspenders. He is not particularly horrible, just pitiful and then very surprised when the young woman suddenly takes the initiative. After so much fuss he does not expect these moves of hers and one can guess that he is having to restrain himself from calling her a whore now that timidity has changed sides.

★

S. takes Elise's hand and sweeps her out of the room and out of the house. They have dinner in the Bois, at the Restaurant de la Cascade. The twilight is an enchantment, in the tall trees lit by the branched lampstands with their globes of milky glass attracting myriad moths whose dance is like a flurry of snowflakes. Lower down, on the road alongside the racecourse, the car headlights glide noiselessly by, and La Cascade is so isolated – so remote from time, so cloaked against the city despite its nearness and its lights tinging the sky with mauve – that Elise forgets the nightmare of that late afternoon, the picture of the man in his long underpants and sock-suspenders contemplating, smug with satisfaction, his companion's artless buttocks; but the arrival of another couple, their affair obviously in its infancy, showing all the signs of the over-indulged pleasures stolen from their brief afternoon encounter, as they get out of their car and make their way to a neighbouring table, clasping hands and talking softly to each other, is enough to envelop Elise in waves of hideous shame: were they not the couple behind the two-way mirror when S. and she were making love for the first time? Anything is possible and S. tells her that that particular show is one of the most prized in Paris, that the voyeurs' room has to be booked days in advance, and that the reason they had to leave so hastily was that the time for each sitting is strictly allotted and other voyeurs were awaiting their turn. . . .

A waiter carefully brings them their *nègres en chemise*, renews the candle which is flickering inside its globe of Venetian glass, and gestures to the ice bucket: the champagne bottle is empty. S. nods indifferently. Elise, whose enjoyment of the pudding, the champagne and the dinner *al fresco* has made her forget momentarily the vulgar and obscene horrors of the afternoon, fights back her tears as she suddenly notices the grim, and almost vicious expression on her lover's face.

'You're a monster!' she says. 'Why did you do it?'

He has absolutely no desire to answer her, although for the first time he is moved to real compassion. What has happened is that Elise's expression has changed: the hard corners of her mouth have softened, her grey eyes, damp with tears, are underlined by a poignant crease, and in the tilt of her head the young woman has something wounded and fragile about her.

'Was it deliberate?' she ventures again. 'Did you deliberately defile our love?'

'Our love'! She has gone too far. If he does not scotch this straight away, Elise will start using high-flown words and inventing high-flown sentiments in which she has not been trained and for which she is not ready. What courses of action are open to him? Should he cut her short, or let her ramble? He decides to develop a thesis for her benefit, one whose pretentious imbecility delights him: that a love untested is not real love. Elise listens, fascinated. No man has ever attempted to seduce her by aiming at her mind, and in any case her knowledge of seduction is largely restricted to what she has learnt from books. S.'s pompous speech reveals to her the depths of her ignorance. The game of love is more complicated than she thought. The pure in heart cannot, she agrees, know how to play it without receiving a schooling in it, although she is at a loss to understand how S. can call the journey to Capri, which he is at that moment suggesting to her, a test. Certainly there are no coconut trees or sandy beaches on that particular island, but Elise has already jettisoned those dull attractions in favour of jagged coastlines, steep cliffs and tempests, and she is all set to be taken to the storm-lashed Ile de Sein when her lover begins to tell her about the Piazza Umberto and how they will eat cassatas *alla Napolitana* there and see the Faraglioni from their window when they fling open the shutters in the morning, how they will visit Axel Munthe who will be waiting for them at San Michele. S. finds such a convincing tone of voice to describe the prospect of Capri that Elise feels like throwing down her napkin, forgetting the champagne that the waiter is pouring into her fluted glass, and leaving at once. S. has some difficulty in restraining her, so enthusiastic is she; then, magically, to give substance to reality, he takes out an envelope in which there are two return tickets to Naples for the train the following morning. Elise forgets the unkind thoughts which have been nagging at her and already sees herself on the train with her lover, her face pressed to the window to watch for the first blues of the Mediterranean as the train rolls into Sainte-Maxime.

The next morning finds Elise at the gare de Lyon, and time is pressing when the ticket-inspector hands her a letter from S. who says that he is unable to leave that day. She should go on ahead and wait for him at the Hotel Excelsior in the via Partenope, where he will join her almost immediately. She travels alone and discovers Naples in a rather melancholy frame of mind. When she gets to the hotel, she finds a telegram waiting for her. S. begs her to excuse him: he has been held up in Paris. She is to settle in on Capri and he will be with her the minute he can get away. The reader will already have guessed that her week on Capri will be solitary and intolerable. The least glimpse of the sea, the sight of a beautiful house, a visit to the Blue Grotto, all tear

Elise's heart in two. Perfections like these cry out to be shared, and later fused together, in bed. Elise encounters a number of lonely people like herself, but they are all either alcoholics, drug addicts or homosexuals, unapproachable in her eyes ever since S. revealed her inadequacy to her and so paralyzed her with shyness. She realizes that these recluses will share nothing with an intruder whose thirst is for love and who is suffering extreme symptoms of sexual 'withdrawal'. As for sharing their pleasures – alcohol and cocaine – it does not occur to Elise: she still has far too high an idea of herself. Capri soon becomes a living hell whose magnificence she is impervious to and which makes her physically sick. The hotel doctor, called in haste, strongly advises her to go back to France as quickly as possible. He has come across many cases of this kind, particularly among widows. A number of these rash women have chosen suicide as a way out of their panic. Elise realizes that this is good advice and she takes the boat back to Naples, which is such a cesspit that it immediately cures her of maladies caused by an overdose of beauty taken in isolation. Her spirits almost restored, she leaves for Paris.

On the platform at the gare de Lyon, S. is waiting for her. How can he have known the date and time of her arrival? – and even the number of her sleeping car so that she finds him beneath her window when she puts her head out to call a porter? It is a mystery for which she will seek no explanation, because the second she sees him again he takes possession of her once more. The worst thing – she notes it immediately – is that his face is as suntanned as hers, and when he calls a porter to take care of Elise's luggage and then grasps her by the arm to walk quickly out of the station, she wonders in a moment of aberration whether the absence of her lover on Capri has not been a bad dream. Why, instead of bombarding her with trivial news she could not care less about – that Oscar has drunk nothing for a week and their father has been set upon in a copse in the Bois de Boulogne – why does he not make any allusion to the failed rendezvous? And what thoughtless cynicism makes him say, to a friend they meet at the taxi rank who congratulates them on how marvellous they are both looking, 'We've just got back from Capri'?

Scarcely have they arrived at Elise's apartment than he takes her in his arms and has no trouble convincing her that their affair reached its maximum intensity on Capri. Too far weakened to resist, Elise surrenders. Henceforth she is his possession. But this naturally means that she no longer holds the same interest for a man neurotically attached to his freedom and determined to possess nothing; and in order to get Elise away from him, S. is now obliged to concoct a scheme contrary to the one which broke down the young woman's defences.

The epigraph to the book comes from Giraudoux's *Amphitryon 38* where Mercury says to Jupiter, 'Like you sometimes I love a woman. But to win her over, you have to please her, then you have to undress her, then dress her again, then to be able to leave her, you have to displease her . . . it is an art in itself.' It is indeed an art in itself, and to displease Elise, S. must use as much ingenuity as he did to please her. There can be no question of going about the treatment brutally; he must play the part of a man who will irritate or disgust her, whose meanness will open her eyes to him, and as women can always be trusted to do on these occasions, she will only need to stop loving him to believe she never loved him at all. It is not the grave defects visible to all which begin a statue's decay; in fact it is perfectly possible to maintain the contrary, that the serious defects visible to all are what exalt a man who would be worth very little without his corruption or his cruelty. It is trivial things which start the decay, like ineptitude at lying.

So S. starts to lie. Yet he must not lie in such a way that he will be believed. Success depends on fabricating futile and gratuitous lies, inconsequential and so thinly camouflaged that, given the slightest thought, they will be detected. When, reeking of perfume, he claims to have just come from a funeral, Elise has no difficulty in identifying the perfume as one belonging to her best friend (S., of course, has bought himself a bottle and sprinkled himself with it before going to see his mistress). When he talks about a well-known person as if he were an old friend and then, only an hour later, apparently forgetting his boast, has himself introduced to that person in front of her, Elise is deeply shocked. She is no less indignant at his claim to have been the lover, a month previously, of a society beauty who, she finds out a week later, has been living in an igloo in Lapland for the past year (or something along those lines). Elise's eyes are opened to a different reality, and she thinks she is seeing a bluffer, a mediocrity, where before, with passion blinding her, she thought she was seeing a satanic enchanter. The rift is finalized when, with supreme arrogance, he invites her for the weekend along with an actor friend of his and cries off at the last minute, leaving them alone together in an hotel in the country well-known as a refuge for adulterous couples. On her return S. asks her, in an intentionally vulgar way, whether she enjoyed 'spending the weekend with her legs apart', thus feigning the indifference which will set her against him for good. Of course she has spent the weekend 'with her legs apart' in the vague hope that this will provoke a scene, either a clash between S. and his actor friend or a fit of jealousy on S.'s part. Not only could he not care less; he now pushes her into the arms of another lover – a publisher – then a third, a journalist. From now on Elise will be part of that small pool of women who slake the thirsts of certain notorious Parisians one after another. S. has served the community. Some time afterwards, he is pleasantly surprised to hear that Elise has taken a decision of her own and gone straight, marrying and settling down with a man who has absolutely nothing to do with the milieu in which S. launched her career.

★

The exercise book in which Stanislas amused himself by noting down his day-to-day adventures with the sister of the alcoholic poet lay untouched in a drawer for six months after the woman who had inspired the character of Elise had her white wedding with a non-descript stranger. Rediscovering the book in his desk, Stanislas reopened it and, with one of those intuitions he felt had to exploit immediately if he was not to be distracted by its difficulties and his own laziness, he took hold of its theme, preserved its day-to-day form and added a sufficient wealth of detail and incident to turn it into a full-length novel. But however great the imagined part of the final version of *Cryptogram*, it did not stop the woman who had inspired Elise from recognizing herself – one is reminded of her sarcastic letter ('A triumph of imagination, I must say . . .'). Yet there was much which was invented because the real Stanislas had few traits in common with the cruel and sardonic S., despite his accumulation of details which tended to be identifiable, and his notable use of the first person narrative which was so misleading that some naive readers were utterly taken in by it.

Certain sections of the press were deeply shocked by *Cryptogram*. Ever since *The Secret Life of an Orgasm* Stanislas Beren had been thought a 'daring' author. The same accusation today would raise either a smile or no reaction at all if levelled at risqué passages which were not central to the book. The author had described the two erotic scenes in the house of assignation coldly and indifferently. The reader had to be fairly depraved to find anything pornographic in the picture of the gentleman in his long underpants and sock-suspenders smugly contemplating the buttocks of a small lady who is committing adultery for the first time and who thinks that the two enormous tufts of hair under her arms are attractive. When the book reappeared in 1956 these pages went unnoticed, having come after the brutal and lyrical revelation of Henry Miller's *Tropics* and, more importantly, after Pauline Réage's *Histoire d'O*. But at the time (1938) there had been cries of indignation. In a letter from Venice (dated 13 October 1956) Stanislas wrote to me:

There were some fools who had called me a pornographer. It was important to reassure them in their foolishness. Remember what Gobineau said: 'We must let fools be fools.' Surely it is an act of charity to let them stay that way? Which is why I threw that bone. One newspaper – let us perform another act of charity and not reveal which one – even called me a pimp. No writer can be happier than when he is taken for something he is not. I was asked in an interview if it was a personal story. I answered in the words of de Musset to whom various people had attributed the authorship of *La Comtesse Gamiani* which he probably wrote with George Sand: 'The man who writes those things scorns doing them, the man who does them scorns writing about them.' To tell the truth, the thing I was most concerned about was telling the story of a man who takes possession of a woman's character and destroys it utterly, to the depths of her innermost inhibitions, then reconstructs it on new foundations; having finished his work, he may delight in seeing an entirely new figure come to life, a character of his own creation. Certainly there was much that was true in the story and I could not have written it without being a little cruel to the woman who inspired the character of Elise Dubouchez. She was not too furious with me. After all, she claims to be a rational, intelligent woman. It is symbolic that she should once more be the victim of an error of judgment about her personality. I still feel a real warmth for her brother, who disappeared so soon after our ludicrous meeting on the landing at Saeta. It is not so uncommon for a schizophrenic to appropriate a character from a novel. On the rue de Seine, before and after the war, there was a man, still young, who used to walk slowly and deliberately up and down. He thought he was Colonel Chabert: he had the complete outfit – boots, frock coat, neck throttled in a stiff collar, stovepipe hat – and he would stride along the street, waving the passers-by out of the way with his cane. A press photographer once caught him in the market on the rue de Buci buying frugal amounts of various fruits, and he published the photograph in a magazine with a funny caption. So the would-be Chabert challenged him to a duel. With sabres, if you please! He wounded the fellow rather nastily. And that's not an isolated case. I feel I should congratulate myself on having met a man with a bit of imagination in his madness, who took himself to be Jezero Skadarsko. After all, what other reason do we write for, than to be believed? But I do regret not having made more of Elise's father. I left him almost exactly as he was in real life; the funny thing is, I should have found it very difficult to invent his death. They found him at home one day, in his apartment on the boulevard Saint-Germain, dressed up like a little girl with white stockings and patent shoes with buckles, and a doll in his arms. I do hope they gave him a white funeral.

The year of 1939 is the year of a little girl whom we shall call Audrey Inglesey, the name she was given later in a novel by Stanislas which has already been mentioned: *Where Are You Dining Tonight?* She is eight years old, and has blue eyes and blonde hair down to her waist. She skis in the snows of Vermont and in the afternoons she practises her piano. Her mother is a painter and her father a conductor. Their house is on the lower slopes of a valley, next to a river whose banks are covered with snowdrifts in winter and tall yellow reeds in summer. The connection between her and Stanislas was the man who turned up at the Saeta offices one morning in October 1938, shortly after *Cryptogram* had appeared. Bundled up in a grey herringbone overcoat (quilted with newspapers to keep its skinny, wheezing occupant a little warmer) and wearing a grey felt hat which, when he took it off, revealed a baldness immediately condemned as frightfully common by Emeline Aureo – the kind that waiters in brasseries have, she thought – the little man held out a visiting card to the secretary:

Maurice Humez
Police superintendent (retired)

He wished to see the 'literary director'. This title was so embarrassing that no one had yet acquired it, and Emeline Aureo judged that, given the visitor's shabby appearance, a moment with M. Dupuy would suffice. At the end of a quarter of an hour's conversation, M. Dupuy, judging himself that M. Humez's proposals were genuinely interesting, led him down to the Rendez-vous des Amis where Stanislas and André were commiserating with each other over some white wine about a spiteful article that had appeared that morning about *Cryptogram* (which, incidentally, was selling very well).

M. Humez, who had retired the day before, was offering his services unpaid. Throughout his life he had read an enormous amount, especially detective novels, and the collection which had interested him most was the one published by Editions Saeta: 'Crime Pays'. Persuaded by long experience that crime did indeed pay, he had seen this bitter reality all but ignored on station bookstalls, except in the first three novels of their collection: *Death of a Foal in its Mother's Arms*, *AC/DC* and *The Derelict*. Thereafter the series had not always fulfilled the promise of its title, and M. Humez was offering, in a disinterested way, to advise the house's authors and even to supply them with subjects drawn from his forty-year-long experience as a policeman. He had been witness to vast numbers of perfect crimes and happy criminals.

Stanislas and André revealed that they were the authors of the first three novels. Without any forethought, and lacking any experience other than their imaginations, they had remedied the fundamental weakness of the detective novel with its fairy-tale ending of the criminal brought to justice.

M. Humez was given an office adjoining M. Dupuy's. Despite the great differences in their respective fields of learning, the two men got on with each other very well. Being brought into continuous contact with suspects had sharpened the ex-police superintendent's psychological insight, and the ex-teacher recognized that his own experience would always remain bookish. M. Humez refused to be paid a salary. He lived in a house in the suburbs at Perreux, took a train morning and evening, had a sandwich and a glass of beer for lunch, and dropped in twice a day at the Rendez-vous des Amis, once for an Amer Picon before his sandwich, then for a cup of coffee during the afternoon. Not once did he ever raise his voice. He contented himself with writing up reports on the manuscripts, noting mistakes of fact and flagging credibility, and occasionally even preparing outlines for authors short of imagination. In the space of a few weeks he had shown himself to be so useful that Stanislas and André found a weight lifted from their shoulders. The success of the *Crime Pays* list compensated for the grave disappointments of other books. A didactic, but prophetic, study of *Mein Kampf* had sold fewer than five hundred copies. Another study, on General Guderian's classes at the German military academy, aroused so little interest among the French public that bookshop returns were as high as 90%. In fact, after Munich and at the beginning of 1939 no one wanted to hear any talk of war, and those who dared broach the subject were considered harbingers of doom, and avoided. Stanislas and André, who had tried to inform the reading public with these two books, might have done better not to have been discouraged quite so quickly; but how, when one loves literature so passionately, can one avoid taking refuge in it from one's disappointments and telling oneself that if the world is going under it's because it wants to, that Nero was a fantastic scene-setter and that the world has sore need of Neros on this eve of apocalypse.

André, relieved of the most time-consuming part of Saeta's activities, wanted to discover America. He had no difficulty in enlisting Stanislas' enthusiasm and convincing Félicité that the future development of Saeta required personal contacts among American publishers. At the beginning of February 1939, they embarked on the *Normandie*. It was André's first voyage on a liner. What follows are the extracts from his diary which refer to the crossing and to the important meeting which occurred:[1]

One would think one was aboard a floating museum devoted to the gastronomic pleasures of France. It is certainly the best of what we have to offer to foreigners, that euphoria that comes from stuffing yourself with high-quality food. We are corrupting the Americans with our foie gras and our champagne and cheeses. They'll go ashore at New York, bloated, nauseous, but happy. They queue up to be worked over by the masseur and lose four pounds that they put straight back on at dinner. Food here has been raised to the level of a religion. Time being limited, they have to eat as fast as they can. Less than four days to go!

The following day:

Aunt Félicité reigns supreme. However absorbed they may be by life on board, however possessed by their gluttony, the passengers are left in no doubt that from her armchair, o₁ ɪe promenade deck, at the captain's table or at her own table, between her husband and myself, this woman rules over a world to which their cheque books will never give them access. One single passenger has found favour – and not just favour; he has seen himself monopolized and tyrannized. It so happens that she knew him twenty years ago when he was conducting the Monte Carlo orchestra for Diaghilev's ballets. He's forty-five, has a magnificent mop of white hair, eyes of opal blue, a fine long nose like a perfumer's and excellent hands – as exquisite as Cocteau's. Anybody who met him in the street would guess, just from the imperious way he carries his head, the way he

[1] 10 February 1939.

stares beadily into the eyes of a wretched passer-by as if he had played a wrong note, that he is a conductor. I don't want to paint a caricature just from the way he looks, but Stanislas and I always have a bit of trouble putting up with the artistic type. Yet as soon as one gets to know John Inglesey, he is pure magic. He gives the impression – and here I am not paying easy tribute – of knowing everything, of having read everything, of meeting everybody during the six months of the year that he's giving concerts. The other six months he spends with his wife, who is a painter, and his daughter.

And the third day:

On the captain's table John was conducting a chamber ensemble, orchestrating everyone's part, then silencing us all for a solo of his own in that gentle, sonorous, almost unaccented voice and, after the last bar, paying homage to the only woman present – Félicité. Had he gone on much longer, we'd have burst into applause. He has invited us to join him in Vermont as soon as we've had enough of New York. Aunt Félicité has decided that we shall go, but to make it quite clear that she hasn't let herself be carried away too blindly, she has told him that he ought to get his artist's locks cut a bit more appropriately. 'John, you can't go any higher – you conduct the orchestras you want to conduct, you play the composers you want to play. So . . . you have absolutely no need for all that hair now.' We were all delighted to see him speechless for a moment, but at dinner he duly appeared with his hair cut. Aunt Félicité made no comment. It went without saying.

When they arrived in New York harbour, the photographers and journalists came aboard before the ship had berthed. They had their list of celebrities: an extremely meagre one, because apart from John Inglesey there were only three or four minor politicians on the voyage. The name of Stanislas Beren evidently made no impact, but the light dawned when someone discovered that Félicité had been Mme della Croce, the wife of the painter whose grandiose 'conventionalism' had beautified several Manhattan banks. Immediately, in all the hubbub of disembarkation, Inglesey, Stanislas, André and Félicité were bombarded with flashguns and questions. The next day the papers were full of their arrival, and since minor events have to be magnified and, if need be, invented, Stanislas was the toast of New York.

Unfortunately this celebrity lasted only a day because the next day the *Queen Mary* came in with a cargo of film stars, a famous violinist, a music-hall clown and the French writer hailed as 'the greatest expert in the psychology of love', the unforgettable author of *The Madonna of the Sleeping-cars*, Maurice Dekobra. André, who had hoped that this first wave of publicity would smooth the way for his 'American campaign', was soon cut down to size when a second wave washed over the first, carrying off perhaps not Inglesey, but certainly the unknown French writer Stanislas Beren, on the tide of obscurity after a moment of short-lived glory. The publishing houses, who granted them appointments reluctantly, making them stand in corridors made draughty by secretaries dashing to and fro, employed armies of lawyers to avoid lawsuits and not a single reader of French. They were sent on to the literary agents – who were no less incapable of reading foreign languages. There was one who had had a digest of *Cryptogram* prepared and then advised Stanislas to change the beginning, the middle and the end of the novel, and especially to cut the 'romantic' scenes. That this man emerged alive from the meeting was largely thanks to Stanislas' restraint of André, who would otherwise have inflicted grievous damage on him. The two friends had no alternative but to resign themselves and admit defeat on all fronts – partly because their 'American campaign' had been ill-prepared, but mainly because in the America of 1939, love of the French had descended to its lowest ebb: French writers were all either communists, pornographers or war-mongers seeking to drag America into the conflict.

The welcome which greeted Stanislas and Félicité on their return to the United States in 1940 was not to be the same: the French were now fashionable, back in favour out of pity for their unhappy country which sparked off wars and was then unable to contain them on her own. Miraculously the first visit was remembered, and *Cryptogram* immediately found a publisher, as did the two books Stanislas wrote between nineteen forty and forty-five, *Trust Me* and *Singtime!*, which I have already talked about.

But the disappointing first approaches and the impression of having been rejected by the great American machine and left on the sidelines of the literary movement which, for two decades, had been rocking the country's intellectual self-satisfaction, would have embittered Stanislas and André for good had Félicité not been fêted and toasted by all New York virtually from the moment she arrived. A month passed quickly; then John Inglesey's invitation was repeated and they left for Stockwood in Vermont.

The conductor's house, on the mountainside, looked down on the great green expanse of Lake Champlain on the Canadian border. After the stone and concrete of New York, whose suffocating force one is unaware of until one is free of it, they drove through a landscape of snow and forests, of charming villages and poetic little towns which belonged to another world. This was where John lived six months of the year, with his wife Laura and his daughter Audrey. Laura spent her days in a studio with wide bay windows facing the pure, cold light of the north; John, installed below the main house in an octagonal music pavilion, lived with his piano and his library; but the heart and soul of the house was Audrey, eight years old, the hyphen between the studio and the pavilion, the messenger reminding both of mealtimes which they shared together, the go-between carrying those exquisite *billets doux* that John and Laura exchanged several times a day, full of impulsiveness and emotion, and which were published after their deaths in an air crash in 1950.

Laura painted landscapes of minute detail, the landscapes of New England: forests of birches climbing the snow-covered slopes of the valleys, village churches with their square bell-towers, rivers flowing deep blue between their banks of snow-drifts in winter and their carpets of tall yellow reeds in summer. She painted for herself, in the way that other people hum or talk to themselves, giving shapes and colours to the movements of her spirit, whose strife, John would claim, she knew nothing of and whose excesses of joy were her only fear. When her mother died, Audrey collected a hundred of her canvases together and exhibited them in one of the Fifth Avenue galleries with a lack of success which would have been complete had not Stanislas and Félicité bought five of them which they later kept in London. Audrey, a victim of destiny herself in 1954, was not to know of her mother's belated success. Discovered by chance in 1970 by a curator at the national museum in Washington, Laura Inglesey's work is today represented in all the important collections of American naive painting.

When Félicité, Stanislas and André arrived at Stockwood, Laura was just thirty. André noted in his diary, '. . . angelic face; voice of the purity of mountain water which reminds you that she could have been a great soprano had she not sacrificed her career to John; hands which caress things before grasping them and mastering them'.

They were still on the front steps of the house, being welcomed by Laura, when they noticed a red dot zig-zagging down among the pines and raising a trail of white powder. The elf came nearer almost without growing at all. It was Audrey. She had a face tanned by the winter sun, eyes like the blue skies in her mother's paintings, and a mass of blonde hair which burst around her face when she took off the woollen bonnet covering her ears.

'I know you!' she said, pointing her finger at Félicité, Stanislas and André.

She kissed them one after the other, brushing the cheeks of the three visitors with her cold rosy lips. John, who had heard the noise of the car, emerged from his pavilion and walked up the steps leading to the house, enveloped in a sheepskin coat, his feet hidden inside his trapper's boots. Audrey took off her skis and ran towards him, hurling herself at him with scant regard for his life and limb.

'He's my father!' she said, with a solemnity which might have sounded false had it not been for her age. 'Yes,' she added, 'and he's the greatest conductor in the world. Did you know that?'

'We thought as much,' Félicité answered, 'but I'm glad you can confirm it for us.'

Audrey did not go to school. This was John's idea. He dreamed of a child who would belong only to them, and speak their language, not a language which was atrophied, reduced to three hundred words imposed as the lowest common denominator by life with other children. A tutor called at the house twice a week, corrected her homework and set her more. At eight years old, Audrey made remarks that were neither the remarks of an adult nor those of a child: things like, 'Yesterday evening, we had one of the most beautiful twilights in the world.' No childish jeering had smothered her personality, nor was there anything of the pasty-faced bookworm about her. The fact that she spoke two languages with equal ease – her mother's French, her father's English – had developed in her an insatiable appetite for games with words and their assonances, and for gentle comparisons which disturbed her listeners; and those adults she came into contact with somehow knew not to praise her personality, aware of the risk of inhibiting it.

As soon as they were sitting in the drawing room where Laura had laid out a tray of tea and toast on the low table in front of the wood fire, Audrey, who had disappeared momentarily, reappeared in a blue satin dress, white socks and patent shoes. Who had she dressed up for, so quickly and yet with so much care? The answer came almost immediately. It was for Stanislas whom she now sat next to, ensuring that he lacked for nothing. Love was born, and that love is the subject of *Where Are You Dining Tonight?*,[1] the novel in which Stanislas portrayed himself in the character of Maximilian von Arelle. But in 1939 we are still a long way from that melancholy evocation of a man of fifty who pins his faith on a memory, and Audrey is just a child with no thought for disguising her feelings. Had she been older, she would have detested Félicité. As it was she was content to ignore her unconsciously, to the point that when she came down to say goodnight to everybody on her way to bed, she forgot to kiss Félicité; Laura had to remind her and she came back covered in confusion at having given herself away so completely. She doubtless learned thereafter to deal with Félicité tactfully, thanks to a feminine shrewdness which surprised everyone by its precocity but deceived no one.

In *Where Are You Dining Tonight?* the first stay at Stockwood is described much as I have just summarized it. Stanislas did not bother to embellish the story of this new-born passion. It was disconcerting enough in itself not to warrant any alteration. The appearance of a child endowed with grace is a magical moment in the life and work of a writer, a breath which passes by and purifies the air he has been breathing. After *Cryptogram*, which had poked fun at the miasmata of an unquiet soul, and the pleasure he had taken in persecuting himself with allegations more imaginary than real, Stanislas needed to rediscover feelings which were devoid of artifice. It is possible that without the enlightened love of this eight-year-old child his work would have been lost to a facile and throwaway cynicism. Audrey rendered Stanislas the invaluable service of reminding him that to love is also to forget completely how to scheme, to feel an irresistible impulse towards a being whose arrival transforms existence to the point that every moment and every gesture are suffused with that other person whom one can no longer distinguish from oneself.

Audrey's intense love affected Stanislas more deeply than he had imagined it would, and it distressed him that he was unable to respond to it with the same passionate generosity. Beneath his napkin, under his door in the morning, in his overcoat pocket, he would find envelopes with the letters S.W.A.L.K. written on their backs, containing those charming poems that he included in the novel. Some were in English, some in French; they contained no references to her feelings but were mainly in the form of invitations to him, to share the exhilaration of a dash at breakneck speed down the hillside, or the melancholy of a boat trip along the banks of the Champlain where the

[1] *Where Are You Dining Tonight?*, Editions Saeta, 1960.

rushes grow so high one is lost in a watery forest, or the joy of a Scarlatti sonata that her father was making her practise in the pavilion that afternoon. Or else she would quote him verses from Eliot and Frost which, she said, corresponded so exactly to her moods that she could stand aside, conscious that she would never say those things better than they had.

She was brave the day they left, her beautiful face screwed up with the effort of holding back her tears, her eyes glistening, her cheeks suddenly a deep shade of red; but when Stanislas bent to kiss her, she clasped her arms around his neck with such desperation that he knelt down to murmur in her ear, 'I shan't forget you; I shall be back.' She tore herself away and ran inside, and from the car they could just see her at her bedroom window, her forehead pressed against the glass.

He did not forget her and came back the following year, in 1940. However improbable it may seem, at the age of nine Audrey had already nursed her love, that strange love sprung from a single look, to maturity, as if, after a momentary rebellion against an impossible situation – her age first of all, and then Félicité – she had resigned herself to make no demands, to take only what was freely offered her; but the intense light in her blue eyes as she watched Stanislas, her sudden moods of melancholy and, occasionally, the pretence of a temperature when her cheeks flushed pink, were reminder enough to anyone who might have forgotten that the fire was smouldering and would go on smouldering for a long time to come.

★

The passages in the novel which describe this child's passion for a man of over thirty, and his respect for her feelings, so fragile that a trifle is likely to shatter them and cause lasting harm to a young soul, are among the most beautiful ever inspired by a love remembered in its minutest details. A man, Maximilian von Arelle, attempts to save from his past a unique experience, something he did not resist the desire to fulfil even at the risk of tainting the perfection of a memory. Slowly, scene by scene – or perhaps one should say frame by frame – as the years go by, we see Audrey getting older, her face and body slowly changing, without her passion ever fading.

The real Audrey was fifteen when Stanislas left for Europe once more, in 1946. In the course of his exile, the bonds of friendship with John and Laura Inglesey had been strengthened. Stanislas and Félicité stayed for long periods at Stockwood, and they also followed John to Washington, Los Angeles, Philadelphia and San Francisco on the concert circuit; but it was at Stockwood that their best moments were spent, and it was there that Stanislas started writing *Trust Me*, after several false starts in their apartment on Fifth Avenue.

The manuscript of *Trust Me*, in a linen-covered folder tied with a pink ribbon, had turned up at the same time as the photos of Nathalie and Vladimir, when Stanislas and I had been rummaging in the drawers that evening in London in 1970. Stanislas had undone the ribbon and wrapped it around his index finger.

'Audrey gave me this ribbon when I finished the final chapter. This is a curious manuscript from the view-point of anyone interested in writers' handwriting. I suffer from an appalling hand, barely legible. In New York, starting at the end of 1940, I had written and thrown away twenty outlines of the first chapter. Impossible. I never got past page ten and I could barely make head or tail of my own hieroglyphs. I thought I was finished. Then we spent Christmas at Stockwood and Audrey asked me, all innocence, what I did in life since I neither painted nor played the piano. Of course, the question was a perfectly normal one; she wanted to know everything about me because she was in love. So I stupidly replied that I *had been* a writer but that now, uprooted from France, having lost my best and only friend in the war, living in a rented apartment whose furniture I did not feel at all at home with, struggling through the day against the English language swamping my mind, I no longer felt capable of anything. So Audrey decided that I should not leave Stockwood without having started on a book. Laura set up a table for me in the room adjoining her studio. I sat on my chair in front of the blank sheets of paper. If I looked up, I could see the valley blanketed in snow. On sunny days the forest of tall pines sparkled with a thousand golden lights and the snow turned blue, but when the sun was hidden behind the clouds it was impossible to see further than a hundred yards and we felt as if we were completely cut off from the world at the centre of a gigantic ball of grey fluff which muffled all sound. A little lower down, the chimney of a log cabin sent its smoke into the still air where it traced hazy, irregular rings like strange aerial jellyfish. The cabin belonged to a trapper. In the mornings he used to put on a pair of snowshoes, whistle up his dog – a silver Siberian husky – and, with his shotgun on his shoulder, trudge into the forest. Or else I would see Audrey, muffled up in red or blue, waiting with her skis over her shoulder for a snow tractor to come along and take her up to the ridge; then a second later there would be a Lilliputian projectile hurtling down between the pines and stopping right in front of my window. Then she would squash her nose against the window-pane and make faces. I began to work with a greater sense of serenity. My handwriting, calmer than before, was now legible, in fact so neat that Audrey, creeping into the study despite her mother's injunctions, was able to read over my shoulder. If I pretended to get angry, she used to settle down cross-legged on a repp sofa and I felt, at the back of my neck, the heat of a piercing stare which compelled me not to put a single page to one side before I had finished it. I wrote the book under her unspoken orders – I should almost say her censure – and when it appeared, Edmund Wilson saw right to the heart of the matter: it was a fairy-tale for the little girl to whom I had dedicated it. After Christmas, when we got back to New York, I had written about thirty pages of the first draft, far enough for most writers to be sure of continuing, but once back, the same inhibitions overcame me. The city was crushing me, devouring me. I could no longer bear Félicité's presence when I was working and I found myself saying the only unpleasant things I have ever said to her in my life. I cannot pretend that she took them well. In February 1941 I returned to Stockwood alone. John was in South America and I shared myself between Laura and Audrey. I did not talk a great deal about Laura in the novel because there was no story to tell. John had known her in Paris, then married her and taken her to America. She was one of those plants which can adapt to any environment: cold, hot, night, day, tropical, arctic. Life carried her along. Lacking any artificiality, she lived for Audrey, John and her painting. It was very easy to picture her, as a child, with the same lovely blonde colouring as her daughter, but the years (she was just thirty) had darkened her hair, and her spectacles – which John spent his time in vain forbidding her to wear – masked the blue of her eyes. In short, Laura was one of those rare creatures with whom a man may find peace, a peace whose surface it would have been impossible to ruffle. Audrey was keeping watch, and in any case . . . the truth is, it did not occur to me. The only thing I was thinking about was my *Trust Me* which really took shape in the February and March of 1941. We were cut off by a blizzard. We had no telephone, no electricity, no heating. For five days the three of us lived in the sitting room, in front of a great wood fire, sleeping under piles of blankets, the room lit by petrol lamps, grilling steaks of bear meat in the embers. The bear meat was a present from the trapper in the log cabin below the Ingleseys'. Where had he killed the bear? I don't think it was anywhere nearby; probably off away in the forests running along the Canadian border. Wherever it was, we had this meat which, once it was marinated, was very decent.

A sort of apathy took hold of us after the second day. The world had forgotten us. When we woke up, the fire was out, the room was in the grip of the ice which covered the bay windows. The light had been shattered into a million pieces by the crystals of snow and it felt as if we were in an aquarium filled with coral. When I relit the fire, the windows began to thaw and through the water running down the glass the tall pines skirting the forest writhed and advanced and retreated, disappearing suddenly to reappear petrified, the menacing guardians of the valley. As the view cleared we made a count of the number of branches which had snapped under the weight of snow. The solitude began to numb our minds and we spoke little. At night Audrey, who was sleeping between us on the mass of cushions piled up in front of the fireplace, would clutch my hand and not let it go, even in her deepest sleep. She was there, unfailingly attached to me, my inspiration and my critic while I mused on the subject of *Trust Me*, which in the course of those five nights – nights sharpened by the suffering of the house weighed down by the snow and the cold, whose walls, beams, roof and door-frames creaked like an arthritic's old bones so that I expected to see our shelter suddenly vanish into thin air, leaving us out in the open beneath our blankets, to be slowly covered over by the snowflakes drifting down in the icy air – had outlined itself so completely in my head that after the blizzard, when the electricity and the telephone were working again, it took no more than two weeks to finish it. Never, after so many initial hesitations, have I written a book so quickly, with such cheerfulness and enjoyment. When I re-read it, twenty years afterwards, I saw its weaknesses and its haste as well as the joy it had given me, but I also saw, behind every page, Audrey's radiant face, her frown when she did not understand a page she had read over my shoulder and her explosion of joy when she tiptoed into the study and saw me writing – very childishly – in a well-formed round hand, the word FINIS. That was the moment when she untied her hair and gave me the pink ribbon. . . .'

This long monologue, which I have reported as faithfully as I can, goes back to that evening in the house in Chelsea in 1970 when we were inventorying the contents of some long-forgotten drawers. With the help of photographs, newspaper cuttings and a faded pink ribbon, the past revisited us in snatches, and it struck me that to Stanislas it was a game to be enjoyed, in which real memories and the novels they had inspired were so far mixed that, years afterwards, he often had little idea of where the truth lay.

Let us move on to *Trust Me*, which is a neat little story, swiftly told, inspired by a completely different vision from the one which had inspired *Cryptogram*, as if Stanislas, regretting the hollow lesson of a lover's cruelty, had sought to erase his cynical outburst. *Trust Me* tells the story of a gentle wooing between a Frenchman and an American woman who meet on the *Normandie* as it is leaving Le Havre. Each is immediately attracted by the other and they are inseparable for the four days of the crossing. But what is there to talk about when they are strolling up and down the promenade deck, hand in hand, for the four hundredth time? Having no friends in common to slander, all they are left with is telling the stories of their lives to each other; and almost by chance these two people, who did not know each other the day before but are now anxious to be interesting, begin the tales of their complacent lives with a white lie. It is inevitable that these two white lies involve a whole cascade of others, and the Frenchman and his American friend, with everything in their favour, find themselves stupidly separated by the dizzying mythomania which has taken hold of them. Through something which began as a game but was soon taken over by the implacable logic of falsehood, they have placed themselves in two irreconcilable worlds. When they arrive in New York they have no alternative but to go their separate ways, or to confess to each other that they have dreamed up these stories for their mutual bedazzlement and that in fact they can love each other very happily without them. Out of pride they choose to go their separate ways.

The novel enjoyed only a *succès d'estime* in 1943, in its American translation, and attracted no attention when it appeared in 1947 in France; but as so often happens, twenty years later an American librettist wrote a musical comedy based on it which played for five years on Broadway before being taken on a world tour. The musical is better known than the novel – whose ending it modified: the couple confess their deceits to each other and marry. *Singtime!*, which appeared in New York in 1944, was better received and became, with the film, an international success. Curiously, these two books published in the United States are the only ones to have been adapted for the cinema and the stage.

*

In counterpoint within *Trust Me*, we can perceive the genesis of *Where Are You Dining Tonight?* which did not appear until 1960. 'What is strange,' Stanislas said, 'is that I have laboured over all my books, except two: *Trust Me* and the second *Where Are You Dining Tonight?*

They were both dictated to me, literally, by Audrey. The first by a little girl with blonde hair and blue eyes, the second by her double, an enlargement of her, the girl who came to stay in Paris in the early fifties after the dramatic deaths of her parents. The two manuscripts are written in the same calm hand, with no crossings out, in complete contrast to my other totally undignified manuscripts, covered with marginal scribblings, omission marks, second thoughts pencilled in, stained orange with rusty paper clips and criss-crossed with the gummed paper I used to repair the pages I had torn up and then picked out of the waste-paper bin after thinking about them. *Where Are You Dining Tonight?* is a completely clean manuscript, with the exception of heavy strokes of red crayon through one or two passages which, when I had finished writing the book, I decided not to publish. Those passages were the ones which were the most important to me: the extracts from the only personal diary I have kept in my life. Afterwards, I burned the diary so that I should not be tempted to re-read it. The pages I copied out for the novel escaped being burnt; but finally I cut them, because on the one hand they seemed to me to be a bit self-satisfied and on the other they interfered with the rhythm of the narrative. I shall be giving you both manuscripts, so you will be able to read them; if you decide one day that you want to publish them, go ahead, but wait until I am no longer in a position to see them. . . .'

Where Are You Dining Tonight? takes up the events I have already mentioned in connection with the stay at Stockwood and the blizzard which cut the house off for five days. The hero's name is Maximilian von Arelle. He originates from central Europe: Austria at best, the Sudetenland at worst. When he speaks French, he has a slight English accent, English a German accent, German a French accent. He lives well, but no one knows the source of his income. When questioned, he answers, 'I am in business. In other words, I should really say that I am a crook.'

This is not in fact true, yet provocative remarks like this sum up his whole personality. Few things irritate him more than the curiosity he excites, but occasionally one feels that he is exciting that curiosity quite deliberately and maliciously. He would prefer to go unnoticed, but that is impossible because he is constantly bumping into people who claim to know him. His defence against the society he inhabits is to be anarchic and insulting. So why does he continue to be part of it? 'Out of cowardice, and because any other society would be equally tedious.'

He enjoys hearing the idiotic rumours which circulate about him.

Some say he is a penny-pinching multi-millionaire. Others call him a sponger, but generous with it. His refined, at times fastidious, way of dressing has earned him a reputation as a homosexual, which delights him.

'Perfect! What better way to reassure all those anxious husbands? Now they can trust me implicitly. I take their wives out while they are having affairs with their secretaries. All the time we're in bed they're thinking that we're at a concert, or visiting some museum or ancient monument. The care with which I groom these ladies afterwards, helping them with their make-up and their hair, and sending them home spotlessly clean, without so much as a crease in their skirts and always with their underwear intact, has assured me an unblemished reputation.'

There are many women in Maximilian's life, which is to say that no one woman holds sway; in any case, there is nothing he likes so much as being alone. On his occasional disappearances, for a month or two at a time, the rumours gain ground and flourish, and when he reappears, we learn – not through him (because he only ever speaks about himself in tones of mockery), but by chance everything comes out somehow – that he has been away in a monastery on Mount Athos or at Solesmes, unless, that is, he has locked himself away in the château of a friend to study some unpublished papers relating to the battle of Waterloo, or plagues in London in the seventeenth century, or the taking of Jerusalem by the Crusaders. Beyond speculation is the fact that he is an avid historian, and his only weakness when someone utters an historical falsehood in his hearing is that he will speak out to re-establish the truth.

His age remains a mystery; however, it seems a fair guess that he was born at the turn of the century, so that at the beginning of his friendship with John Inglesey in 1939, he is not quite forty. He will be fifty when Audrey, after the death of her parents, comes to stay in Paris. The word amongst his women friends is that Maximilian at fifty is much more handsome than in his youth, with his grey-blond hair waving over his temples, his leaner, more assertive nose, and the pale lines of the crow's feet around his eyes in an otherwise bronzed complexion. Naturally, no man finds him even remotely attractive. Maximilian's success with women is beyond the realms of their perception; but it must be said that he plays a brilliant hand. Time is the key. While his rivals are either impatient or failing to give the matter any thought, he devotes to his companions all the time that they need. Two or three close friends, no more, know that this idle man is actually a tireless worker who has evolved a methodology which does away with work. In his office, where with the aid of three telephones and a telex he conducts exchange deals all over the world, not a minute is lost. On the other hand he is quite capable of waiting an hour for a woman who is trying on a hat or a dress, or visiting her favourite hairdresser and telling him her life story or asking him for advice about her lover who is threatening to leave her or her husband who is standing for parliament in some far-flung constituency in the provinces. A man as available as Maximilian possesses a priceless asset, and there are dinners where he is surprised to find that he knows, intimately, all four or five attractive women at the table.

When Audrey arrives in Paris, armed with her innocent faith in the man she has loved since childhood, Maximilian is in the thick of a stormy affair of which, for the first time in his life, he is no longer the master. Madame de C. wants him for herself alone, as exclusively as she wants her husband. She cares nothing for moderation or refinement of feeling. Maximilian has to wage a constant battle to preserve his freedom, but at the same time cannot bring himself to break off the liaison. The resulting unsettled state of affairs is difficult to conceal from Audrey. Her hope for something exalted and wonderful has, she believes, been dragged down into something horribly sordid, but of course the truth is that she has found herself in one of the most everyday situations there can be. One has to picture this beautiful and disarmingly ingenuous young girl landing in France; she has been brought up in the snowy cocoon of Stockwood, by a father whose greatest passion was the music of the Romantics, a mother who took refuge in a universe of naive landscapes and fairy-tale characters and a tutor whose only link with the outside world lay in the abstractions of mathematics and chemical formulae devoid of meaning. Nothing in that upbringing has prepared her for her discovery that the object of her childhood passions, then her adolescent passions, is in the thrall of another woman from whom, with unusual weakness of will, he is unable to free himself and so welcome her, paragon of purity, into his open arms. Only in the light of this can one understand how deep and grievous is the wound. But Audrey is possessed of remarkable resources of dignity and nobility. The discovery of the shocking world outside Stockwood where she has for so long been confined, without erasing her disappointment – so deep that it seemed quite unreal – that discovery preserves Audrey from despair. She possesses a savage energy too, and a contempt for the dimension of time. She moves into a large studio on the quai Anatole-France, buys a piano and begins to study with a teacher at the Conservatoire. Though an exaggeration to say that she is a virtuoso, she has certainly inherited her father's particular gifts: a generous approach to Italian music of the seventeenth and eighteenth centuries, and a fingering so light that her hands seemed to be sketching arabesques above the keyboard without touching it. Outside her lessons and practising, she plays only for her friends, a small group of Americans who live like students and constantly dream of composing or painting or writing. They start a magazine, the *Paris Review*, and publish their first efforts.

It is during one of their evenings together in her studio that Maximilian discovers the real Audrey. Until then she has been a plaything to him, endearing and graceful, but in her studio, quite suddenly, her character is illuminated by a mysterious inner glow. The room is plunged into semi-obscurity and Audrey's friends are sprawled on the sofas, or sitting on cushions on the floor. Audrey's profile is outlined by the flickering, waxy light from the candles in the piano's candle-holders as she bends over the keyboard. The chiaroscuro idealizes the fine and beautiful face with its long blonde hair. She dresses in Arab and Indian robes with billowing sleeves drawn tight at the wrist and a black headband is tied across her forehead. When she plays, no one moves, all eyes are turned towards her, but as the last chord sounds the darkness of the studio comes alive. More candles are lit, mounted in the necks of old chianti flasks. Red wine is drunk from thick green glasses as the camembert and *biscottes* are passed around. Somehow one or two girls always manage to look like Zelda Fitzgerald, but the boys seem to prefer the Bill Cody look: long, drooping moustaches and shaggy hair. In the Paris of the fifties this small, tight-knit circle is closed to all, or almost all, Frenchmen. Maximilian is tolerated only out of respect for Audrey. But he cares little whether he is tolerated or not: he is there to discover this magical girl arrived from her cold Vermont, and though he may not yet be sure of his feelings for her, he can feel a strange and desperate emotion rising in himself. His casual and cynical existence begins to appear in all its vanity to him, and he suddenly despises himself for being so weak about Madame de C.; the only reason he cannot bring himself to break with her is because she provides him with a degree of sexual excitement he has never known before. As Audrey plays on in the semi-darkness of her studio Maximilian sincerely believes his salvation has come. His greatest wish is that she should never stop playing, that the music should not be replaced by the artistic small talk of her friends at which he, lacking their youth, is so inept. In an effort which surprises him, he pounces on the books they discuss and the authors whose names are dropped like passwords, but no sooner has he read Carson McCullers' *The Heart is a Lonely Hunter* or Mary McCarthy's *A Charmed Life*, than the little group has switched its admirations to other targets. What Maximilian lacks is not so much their youth, but the flair to stay ahead of these young aesthetes; whenever he thinks he has discovered a novelist, a poet, a playwright or a composer before they have, they listen to him with such exaggerated politeness that his error is obvious to him: he has been talking about a nine-day wonder; he is not with it.

Ever since Audrey has realized that Maximilian is not free, she has arranged, though without avoiding him entirely, never to be alone with him. She puts between them the young men and women who talk so easily and familiarly about people and ideas, about studying at Swiss and Italian universities, about concerts they have been to in Aix, at the Albert Hall, at Glyndebourne, in Rome, in Salzburg, in Bayreuth and from which they have come back crazy about Furtwängler's interpretation of the Ninth Symphony or Wieland Wagner's production of the *Ring*. A number of them are Nadia Boulanger's pupils; she has opened a conservatory for the young Americans at Fontainebleau. Maximilian himself has always loved music of course, but only as a discriminating amateur, and this avalanche of names and references, these appraisals of singers and musicians, leave him standing. So his life is turned upside down as it dawns on him that he has been defending himself against his emotions with his all too ready sarcasm when he should have been surrendering to them wholeheartedly. Sitting on the floor in the darkness of the studio, he sees Audrey's white hands re-inventing a Scarlatti sonata or a piece by Lulli and suddenly senses that his life has been a sham of avoidance and selfishness. But there is still Madame de C. whose hold is as strong as ever once he leaves Audrey to the friends who have made her their queen and at the same time made him aware of how old he is at fifty. He even finds himself obsessed by the ridiculous notion that these men of twenty and twenty-five are more attractive than he is. There is only one solution: he must tear himself away from Madame de C. and make his escape once and for all. The terrible thing is that this means he will have to leave Audrey too. In the nineteenth century, the hero of a novel languishing under an unhappy passion might have challenged a professional duellist or offered his sword to Greek rebels or gone to Italy to explore Vesuvius and Etna. Maximilian decides to leave for New York. Resisting the temptations of drowning his sorrows or renewing the pleasures of the flesh with some other woman, he turns instead to work, with an application and frenzy unprecedented even for him. When he returns to France six months later, Madame de C. is exorcised and he wonders just how he could have shackled himself for a year to a woman who forgot him as soon as his back was turned. Apprehensively he telephones Audrey. A man's voice, still thick with sleep, answers him in English.

'Excuse me, we went to bed so late last night. . . . I didn't catch your name.'

'Maximilian von Arelle.'

'Oh! Maximilian, of course. This is Johnny. . . . You want to talk to my wife?'

'I wish to speak to Audrey.'

'Audrey's still asleep. Where can she call you?'

Maximilian replaces the receiver without answering. It has already been one of those days when nothing goes right. Having cut his lip while shaving and burnt a finger trying to toast some bread, he then had to drink a black coffee because there was no tea in the kitchen. Which one was Johnny? He cannot remember: the fair boy with frizzy hair, or the tall, thin boy who bit his nails? He has seen them all a hundred times, spoken to all of them and known none. Some had been scornful; others had respected his age which annoyed him even more. Johnny? He tries to put faces to the voice like a series of masks and still cannot find the one who might have been close enough to Audrey to marry her – unless she simply chose one of them at random. Maximilian finds out what it is to be unhappy. He has voluntarily lost Madame de C., which is a deliverance for a man in love with his liberty, but now he is more of a prisoner than ever, bound fast by a small blonde girl whom he now knows to be a wife. At first he thinks that Audrey will refuse to see him; but on the contrary, it is she who calls him at his office and suggests they meet at the Café de Flore. When she pushes open the door, he does not immediately recognize her. In a few hours of torment he has had time to etch a new portrait of her on his mind. Maximilian detests the marriage so much that he already imagines Audrey pregnant, with bags under her eyes, her hair shorn, neglectful of her appearance, having lost all her disarming girlishness; but the Audrey who comes into the Café de Flore and stands motionless by the door for a moment, scanning the tables – this Audrey is the true and perfect copy of the one he left, the young Audrey of Stockwood. Nothing has altered her beauty or her grace, or the gift she has kept from her privileged childhood: her transparency. Amazed, he stays seated, not even raising an arm to indicate the table where he has been waiting for half an hour, having arrived early to try – in vain – to calm himself down. Audrey's slight shortsightedness prevents her from seeing him for a moment, but the moment she does, her face lights up with the same childlike joy that made her so precious to him at Stockwood. As she sits down at his side, Maximilian is in the depths of despair: he realizes that for the first time in his life he loves someone. He has known passions and known the real reasons behind them, but never this kind of fear. Audrey's lips on his cheek snap him out of his dreamy inertia. The barriers she erected when she discovered he was not free seem to have melted. He finds her just as he might have imagined her, arriving from Stockwood, animated by that irresistible vitality which she brought to him as a child of eight years old. Maximilian's heart is filled with joy. Perhaps her marriage is a nightmare and all he need do to awake from it is open his eyes to reality, to the café with its brown seats, its highly-polished tables, its copper piping, Paul Boubal leaning on the till, ruling over his regulars, and the waltzing of the waiters in their white jackets (Pascal, the best-known of them all, his broad yellow skull underlined by the black bars of his eyebrows). The atmosphere is thick with smoke, and with the rain outside, the clothes of many of the customers are giving off a smell of damp wool. At the next table there is a young man, his right hand decorated with an amethyst, writing in a score-ruled exercise book; he stops, looks up absently, and lifts a demi-baguette of ham to his mouth. He is on his fifth coffee. Despite the lace curtains masking the scene on the terrace and the boulevard Saint-Germain, the silhouettes of cars can be seen moving slowly past on the glistening road surface, and each time the glass doors opens the people coming in shake themselves like wet dogs. At that moment Maximilian realizes that Audrey's presence at his side is contradicted by one thing: her face is not damp with rain and the coat he has helped her off with is dry, yet she has not even an umbrella. Where has this unreal person come from, whom rain runs off without wetting, like water on the leaves of a geranium? But she is quite real; she has a voice, and her hands with their short nails are lying flat on the table.

'I was lucky. Johnny dropped me right in front of the door.'

Maximilian smiles, reassured. There is no magic in this apparition. But now he must ask the question. 'Does he know you're meeting me?'

'Of course. He wanted to wait for me. I told him not to, because you'd take me to dinner and then maybe to the cinema, and possibly even to have a drink in one of those places where you love to while away the nights like an old roué scared of sleeping on his own.'

'Audrey – are you married?'

'Yes.'

'Do you love Johnny?'

'What about you, do you still love Mme de C.?'

'No.'

'About time too!'

'What you mean is it's too late.'

'Too late, why? Didn't I tell you at Stockwood that I would love you for ever?'

'Even after marrying Johnny?'

'Oh, Johnny's perfect: he's good, generous, utterly honest and like me he loves music.'

Maximilian hesitates to ask her the question which has been torturing him since the second he saw her come into the Flore. He is afraid of the answer and, at the same time, he knows he will live in constant anguish if he cannot bring himself to ask it.

'And do you make love with Johnny?'

'Oh no – but he's my husband and I have to sleep with him.'

And then, as she notices his look of utter misery, his pallor, the catch in his throat as he orders two large whiskies from the hovering waiter in order simply to get rid of him (forgetting that neither of them drinks whisky), Audrey corrects her 'I have to . . .' with a few words which suddenly illuminate her new life and explain how she has kept her 'transparency', the radiant look of a girl raised in a greenhouse. Without a single embarrassing word, she tells how Johnny – of all the friends at the soirées in the studio the one she liked best – as a result of being wounded in the war, is incapable of making love. At night, he holds her in his arms and she falls asleep. Maximilian blurts out the question with a vehemence he would not have thought himself capable of.

'You mean he hasn't penetrated you?'

No sooner has he said the words than he looks at Audrey's angelic face and is filled with remorse for their appalling crudity; but she does not blush and seems to find Maximilian's question perfectly natural.

'No, the poor boy can't, although he makes me want him to. If you hadn't come back one day soon, I think I'd have given in to Ronnie or James.'

Simultaneous with the joy that overtakes him, which he knows he must at all costs not show, Maximilian cannot help thinking that seven days earlier, when he should have been planning to stay in New York for some weeks longer, he was seized by an irresistible desire to return to Europe as if he had a premonition of the dangers Audrey was exposed to. She is there next to him, so present that he begins to mistrust the reality of her. For example, he wishes she would perfume herself, but this is a detail she has always overlooked, and now he wishes he could smell her skin because he is convinced that this body, so young and so white, has a scent of its own that is far more attractive than any artifice. She is wearing nothing underneath her V-necked sweater, and although there is nothing consciously teasing about her, the triangle of white skin edged by the black wool is so candidly erotic that no man could resist the temptation to reach out and touch it with the tips of his fingers. Which he does. Audrey smiles. This is not the place, she says. They have waited twelve years, they can at least wait one more evening, and anyhow she wants him to take her to a small cinema in the Latin quarter to see a film by René Clair, *La Beauté du diable*, because, she explains, she is a great René Clair fan and has seen all his films but this one. Did she not come to Paris to cultivate herself? She wants to see everything, hear everything, understand everything. This avidity is, she concedes, very American, but then she is an American by her father and she has never lived outside Vermont – apart from the few months she spent in New York where her curiosity was awakened. In short, she is looking for a mentor and she wants Maximilian to be that person. Johnny and his friends are marvellous talkers, but they are only interested in themselves and live in their closed circle in Paris as they would live, utterly uninfluenced by it, in a small town in the United States. Maximilian enumerates his short-comings: apart from historical works he reads little, goes only to concerts to accompany a lady friend, and visits exhibitions only because he is well-known enough to be part of the smart set who are always invited to private viewings and because galleries and museums on opening days are pleasant places to meet people. Of course he is well-travelled and well-versed in Italy, Greece, Spain, Portugal, France and so on, but to be honest, this is partly because of a need to fill out dull conversations with people who continually bore him stiff with remarks like, 'What? You mean you've been to Madrid and not visited the Prado? What? Not seen the Carpaccios in the Accademia? And when you went to Leningrad before the war, you didn't rush straight to the Ermitage?'

'Audrey, your wish is my command. We'll go to museums together, to concerts, to Vézelay, to Mont-Saint-Michel, we'll walk around the

Tower of London behind a beefeater if you like; but you must promise me, you must swear on your honour that if one day we find ourselves standing looking at the sun setting over a red-tinged sea, you won't say, "Isn't that nice?" and that, in fact, you'll never say that about anything.'

'I swear it!'

'Good. Let's go and see *La Beauté du diable* – which is entirely inappropriate, because your beauty is the beauty of angels.'

'Even after I fall? After the sin.'

'You shan't fall. I shan't lay a finger on you.'

'Oh no, come on, that's not fair. When I've been waiting for you since I was eight?'

It would require a singular strength of mind to resist her. That night, having stayed in the cellar at the Club Saint-Germain until two o'clock, Audrey follows Maximilian to his apartment, and what she has been waiting for for twelve years, with an ingenuousness only just blunted by her existence in Paris among her band of friends, finally takes place. Women who love to the point of making themselves loved can shape their lovers to their own wills. Although in his fifties, Maximilian, in Audrey's inexperienced hands, becomes a young man once more. He suffers hope with a pounding heart again, buys modest chrysanthemums to decorate his apartment where before he was stupid enough to have nothing but orchids, and arranges to meet Audrey at métro stations, outside cinemas and in theatre foyers. They go to the Comédie Française to see Raimu play Molière and Jean Marais Racine, and they join the club of the film library where Joseph Kosma plays a piano accompaniment to the silent films. Audrey demands that they see *Paris qui dort* and *Le Sang d'un poète* five times. Their love manifests itself in a wild quest for all the things that thrill Audrey and which Maximilian enjoys as novelties.

And Johnny? He puts in very few appearances in the novel, although Audrey often refers to him in the way he drives her to her meeting places and sometimes even comes to fetch her in the morning after she has telephoned him. Maximilian, to begin with, is unperturbed. Love blinds him, making him think he has the better part of Audrey, her body, her gaiety, her passion; but blind love is as brief as summer lightning, and when reason gets the upper hand again – oh gently, very gently! – he thinks about Johnny more often and asks himself who really has the better part of Audrey? The lover, or the husband? He is not certain that he will be the eventual winner, and as the months pass, he becomes less and less certain. Johnny's discretion and self-effacement exasperate him. He wants to look forward to possessing Audrey for himself, but how can he dispute title to her with a co-operative ghost who, apart from anything else, often goes away on business, either back to America or to Milan where, in the La Scala library, he is working on a monumental history of Italian opera commissioned by a generous foundation in California. The work is a true Penelope's web, which Johnny takes great satisfaction in endlessly rewriting and expanding with new information. One day, by a subterfuge, Maximilian eventually catches sight of the mythical husband, who is neither the fair boy with the frizzy hair nor the tall, thin boy who bites his nails. Horribly wounded in the Rangers' assault on Omaha beach, Johnny must be nearing thirty, although he does not look his age. Maximilian is struck by the gentleness and character of the face. The blond beard is cut in Edward VII style and in the look beneath the thick eyebrows there is a charm so unassuming it is impossible to avoid it. How Maximilian did not pick him out from the other members of the little group in the studio is incomprehensible. The danger to Audrey could never have come from the other young Americans, all intoxicated by their pretentious aestheticism and their entry into the secret societies of expatriates in Paris, or Rome or London. She would not have given in to that, however seductive the men of her age might have been. What had happened was that she had given herself to the man whose character most nearly matched her own; and she confessed to Maximilian that she had done it to punish him for his affair with Mme de C. and his disappearance. The tenderness, their immense tenderness, had come later.

'When you leave me,' she says to Maximilian, 'I shall always have Johnny to take me in.'

Maximilian is clear-sighted enough to foresee that, of course, it will be she who leaves him and that he will have no one to shelter him from his renewed and inevitably hateful loneliness. In the meantime he prefers not to meet Johnny, and Johnny has the good manners to adopt the same attitude. There is no knowing how long this simultaneously comfortable and uncomfortable situation might have continued had Audrey not fallen ill. The Paris air has attacked her weak lungs. She agrees to leave for the mountains. The name of the place is not disclosed in the novel. Stanislas took great care, as we shall see, to jumble the images, suddenly becoming aware that he was copying too much from reality, that in the course of the narrative the distance between himself and Maximilian was being pared down to the point that, on certain pages, carried away by his own impulse, he was telling the story of Audrey, not in the third person, but in the first. The corrections he had to make are the only alterations on the manuscript, whose calligraphy is so perfect one would think he had made a fair copy of his draft. But of course the reality was not like that and we know that Stanislas always attributed the spontaneous generation of *Trust Me* and *Where Are You Dining Tonight?* to some sorcery on the part of the little girl from Stockwood.

When Maximilian learns that Audrey cannot live in Paris, he knows at once that it is over, he has lost her, and Johnny has won. In the capital Audrey and Johnny are invisible, lost in the crowd. In the mountains they will be constant objects of their neighbours' attention and it will be impossible to avoid Johnny. Maximilian will be able to spend only an occasional day or two close to her; they may be able to make love in a nearby hotel, if there is one: but these will be brief, stolen moments that will leave behind a gnawing taste of regret. If he were to implore her to stay in Paris, she would stay, but for several weeks now she has looked so pale and ill that even love-making fails to bring the colour back to her cheeks for long. Maximilian has foreseen the physical malaise which now takes hold of him and almost happily he acknowledges it: it is all true, he does love Audrey, he has not simply surrendered to the lures of young flesh. So like a young man of twenty he starts to keep a diary. An apocryphal diary, of course – he has to save face.

The final version of *Where Are You Dining Tonight?* does not contain the extracts from the diary attributed to Maximilian. When he re-read the manuscript, Stanislas saw in it a rupture of tone and even a faint implausibility. Instead of telling a story he was lending his own voice to the hero of the novel. However common it might be for a man who loves and is loved to exclaim ingenuously, 'My whole life is a novel!,' it was hardly in the character of Maximilian, who had only ever dictated business letters or reports on the running of the companies under his control. The author saw that the dividing-line between Maximilian and himself should never be crossed, and that to do so would be clumsy and unbalance the novel. Should we see in it a reflex motivated by reticence, a fear that he would be showing more of himself than he wanted to, in however fictionalized a form? Readers tend to identify the author with his hero so deeply that some sort of barrier has to be erected if he wants to avoid being misunderstood.

These pages from the diary which slow down the narrative present more interest for our knowledge of Stanislas Beren than does the novel itself, for all its accomplishment. Maximilian's cynicism at the beginning of the story gives way to the magic of a love to which he surrenders with a delicious abandonment. Afterwards he must suffer the heavy burden of melancholy, a form of despair attenuated by experience. Returning from a visit to Audrey, in the aeroplane bringing him back to France, Maximilian writes:

Between – and Paris,
15 April '53.

A man between the ages of forty-five and fifty-five (a vague manner of speaking which actually makes the man younger without implying that he is trying to conceal his age – nothing could be farther from the truth: he happily owns up to it on most occasions for the sake of our feigned amazement when he gives an exact number), a man who has dreamed many dreams in his life. Daydreams, and dreams at night asleep. From his daydreams he draws his sustenance; his dreams at night he remembers rarely, because he is too lazy to note them down. Yet one of his dreams has recurred often enough for him to remember it as if these images really belonged to the life he lives.

He is in a landscape, a nondescript sort of landscape; if one were to take a panoramic photograph of it, nobody would be able to identify it: some would say it was the Perche, some the Vosges or Normandy, others might – supposing they were reasonably well-travelled – situate its colours and contours in Derbyshire, or in Hessen or the canton of Vaud, or quite possibly in Vermont. The one thing our friend knows for certain is that every time he finds himself walking through this scene in his dream, the weather is fine, very fine. The hills, and the distant mountains capped with snow, are bathed in a cool light, and a blue breath of mist rises from the forests sheltered by the valleys. The fields are not enclosed, but they are not to be crossed unless there has been a frost and the furrows are still hard as stone. There are no hedges bordering any of the paths or small roads. Our hero has the impression that he is utterly exposed, visible to everybody, and yet the countryside is deserted, left to its own devices although men's work is certainly responsible for the way it looks. The season is not always the same, but by one or two signs it can be narrowed down to the middle of autumn (the orchards glutted with apples), or the beginning of winter or even shortly before spring. In winter he sees several half-frozen springs: a trickle of water makes a small hole in the icy surface of a grey stone trough used by the animals. Another day, the lucerne is growing steadily. It is not difficult to imagine these hills in summer, green to begin with, then gradually yellowing and turning russet. To say that there is nobody to be seen is not quite true: there are certainly very few cars, but there are tractors and here and there a farmstead, picturesque with its sloping roof and wooden balconies. Pine logs are stacked around the doors and judging by the size of the stacks it must be some time in winter. The charm of the scene is due, above all, to the beautiful light, the gardens exposed to the sun, well protected from the cold winds, and miraculously bursting with flowers. How? Or is it an illusion? In dreams everything is accepted, and our walker scorns the voice of the real world telling him over and over again that there are no flowers in winter apart from snowdrops and edelweiss. Disagreeably, but inevitably, the fields reek of fertilizer. The first reaction is one of sharp distaste, but as the walk progresses, the smell begins to have something quite pleasant and reassuring about it.

The man, nearer his sixties than his fifties, does not walk alone in this landscape, nor is his guide, who knows every small path and all the best short-cuts, unknown to him. Sometimes he turns his head to see her in profile, but only occasionally: he is afraid she might vanish in the cold air. Respecting her anonymity, he avoids looking at her, but listens closely to her voice and savours the slight accent. He has always loved accents: B.'s English, G.'s Spanish, even H.'s German and L.'s Creole. He has no hard and fast rules, having loved French women too, but he has a weakness for those who have difficulty saying r and u and remembering the gender of nouns. His companion on these country walks says nothing out of the ordinary, nothing earth-shattering. In fact, the thing she talks about most is how sad they will be when they part, which implies that they have spent several days together, perhaps several nights together under the same roof, and that this walk is unhappily the prelude to an imminent separation. They have many things to say to each other and do not say them. The dream has it that they are both, if not shy, at least reserved. And perhaps in their past they have exchanged the few words, the few clasped hands, the few looks which are enough to form a bond for life. It has become clear that they love one another and that the anguish of this walk fades away in the calm and limpid countryside, then returns as they get back to their starting-point. It is then that the man feels a lump in his throat and one single desire, to run away, so as not to have to see the tears in the steady blue gaze of his blonde companion, tears which will reassure him of the love he has been able, even at his age, to inspire, and which will plunge him into despair because the dream is coming to an end, because, in a moment, the deafening noise of the aeroplane's engines will drag him from his easeful sleep.

Even though his freedom is not as great as he could wish it, Maximilian does see Audrey again, not at her home, which he will never set foot in, but in the hotels of the two towns near the place in which she has sought refuge from her illness. Another passage cut from the final manuscript strikes this very Berenian note:

I must write a guide to hotel rooms. I shall be able to put a great deal of my experience into it, and few of the rooms will find any favour at all. Actually, I could get used to sleeping in them if I stayed for a long time, but I am a nomad and their ugliness and impersonality offend me before that can happen, even if they are occasionally dispelled by a naked body crossing from one side to the other wrapped in a bath towel. There is another hotel phenomenon which deserves a book, too – revolving doors. Perhaps I shall write a guide to the revolving doors of the great hotels and the women who pass through the glass as if by magic suddenly to materialize in all their beauty.

On another occasion, again on the flight back to France, Maximilian notes:

Between – and Paris,
16 May.

A letter I shall never finish: Do you remember the concert we went to, Beethoven's 3rd Piano Concerto played by Sviatoslav Richter? I was so taken by the music that I forgot your presence at my side. I could not even smell the scent of your skin that I love so much, and I did not even think to stretch my hand towards yours. When the last note was played and Richter stood up, with his customary stiffness, to acknowledge the applause, your presence was a genuine surprise, the loveliest surprise I could have hoped for as I came back to earth.

On the other hand, if you are not there with me, the music speaks only of you and I scarcely listen to it at all, deep instead in my memories of your face, your hands, your voice, your body.

The novel draws to its close. The distance – as much moral as physical – is too great. Both partners accustom themselves to the dreamy poetry of being apart, as the last paragraph quoted from the 'apocryphal diary' shows. There is thirty years' difference in age and several hours' flight between them. Audrey has always felt a great affection for Johnny, and because he knew, during the stormy days at the beginning, how to safeguard the serenity which placed his love for her above his own sensibility, she realizes that he is her true sanctuary in a life diminished by her illness. When they are alone together in their house in the country, she feels herself moving towards this man who shares her passion for music more than Maximilian can. In the mornings she plays for him, in the afternoons she helps him to organize his thousands of notes on Italian opera. With Maximilian she continues to sublimate her childish love, with Johnny she lives in the peace of the heart and, inevitably, the peace of the senses. Maximilian will always be the only man she has loved, and that certain knowledge is so untouched by changing fortunes that she has almost no need of him to nourish it. Neither will make any protest, both are conscious that the separations provide a kind of grace which lovers so often lack. Moreover, despite the precautions she has taken, despite the pure mountain air she breathes, Audrey can no longer conceal from herself that her health is deteriorating month by month. On some days she suffers extreme fatigue and can barely speak. The remissions become shorter and shorter. Johnny has to bear the cruel irony: when she is exhausted, Audrey belongs to him; when she revives, she telephones Maximilian and he comes to her. But little by little the lover's portion is whittled away by her illness. Neither really suffers; one cannot even be sure that Maximilian has noticed, until the day he arrives in the town where she normally meets him twenty-four hours earlier than he expected to, and goes to a concert. From the circle he notices Audrey and Johnny sitting in the stalls. Deaf to the performance of *Firebird* conducted by Markevitch, he observes the couple. It is the first time he has seen them together. Both are listening with intense concentration, but this concentration, in contrast to the way he had listened to Richter playing Beethoven, is not a case of each submerging himself, it is a delicious communion conveyed by an exchange of looks and, once, a tender gesture – Johnny lays his hand on Audrey's for a few seconds then takes it away as if not to influence her – and when the last bars of *Firebird* have died away, Maximilian knows by their behaviour that their union is perfect and that, for them, the entire hall packed with music lovers has ceased to exist. They do not applaud either, because what they have felt is beyond noisy enthusiasm.

Maximilian waits until all the other concert-goers have left, to make sure that he does not meet them in the foyer; then he walks the streets where the cinemas and bars are closing, disgorging onto the pavement a shivering crowd which hurries off to its warm apartments and rituals before bedtime. The great, heroic solution would be for him to make his way to the airport and take the first flight regardless of its destination. His desire to see Audrey one last time is stronger. He wants to kiss her fragile, now almost diaphanous, face without confessing anything of what he has seen. When he leaves her three days later, he is proud of having kept the secret; he feels almost happy to be going. They have walked in lovely forests of bare trees, crossed the lake in a paddle-boat to take a piping cup of tea in a small tea-shop whose waitress, dressed in national costume, bent low over their table to reveal a plunging view of her maternal, milky-white bosom; they have slept in the double bed in the hotel room in which Audrey, wrapped in a bath towel – more to hide her thinness than out of modesty – walks to and fro, dispelling, as always, the ugliness of the furniture, the gaudy, wine-coloured rug, the bad copies of Redouté's engravings of roses. He has held Audrey's hand at night and been hardly able even to doze, worried by the tremors she is sending through his own fingers, a coded message telling him of her dreams and of the exhausting struggle taking place in her body. On the last morning Audrey dresses slowly, moving around the room, and he says goodbye, his lips together, to all of her: her stomach, her legs, her breasts, her shoulders.

At the airport, when the loudspeaker announces his flight, he lingers one last time to taste the lips of the only woman who has inspired in him a love untainted by any vanity or boasting. Audrey's chin is trembling a little. Does she know too? The stewardess comes to fetch Maximilian and he has to walk quickly to catch up with the others; he turns round only once to see the bulky silhouette of Audrey in her fur coat, a silhouette which bears no relation to her own, so slim and so transparent. From his window seat in the aeroplane, he can still see her on the spectators' balcony where she stands shivering, the cold making her eyes water and the tears roll down her cheeks, although she is overcome by a mysterious sort of bliss as if the departure of her lover has detached her from everything. She waves, without seeing Maximilian but in the certainty that he will be sitting somewhere where he will be able to make her out in the crowd watching the take-off. This will be Maximilian's last memory of Audrey. When she goes home, having caught a chill from standing on the balcony whipped by an icy north wind, she will go to bed never to get up again.

Where Are You Dining Tonight? appeared in 1960, six years after the death of the woman we shall go on calling Audrey as the novel called her. We may safely leave it to the detectives and the forensic pathologists of literature to investigate her and find out her real name and where she lived. In which town, for example, did she meet Maximilian at the end of her life? Which hotel? The doctors' diagnosis will be published, and the exact date when, as they say, she breathed her last. Her letters and her juvenile poems will be published too. There will be photographs of her with her mother and father at Stockwood, a number of others showing the Ingleseys and the Berens together (in which Audrey does not feature because it was she who took them with a bellows camera which Félicité had given her). In all, there is only one snap to be found of her and Stanislas together, the work of one of those street photographers who tout for customers among the tourists at the Arc de Triomphe. Her beautiful blonde hair is flying in the wind which was blowing along the wide pavement that morning. She is in a dark suit and has slipped her arm into Stanislas'; she comes up to his shoulder. Stanislas is wearing a cap made of the same cloth as his jacket, a small-checked tweed. Although, curiously, there is a resemblance between them, no one looking at the photograph could mistake them for father and daughter: they are obviously lovers. Of course the indiscretion of literature's detectives and pathologists knows no bounds, and Johnny, now living in California where he is teaching the history of music at Berkeley, will be brought in for questioning. He will refuse to talk or to explain why he was so co-operative. He considers that no one would understand that he did it out of love. To know everything, the investigators would have to open Stanislas' heart with a scalpel, but this operation is not without its dangers when attempted on a living subject who will defend himself.

So then we have the witnesses. They were few. The lovers had conducted their affair in private. However, it is important not to wait too long to question those who knew, for they are, in general, older than Stanislas. The majority will probably keep their counsel. Stanislas himself will say nothing. Has he not written a *novel*? Can he not be left in peace? To make absolutely sure, he disappears the day the book appears in the bookshop windows. He has asked for a slip to be inserted in all the review copies: 'With the compliments of the author, at present out of Paris.' Stanislas has left on his last fugue. He is fifty-two years old, and no one supposes this time that he has returned to his childhood mountains, or simply gone to Venice or London. If we look further, we shall find him in Lisbon. He has found some old friends there, men known only to him, but all good drinking companions. Georges Kapsalis and Félicité are in Paris, Félicité at the Ritz – of course – in the room which is kept for her overlooking a small, walled garden. She receives her friends here, because for several days now walking has been so painful that she can only get about in a wheelchair. There will, in a month's time, be an improvement, and she will leave for Venice, against her doctor's advice. She is sixty-five, which is not the end of the world, but the mechanism is quite worn out, even though the spirit is still alive with a lightning wit belied by her semi-invalid state.

When I took her the first copy of *Where Are You Dining Tonight?*, Félicité pursed her lips as she weighed the book in her hands.

'Years, and days, and nights are reduced to three hundred grams of paper. It's an insult.'

She opened a page at random, put on her reading glasses, read a number of lines, then her bony index finger jabbed at a typographical error.

'Dear M. Dupuy would not have missed that. He will turn in his grave . . . I wonder what he would have thought of this novel?'

'Well, he was not an indulgent man, but I think he would have liked it.'

'He was a romantic, then.'

'A romantic with his fair share of sarcasm.'

'Anyhow, he knew what was what. Without him your little business wouldn't exist. . . .'

I was used to it: in her bad moods, she poured scorn on everything. But it is true that without Georges Dupuy I would certainly not, in my twentieth year, have taken over a 'little business' which was healthy, selective in what it published, and respected.

She had read the book in manuscript, and it was more than likely on her suggestion that Stanislas had not published the passages from his own diary under the pretence that they were Maximilian's writings. But she would only have suggested it to him, and now, with me standing there, she was reluctant to delve and see whether Stanislas had listened to her. Knowing her tricks, I let her turn the pages with an unconcerned air. She seemed relieved not to find any trace of what was worrying her.

'Will you leave me this copy?'

'I brought it for you.'

'The hotel porter is very anxious to read it. One of the gossip-writers is claiming that it is a *roman à clé*. No porter of any great hotel can afford not to be interested.'

I smiled.

'Why are you smiling?'

'Because I know you.'

Her fit of peevishness masked the emotion she felt at the appearance of each of Stanislas' books. She seemed to be musing again. 'A love story! In 1960! Stanislas is mad. I should have advised him not to publish it.'

'It's not just a love story, it's the story of a particular love.'

'A pretty nuance, but I know where you got it from. You've been walking around with Nimier's book in your hand for a week: *Histoire d'un amour*. . . . But you never knew this . . . what did he call her? Ah, yes . . . Audrey. Did you know Audrey?'

'I caught sight of her once.'

'An adorable child. She was terrifying: so much of a woman at eight years old that one wondered what kind of a dance she'd be leading men at twenty.'

'She didn't lead any man a dance.'

Félicité never listened when one contradicted her.

'I don't know,' she said, 'what Stanislas saw in her. Oh, her hair was lovely, her eyes a disturbing blue. But her voice . . . so little-girlish! As if she hadn't grown up. A good pianist, even so. Uncomfortable as soon as she got away from Ravel and Debussy. As I say, she just hadn't grown up! They had dinner with Léautaud one evening: he looked at Audrey's bosom – I think he even hooked his finger inside her blouse to judge better – and said with disgust, "No breasts at all." They say he then spat in his plate, the old lecher. It reminds me of a Félicien Marceau novel where the father gives his son a piece of advice: "Never marry a woman without a decent bosom. At forty, life will seem like a desert to you."'

She clapped the book's cover with the palm of her hand. 'So miracle cures still happen, do they, and now we have Audrey changed into a tender and true-hearted girl. Literature is wonderful isn't it? Anyhow, I hope you'll sell a few copies. . . .'

'Twenty or thirty thousand. . . .'

'Who is going to read it? Stanislas always preferred to keep himself hidden. This book is quite shameless.'

She must have seen that she had upset me, cut me to the quick. The novel was very close to my heart, as well as being the first book by Stanislas that I had published since Monsieur Dupuy had died.

'Don't look so long-faced! I didn't say it was not a fine book. I simply didn't like his model and, after all, don't I have every right not to?'

Had she felt threatened by Audrey? I don't believe so. The novel gives no inkling of the existence of a wife, and Maximilian, apart from his passionate entanglement with a certain Mme de C., is a free man. Stanislas enjoyed about the same amount of freedom as his *alter ego*, with the exception that he had not brought Audrey into any of the circles which were connected with Félicité. The latter had few grounds for complaint: he had always respected her, and when he came to tell the story of his secret life, he had done it behind the mask of the all-embracing novel. Félicité had shaped her philosphy a long time before: her attitude to Stanislas had nothing to do with resignation. And Johnny's treatment of Audrey was no different: he was convinced, at the beginning at least, before she fell ill, that his wife would come back to him. Félicité had never doubted that Stanislas would come back to her either. And against that terrible strength, all third parties, lovers and mistresses, are powerless.

I heard, the same day, a quite different version of Audrey. Georges Kapsalis came into the offices in the late afternoon to collect a copy of the book. I took him down to the Flore, just for the pleasure of sitting facing the door at the same table where Maximilian waits for Audrey. Together we read the page describing her entrance. The rain was lashing the boulevard Saint-Germain as it had done in the novel. A girl came in, in a raincoat and blue beret, which she immediately took off, freeing a mass of blonde hair. Her face, pink with cold, lit up in a radiant smile as she noticed, by the table nearest the cashier, a black boy with long eyelashes.

'I didn't find Audrey as beautiful as Stanislas makes her out to be,' said Georges Kapsalis. 'We dined together on two occasions and one evening I found myself sitting behind them at a concert. I must have been staring very hard at the back of her neck, because she turned round and smiled at me. It was a charming smile, I remember . . . like the smile of the girl in the raincoat and beret who has just come in. Frankly, I don't want to be unkind, but she seemed banal to me, one of those averagely beautiful girls America is so good at, the twenty-year-old Shirley Temple type. Audrey had a prettier nose, I suppose. But what captivated me about her was her voice. She must have got it from her mother, who was a soprano as you probably know. An exquisite sound. Often we think we know a woman by her eyes or the shape of her lips. One's picture of Audrey – she didn't speak very much and you had to guess at her personality – came from her voice. If these glasses were crystal, I could give you its exact tone by tapping one with my finger. As soon as one had that note, one conjured up a picture of her transparency. Stanislas used that word several times when he described her in the novel. Yes, "transparent" like crystal, that's the word. The first time I saw her I told myself that I would not have paid her any attention had I not known that she was Stanislas' new mistress. But the second time I could not take my eyes off her, despite there being three other ravishing women present at the same dinner; that was the evening she played a difficult sonata by Debussy, and with a brio which was disconcerting, coming from a woman who was not a virtuoso. I suppose that having inherited her mother's voice, she had inherited her father's talent too. You'll tell me that she might have played the piano as well as her mother painted – I'm very suspicious of naïve painters, so often they turn out not to be naïve at all! – and she might have sung like her father who had the worst voice in the world. But she was lucky: the genes made no mistakes and she got the best of both her parents. I often wonder what would have happened if she had lived. Thirty years' age difference, it's a big gap. It doesn't really matter at twenty and fifty, but by the time she was forty, she would have been celebrating Stanislas' seventieth birthday.

'There was an odd thing about that husband of hers. A year or two ago, I read an article in an American magazine: a man called Johnny Smith, or Brown, I don't remember – and maybe it was a namesake of his, in any case – was accused of indecent behaviour with some young boys in a college where he taught music. Stanislas might have thought it was kinder to portray him as impotent than as a paedophile. The point about that is that the novelist claims all sorts of licence for himself, and has every right to. . . .'

The girl with the blue beret stood up and put her raincoat on. Her friend followed her and they walked out, to return almost immediately: the handsome black boy with the curled eyelashes did not want to get wet. Their table had already been taken and they came and sat down next to us, face to face. They were American: he had a deep, bass voice, she a trace of Irish in her accent. At one point their hands joined in mid-air above the table, a soulful interlacing of long black fingers with mauve nails and short white fingers, plump and pretty.

'That,' said Georges Kapsalis, 'is no odder than Audrey's love for Maximilian.'

*

We parted a little later. With his book tucked beneath his arm, he took cover under a black umbrella with an engraved silver handle. I had not argued with his portrait of Audrey. I had heard two different opinions in the same day. Neither satisfied me. In fact, I had lied – a harmless lie – to Félicité Beren when I pretended only to have caught sight of Audrey once. One morning Stanislas was waiting at the school gate to take me to lunch. Next to him stood a girl, or young woman, in a beige coat, with a funny little hat on her head, a sort of toque of brown velvet pinned in place on top of a mass of blonde hair wound into a chignon. On her arm there hung a leather case like the cases musicians use to carry their scores. I thought she was pretty, no more; but she was so young, and her extreme youth – accentuated by the difference in age between her and Stanislas – dazzled me, sparkling like a divine gift, sweeping notions of beauty aside, making me oblivious to the un-fathomable blue of her eyes or the harmony of her pale face and blonde hair. She was so *young*. She made me think of a Nattier, and in particular very much of the portrait of the duchess of Chartres.

We lunched in a Chinese restaurant in the rue Monsieur-le-Prince. Audrey had a wonderful time eating with chopsticks while Stanislas and I had to beg some forks from the waiter. If her voice was little-girlish or like the tinkle of crystal, I would have noticed it, but I have no memory of it, although I can however remember the question she asked me about my philosophy year, about music, about what I was reading. I seem to remember – despite what Stanislas might have said in the novel, which is largely invalidated by the extract from the unpublished diary, in any case – I seem to remember that she had a slight accent and that two or three times she used anglicisms which neither of us felt any urge to correct. Contrary to those women who are duly briefed by their lovers to conquer their best friends, Audrey attempted nothing of the kind and I instantly liked her, from that first and only meeting, for her naturalness, and the way she put herself on an equal footing – as if we had known each other for ever – with a boy whom she considered as old as herself, or nearly so. Her music-case, containing the Scarlatti scores she was studying at the time with Marcelle Meyer, corresponded to my schoolboy's carpet-bag, stuffed with books, battered and frightful. At the end of lunch I had the impression that we had forgotten Stanislas, but he had not been excluded by us, he had excluded himself, withdrawn into a reverie the reason for which was easy to guess. Would Audrey and I pass our mutual test? She passed it very well as far as I was concerned and, some days later, Stanislas told me I had got 'good marks' from Audrey. All in all, the impromptu lunch was a success and I got back to the *lycée* in time for the afternoon classes feeling reflective and vaguely emotional. Because of Félicité, and although she was fully aware of the double life he was leading, Stanislas could neither be seen in public with Audrey, nor take her to visit Félicité's friends. Or perhaps he felt happier as he was, having her all to himself: he was making enough of a sacrifice already, with her going back to Johnny the moment he left her. Or, then again, he might have felt a need to make sure there would be witnesses who, one day, would swear that Audrey had existed. Years later – it was after Félicité's death – when we were walking along the quai Anatole-France, we passed beneath the windows of her old studio. Stanislas caught me by the arm and pointed to the bay on the top floor. 'She did exist, you know she did,' he said to me. 'You saw her, you have the proof.' The proof! As if he now doubted it, because his beloved Audrey had been dead for twenty years. The news had reached him in the spring in Cannes where he was heading the jury at the Film Festival. He had stuffed the telegram into his pocket and watched the screening of the next entry without saying a word.

Three months after Audrey's death, the *Paris Review* published an article about her. Its author, Peter Kilroy, had been part of the small group of dogged would-be artists in the studio. The group had split up after Audrey had left Paris. Several of its members had gone back to America. Others had drifted on to Italy and Greece and could not bring themselves to leave old Europe, imagining hopefully that these countries would one day bestow on them a talent which, for the moment, eluded them. Today Peter Kilroy is the only one who enjoys any reputation, from his first, savagely funny book *Did Eleanor Eat Franklin?*, a merciless satire on a rapacious widow who, out of a thirst for his legacy, casts a veil over her husband's infidelities. In 1954 Kilroy was writing for the *New Yorker* and it was he who opened doors for Stanislas and introduced him to the very closed circle of that magazine. The portrait of Audrey in the *Paris Review* suffered from too turgid a style. When I told him so, some years later in New York, Kilroy confessed that 'it was an exercise in style. I am more at ease being nasty about people than I am being poetic about them. I haven't repeated the experience. But my old friends enjoyed the piece, you know.' Nevertheless, Audrey was instantly recognizable, just as she must have appeared to those young people avid for ideas and excitement: a fairy sister, an idealized mediator between them and the talents they pursued. One detail, however, was disturbing: Kilroy gave Audrey green eyes and auburn hair, while everyone else agreed that she was a porcelain blonde with blue eyes. Likewise, he claimed that she only liked playing Satie, and that one only needed to hear *The Three Distinguished Waltzes of the Offended Dandy* to bring her instantly to mind. Even if everyone was agreed on her talent as a pianist, it seemed that each had his own idea on the composers she interpreted with the greatest fervour. From Scarlatti to Satie there is an enormous range, and it is possible that she had a series of passions, each of which ruled her briefly, for one or another of these composers. We should add one other curious note: in 1970, two theses were presented, one at the Sorbonne, the other at the University of Indiana, on women characters in Stanislas' work. Pierre Levy in Paris states that Audrey died in Switzerland and that Maximilian used to meet her in Lugano, while Thomas O'Brien's conclusion was that she had returned to America and was living in Sun Valley. What had given them grounds for such certainty? When he read the two theses, Stanislas said to me, with an expression of mock dismay, 'Soon Audrey will be buried under a pile of errors and misconceptions. The truth is so much simpler.'

Faced with so many disputed facts, the wisest course is to rely on the portrait in the novel. There, sheltered from false witnesses, Audrey has won a reprieve from obscurity and will continue to live as long as Stanislas is read. Like Sosius proclaiming that 'The true Amphitryon – Is the Amphitryon where one dines', the true Audrey is the Audrey that Stanislas, alias Maximilian, loved. The one weakness of the book is the character of Maximilian. Preoccupied with not putting himself on show in any way, Stanislas has overworked the hero's character so that the reader is not tempted to confuse him with the author. The drawbacks are obvious. Stanislas is not, for example, at his ease when he talks – as he has to, despite its minor importance – about Maximilian's professional life. We guess he is a currency dealer, but no man in that profession has ever more than minutes to spare, nor has he Maximilian's free spirit. Stanislas is vague on this point for the simple reason that he had never taken any notice of exchange dealings and had not bothered to inform himself. He constructed a character, with paste and scissors, who is amusing but often appears in an unpleasant light. The origins of his hero are left a mystery. He makes a brief entrance in his forties, then we lose sight of him for a time and meet up with him again when he has turned fifty and Audrey is twenty. He is careless, cynical, sure of himself, judging that when pleasure is past, the greatest compliment one can pay a woman is to leave her in as little time as it has taken to seduce her. How, then, has this man who detests chains, let himself be bound to Mme de C. who exercises a purely physical attraction over him? When he is finally cured of this woman (who is not even fond of him) and can at last love Audrey, he falls into the much worse trap of a love condemned to brevity, and the knowledge of this brings on a mood of melancholy which is somehow incompatible with the character described at the beginning of the book. Equally surprising is the way Maximilian's reaction to the death of Audrey is glossed over – just as Stanislas shrank from showing any reaction in his own life. He only talked about it when forced to, because someone mentioned Audrey in front of him, or in an unguarded moment, as he had done on the quai Anatole-France when we were walking underneath the windows of her old studio, and on one other occasion, in Spain, at Ampurias. But then what are we to make of his abrupt flight in 1960, when the novel appeared?

*

Where was he? Although used to his disappearances by now, Félicité was beginning to worry when chance came to our aid. In our *Crime Pays* collection, still in the hands of Maurice Humez, by now in his eighties, we had a young Portuguese author much liked by Stanislas. Mario Mendosa turned out two detective novels a year for us, earning enough money to get by in Lisbon and lead the café life he enjoyed, and enjoys still, because it is in Lisbon's dark and decrepit cafés that its poetry and prose are born, around marble tables ringed with brandy stains and in the acrid smoke of cigarillos. It seems that Mario's early life had been very dramatic. People said – but what won't people say to while away the early hours? – that when he was sixteen he had been detained for armed robbery and when he was twenty he had killed a man. After a year in custody he had been tried, and eventually acquitted on the grounds of insufficient evidence despite the judges' and jury's conviction that he was guilty. In prison, Mario had been assigned to the library where he had swept up and stuck labels on the books. To begin with, he had been able to sort and stick a hundred labels a day. Towards the end, he was down to one a day: the rest of the time he read. Not just anything, but Camoëns' *Lusiads*. What had happened inside his head, left untouched for years? How was Camoëns' lyricism, his erudition and his nostalgic sense of greatness, able to seduce a young man who was not only withdrawn, but as secretive and devious as most convicts are, seeing enemies everywhere? Out of prison, he had continued to read, learnt French and begun a novel which revealed his intimate knowledge of Lisbon's low life. When it was published the book had immediately been translated into French for our collection. Maurice Humez held quite rightly that Mario Mendosa had something more than a hack writer of detective novels. In each of his books – we had just published the fourth – it was Lisbon which was the central character, a 'sad city teeming with life', according to the verse of Armindo Rodriguès. Mario loved his city so passionately and so single-mindedly that when we invited him to Paris he showed no interest in any aspect of the French capital. After a week we had to put him on a train back to Lisbon, and we said goodbye on the station platform to a happy man anticipating the reunion with his city and his friends, a small group of intellectuals among whom he enjoyed an ill-won but definite prestige. He was supposedly preparing, in secret (although it was no secret to any of his friends who were treated to countless references to it idly inserted into the conversation), an epic poem to the glory of Lisbon, a modern version of the *Lusiads* which had so changed his life when he read it in prison.

It was a not insignificant part of Mendosa's admiration for Camoëns that they were both blind in one eye, with the exception that the author of the future verse epic on Lisbon had lost his eye in a street brawl which had turned nasty. The appearance of the 'new' Camoëns was rather sinister. When his trial was over, he decided to wear nothing but black, and now dressed in suits of such shiny material that in the dim lighting of the cafés they took on a greenish hue. Even his threadbare shirts, whose frayed collars he patched himself, were grey rather than white and in place of a tie he knotted about his neck an old and crumpled velvet ribbon. He was tall and thin, and when his long bony feet were made even longer by his down-at-heel boots, he seemed to have trouble walking in any other way than a waddle, the waddle of a duck hiding premature baldness beneath a black Homburg. There is little to say about his face apart from the fact that it inspired about as much gaiety as his dress. With his sallow complexion and coal-black eye (the other covered by a smoked monocle), his silent presence was as solemn as an undertaker's, but once he had the floor a sort of genie possessed him, nourished by a vocabulary at the same time pedantic and slangy. He had an amazing repertoire of stories which, told in the low and shushing tones of his sonorous voice, sounded all the more outlandish. Stanislas had met him in Paris where we had, inevitably, spent long hours at the Rendez-vous des Amis, much longer hours than at the Louvre or the theatre.

Just as we were despairing of ever finding out where Stanislas had taken refuge from his book I was summoned by a short and urgent note from Mario Mendosa: 'He is here!' he wrote. 'You must come quickly!' Mario was waiting for me when I stepped off the 'plane, and as I presented my passport I could see his head above the crowd milling around the doors to the arrivals lounge. His Homburg was raised in recognition, uncovering his shining scalp. Stanislas, after spending several days in one of Lisbon's luxury hotels, had moved out to a slum in the Alfama quarter where he was drinking so heavily that Mario and his friends were beginning to worry. We took a taxi as far as the foot of Saint George's castle. From there we had to walk, up narrow, stepped streets, in a heat which seemed scorching to me. The air was laden with the pleasant smell of grilled sardines, and barefoot children ran round our legs continuously, throwing metal quoits at each other which jangled as they bounced down the steps, watched by the women sitting in the shade of their porches, sewing or pounding garlic in wooden mortars. Getting off a 'plane and finding myself only a few minutes later walking through narrow streets accompanied by a man in black was so unreal that for a moment my reason for being there was forgotten. Alfama smelt of spices – saffron and pepper – and fried fish, and here and there, more pungent than anything else, the oily water which the women emptied into the gutters. I was blinded by the glaring furnace-whiteness of the houses studded with brightly-coloured patches in their windows. Mario exchanged greetings with the few men we came across: all in shirt-sleeves, carrying their jackets over their shoulders and, in the other hand, an umbrella, or a toothpick with which its owner would absent-mindedly attack his gums. We came out onto a small square just below the stone plateau which raises the castle up above the city, red and honey-coloured as if it were ablaze in the dazzling light. Mario, who had barely said a word, pointed his finger at a sign-board: 'Pensaō Amanda – Comodidades', in front of a house a little better cared-for than the others with tubs of pink geraniums on wrought-iron balconies. A Virginia creeper climbed around the doorway. The door was open on an entrance hall which was shrouded in complete darkness. Mario clapped his hands and something moved at the far end of the hall, an amorphous black mass which, as our eyes adjusted to the darkness, we could make out to be a woman sitting in a creaking armchair, probably made of cane. Her hands, forearms and calves appeared to us slowly out of the dark shadows that still obscured the body to which they were attached.

'Senhora Amanda!' said Mario imperiously.

An unexpectedly childish and simpering voice – or perhaps she was speaking in an affected way, taken by surprise in the middle of her siesta – answered, 'Oh, it's you Senhor Doutor!'

She rose clumsily to her feet and walked towards us in the narrow corridor where she had been dozing, keeping one eye on the comings and goings of her lodgers. Walking is perhaps an exaggeration. She gave more the impression of rolling between the damp walls which contained her. On the doorstep of her *pension* the Senhora Amanda was finally revealed, and although I was left in no doubt that she had once been a splendid woman, from the jaded beauty of her black velvet eyes and her voluptuous mouth with its finely rolled lips and magnificent teeth, it was obvious that age and dropsy had taken their toll.

'We've come to see the Frenchman,' said Mario.

She raised her enormous forearms in a gesture which might have been interpreted either as impotence or despair.

'Senhor Maximilian has gone, two days ago. He left his suitcase. He has not paid his bill.'

She groped in the pocket of her apron, in search of a piece of paper which did not seem to be there.

'Concha!' she shouted in her shrill voice.

A small girl that we had not noticed, hidden behind the cane chair, appeared with the bill in her hand. I paid the twelve hundred escudos. Mario had said nothing to me about Stanislas calling himself Maximilian. Why had he taken so much trouble to differentiate himself from the hero of *Where Are You Dining Tonight?* and then assumed his name in a country and city where, apart from Mario Mendosa and one or two intellectuals, he was totally unknown? Senhora Amanda showed us the stairs and where to find room 3. It was unbearably dismal. There were two suits lying on the floor, stained and crumpled. Dirty washing spiled out of the bowl on the washstand and the 'comodidades' turned out to be a jug and bowl in flaking enamel standing on a slab of rough marble, with a soap dish and a towel full of holes. The quilt had been pulled up over the unmade bed.

We threw the belongings into the suitcase. Downstairs, Senhora Amanda wanted to apologize. The room was not her neatest and tidiest one. She found it so hard to climb the stairs with her swollen legs. Without warning, modesty was abandoned and she lifted her skirt halfway up her thighs, uncovering a mass of purplish flesh.

'I haven't said anything to the police,' she said. 'What shall I say to him if he comes back?'

'Tell him I came to pick up his things. But he won't come back.'

'Such a nice man!'

Mario shrugged his shoulders and we went back down from Alfama to where the taxi was waiting.

'It'll be difficult,' muttered Mario; 'but you can't lose your temper with that old whore, she doesn't know a thing.'

'She's not a whore, is she?'

'Not any more, but she was once. Her man's in and out of prison all the time. The police keep an eye on her.'

'So they'll have been keeping an eye on Stanislas too?'

'Maybe. Unless he's given yet another name. Maximilian von Arelle! What kind of a name is that to invent?'

'It's the name of the main character in his latest novel.'

'I haven't read it.'

'I've brought you a copy.'

★

Mario and I met again that evening before dinner, in a café on the praça dos Restoradores. Two of his friends were listening to him telling a story; I assumed he was talking about Stanislas because he stopped as I came nearer, but not before I had time to notice that his face was animated by an excited expression which I had not seen before. The two men had already been told the whole story. One was a poet whose name I have forgotten, the other a police inspector, also a poet in his off-duty hours. In an eating-house which smelt so foul it was almost impossible to draw breath, we ate a marvellous grilled *emperador*. We talked, not about Stanislas, but about poetry. The three men knew everything, were continually on the look-out for news of a new poet, anywhere in the world and however minor he or she might be, inquisitive in a way it is impossible to imagine in France, where poetry is exclusively the province of self-important cliques. From time to time Mario winked his good eye at me. It was obvious that he was out to impress me, but at the same time we were not losing sight of our target. They left me at the entrance to the hotel and Mario muttered in the direction of my ear, 'We're looking for him. The chances are good.'

I spent the next three days taking my mind off my anxiety by walking around the city, sometimes on my own, sometimes in the company of Mario Mendosa who appointed himself my mentor. We tasted fried cod washed down with *vinho verde*, and Mario knew dozens of places where, according to him, the madeira and port were incomparable if they were drunk in the right frame of mind – and there were always friends to be found in these places. I was amazed to find so many poets in Lisbon, as against the small number of novelists. Mario was proud to be able to introduce 'his' French publisher. They had all met Stanislas at least once or twice since he had arrived in Portugal, and they were at a loss to understand why this author who was so well-known under his real name now insisted on being called Maximilian von Arelle. Did he drink? Yes, a great deal, they said, and more than once Mario and his friends had had to escort him back to his hotel and hand him over to the porter to look after him, and later to the *pension* where they had had to carry him upstairs and see him to his bed.

'It's been good for him,' Mario said. 'He was a man who needed to liberate himself.'

To liberate himself from what? I was eager to solve the mystery even though it was inevitable that Stanislas would eventually give up and go back to Félicité in Paris. On the third day the porter gave me an envelope containing a piece of paper tablecloth on which the inspector-poet had written: 'Posada de Lord Byron, Sintra.'

*

The *posada*, below the road to the old royal palace, was a pretty-looking and well-proportioned house at the bottom of a vale where the magnolias with their waxy leaves, the camellias with their red, ruby-coloured and white flowers and the mimosas with their withered clusters proliferated in a riot of foliage, covering everything and threatening even the house, overflowing onto the verandahs and coming in through the windows unchecked by the owner, an old English woman with carefully curled white hair. The contrast between Mrs Simpson (no connection with the morganatic duchess) and the Senhora Amanda was so striking that it brought a smile to Mario Mendosa's baleful face. Mrs Simpson seemed delighted to see us, as if she had been waiting for us for some time.

'Did you find his suitcase at the airport?'

This was probably how he had explained his arrival without any luggage, and Mrs Simpson immediately assumed that we worked for the airline which had supposedly lost his suitcase. Her delight at our appearance was such that it prevented her from answering our initial questions, and it was only after she had brought us a tray of tea with sugared eggs – a Sintra speciality – and *torradas* grilled to perfection that she seemed to begin to understand our interest in Stanislas. She, like Senhora Amanda, called him Maximilian von Arelle. Yes, a charming man, a man of great erudition. He knew everything about Byron's residence in Sintra and could recite page after page of *Childe Harold*, which was begun in this very house that had now become a *posada*. He spent his days walking in the park at La Pena, had a slice of toast and ham and a cup of tea for dinner, then sat up until the early hours reading in an armchair next to a wood fire, for the days here in Sintra might be very hot, but that is of little help when the nights are cool and the damp air from the forest lies like a blanket over the house, making the windows and walls stream with water the next morning.

'I had to take him into town, to a gentleman's outfitters, so that he could buy himself a pair of trousers and some shirts and a sweater to keep him going until his suitcase was found. He's really rather an overgrown child, I'm afraid. . . .'

The Senhora Amanda must have seen him in a somewhat different light.

'He insisted on me calling him Maximilian and he calls me Dolly . . . that's my first name, although I don't look a bit like a doll. . . . He shouldn't be long, unless he's got lost like he did yesterday . . . oh, I do hope he doesn't try to carry out his idea of spending a night in the Capuchin monastery. . . . It's an absolutely sinister place, but he seems to be irresistibly drawn to it. He assures me that if he spends a night there, in the cork-lined grottoes where those poor souls used to live, he will be able to share their dreams. One wonders what kind of dreams the Capuchins can have had . . . well, I suppose Catholics are like that!'

'They used to dream about beautiful, naked girls with plenty of flesh on them, and cream cakes and roaring fires,' said Mario.

Mrs Simpson gave an embarrassed giggle.

'I should never have thought you the sort to make jokes, Mr . . . Mr . . .?

'Mario Mendosa.'

'And what do you do at the airport?'

'Madam, I am a poet and novelist.'

She seemed surprised that a man with one eye could write.

'Doesn't that bother you?' she asked, pointing at her own eye.

'No more than it bothered Camoëns.'

'Oh, yes . . . and Cervantes.'

'No, not Cervantes, he lost a hand. It's true it was his left hand.'

'Hmm, that must have been very awkward. . . . And what about you, do you write too?'

'No, I'm a publisher. In fact, I'm your lodger's publisher.'

'Oh dear, how extraordinary. We're completely at cross purposes. We're talking about two different people. Baron von Arelle is a currency-dealer. . . .'

'In his spare time maybe . . . the rest of the time he is a writer, I assure you.'

'Well, he's a dark horse . . . and here's me taking you for airport or customs people. . . .'

I decided not to trouble her any further. I also felt sure that it would not be a good idea to bump into Stanislas as we left. We could count on Mrs Simpson to tell him that we had called, and would call again the following day at about the same time. Should he not want to see us, he would have plenty of time to get away and find himself another refuge. I left an envelope with about a thousand francs in escudos in it, in case he had run out of money. Mrs Simpson was sorry, and were we sure we did not want to stay for dinner? Mario had understood and made our excuses: we were to have dinner in Lisbon.

It was impossible to turn on the narrow road cut into the hillside which led down to the *posada* at the bottom, and we had to go back up to the paço de Sintra. The coaches were taking on their last batch of tourists and the pedlars were packing up their cheap souvenirs: dolls of Ribatejan *campinos*, *minhote* peasant women and Nazarré fishermen, models of the local horse-drawn carts, gingerbread donkeys and corn-dolly charms. Sintra was returning to normal. From the forest, drifting into sleep, there rose the blueish mist which would soon descend on the valley. I was about to turn the car around when Mario stopped me, putting his hand on the steering-wheel.

'There he is! He looks better.'

Stanislas was crossing the square a few yards away from us, just as Mrs Simpson had described him, in corduroy trousers and shirt-sleeves, a sweater knotted around his waist. I had never seen him with a walking-stick before. This one was more of a knotted cudgel, like the kind a herdsman will hurl, boomerang-style, at the head of a stray bull. The massive handle was drilled and threaded with a leather strap which he had wrapped around his wrist. He must have bought it from one of the pedlars on the square outside the castle. It was in Sintra that he adopted the habit of carrying a walking-stick. Later on, in London and Venice, he had a stand full of them and never went out without choosing one which matched his mood. His sticks were not used to help him in walking, but he liked to stop and rest his weight on his 'wooden leg'. In fact, the main function of his sticks was to provide a rhythm for his inner voice, and often as I waited for him in a garden or park in Paris (he liked to arrange to meet in such places), I could tell his mood at a distance merely by the way he was holding his stick. When he re-appeared in Paris, the new habit gave rise to one or two rumours: he had had a skiing accident (he didn't ski), fallen from a horse (he didn't ride), was suffering from arthritis or rheumat-ism (he never had either). No – his sticks were toys to him, and something which satisfied his passion for collecting: going into bric-à-brac shops, spotting a gold, ivory or silver handle, then seeking out a craftsman who had stocks of malacca, bamboo, hazel, oak or ebony. And had he suddenly tired of his walking-sticks he would have had to answer for it to the photographers. Edouard Boubat de-manded a stick for the photograph he published of him in *Miroirs, autoportraits*;[1] and when Marcel Jullian launched his charming *Idée fixe*,[2] an open invitation to authors of all kinds to confess their ob-sessions, Stanislas suggested that he contribute fifty pages on his walking-sticks. The idea amused him but was destined to remain just an idea. Or perhaps he had the feeling that he had said most of what there was to be said in a letter he wrote me from London on the subject:[3]

[1] Denoël, 1973.
[2] Plon.
[3] 1 July 1976.

Collecting canes is no odder than collecting stamps. A stick gives one bearing. I do not like hands in pockets or women without hats. Coco Chanel used to wear a straw hat when she was in the bath. Perhaps that is going a little far, but she definitely had the right idea. Just suppose the plumber had barged in without knocking to mend a tap? Well, I share the same apprehension. Should some Sganarelle or other slander me, what am I to do? Hand me my cane and I can give him a beating, the sovereign remedy. And people have been driving asses with sticks since antiquity. That is the impulse behind Aristophanes, behind Molière, behind Goldoni and Marivaux. Not to mention all those minor playwrights. Nadar used to photograph his contemporaries cane in hand: Barbey d'Aurevilly, Emile Augier, even that marvellous clown of an anarchist Mikhail Bakunin. There is Boni de Castellane's very pretty cane, the more solid canes of Flaubert and Apollinaire, and General Leclerc's too. And what do you think all those crutches in Dali's paintings signify? They are canes, of course. Dali never walks anywhere without his cane. Have a good look at Van Dyck's Charles I, and Rigaud's Louis XIV and you'll see: both have canes. Note, however, that they are both holding them in their sword hands, Louis XIV in his left, Charles I in his right. You remember the story of Lauzun in a fury, breaking his sword in front of Louis XIV and saying, 'Never in my life shall I serve a prince who betrays his promises so shamelessly.' Louis raised his cane, then, thinking better of it, opened a window and threw it out with the words, 'I should be too vexed with myself if I struck a gentleman.' God does not use a cane, but his bishops are instructed not to show themselves in public without their crosiers. I shall not lack for material if I ever write a study of the habit.

So he developed this habit in Sintra, quite by chance, in the idleness of days when anything was worth trying if it helped to bury the bitter memories which had come crowding back when *Where Are You Dining Tonight?* was published.

He walked by the car without paying any attention to us, absent, perfectly at ease with himself as people are when they have been through a stormy internal struggle. Whenever he returned, calm again, from one of his fugues, he liked to say, 'I have come back from a long way off. I could not see myself any longer. The reconciliation was difficult, but you know how it is: old couples like me always end up getting back together again. The fear of emptiness, or the fear of adventure, always gets the better of our temptations. But there is no need to preach to oneself; it is only with oneself that one is really at ease. I am against the kind of divorce which separates a man from himself. As long as we can show ourselves a little indulgence, then we can rest content with ourselves.'

At Sintra, the excesses of the last two weeks had left no mark. Once more I admired his physical resilience. He had certainly grown thinner, but it was the kind of thinness which makes the body lean and hard. I thought I could hear him repeating the words he used when he came back from one of the long walks he used to take in all three cities – London, Paris, and Venice – whenever he was not up in the mountains.

'I feel purified! I have burnt up my alcohol, coughed out my nicotine, eliminated my cholesterol and my toxins, emptied my brain of all its polluting vapours. I am a new man.'

Then he would pour himself a glass of whisky and light a cigar, and at lunch he would eat like a horse, drink several cups of coffee and an armagnac or a plum brandy from the supply sent every month by a reader in Switzerland – even if all this indulgence meant going for another long walk in the afternoon or to the gymnasium where he would follow a routine of (fairly) violent exercise, steam bath, cold plunge, and massage. More than a healthy state of tiredness, he sought in these long walks an outlet for the feelings which nagged at him.

'I should never have been a writer . . . I should have been a country postman, a hundred years ago when they did not even have bicycles. Ten leagues a day encouraged a man to sound thinking, schooled him in a huge range of human experience. The country postman bore the news of births and marriages and deaths. He pestered the widows, advised the widowers, influenced the elections. He lived to a ripe old age, steeped in wisdom, desiccated, all skin and bone, his face wreathed with wrinkles from the fresh air, a wizened elder of the village to be consulted on everything from troubled hearts to troubled pockets. A wonderful life in the service of others!'

Stanislas continued on his way, turning down the road leading to Byron's *posada* where Mrs Simpson was probably beginning to worry about her lodger. If he did not want to see me, it would be easy for him to leave there and then. I had found him, but I had not found him in order to force him in any way.

★

When we returned the following day, Mrs Simpson beamed with delight and exclaimed, the moment she opened the door, 'He's waiting for you at the castle.'

'In this weather?'

'He didn't even notice it was raining. I had to run after him with my husband's anorak. The rain here goes straight through ordinary raincoats. Have you got anoraks?'

'It was hot and sunny in Lisbon when we left.'

'Well, Sintra's not Lisbon, I'm afraid. It's hardly even Portugal. The forest has to be watered every day. I'll lend you both something.'

She took two yellow anoraks down from a coat-hook.

'These were left here by some guests. They were going off somewhere nice and dry . . . I'll have a fire going by the time you get back.'

The rain was pouring down in a solid wall. Mario declined the anorak he was offered, gesturing at his umbrella, which was about the size of a beach umbrella. Black, naturally. Mrs Simpson had told us we would be wise to walk up to La Pena, in case Stanislas had got tired of waiting and decided to come back down through the forest. Walking under the trees, we imagined we would get some protection from the downpour, but this turned out to be an illusion. Raindrops were replaced by bucketfuls of water every time a gust of wind shook the thick foliage of oaks and beeches. The winding path skirted round waterfalls, then took us across streams, ponds and stagnant pools. We were trudging through an aquarium, our footsteps muffled by the sodden ground and our clothes gradually being impregnated by the thick smell of leaf mould. Forests have no magical spells to secrete, only death and decay, and the trees are columns of despair, fed by thousand-year-old corpses devouring their roots. Fear is what keens the senses of the walker who has lost his way. Without the arrows to keep us on the path, we would quickly have got lost in the glaucous light filtering through the lower leaves and the almost impenetrable undergrowth of giant ferns. Yet it was impossible to fall completely under the evil spell of the forest with Mario for a companion. Although his head and shoulders were protected by his umbrella, his trousers were soon wringing wet and his old laced boots had let in so much water that with every step they emitted a squelching noise like a slobbering kiss, which he, tight-lipped, did his best to ignore, furious at having to flounder in the mud, to pick his way through puddles, to cross rickety, hump-backed bridges over ponds and lose his footing on slabs of granite. In these surroundings, Camoëns' disciple looked distinctly absurd. Absurd and comical, chewing over his rage at having to venture into this jungle: Mario, child of the Lisbon streets, troglodyte of dark cafés which foster the traditions of hermetic poetry consumed by the melancholy of being. As we stopped to get our breath at the edge of a pool by a picturesque blue waterfall, he sighed heavily, 'If this is an initiation, I'd rather have stayed innocent.' Perhaps we were being made to work for our reunion with Stanislas – that is, supposing he was still waiting for us at the castle and had not slipped off somewhere else in his elusive and sarcastic way. La Pena eventually came into view as the path rejoined the road. Raised on its foundations of grey rock, its soaring towers reached up to snag scraps of cloud shredded by the wind. All of those who have fallen for Byron's Eden have talked about the castle of La Pena, and after Beckford there is nothing I can add. I might just say that to its two present visitors it did not even seem real. I had an intense desire to topple the walls with a well-placed kick in the papier mâché, but this extravagantly pretentious edifice had been built to withstand every challenge, including time. The dreams of Facteur Cheval or Gaudi seem muted and commonplace in comparison with Ferdinand of Coburg's dream at La Pena, his precursor of Disneyland. I looked at Mario: soaked, his trousers corkscrewed around his skinny, stilt-like legs, a café-crawler splashed with mud, imperturbable, and with the offended air of an inveterate city-dweller who finds he has wandered into a courtly romance, he was irresistible. I burst out laughing, which was almost fatal, and I had to pretend that I was laughing at the vulgar architectural tastes of this Saxon prince and the trick which Stanislas had played on us by dragging us from the *pension* of Senhora Amanda to the castle of La Pena.

'I bet,' said Mario, 'that we won't find him. He has gone off to amuse himself somewhere else while we've been getting ourselves lost in the forest. I've always hated nature, but without knowing why. Now I know that my instincts were right.'

He held up a finger sententiously and, finding that the rain had stopped, shook his umbrella and closed it. We were just going under the postern gate when a familiar French voice shouted over our heads, 'I am glad to see you well! Horatio, – or I do forget myself.'

'Hamlet-Maximilian-Stanislas, the joke has gone far enough,' answered Mario, looking up at the grinning face poking out between the battlements.

'Be thou a spirit of health or goblin damned, bring with thee airs from heaven or blasts from hell, be thy intents wicked or charitable, thou comest in such a human shape that I will speak to thee, oh Mario, poet and Portuguese.'

'Oh, I see, I suppose you think I don't know my *Hamlet*. My dear Stanislas, I know it by heart.'

'Come on up, gentlemen. I am out of patience with waiting for you. Come on, it's splendid up here.'

Stanislas was waiting for us on the rampart, dishevelled and radiant, leaning on his walking-stick with Mrs Simpson's anorak over his arm. The shreds of cloud, which a few moments previously had still been hanging over the castle, had disappeared and sky of a shy china blue was opening up.

'Welcome to my home!' said Stanislas, spreading his arms.

Mario could not have known that Walker's thesis of 1957 had sought to trace a father for Stanislas among the Coburgs, but I had not forgotten his sweeping denials of the American student's claims. There had never, as he said, been a single artist in the Coburg family – whose only achievement had been to supply kings to European dynasties exhausted by inbreeding. For Stanislas to make a reference to this, making fun of La Pena and himself at the same time, was a sign that he was at this moment recovering his old bluff cynicism, mocking himself by mocking others. It also signified that he was ready to return to the fold and that we had arrived neither too early nor too late. But why did he look so much older now, despite the calm, rested expression and the eyes sparkling with irony? He was not an old man, only fifty-two, but he suddenly looked his age, as if he had been through an ordeal which had not left him unscathed. This confirmed what I had sometimes suspected in him, a great weariness with the life he led ordinarily, with the whole social parade which living with Félicité had imposed on him, even though he was so much at his ease in it that he would never give it up. Who can say that he has not, occasionally, experienced the desire to destroy himself because everything is perfect down to the last but one detail and suddenly that detail means more than all life's benefits together? Stanislas' crisis was past, however; he was returning to the world of order. Another few months and he would be starting a new book, because like the drug addict, the writer who stops writing will begin to suffer withdrawal symptoms.

We made our way back to Sintra along the road. After the rain the scents of the forest greeted us in repeated waves of flowers and leaf mould and the fresh smell of wood swollen with water. Stanislas walked cheerfully along between us, ignoring Mario's bad mood. He made no reference to the last two weeks, but took great pleasure in telling us of an encounter the day before when his footsteps had led him to the Hotel Seteais. And who had he bumped into there? He gave us a thousand guesses, but of course we were not to know that Jacques Chardonne was spending a few days in that particular hotel which was perhaps in its time the most beautiful in the world. He and Stanislas had met in the hall.

'I should imagine that even in the middle of the jungle in Borneo he would still be wearing the same bow tie as in Paris, the same beige Eden hat, the same grey striped suit and pink shirt. We didn't talk about Portugal at all. No. Only about Cioran of whom he has a very high opinion. He has some good quotes of his. I have one too, which is quite good: "Dress is the main reason we flatter ourselves that we are immortal – how can one possibly die when one is wearing a shirt and tie?" His bow tie was certainly very handsome, blue silk with white polka dots. Do you know, we spent an hour talking about our carcasses which dress themselves up as a defence against nature. I reminded Chardonne of that question once asked of a man who was always as elegantly turned out as he himself was: "When you put your hat on, who could tell that you have just been wading through blood and guts or that there will soon be worms gorging themselves on your fat?" We sat down and had a cup of tea, which was perfectly jolly despite the gloomy topic of conversation. After all, only pessimists really see the face of the world properly, and it is a pretty comical sight. The terrace at the Seteais overlooks the valley, above the forest and the gardens which stretch down to the road. On the other side there are rows and rows of vines crowded onto the slope. Chardonne tells me their red wine is excellent. I enquired after its name: Colarès, apparently. We must go there tomorrow and buy a demi-john. . . .'

'What would we do with that?'

'Give it to Mrs Simpson, of course. It might make her dinners less dull. There is nobody like the English for being impervious to the country they live in. The French can be pretty insensitive sometimes, I suppose. . . . Chardonne pointed out a little village called Cabriz at the bottom of the valley, full of white houses with pantiled roofs. One of his friends has settled there with his wife and his dog, and he is writing a novel which is entirely set in north Africa, right in the interior. He has to shut his eyes to write, so that he can forget his lush garden and his border of agapanthus, or the edge of the forest with its blue vapours. But we are all the same, are we not? Writers are not painters from nature. They have to re-create it all in the dark-room of the imagination. I have never managed to write a single line on Venice when I have been there on the Largo Fortunio, nor on London when we have been staying in Chelsea.'

'What about Lisbon?' asked Mario.

'That will be for later – much later.'

*

That 'later' came with *The Bee*,[1] when Roger Sanpeur leaves Italy after his failed suicide attempt and goes to stay in Lisbon for several weeks to write one of the detective novels from which, to his shame, he earns his living. The novel is set in Hamburg, a place Sanpeur has never visited, but he has conscientiously bought a guide and a photograph album of the city. Whenever he looks up from his table, he can see through the window the narrow Alfama street with its children playing and its matrons grumbling. The *pension* is run by a fat woman with a greedy mouth and elephantine thighs, and the room next door houses a tall, unkempt man dressed all in black and pacing up and down reciting *The Lusiads*. In the Lisbon which surrounds him and ought to command his attention, Sanpeur is like a foreign body, immured in his detective novel and immune to the charms of the city and its sounds. *The Bee* has a number of pages on Lisbon which are among Stanislas' best.

The day after this reunion at Sintra we flew back to Paris. Mario Mendosa escorted us to the airport and his melancholy hidalgo's silhouette stayed motionless on the other side of the passport desk until he was certain that we had boarded our flight. I think he watched Stanislas leave with a mixture of regret and relief. He had witnessed a man drowning and then surfacing in the most unexpected way. At Sintra we had dragged him into a forest which confirmed his loathing for nature. And when, in 1970, he published a fragment of his *Lisbonenses*,[2] we recognized, like a description of hell, the ascent through the sodden forest of La Pena and the encounter with the ghost of Hamlet on the battlements of the castle.

'He and I are the same,' said Stanislas. 'He stores everything away. Sometimes I feel ashamed and think I ought to have a notice pinned to my back, warning people: "This man remembers everything, uses everything, without scruple." I am incapable of inventing anything.'

'But you re-invent.'

[1] *L'Abeille*, Editions Saeta, 1963.
[2] Livraria Bertrand.

'Only because I have afterthoughts.'

Back in Paris Félicité greeted Stanislas as if nothing had happened. They had better feelings to share with each other than the base coinage of reproach and recrimination. Their life continued as before, the only slight difference being that Stanislas had discovered, six years after Audrey's death, the immense depth of the love he had been offered by the little girl from Stockwood. Writing and publishing *Where Are You Dining Tonight?* had educated Stanislas about himself more than any other of his books. Lived, Audrey's love had been a lyrical, delicious adventure, but from the day that it had been recomposed, image by image, emotion by emotion, written down on blank sheets of paper in a hand so neat it could only have been inspired, this love became a heart-breaking reality which would profoundly affect the rest of his life. By devoting a book to her, Stanislas had restored to life the dead girl, so young and pale, who had listened enthralled to *The Firebird* conducted by Igor Markevitch. She lived again and said those disarming things which had blossomed in her heart and nowhere else; one could breathe her perfume, catch that look in her sky-blue eyes, anticipate the pressure of her hand, and believe that she would suddenly arch her lovely white, naked body striped with a strange scar on her stomach, and press it against the body of her lover who was only ageing because she was too young and pure for him. Men left deserted by infidelity or bereavement – which resemble one another so closely that people feel infidelity as a kind of bereavement and bereavement as a sinister infidelity – men who have only memories which are rapidly extenuated, sickly letters or photographs which fail to do justice to the loved one, have the good fortune to forget gently; but reckless writers dig their wounds deeper and an incurable disease, self-inflicted, drives them into the bitter-sweet pains and pleasures of incomplete memories and the frantic search to complete them. So it was with the memory that Stanislas decided to retrieve in my company two or three years later. I was working in my office at Saeta one morning when he appeared in the doorway in tweed jacket, grey trousers and cap. I thought he had come to sign the review copies of *The Bee*, but no, he had decided to take me out to lunch in a little restaurant on the Orléans road. It would give him an opportunity to try out his new car – an Italian-registered Maserati. At ten o'clock that evening we presented ourselves at the Spanish border at Le Perthus. It was shortly after midnight when we arrived, almost groping our way, in Ampurias. Early the following morning, from the balcony of my room, I saw him on the beach, in shirtsleeves and with his trousers rolled up to his knees, walking along the water's edge in the waves breaking gently on the sand. Still red from the rising sun, the sea moved lazily between the two headlands of the bay and two fishing-boats anchored a short distance out swayed on the swell, their *lamparos* swinging.

Throughout the unexpected drive we had hardly said three words to one another, deliberately on my part, for fear of interrupting him in the thoughts which had got hold of him and propelled us down that long road to be eaten up by the blue Maserati – his most recent toy. It was not simply a question of trying out a new car, that I was certain of from the moment we had raced past the restaurant which had been the pretext for this sudden mad dash. Had he actually had any intention of stopping there? No, and nor were we on our way to meet a woman, with whom he would have had no use for a witness. But it took me a long time to work out that we had come so far in pursuit of a shadow. Yes, Audrey, ten years earlier, around 1952 or 3, had come to spend a month in Ampurias with Johnny and some of their friends. In the same hotel where we were now staying, they had taken the four rooms overlooking the sea. Ampurias was nothing at that time, just a fishing village with one or two Roman ruins to attract the most dutiful tourists. The Costa Brava was perfumed with thyme and myrrh, before the smells of suntan oil, petrol and the tenacious dust of the great blocks of concrete had taken over. Audrey's friends had brought books and guitars, and developed a taste for Spanish pastis, drunk with water dripped drop by drop onto a lump of sugar balanced on a perforated teaspoon. These children from a prefabricated civilization were amazed to discover the taste of fish brought ashore in the nets at daybreak, the smell of hot bread wafting from the ovens built behind each house, and Catalan wines to roughen the throat and sherries to set it on fire. This, to them, was life *à la* Swiss Family Robinson. Another few years, and the Costa Brava would be transformed into a rubbish dump. Without knowing it, they were tasting its last days of simplicity and freedom.

Stanislas had arrived one night when they were sitting on the beach in a circle, singing. At first, despite the torch burning in their midst, he was unable to distinguish Audrey from the other young women in the small group, but then recognized her voice as she began to sing a Catalan ballad she had learnt, the day before, from a woman of the village. Hidden behind the hull of a wrecked fishing-boat, he had waited for them to leave, then found a room in a bed and breakfast, and the next day sent word to Audrey through one of the local children to meet him on the road out of the village. The sun had tanned her delicate complexion, and when he saw her coming towards him as he waited for her, motionless, leaning against the trunk of a pine tree, he found her so lovely that his heart was gripped with a terrible sadness. She would never belong to him, to him alone. He would always have to share her with Johnny, with her friends. But his despair was banished when he held her and looked into her eyes again and stroked the nape of her neck beneath her long blonde hair. She belonged to him too. They had walked in the pine forest, to a cove where a fisherman had lent them a boat. They had rowed as far as a creek with water the colour of opal. There were no paths leading to the half-moon of white sand at its edge. The only access was from the sea. Audrey had stripped off her brightly-coloured gypsy dress and dived in, reappearing with a tawny pelt of hair clinging to her head. They had swum towards the beach, where the sand was so soft they had sunk in up to their ankles. She had stretched out on her back and he had undressed her. She had smiled at his surprise that her breasts were as tanned as the rest of her body. With her friends she swam as they did, half-naked. When Stanislas had taken off her briefs, he had seen the narrow mark of her bathing costume a fraction above the curls of hair glistening with water droplets like an open jewel-case. He had wanted to put his lips to it, to drink this sparkling dew, but she had taken his head between her hands to draw it up to her own face. Looking down on this wide-eyed and happy face, Stanislas detected in it a reflection of the sky, a blue glimmer misted over by the nearness of joy. It is one thing to embrace beauty in the shadows of a bedroom, it is quite another to embrace beauty in a sunlight without shadows.

Stanislas had spent a week at Ampurias, with Johnny and the group of friends unaware of his presence. They spent the mornings lounging in their rooms. In the afternoons it was he who did not show himself. In the evenings he saw them on the beach, always singing or dancing or reciting poetry. He could not envy them. He was the thief, not Johnny or his friends. It was to him that Audrey gave the most beautiful thing she possessed, the pleasure of her suntanned body lying on the sand, those seconds when her misty gaze betrayed the birth of a climax beyond which she would subside into nothing more than a limp form in her lover's arms.

This could have lasted all summer, had Stanislas not invented to himself a reason for leaving. It was more important to preserve a perfect memory, however brief, than to tarnish it by risking one final rash encounter. It was this memory which we had returned to Ampurias to find, one morning in June. The hotel had had another floor added. Underneath the windows the beach was spotted with orange umbrellas and red pedalos. A man with his stomach hanging over his dirty shorts was raking over the sand and picking up the cigarette butts to unwrap the last shreds of tobacco and fill his pipe. We wanted a rowing boat. They had only motor dinghies. A fisherman offered to take us to the creek, one of many scraped out of the red rock. Stanislas asked him to stop as we rounded the first point. There was the half-moon of sand. But the beach was dominated by a house of ochre-coloured stone. Steps had been cut into the red rock. A little further on, there was an hotel and a concrete jetty which had changed the beach completely. The sand must have been used in the construction of the slab of concrete because only the shingle was left. The next two creeks had suffered the same fate. Stanislas asked the fisherman to turn back.

'I must have dreamt it!' he said as we got back in the car.

We were back in Paris that evening, unshaven and exhausted.

Stanislas did not talk about Audrey again, except on that evening when we walked under the windows of her old studio on the quai Anatole-France, but I had no need of confessions, nor even veiled references. He never stopped thinking about her. A love relived is a sort of sublime anthology of long periods of waiting, of doubts and fears. Its span is compressed into a few intense scenes and the times between, the disappointments, are forgotten; when separation, even the cruellest kind, saves it from outstaying itself and the lies which follow, the past is established in our memories like a magic butterfly mirror reflecting two faces filled with wonder.

There were still a few years left to him to spend with Félicité which helped him in this delayed crisis. There is nothing to be gained from self-delusion. He respected her sufficiently to be able to find a peace with her which he would never have found had she not continued to remind him of the discipline which she had made her guiding principle. Thanks to her, he faced up to what could not be otherwise. There were other women. Without being unkind, let us say that they were passing attractions.

Where Are You Dining Tonight? was a success from the day it was published. Of all Stanislas Beren's novels it is the one which has found the most lasting popularity. To say that he was insensitive to this fact would be an exaggeration, but what effect it had on him is difficult to say; any pleasure he might have derived was well disguised. In a letter from London in 1970 (undated), ten years after the novel appeared and two years after Félicité's death, he wrote to me,

I beg you to say no, as categorically as you can and once and for all, to this producer, to all producers. I do not want to see Maximilian von Arelle and Audrey Inglesey on the screen. The reasons for this are personal ones, emotional if you like. They have suggested a ridiculous cast list, but that is not really the point at all. The fact is that nobody can play the parts. I can see exactly what the cinema would make of the story of Audrey and Maximilian. It would be a laughable melodrama. I should never have written the book, let alone published it. I made a mistake and now it is too late to do anything about it. Every time I look at it, all I see are weaknesses and compromises which, of course, explain why it was such a success. I made no attempt to please, but it made no difference. People liked the book all the same, and I am left with a faint feeling of shame. I always remember that Athenian orator being applauded by the senate and cutting them short by asking, 'Have I uttered an inanity?'! The huge sales of the book have that effect on me. Likewise the rave reviews, which I simply could not understand. The remedy would be to find a magician who could turn the clocks back and destroy the manuscript. But since I don't know any magicians, there's only one solution: I am going to write the truth about Audrey, without any of the masks and devices I clothed her in, without the over-woolly character of Maximilian. The intuition that this was what I would have to do came to me that day we went to

Ampurias to find the little creek where I had made love to her. The folly of men had disfigured what was, for me, almost a shrine. I owe it to Audrey's memory to tell the whole truth. I have started writing the book; in fact, it is almost finished. In a month's time I shall put the manuscript in the safe I showed you, in a parcel with your name on it, and you alone will have the right to open it after my death, in ten, twenty years' time. Then you can publish it, if you think that completely rewriting it was the right thing to do. As for the title, at a pinch we could use the same one. Aren't there three or four different versions of Lady Chatterley? But having said that, I did have an idea for an amusing variation. It goes back to 1962 – at least I think it was 1962 – when I had been walking through Hyde Park, ended up at Speakers' Corner and found myself listening to a cadaverous madman predicting the end of the world for that very evening. There were four or five of us listening to his rantings and suddenly I felt a friendly presence at my side: Evelyn Waugh, battered boater askew and cane under his arm, was listening with infinite attention and politeness to the bag of bones standing on his soap-box. He took me by the elbow and we walked back into the park a short way. I think we knew one another well enough not to have to go through all the preliminaries, and we were certainly too well brought up to mention our books to each other. Eminently subtle as usual, Evelyn made an opening remark which brought together the gloomy prophecies of our half-starved orator and the title of the book I had sent him shortly before. 'Well, Beren,' he said, 'where are you dying tonight?' So there you have it, the title of my 'remake' ready-made, and a tribute to those marvellous verbal slips that Evelyn Waugh so enjoyed. Don't bother trying to persuade me that it's a bad title, or that the sales people won't like it. I do not care. It is the whim of an ageing writer. Respect it. Between *Where Are You Dining Tonight?* and *Where Are You Dying Tonight?* the public can choose. I fear it will choose the former, but time will be a better judge in any case. Shall I still be read in the year 2000? I am not in the least bit certain.

The terrible thing that I cannot get away from is that I drained myself completely in writing *Where Are You Dining Tonight?* Very unwise. Afterwards I managed to write one or two reasonably competent and slightly satirical novels like *The Bee* and *Three is a Crowd*, which people enjoyed. For me, they were the products of craftsmanship, polished prose, but I am undoubtedly the only person who sees the weariness behind those stories. When he gets to a certain age, a playwright or a novelist begins to imitate himself. Do not fling Stendhal in my face just because he wrote *La Chartreuse de Parme* when he was fifty-five. He had been accumulating dynamite all his life. I used up the last of mine a long time ago.

In the second version of Audrey's story I have sailed as close to the wind of my memories as I could. For example, the first version had nothing to say about Audrey's body. That is a grave omission. Perhaps you guessed as much the day I kidnapped you and took you to Ampurias. The pleasure I experienced with Audrey on that half-moon of white sand was the most intense pleasure of my life. I did not want to relive it. I only wanted to see the place where I experienced a terrible explosion inside myself. The second version will tell how we made love. There are details (our moral guardians will call them crude details) that cannot be published while one is alive. Do not imagine that that frail and poetic child was somehow a wanton. Far from it. The heights of tension that we reached in the course of our secret meetings probably stem from the miraculous balance which Audrey brought to bear on her modesty and her spontaneity. And whatever my reputation might be, I am not an erotic writer. If you insist on pretending to have read my books and to have enjoyed them, you will remember that I prefer suggestion to description. (The story of Elise at the house of assignation in *Cryptogram* ridicules eroticism, does it not?) *Where Are You Dying Tonight?* is the confession of a revelation, the dazzled amazement of a man each time he penetrates the woman he loves. Not one of our pleasures is forgotten. I am well aware that some of them were childish, but physical love can easily bear such childishness. It is both a game and a joyful investigation. How otherwise can we explain the moment after the climax and before desire revives, when we are assailed by a crushing sadness? The game is over and while it draws breath before it begins again, we feel abandoned, excluded from paradise. Brasillach once said that Mauriac had found, in the sadness of the flesh when love was over, a proof of the existence of God. People thought this was just Brasillach being witty, but perhaps there is some truth in the idea that coming inside a woman is a creative act, regardless of the modern, risk-free ways. There are only two sorts of creator on this earth: artists, and men who fuck. These two are gods.

It is possible that you will be disappointed by the second version and that you will hesitate to publish it because you will say to yourself that a book in which sexuality has such prominence runs the risk of damaging me as a writer; but think on it: it is my will. The thought of what people will say does not bother me – and it will bother me even less when you have done me your last kindness and put me in the cemetery at San Michele next to Félicité. This book will be my one moment of honesty, which I owe more to Audrey's memory than to anything else. What we experienced together was not just her childish fancy on the one hand and my middle-aged vanity on the other. Remember that we were condemned to secrecy, or at least to the appearances of secrecy since Johnny and Félicité knew, and had to feign not knowing. We respected them both, but neither of us owed anything to our partners physically. Without going into details, I am sure you have guessed that Félicité and I had had no physical relations with each other for years, and as I said in the novel, Audrey had been somebody's wife but nobody's mistress. I was not the first man to hold her in his arms. She and Johnny slept together, and with great tenderness, I am certain. He may well have caressed her. But I was her only lover. The private beauty of her body filled me with anxiety. Her vagina was a minor work of art, scarcely shaded, a faint incision between her two long thighs. Yet it was a living thing, pulsing with the startled breath of those oysters that carpet the coral forests of the Pacific, a strange mollusc or exotic fruit like the Barbary figs that an Andalusian peasant splits open with one cut of his pocket-knife and brings to his lips, just as I put my lips to her, indifferent to the myriad pricklings of the skin. Her breasts were such a source of wonder to me that for fear of seeing them grow old, I wanted to photograph them in the bloom of youth. We spent a few days in a small hotel at Montfort-l'Amaury. The window of our room opened out onto the garden where luncheon was served in summer. A pleasant murmur of adulterous conversation mingled with the soft clatter of cutlery on plates and the head waiter's instructions to his staff. A little later a violinist – undoubtedly a virtuoso – who was practising in his room in the other wing of the hotel, spent half an hour rehearsing a passage from the Beethoven concerto in E major, and it was so light-hearted and playful and produced a mood of such happiness as we listened to it that I decided to take out the camera and photograph Audrey; I must have taken about thirty pictures, from every angle, playing with the afternoon light which slanted through the window and flooded the bed where she lay, the chair where she sat in profile, and the armchair she dropped into languidly at the end. Back in Paris, I took the film to a photographer who developed it in front of me. I have no idea what absurd little mechanism in the camera had failed to work, but every negative came out black. All one can do about that kind of thing is sit back and enjoy the comic fatalism of it. I did not try to repeat the experience, but the memory of that 'modelling session' in a rather ordinary hotel room, to the sudden sweet accompaniment of the violinist practising, stayed so crystal clear and perfect that for the first time in my life I believed in sensuality. Audrey admitted that she had found it as exciting as I had, and so intensely sensual an experience that she did not want to go through it again for fear of blemishing its perfection. For us this was the end of all our false modesty and the end of the last taboo which could have prevented us from loving each other totally. I hope it doesn't sound as if there was anything kinky in our relationship. Audrey had nothing in common with Paul Morand's Hecate followed by her pack of Arab children. She explored love with an enthusiasm whose innocence and purity still scare me when I think about it. It all seemed so natural to us. . . . I know you might have thought me indifferent when I heard of her death, but you know as well as I do that I find it very hard to show my feelings. I kept saying to myself that we had no regrets, neither myself among the living nor she beneath the earth. Love's cycle had been completed. We could have repeated the same gestures, but surprise would not have met with pleasure as it had done before. I accepted our separation as a providential end to our affair. I could not say to myself that we had not dared to do this or that and therefore I would always have regrets. No. We had tried everything, and it had all been successful; even those marginal things which can upset the delicate mechanism of desire rather than pacify it. What risks might we have run if we had gone on? Violence? Too awful to think about.

So the few witnesses to Stanislas' affair with Audrey had no knowledge of its essence as revealed in this letter. Even Félicité, for all her intuition, did not guess. It was probably the only secret he had from her. She was wrong in thinking it was Vladimir and Nathalie who had almost taken Stanislas from her. The real danger came later. That she was unaware of it was a good thing. She had seen *Where Are You Dining Tonight?* as an outburst of romanticism, an adventure of the kind they had tacitly agreed he could have as frequently as he liked on condition that it was not aired in public. When the book appeared, Félicité made her feelings of annoyance plain, as I have already said, but this was because she expected *more* of him. I can still hear her saying to me:

'With their habit of making love out to be greater than it is, and inventing paroxysms of passion everywhere, French writers have manufactured a lot of non-existent feelings which their idiotic readers run off after without watching where they put their feet because they're utterly convinced that they have only to reach for the heavens and it will be theirs for the taking. What happens? They take one step and fall flat on their faces, and they're wretched for the rest of their lives. I had hoped that Stanislas would not go and swell the numbers of such dishonest men. He has plenty of better things to say.'

These 'better things' that Félicité was expecting of Stanislas remained unsaid in her lifetime, unsaid until Stanislas decided to sit down at his long painted table in the library of their apartment on the Largo Fortunio, with the window open on the canal that rang with the gondoliers' shouts on tourists' fine afternoons, and eventually write the true story of his relationship with Audrey.

Two novels had appeared since *Where Are You Dining Tonight?*: *The Bee* in 1963 and *Three is a Crowd* in 1967. The wound that had been opened up by the writing of *Where Are You Dining Tonight?*, the bitter idea that the book was a failure because it had concealed the real reason behind his passion for Audrey, made him judge these two later novels as mere stylistic exercises. With heartfelt disdain he referred to them as 'formula novels'. Yet in both there is a nicely observed comedy in the portrayal of young men who love beyond their means. Of the women that they desire, one is bored and available to the first man who can make her laugh, and the other thinks herself an intellectual and will succumb to the first man who can surprise her. Neither, of course, will have anything to do with shy, fumbling men. Roger Sanpeur, in *The Bee*, is a failed writer who conceals the fact that he writes pot-boiling detective novels. In *Three is a Crowd* Abraham Siniaski, scion of an enormously wealthy family, ruins himself by his attempts to set up a series of madly grandiose schemes to dazzle the woman of his dreams. Sanpeur is in love with the Princess Albina Sansovino, a beautiful Roman lady bored to distraction with having to sit in her palace all day long. She discovers she has not married a prince, but a whole family: an overbearing mother-in-law who, forgetting that she herself was the toast and the talk of Rome for her escapades in the nineteen twenties, visits her every day to lecture her on her behaviour, and not alone, but with an endless host of aunts and uncles and cousins in tow. When she is not wagging her finger at

Albina, she is pointing it at family portraits and instructing her in the Sansovinos' history. This heraldic babbling so exasperates Albina that, in order to escape it, she is ready to fall into the arms of the first man who whispers a four-letter word in her ear. Roger Sanpeur is not unattractive, but he is petrified by the fear of failure, the kind of man that women can only encourage by physically attacking them. When Albina discovers that her would-be lover, under an American pseudonym, writes detective novels whose hero is a private eye with an insatiable sexual appetite, she is convinced that Sanpeur is playing a game with her. Identifying him with her station-bookstall hero, she pays him a visit in his third-rate hotel. For Sanpeur this stroke of good fortune is so great and so unexpected that he miserably fails to rise to the occasion. Humiliated, with Albina's mocking laughter ringing in his ears as she leaves, he decides to commit suicide but – supreme failure – the gun misses. The sad fate allotted him condemns him to writing stories about supermen that he will never be able to emulate.

Siniaski, the hero of *Three is a Crowd*, has fallen for a French woman called Margot Dupuy. A blue-stocking, she holds open house one evening a week to which there throngs a crowd of would-be writers, privately-published poets, dubious music lovers, Sunday painters and large numbers of ladies nearing maturity whose finer feelings have been denied them by sensible, down-to-earth husbands. Margot herself is under no illusions about the mediocrity of her guests, but from time to time her gatherings are illuminated by the presence of a real painter or writer and she knows that if she perseveres she will eventually eliminate the mediocrities and have nothing but real artists. In the midst of this dreary collection of guests who fill their pockets with *petits fours* and drink too much champagne, Siniaski is an outsider, laughed at behind his back and buffeted from guest to guest like a ball until the day that one of the rare illustrious visitors (a writer who bears an extraordinary resemblance to François Mauriac) shows an interest in the young financier, takes him off to a corner of the drawing room and talks to no one else for the rest of the evening. As he leaves, he tells Margot how grateful he is to her for giving him the opportunity of meeting a man as remarkable as Abraham Siniaski. Margot immediately collars her suitor and takes him to her bed, only allowing him to leave the next morning, and she is so carried away by his all-round performance that she divorces her comfortably-off banker husband and marries him. The discovery that he is bankrupt is at first a mere detail, but however above such worldly things she may be, it soon takes on considerable importance. How can one hold a salon in Paris without the wherewithal to feed and water these artists with their unquenchable thirsts? It takes her less than three months to throw Abraham over and re-marry her complacent ex-husband.

The cruelty of the portraits of the two women meant that when the books were published the gossips had a field day. 'Informed sources' claimed that Princess X . . . had provided the model for Albina, and that Margot, in real life, was Madame Y. . . . The two ladies in question voiced their indignation so loudly that no one was left in any doubt about their vanity at being portrayed in a novel. In a letter from London dated April 1967, shortly after *Three is a Crowd* was published, Stanislas wrote to me:

Marvellous reports! Many thanks. In fact Madame Y . . . never crossed my mind when I was describing Margot Dupuy. In any case, I hardly know her, having been introduced to her only once at Marie-Louise Bousquet's where she was trying to pick up the crumbs being dropped by that charming – and so spirited – woman. I cannot have talked to her for more than three minutes. I think she probably did invite me to one of her 'Wednesday evenings' but I had been warned and I declined politely. I seem to remember a reasonably attractive woman who steered into my field of vision – right under my long nose, in fact – two wobbling white breasts ready to burst out of their constricting bodice. I took this as an invitation to slip a *billet doux* into the glory-hole between them, another invitation, I might add, that I did not take up. I adore the idea of her trumpeting all over Paris that she was my model in *Three is a Crowd*. If what you say is true, and that she has taken her indignation to the point of buying up dozens of copies to distribute to her friends who haven't already read it so that they can share her outrage and see what a nasty piece of work I am – then congratulations are in order for all of us. Of course the cruellest thing we could do now would be to publish a denial, stating that my Margot Dupuy is not Madame Y . . . at all, but Madame Z. . . . That she would never live down. You'll remember that Princess X . . . reacted in the same way when we published *The Bee*, though less noisily. Actually, she had better reason to. Albina Sansovino owes more than a little to her. I was inspired by her quite unconsciously, despite the fact that four or five years ago we had a fling together one weekend on Ischia. She is a loveable person in the true sense of the word and, unlike Roger Sanpeur, I did not turn to jelly when we were able to get away from the others for a few minutes. I take my satisfactions where I can.

Félicité is a little better. We shall be going to Venice at the beginning of May; I hope you'll be able to join us there when Saeta goes into its summer recess. We can talk about your idea then. When it comes to writing a novel my imagination is floundering rather feebly at the moment, but the idea of a *Cardinal de Bernis in Venice* is an amusing one. I am turning it over in my mind. But apart from the adventure that Casanova talks about in his *Memoirs*, who else can tell us anything about Bernis' ambassadorship at the court of La Serenissime? I am eager to question Paolo Carlotto on the subject because, sitting in his dusty palazzetto, he is the very incarnation of Venice's past. The moment I utter Bernis' name to him, out will come the step-ladder and down he will climb with ten books and fifty documents on the man. Thank you for sending me Roger Vailland's pamphlet, but Vailland does not talk about Bernis so much as himself. Which is what he is best at.[1] Have you ever noticed how former surrealists, once freed from Breton's moralizing yoke, frantically seek to justify their poetic and political ideas in erotic researches? For them, the idea of 'everything present in everything else' is just a sexual version of a round peg in a round hole. Coupling is the basis of all ontology. Who can say better than that? You can find the same labours in the Tibetans' Tantric philosophy. Fornicating for hours without reaching a climax – some even say that certain monks manage it for days on end – becomes the slow progress towards ecstasy, an attempt to return to the womb. In this one can see a sort of un-creation, the opposite process to that of creation, which should, like taking apart one Russian doll after another, eventually reveal the Meaning Of It All to those who have kept their pleasures in check the longest. That said, though, what a writer Vailland is! Personally I prefer his cold and scornful insolence to his cynical erotic acrobatics.

P.S. One can never restrain oneself sufficiently, either from climaxing or, in my case, talking about my books. In the article in *L'Express* I see there is a very fair criticism: I have not properly explained what it is about Abraham Siniaski that fascinates the famous writer who has strayed into Margot Dupuy's salon so much. What do they actually talk about? Abraham's tastes go no further than Albert Samain and Marcel Prévost, and he is totally ignorant of

---

[1] Roger Vailland, *Eloge du Cardinal de Bernis*, Editions Fasquelle, 1956.

the works of this revered figure who takes him by the arm and, to the ill-concealed fury of the mistress of the house, neglects her and all her other guests. I have given some thought to this and it has filtered through to me that the famous writer, having smelt out a financier, then spent two hours asking questions about how to fill in his tax returns and how best to place his royalties. There can be no other explanation. But Margot Dupuy will never know.

I joined them in Venice in June. Stanislas was in the thrall of a genuine passion for Bernis, reading and re-reading his *Memoirs*. In his study he had set up a low table where he was accumulating various books and documents lent him by Paolo Carlotto. There was a pile of notes which had begun the task of reconstructing Bernis' movements during his Venetian period. But Carlotto had been stuck on one detail: what name was to be given to M.M., the two initials designating the Superior of the convent at Murano mentioned by Casanova in his *Memoirs*? The convent's archives had either been burnt or dispersed by Bonaparte's soldiers in 1797. Nevertheless, Carlotto was optimistic. He and Stanislas spent their mornings at Murano, questioning the local people as if Bernis had only left the day before and presenting themselves at the few patrician houses where some of the records might still conceivably be found.

In the afternoons Félicité would leave her room. By now almost a skeleton, she weighed no more than a child, and Luigi, the portly and taciturn Venetian who had been in her service for thirty years, would pick her up effortlessly in his arms to take her down to the motor-boat moored by the door opening onto the narrow canal. The day of the gondola was past, with the exception of the traghetti and the tourists who had themselves taken out in the evening to the accompaniment of a guitar or an accordion and a gondolier singing *O sole mio*. They had been replaced by the long motor-boats, highly varnished and maintained with pride. With the respect of a man taking the holy sacrament, Luigi would solemnly place Félicité in the boat, inside the glazed cabin if it was raining or on the wooden seat at the stern when the weather was fine. Her maid always saw to it that she left well wrapped-up, her black hair (of course it was dyed, and she had other vanities besides) enveloped in gauze to prevent it flying away in an unkind gust of wind. For these excursions she had given up her celebrated felt hats by which everyone had once immediately identified her. After all, fashions had changed, despite countless revivals. Seeing her alone on the wooden seat, stiff-backed, her hands in a muff, she might have been taken for a mummy removed from her sarcophagus and dressed up for some macabre practical joke. Her sorties lasted an hour or more, through the canals and now and then on the lagoon if the water was calm. She liked to go to Torcello and Burano – for her more beautiful than anywhere else – and she no longer visited her women friends as she had in the past. For the most part they had either died or gone back to England or America. The palaces which had once given private concerts and sumptuous balls, or *soirées* where young men dressed a little too finely had recited vilipendious verse against the scourge of capitalism, and tea-parties where the last generation of Venetian dandies had mixed with singers and actors from touring companies appearing at the Fenice, these palaces had one by one closed their doors. As she glided by one of those façades with its crumbling balconies and its windows sagging dangerously – a sure sign that the foundations were giving way, rotting from age, woodworm and the polluted water – Félicité relived the parade gone by. Depending on her mood, she sometimes went out alone, sometimes stopped and picked up companions whom she referred to, quite without arrogance, as her 'occasional friends': Maria Bomponi, a voluble French woman married to an Italian lawyer, or Adriana Salpucci, a former singer in retirement now from the seductions which had once taken her a long way in her career. With the first fine weather Georges Kapsalis had arrived, and it was his happiest duty to sit on the wooden seat at Félicité's side. The breeze from the movement of the boat prevented him from wearing his Borsalino and he adopted instead a checked cap which clashed with his close-cut suit, his tie held in high relief by a pin mounted with a pear-shaped pearl, and his cream kid gloves tightly clasping the silver knob of his cane. They had many memories in common and could talk for hours, about Peggy and Daisy, and Mary and Grace and Carlos and Mimi, and Apostolis and Etienne and Paul and Jean.

During my stays I accompanied her too, often with the almost intolerable feeling that the feverish gaze in this emaciated face was seeking to see everything and then see it all again with the single idea of soon taking to the cemetery of San Michele the indelible image of Venice. To me she spoke little. We had not got the common currency of Christian names to exchange and I had not known the society whose heights of luxury – and absurdity – her memory sought to rediscover. We exchanged complicity more than conversation, and when perhaps her gaze would light on a palace dear to her, a romantic canal or a once proud, now dilapidated façade, she would point it out to me with a touch of her hand on my arm. And I would look and something to her anguish would convey itself to me, producing a lump in my throat. She understood without my saying a word.

'Don't worry on my account, Georges. I've had a beautiful life. I've never been bored and I've been able to love the beauty around me. It has made me demanding, capricious I suppose some would say because I haven't always done the done thing, but that was because I was too lucky: three husbands who had the courtesy not to outstay themselves, then Stanislas until my last breath. . . .'

We would go back for tea, a ritual she had always observed. At her silver tray with its pretty Minton cups and its toast and cakes, she officiated without anyone daring to serve himself. Woe betide anyone who might have tried to reach for the sugar or a slice of lemon without asking: a slap on the hand would bring him back into line and Félicité would then offer a lump of sugar with the tongs or spear a slice of lemon with a tiny, two-pronged fork. If there were friends, Stanislas would appear, drink his Ceylon tea standing up, then return to his work. I liked it when she and I were alone and our conversations would come back to the man, shut in his study, who was uppermost in our thoughts. Now and then Félicité would manage to ask an embarrassing question.

'Who is the woman he has loved most in his life?'

'You, of course. Who else?'

'Please don't be stupid.'

I knew that I somehow had to avoid saying Audrey, so I pretended to ponder the question.

'Nathalie, maybe?'

She did not seem convinced.

'Surely not Elise?' I said.

'She deserved better treatment than what he put her through in his novel, perhaps even in real life. . . . But then, no, she wasn't his type. Who then? Did he ever talk to you about Eva Moore?'

'Never.'

'He wrote to her for over a year and then suddenly he turned his back on her.'

I thought about the letters I would one day have to retrieve from this unknown woman, in exchange for her three sickly notes. Absent-mindedly I reached over towards the plate of biscuits. Félicité stopped me.

'No, Georges. You really must watch yourself. The Garretts run to fat far too easily. Your grandfather was three stone overweight and when your father was called up even he was a stone overweight. You come from a long line of fat people, don't forget it.'

'So why this tempting spread? You're not eating a thing.'

'It's as it should be.'

'But the cook must be furious when all the cakes are sent back.'

'Of course she isn't. She takes them home with her. Have you ever seen her children? All as fat as pigs. . . . I wonder whether Stanislas still thinks about Audrey, eleven years later.'

'He thinks about a good many things.'

'Oh no, there's every chance he might have ended up thinking of nothing else if you hadn't given him that wonderful idea of doing *Bernis in Venice*. It really has taken hold of him; although I'm not sure that he will actually write the book. No, I don't think he will. It would mean getting inside somebody else's skin and Stanislas has never been happy outside his own. He has his limits, I know him. Yet there have been occasions when his understanding of people has gone almost too far. He can violate their souls when he wants to. As Jean-Paul Binet said to him one day, "I do open-heart surgery, but you, you do open-soul surgery." Nathalie delighted him because he found there was nothing there . . . unless of course the single-minded pursuit of futility can be fascinating . . . yes, probably that was it . . . or it could be quite simply that she always wore white underwear. White underwear! Can you imagine? But when Stanislas looked inside Audrey, he found a kernel as hard and as pure as rock-crystal. . . .'

'And what did he find in you?'

'Oh, in me he must have come across an obstacle, or perhaps a looking-glass where he would always look at himself without false shame or false pity. He knew straight away that we couldn't lie to one another. We would have shattered the looking-glass. He wasn't capable of being properly unfaithful to me. . . .'

It was a blessing that Félicité still put her faith in appearances. I could hear Stanislas saying, 'I cannot tell lies. I dissimulate. . . .'

'With his dear Paolo Carlotto,' Félicité was saying, 'he has found a guardian angel and a great supervisor. I do wish you'd persuade him to go out more though, to sit outside, to go and bathe at the Lido. If he spends much longer stuck in Paolo's library, he'll come out looking like a Venetian maggot.'

I had to hide a smile. Paolo Carlotto, so completely Venetian that he became homesick whenever he went any further than Padua – and even Padua was too far for him since they had closed down the Brenta ferry – Paolo, an 'old man of fifty' as Balzac would have called him, was so much at home in the eighteenth century that he had extended it into the twentieth with his keen appetite for all kinds of minor intrigues and conspiracies. Fate might have condemned him to a life of observation, but nothing kindled his enthusiasm as much as the success of a friend in a plot hatched by himself, the 'senza cazzo'. Highly respected, the correspondent of numerous learned societies, consulted by historians in every country, owner of the finest library in Venice completed over six generations with a singleness of purpose which had more than once forced the Carlottos to resort to dishonesty, Paolo knew no greater pleasure than to launch his friends on adventures that he could never have seen through successfully himself. So it was that two weeks earlier Carlotto had introduced Stanislas to a young girl convalescing with her parents, who kept house for him at the palazzetto. There was nothing specifically 'Venetian' about this, until it became clear that the girl was a nun, from an order in Brescia. Still pale from her operation, with beautiful velvet eyes, a mouth the pink of a pomegranate, and dressed in black lightened by a white band encircling her face and a white collarette at her neck, Sister Annunciata inspired desire rather than respect. But she was a modest girl, quiet and demure, giving no cause to suspicious minds, spending her days helping her mother with the housework in the palazzetto. Which was where Stanislas had first caught sight of her, sitting on a chair polishing a silver candlestick held between her legs. Her short skirt, pulled down by the weight of the candlestick, uncovered two neat knees sheathed in black. Paolo had intercepted Stanislas' gaze and remarked that the twenty-year-old nun had not smoothed her skirt down to cover her knees; on the contrary, he declared, she had begun to polish the candlestick with a frenzy which was positively symbolic.

Let us not over-idealize Stanislas' seduction. Sister Annunciata was quite ready. Thanks to the hospital, her operation and her convalescence with her parents, she was beginning to measure the thankless future in store for her if she stayed in her convent in Brescia. Paolo provided the room, on the first floor. The young nun came up at midnight by the service stairs. She did not compound her sacrilege by appearing to Stanislas in her black robes and certainly lost a little of her charm by not doing so, but her innocence and her natural gifts made up for it. At about four in the morning Stanislas would walk briskly back to the Largo Fortunio through a silent, sleeping Venice like an elaborate stage set abandoned by its actors. The adventure was limited to these three or four nocturnal hours, but Paolo Carlotto was jubilant. His friend had not been content to study Bernis' life in

Venice. He had, in his cynicism and licentiousness, become Bernis; and did not take the affair any more seriously than the young ambassador and priest had taken his. In July Sister Annunciata refused to go back to her convent and re-assumed the name she had had before, Adriana. Her skin, Stanislas would say, had the taste of nectarines ripened in the sun. Paolo expressed his satisfaction at her singing in Venetian dialect as she helped her mother with the housework at the palazzetto. The following year, when Félicité died, Stanislas saw her once more in circumstances I shall reveal shortly. A little later she asked his permission to marry, permission immediately granted on the likely condition that their occasional pleasures should continue. Gratitude was part of Adriana's nature and the well-behaved, even pious wife, so proud of her husband playing the violin in the orchestra at the Fenice, never forgot anybody. I saw her again at the cemetery on San Michele as Stanislas' coffin was being lowered into its place beside Félicité's. She was there, in a black suit, her glossy black hair covered by a net, kneeling on the marble step and weeping with her face in her hands. I remember thinking what lovely legs she had. I feel no guilt for noticing them at that moment; Stanislas would have noticed them with the same pleasure.

*

After dinner, before departing to join Sister Annunciata, Stanislas would sit for a while in an armchair at the foot of Félicité's bed, reading to her from Saint-Simon or Chateaubriand or Stendhal. Her mind dulled by painkillers, she would listen drowsily and then drift into sleep, her head wobbling on her thin neck with its pronounced dewlaps. Stanislas would leave the room on tiptoe, turning all the lamps down. In the neighbouring room there was a night nurse who slept on a camp bed. They had had a great deal of difficulty finding a nurse who did not snore. The latest one dropped into such depths of sleep that no call or bell, however loud, could wake her. Signora Barberini had had to be attached to Félicité by a length of cord which the latter would jerk sharply to wake her. This lady had been a dresser at the Fenice; and she had, she claimed proudly, followed Diaghilev's funeral procession, dressed Eleanor Duse's hair and for a second held in her hand the sexual organ of Gabriele d'Annunzio who liked to drop his trousers and pay his respects rapidly in this way before buttoning himself up again. These and similarly colourful stories whiled away the hour between three and four when Félicité regularly woke up and could not get back to sleep. At daybreak she called for her maid to help her with her toilette, then she read until breakfast. The pile of books and papers was always waiting on her bedside table: press cuttings, reviews, slim collections by young poets. She scribbled notes in a small pocket-book and talked sufficiently succinctly to Stanislas about her reading for him to be able to answer each submission with a letter which was both genial and to the point. Occasionally, when Félicité was unusually complimentary, he would open a book and read it to the end, but he was deeply absorbed in the preparation of his *Bernis in Venice* and he preferred not to be deflected from it.

In 1967 they stayed in Venice until the Biennale, then flew straight to London. Félicité was deteriorating daily. Only her voice, with her last reserves of strength summoned by her pride, remained strong and vibrant. In the spring of 1968 she almost succumbed to a particularly virulent strain of influenza which brought London to its knees for a month. Félicité battled frantically, hurling abuse at her doctor.

'I will not die here! I am going to die in Venice.'

She had just enough time to be taken back to the Largo Fortunio, to ask for her bed to be turned towards the window overlooking the Grand Canal. Propped up on her pillows she spent a whole day, her gaze damp with tears, murmuring at regular intervals, 'It's so lovely, so lovely. . . .'

At nightfall she closed her eyes, for the last time it seemed to us. Stanislas dozed in the armchair beside her bed, starting when he thought he could no longer hear her breathing. As the sun rose the following morning she opened her eyes. Her gaze was already veiled with a blueish bloom, but her voice was as imperious as ever.

'Stanislas! Go to bed.'

He did as he was told and I took his place in the armchair.

'Open the Musset.'

'But you don't like Musset.'

'Do as I say. Page ninety-eight . . . read it to me. . . .'

> *Dans Venise la rouge*
> *Pas un bateau qui bouge;*
> *Pas un pêcheur dans l'eau,*
> *Pas un falot.*
>
> *Seul, assis à la grève*
> *Le grand lion soulève*
> *Sur l'horizon serein*
> *Son pied d'airain.*[1]

[1] In Venice blushing red/ Not a single boat stirs;/ Not a single fisherman afloat,/ Not a single lantern./ Alone on the strand/ The lion raises/ To the horizon serene/ His great bronze paw.

Her shoulders heaved as if with a silent fit of coughing, and I moved closer. She was simply stifling her laughter.

'How ridiculous,' she said. 'Poetry for tourists. Read me *Et les palais. . . .*'

> *Et les palais antiques,*
> *Et les graves portiques*
> *Et les blancs escaliers*
> *Des chevaliers*
> *Et les ponts, et les rues,*
> *Et les mornes statues*
> *Et le golfe mouvant*
> *Qui tremble au vent. . . .*[1]

'Stop,' she murmured. 'The rest is too stupid for words. You can't write about Venice: it's courting suicide. Venice is a painter's city. . . . You must get your hair cut. It's far too long.'

Stanislas returned towards midday. He had been with Paolo Carlotto to see Franco Lombardi at San Vio, Lombardi who knows everything about Venice that scholars do not and will never know. They returned with the answer which they had sought without success until then: the Superior at the convent at Murano had been a Morosini. Yes, there had been a doge in that family. He had immortalized his family name by firing the incendiary cannon which had blown up the Acropolis, then occupied by the Turks. There had also been a countess Morosini who had inflamed the passion of d'Annunzio. She had gone mad. As for the voluptuous and beautiful Mother Superior, a portrait of her had been sold a year previously to an American collector whose interest in Bernis' and Casanova's mistress extended to his writing a book on her. Franco Lombardi had promised to unearth the collector's name and his address in America. When Stanislas related this incredible conjunction of circumstances to Félicité she looked at me, certain that I had understood: *Bernis in Venice* would not be written, but Stanislas had to be left to pursue his chimera of the moment.

In the afternoon she seemed distinctly better and asked for some tea. A tray was brought to her bedside. As she raised the cup to her lips her hand hesitated and dropped back. The tea spread over the

---

[1] And the antique palaces,/ And the imposing porticoes/ And the white stairways/ Of the noble houses/ And the bridges, and the streets/ And the sad statues/ And the shifting bay/ That trembles in the wind. . . .

embroidered top of the sheet. Félicité Beren was dead. On the orders of Signora Barberini who now appeared, we were ushered from the room and the next time we saw Félicité she had been laid out on her four-poster bed in a gown of white lace, with black slippers on her feet and her jaw held in place by a bonnet-string. Stanislas, paler than she, did not say a word. Behind him Georges Kapsalis, Paolo Carlotto and I stood in silence. The priest came and went, having blessed her and placed a box-palm between her crossed hands. Carlotto was the first to leave; then Georges, who had always known the right thing to do, took me off to dinner. On our return we found Stanislas in the armchair by her bed, a glimmering lamp illuminating the same book he had been reading to her the day before: Chateaubriand's *Posthumous Memoirs*. At midnight he sent us away, turned out the lamp and stretched his legs. A candle was burning on the bedside table.

Stanislas woke me around eight o'clock.

'Take my place. We must not leave her alone.'

I heard him taking a shower, cleaning his teeth and shaving, then there was silence. Georges came to join me.

'He's gone out.'

*

Later I found out from Paolo Carlotto that Stanislas had appeared at the palazzetto at ten o'clock that morning, wanting to see the former Sister Annunciata immediately. It was not the best of times with both her parents up and about, her father painting a door in the small courtyard and her mother chasing the dust in the drawing room. Paolo had had to send one off to the Giudecca with a letter and the other to the market. Annunciata-Adriana had not had time to change.

'Stanislas can be an absolute rake. He certainly didn't take long over it. Little Adriana was left dazed on the bed, still in her black dress which I'm sure he pulled down when he left because he's such a tidy man. You know, I think he just had a desperate need to escape from the idea of death. I've drawn up a little list with all the references I could find to the chroniclers of the eighteenth century who talk about similar adventures: Jacopo Lorenti, Luigi Caretto, Orlando Lodenbacci, Antonio Bruno. All Venetians, isn't that interesting? Might it be an impulse peculiar to Venice?'

Félicité was right. Stanislas eventually dropped the idea of a *Bernis in Venice*. He had enjoyed the research but after writing the first few pages was put off for good. His own temperament was so different from the cardinal's that he found it almost impossible to get inside the man's character. Roger Vailland had summed him up in a few brilliantly apt pages; and Vailland, though he was not Bernis, would have liked to have been, which was what mattered. Vailland's misfortune was to have been born in the twentieth century when he was made for the eighteenth. Stanislas was a man of his age and consequently found it difficult to step back into another period of history.

Ideas have a life of their own, however. As Stanislas was amassing his notes and background reading, the American mentioned by Franco Lombardi had already begun his book *The Loves of Cardinal de Bernis*, which appeared at the same time as Holger Zerfüss in Munich published his monumental and teutonic biography of the cardinal. Paolo Carlotto hid his disappointment well. Although he had not succeeded in inspiring Stanislas, there was always the consolation of the Casanovian adventure with the pretty nun.

The day after the funeral at San Michele we left for Paris, dropping Georges Kapsalis at Milan where he was to catch a train for Cannes. We had not read any newspapers for several days, still less listened to the radio, but as we crossed the border at Vallorbe the customs officer advised us to fill up with petrol in Switzerland and, if we wanted to be on the safe side, to take an emergency can as well. In his broad Vaudois accent he added, 'If you are mad enough to go into the lion's den you might as well give yourselves an escape route.'

What lion's den? I don't think we even bothered to ask him to explain. It was a sparkling late spring in the Jura and we saw no wild animals, no lions at any rate. The petrol stations were all open and everyone was working. Nearing Paris on the motorway, however, the atmosphere changed: we were alone on the road to the capital. To our left, on the southbound carriageway, the cars were bumper to bumper, laden with luggage and furniture just as they had been in May and June 1940, twenty-eight years before. 'The rats are leaving!' said Stanislas. 'Hitler must have come back to life and sent General von Briesen to take Paris again. If we don't get stuck in any traffic jams, we shall arrive just in time for the march-past on the Champs-Elysées. I wonder if he still has his black horse? Do you think the Reichswehr still knows how to goose-step?'

The Reichswehr was not marching down the Champs-Elysées when we arrived. On the place de l'Etoile the crowd was watching a group of young people, students it was said, urinating on the flame of the Unknown Soldier. All public transport had come to a halt and the roads were empty of traffic, apart from one or two cars and pretty girls cycling by, their skirts billowing, just as they had during the German occupation. The sun shone, the street-sellers handed out red balloons, and with the cinemas all closed, whole families of Parisians strolled along pavements unencumbered, for once, by cars. In short, it felt exactly like a public holiday or one of those English Sundays when there is nothing to do but stare at shop-windows. I took Stanislas down to the Left Bank. The beginning of the boulevard Saint-Germain was utterly deserted, the shutters of the apartment blocks all closed. Police vans and ambulances drove by us at speed towards the boulevard Saint-Michel. I stopped outside the Saeta offices. There was no one there and I went to collect the key from the concierge, who said that Emeline Aureo had taken it. Age had taken its toll of Mlle Aureo and I had been forced to ask her to retire. We went to the rue de Sèvres, where she lived. The appearance of Stanislas on her doorstep had the effect of a thunderbolt on the wizened little woman who had taken to dyeing her hair straw-blonde, ever since Félicité had lectured her on the subject of white hair, which of course, according to her, was something no woman could allow herself.

'You here, Monsieur Beren! You owe it to your readers to take better care of yourself. You must hide, the revolutionaries are burning everything . . . even cars belonging to innocent people.'

'So there are still innocent people living in Paris, are there?'

He was thinking of the youths, the sons of the well-off middle class, who had been pissing on the Unknown Soldier in front of a crowd of passive onlookers. Emeline Aureo had not understood the question. She took a canary-yellow coat down from the coat-hook, thought better of it, and chose instead a grey jacket which seemed better suited to the occasion.

'We must try not to get ourselves noticed,' she said. 'Thank goodness you didn't bring Madame Beren with you!'

'Yes, thank goodness!'

'I hope she's not too tired, at any rate?'

'Oh, I am afraid she is, Emeline, very tired.'

'You shouldn't leave her alone then.'

'I shall join her as soon as I can.'

When she discovered the truth some days later, she was extremely upset with Stanislas, and I had to try to explain to her that it was just his way of shutting out a grief which would not leave him in peace.

We went back down the boulevard Saint-Germain with the police vans and ambulances still howling past us as if we were in some American film. Muffled explosions could be heard in the distance.

'I came back to get the key,' she said, 'because all the office staff have left.'

She had never retired, and did not intend to. We expected to find the offices in chaos, but no, everything was in its proper place: manuscripts in piles on the readers' tables, typewriters under their dust-covers, and in the in-tray one or two letters delivered by hand.

'There's no post any more. But you can still get through on the telephone if you dial direct. You could ring Tokyo, for instance. . . .'

'But I don't know anybody in Tokyo,' Stanislas objected.

'Oh, I only meant it in a manner of speaking. But actually it wouldn't be quite as ridiculous as you think: just before you left London the rights department had an offer from Japan. Wait a moment . . . I wonder if I can find it . . . yes, here it is. They want to translate *Three is a Crowd*.'

Stanislas smiled. 'Is there anything you don't know about?'

She had refused to give in to retirement. Her entire life had been played out in these dusty offices where Stanislas had forbidden a single desk to be moved. Everything was to stay exactly as it had been in the days of André Garrett and Monsieur Dupuy. Emeline Aureo was his watch-dog; once I had even had to beg the cleaning woman to use her broom to dislodge the cobwebs in the corners of the ceiling, against the express instructions of Mlle Aureo. After that, she was always referred to as 'the spider' in the office. Of course she was no longer asked to wipe my nose or take me for a walk in the Jardins du Luxembourg to see Punch whacking the policeman with his big stick, but if time had been rolled back and I had become a child again, she would not have thought twice about it.

'It's like a graveyard here,' said Stanislas. 'I suggest we go to the Latin quarter.'

At this Emeline spread her arms wide, as if to say it would be over her dead body if we went into the 'lion's den' that the Swiss customs officer had warned us about. Stanislas was probably the only person who could have calmed her fears. He kissed her on both cheeks. *'Morituri te salutant!* Emeline, we leave you to guard the building. Let no man enter till we return!'

We left her behind and she stayed in the offices for twenty-four hours, not even daring to go down to the café and fetch herself a croissant and a cup of coffee. Had we left her there and not gone back for a month, she would probably have died. But there was not enough going on in Paris to keep anyone amused for a month. After dropping in on the main amphitheatre at the Sorbonne to hear Sartre tell us about the revolution in front of an invited audience of leftist ladies in Chanel suits, and a concierge harangue us about her problems with the rubbish piling up onstage at the Comédie Française, we had heard enough. The streets offered better fare. Stanislas jotted down the revolutionary slogans in his notebook: 'Under the streets are miles of golden sand', 'No laws, no oppression', 'Make love not war' and, on a wall, scrawled in blue, the injunction to passers-by: 'Be happy.'

'A breath of something has come and gone,' said Stanislas, 'and now the philosophers and politicians are running after it with their nets. Can you imagine Sartre ever writing, "Under the streets are miles of golden sand"? He's never seen a beach in his life. What a shame that André Breton died without seeing his grandchildren writing, "Let those who can no longer see think of those who can." They think they're making a revolution, but what's really happening is that they are ridiculing those who call themselves their masters – which is much better. They ought to be allowed to go as far as they want. What a marvellous atmosphere! The only thing wrong with it is the number of grotesque characters crawling out of the woodwork. . . . At last I can justify my laziness which prevented me from ever taking an interest in politics. . . .'

Which was quite true. He had never been interested in politics, and anyone seeking his signature on a petition had always been politely shown the door.

'I never sign other people's writings,' he would say. 'In any case, there is a spelling mistake in yours. Nobody is infallible when it comes to spelling, but I only answer for my own, which is quite enough for me.'

Nothing was more guaranteed to make him laugh than 'ideas'.

'They always make me think of Anatole France's reply to a journalist who asked him his opinion on some form of government or other: "You want an opinion? From me? You would do much better to go and ask in the café on the corner."'

Opinions or not, the upheavals of May '68 wrought a change in him, leaving him more pensive than one might have expected. To him, the demonstrations signalled an outbreak of romanticism in the flat calm of the complacent nineteen sixties, a vitality which for once had interrupted the preening of the bourgeoisie – his own as much as anyone else's. His pretence of being simply an observer was unconvincing; until the beginning of June, when calm was restored, he spent his days walking in the tinder-dry parts of the city and going to meetings whose militancy was hard-pressed to conceal their empty rhetoric. Every morning he greedily devoured the newspapers. Occasionally he telephoned me.

'A very thin day today, not even the ghost of a commentary to get my teeth into. One can tell that summer is on its way. The romantic fever has run out of steam, and all these beautiful people are leaving for Saint-Tropez to recover from their exertions. I think I might go with them – perhaps I should find that delightful creature I saw being carried shoulder-high yesterday, brandishing the black flag and naked to the waist: she had lovely breasts, worthy of being bared to the sun.'

He did not go south, however, but went instead to London for the summer. The only record I have of that period is two letters from him. The first is dated 4 August 1968:

Where has she gone, that lovely girl with the bare breasts on the place Edmond-Rostand? I keep seeing her in my mind's eye, a symbol of freedom on the march, of victorious revolution, a great ground-swell to strip off our inhibitions and our clothes. The greatest slogan of the revolution was 'A bas les soutien-gorges'. Look at the engravings of all those fashionable women at the end of the eighteenth century: they let it all hang out. I remember a little book by Raymond Dumay, a diary of the Liberation of Paris. He had seen the signs in a girl bathing bare-breasted on the bank of the Seine. I think it was called *The Breasts of Liberty*. It will take a bit of time for the fashion to catch on, but you'll see; soon women will walk about with their breasts open to the air. That will be the noblest achievement of our mini-revolution of 1968. But how on earth can I find out the name of that plucky young lady perched on the students' shoulders?'

The second letter, dated 25 August, came in answer to a question I had put to him on the telephone: was he working? It worried me that he did not seem to be getting down to anything:

You caught me off guard and you have every right to think me evasive. Blame it on my slow brain. In fact, I am hovering between two ideas at the moment. One is a history of the imprisonment and liberation of breasts through the ages – a sort of re-appraisal of our various conquests, together with the thoughts of a moralist on the subject. Why have women been so keen to show off their breasts at some periods of history and just as keen to keep them covered at others? What is needed is a massive enquiry, canvassing both the sexes concerned, not to mention a study of the breast in painting and theatre – where I have already observed three illustrious bosoms, namely Dorine's in *Tartuffe* (oh! Gabrielle Dorziat), Mari-Gallia's in Valle-Inclan's *Divine Words* (oh! Germaine Montero) and Stella's in Crommelynck's *The Magnificent Cuckold* (oh! Hélène Sauvaneix). There must be plenty of others which, with the help of a researcher, I shall unearth, but those three, and the emotion they aroused among the spectators, have left a deep imprint on my memory. So you see how a fleeting image, the image of an ardent revolutionary waving her black flag and showing off her breasts to the May '68 crowds, has given me much food for thought. That's what is so noble about the whole thing. I might add a footnote about the hysterical girls who strip off when Mick Jagger struts onto the stage, but they are just letting off steam. I saw some photographs of the Woodstock festival. 'Three days of peace and love', and a marvellous and moving thing, but on closer examination those particular naked torsos revealed a lot of platitudes. Might it be that mammary modesty springs from large numbers of pretty girls not having pretty breasts? I predict that in the Great Undressing to come – like a last gulp of fresh air before we drown in the black waters of the New Puritanism – the beauty of the bosom will be utterly irrelevant. No doubt we shall even see poached eggs on show. In which case I think I prefer modesty.

The other thing on my mind this summer is much less serious. I am utterly alone in this wonderful city, glinting in the sun. There has been a mass exodus of its inhabitants, to the Balearics, the

Canaries and the Greek islands. Walking around Chelsea and Kensington I feel as if I am lost in a gaudily painted temple. The doors fascinate me. What race besides the English would dare to use such colours? And why here, here alone, are these poisonous greens, mauves, violets, dingy blacks, gory reds, chocolate browns and liverish-shit colours so harmonious and attractive? Taken as a whole, they are actually *beautiful*. What is worse is that there are even Victorian porches with their black and white columns and triangular pediments which have had their doors modernized, Art Deco-style. Quite ludicrous and yet somehow it works. . . . I can't begin to imagine the same jarring variety in Paris where, in any case, only two colours are tolerated: fake ebony and fake oak. I have been trying to guess what the people living in a house with a particular colour door must be like, their characters, the partners they have chosen, their favourite pets, their favourite drinks, their secret vices. An interesting extension of this door-to-door survey has been an examination of the knockers. Now the variety of knockers is staggering. Many are in the form of hands, often covered in rings, holding the oddest collection of objects: white marble balls, hammers, riding crops, negroes' heads, and so forth. I am positive that one day I saw – I know you'll say that the older I get, the more obsessed I become – a phallus held delicately between a gilded thumb and forefinger. It had been rubbed so smooth with use that it was a shadow of its former self, but I got Harry Dawson to give me his opinion and he confirmed my first impression. Lifting it, he found the date – 1749 – underneath, which it seems is corroborated by a delicately crooked little finger: a practice which he says was once highly fashionable but is now no longer in vogue. (He calls it 'the original golden handshake'.) 1749, if you remember, was the year that *Tom Jones* was published. England was at the height of its libertinism, before the nineteenth century stamped out the fires of joyous lechery as well as freedom of speech. Both direct consequences, alas, of winning Trafalgar and Waterloo. What a shame that the English started taking themselves seriously! At any rate, you can see that I have plenty of work to be getting on with, and I have not forgotten, either, that I must keep you supplied with things to publish. You shall have your book very soon. What am I saying? One . . . two books . . . if not more. . . .

Stanislas had always cloaked his sadness, sometimes in black humour, sometimes in silence. All things considered, the former was the better of the two because it left some small space for hope. His friend Harry Dawson, an antiquarian and expert on bronzes, used to meet him in the Garrick in the evenings and they would dine together. Harry wrote to me: 'He seems very well and has not said a word about Félicité. Our conversation revolves around utterly useless things like his collection of walking-sticks, his paperweights, door-knockers. But have no fear – we're not about to start shuffling to Saint James's Park every morning with bread for the gulls and geese. The prognosis is good, and I suspect (perfidious, this) that Stanislas is well on the way to writing another book.'

The book in question was *Salvation and Death of a Hero*, a strange piece of work that he wrote in two months (October and November 1968) in Amsterdam. Why did he write it in Holland? 'Because of a travel poster,' he said later. It was as good a reason as any, and he had need of new surroundings to distract him from his memories. The novel – if one can call this long incantation a novel – baffled the critics. With its soft-spoken melancholy and its spectral characters trailing mysteriously prophetic messages in their wake, it could not be slotted into the established Beren *oeuvre*. Apart from any other difficulties, death – or rather the idea of death – is ever present. I have quoted one passage from the beginning of the book, where Stanislas gives us the key to his meeting with Félicité forty years earlier, one evening when they went to a Debussy concert. Félicité is behind every word and sentence of the book, invisible but so clearly there that no image can come to life without her inspiring it. Doors open onto the void of death, but every gesture of a man who wants to die is destined only to make him live his grief more acutely.

The writing of the book provided a genuine release for Stanislas. He delivered the manuscript to me in December 1968 in Paris.

'Don't publish it now. Let us wait a year. In a year's time I shall re-read it and we shall decide together if it is worth it.'

Salvation and Death of a Hero was published by Editions Saeta in the spring of 1970. Stanislas was unsurprised by the divided opinions and the reactions both of astonishment and smug dismissal. It had always been expected of him that he would go on reproducing his other books, and here he was publishing a novel which bore no resemblance to any of its predecessors. Curiously, for the first time in almost forty years, Béla Zukor found something complimentary to say about Stanislas' work: 'All his life Monsieur Beren has gone to enormous lengths to write bad books when he could so easily have written a good one . . . though let us not get carried away . . . a readable book which shows that beneath the expensive, mundane, snobbish and dandified exterior, there may be a man of sensitivity. I say "may be": what I mean by that is that it is no doubt a complete confidence trick, but I cannot deny the enjoyment certain passages gave me. It must be old age making me indulgent.' This piece was Béla Zukor's last; he was discovered the following day, dead in his apartment.

'So I have finally lost my number one enemy, have I?' said Stanislas when he heard the news. 'May he rest in peace. You know what the gossips will say, don't you? That he died because he failed to drain off his bile the day before. It was his hatred that kept him healthy. I have no doubt that he will be replaced.'

To the tentative and lukewarm reception of *Salvation and Death of a Hero* Stanislas remained indifferent. Detached from him and passed on to the public, the book no longer interested him. I was aware that this would happen, as it had done before. It was for this reason that he kept his finished manuscripts locked in a drawer for as long as possible. I had had to resort to subterfuge, almost to theft, to get hold of *Where Are You Dining Tonight?* and *The Bee* and *Three is a Crowd*, and it was no different with *Salvation and Death of a Hero*. However, the task was made easier for me by a set of circumstances which were somehow linked to all the games of chance he played against life and which life, in return, played against the fruits of his imagination. In that year, 1970, thirty-seven years after the fatal accident, Nathalie reappeared in the most unexpected way, sparking off a final, the final, passion. Obviously this passion could not compare with the fascination of the first, and yet it was an attraction which arose, phoenix-like, from the ashes which Stanislas would have been justified in thinking long since dead and cold. Yes, the Nathalie of *Singtime!* returned, personified with uncanny likeness by Mimi Bower, a bubbly blonde whose charms had been rewarded with the title of 'Playmate of the Month' in a 1968 issue of *Playboy*, where she appears naked on a bicycle in a Japanese garden. With a Russian mother, a father in the Canadian Mounted Police, a Mexican first husband whom she had speedily divorced, and now with a producer of Polish origins in tow, she was the perfect choice to play Nathalie in a part where conversation was peppered with borrowings from every language. She was – and there is of course an extra, sad note to 'was' because of Mimi's death in an air crash in 1972 – she was one of those girls made particularly delightful by blue eyes of an exquisite candour. The issue of *Playboy* which contributed to her rise to fame featured her in shorts and blouse on the campus at Berkeley where she was studying biology. The other shots were of her swimming naked in a swimming pool and reading Freud *sans culotte*, sprawled on a large sofa covered in zebra skin. It was the idea that these pretty haunches would be thinking about Freud between the sheets with him that had captivated Ladislas Serkinski, the producer of *A Thousand Years to Love* and several other widely differing cinematic successes. The day that Mimi, who read books with unusual perception, told him that she wanted to play Nathalie in *Singtime!*, he gave the novel – recently published in its American paperback edition – to his secretary, who read it for him. On the basis of an enthusiastic report from her, Serkinski sent a telegram summoning Stanislas to Hollywood. Stanislas' reply was equally offhand, summoning Serkinski to Paris for lunch the following Monday. The contract would never have got signed if Mimi, in her determination to see her idea through, had not dragged her producer onto the 'plane by force.

I was present at the lunch. Stanislas, his thoughts elsewhere, let Serkinski talk on uninterrupted about the novel, with an enthusiasm which might have led one to believe that he had actually read it. A false impression: the producer had only seen a two-page synopsis (cut down from the ten pages he had first been presented with). So he knew the plot, and something of the characters because of what Mimi had said about them.

Mimi Bower at once appeared as she was, a guileless and gorgeous creature whose face and figure put her at a disadvantage: how could she be taken seriously with her pink cheeks and large blue eyes sparkling with fun and curiosity? Instead of listening to what she was saying, one found oneself looking at her more and more greedily by the minute. That morning I had shown Stanislas the issue of *Playboy* which had brought Mimi into the public eye, and together we had looked through the colour photographs of her. In one sense they did justice to her, but in another they fell far short of revealing the real Mimi Bower. Certainly she was as fresh and graceful and natural in her pictures as she was in the flesh; but there was something devilish about her too, for in the twenty-four hours since her arrival, she had not only been to have her hair cut like Nathalie's, but also gone shopping for a white sweater two sizes too big for her, a straight skirt, flat shoes and a beret which she was wearing rakishly tilted to one side of her head.

When he saw her, Stanislas paled. I heard him murmur, 'It's her!' Serkinski was forgotten. I sensed Stanislas lost in his memories, desperately trying to find something which would contradict the reality of this resurrection. When Mimi said two or three words in

Russian, I thought he would get up and leave. The situation was untenable. Mimi's over-eagerness was about to lose her gamble. Her natural grace saved her. Serkinski had many faults but he was no fool, and he had seen the danger. The subject of the film, the contract and casting, was dropped, and Serkinski began to behave as if his reason for coming to Paris had completely slipped his mind. He had a natural gift for mimicry: one minute he was Clark Gable, the next Charles Boyer, Marlene Dietrich, W. C. Fields, John Wayne – a repertoire which, in the circles he moved in, was always well received. Stanislas listened with a sort of frozen politeness and, paradoxically, it was only Mimi herself who saved the lunch from fiasco. At first her effervescence had drained away with the realization that she had identified herself with Nathalie too soon, but her confidence returned as Stanislas' expression softened. She became certain that he was no longer seeing Nathalie through her, but her, Mimi, through the fatal accident on the Moyenne Corniche and the girl-child to whom living had been such a joy. One would have had to be blind not to see that there was a storm blowing up, that two people unknown to each other an hour before had found themselves on the crest of a wave and could no longer see those who, still in the troughs, were swimming frantically to stay afloat. Mimi's twenty-two years against Stanislas' sixty-two: in some cases the difference is minimal. They were not going to marry or have children or grow old together. They were simply going to leave the table as quickly as possible, walk out of the restaurant without a backward glance, and make love while I discussed with Serkinski the contract to be signed between himself and Editions Saeta for the sale of the rights to *Singtime!* When they got up to leave, the producer began to talk slightly faster, with what I detected as a trace, just a trace, of anxiety, a hint of disappointment. This game did not include him. But his dignity, if not his self-respect, was in no danger. In reality, he was a happily married man, with a wife and children. For a short while, the desirable girl riding a bicycle naked in a Japanese garden had provided a diversion, but the day she became a star that amusement would represent a risk that Serkinski, who played hard in business but always safe in love, was unwilling to face up to. I think the events in the restaurant left him feeling a kind of cowardly relief. Mimi had been part of the furniture of his life, a little more than a Rolls or a Cadillac perhaps, but less than a big-budget production with forty elephants, twenty lions, ten crocodiles and a hot-air balloon.

I have not given the name of the restaurant. A grave error, Stanislas would have said. 'One does not lunch in *a* restaurant. One specifies which restaurant and where. One does not drink *a* wine, either. One drinks a burgundy or a claret of such and such a year, such and such a growth. Life is rich in details that novelists neglect because they know nothing of it, spending their lives in libraries, eating paper and drinking ink. Whenever I hear a man in a bar ordering *a* brandy I know he is a peasant who would be quite happy if one served him a cooking brandy. . . .'

So this lunch took place in the Grand Véfour, where Raymond Oliver had booked us the table dedicated to Jean Cocteau – the memory of whom had come to us as we walked through the gardens of the Palais-Royal, talking about the last time Stanislas had met him in the small apartment in the rue de Beaujolais. The mood was one of melancholy, as befits a garden at lunchtime when the children have disappeared and only the old people with time on their hands are left.

Exactly when Stanislas and Mimi slipped away I cannot really say. Perhaps we did not even see them go, so expected and inevitable was it. Serkinski had taken out his notebook and was making notes about the contract. Good manners demanded that neither of us make any reference to their abrupt departure. Serkinski drank several cups of coffee in quick succession, then began to smoke some quite horrible Italian cigarillos, acrid and evil-smelling things for which, he explained to me, he had developed a taste during the Italian campaign with Patton's army.

'Completely unsmokable as far as everyone else is concerned,' he said, 'but they bring back so many memories. I met my wife in Naples, you know. She's Italian.'

He looked at his watch.

'Three o'clock! They'll be in bed screwing by now. Does your friend always conduct his affairs at this speed?'

'Not all of them.'

'It must be some kind of record. I'll tell you, just to put things in perspective, that Mimi is not an easy girl. She'll show you her ass quite happily, but you try and lay a finger on it. . . . She's a sweet kid, a lovely girl, and she tells me everything, so you can tell your friend that he's only her number three. No kidding, and in her career, with her figure. . . . Mister Beren is some kind of champion. How old is he?'

'Sixty-two.'

'Well, he doesn't look it – and doesn't it give the rest of us something to hope for?'

The tables were emptying. We were among the last, and Serkinski rocked back on his chair in the pose of a man whose lunch has given him food for thought. I have not described his appearance – a matter of no great consequence in any case – but to be fair, he had none of the qualities one associates with one's idea of what film producers look like. He was not corpulent, nor bald, nor did he have a shock of white hair or wear loud ties or dubious jewellery. He was a compact man with a gaunt and expressive face and hooded eyes of a deep, shining brown. It was easy to imagine him as one of those men who fly into towering rages and subside again almost immediately. From the attention he was paying his surroundings in the Grand Véfour I could tell that he was sizing it up, engraving the flawless murals on his memory, for the day when one of his productions would need a set like the restaurant where he had decided to buy *Singtime!* and lost Mimi Bower.

The following day I drove him to the airport. Mimi and Stanislas had not reappeared. Serkinski caught me by the arm as I was about to leave.

'When you see Mimi again, you can tell her I'm happy for her, but that she mustn't forget to keep her work and her love-life apart. She can do it: although she hasn't quite made up her mind about her ambitions, she's a first-class kid. I'll tell you quite frankly that I prefer to see her fall in love with a man of sixty than with some gigolo who's going to wear her out looking for thrills and eat up her first big fee. But I've had time to appreciate how intelligent she is, so I don't think there's much chance of that happening. She reads for me, you know, and that's an incredible help. Whenever I see a page of type I get this feeling of *angst*. My analyst tells me there's very little chance of a cure. We spent months and months going back over my childhood to try and see how I was traumatized into becoming allergic to books, but we couldn't find anything. On the other hand, the angels gave me a great gift by making me an excellent judge of faces. I knew everything about Stanislas Beren within five minutes of meeting him yesterday. I can tell from the lines on his face that he has that strange mixture inside him of certainties and uncertainties which make the most interesting creative artists into what they are. It's the price you pay for talent. You can see it in his look and the mobility of his mouth when he pays his listener the compliment of uttering a few words.'

'I assure you that he does talk,' I replied, 'but it depends on his mood.'

'Does he get himself analyzed regularly?'

'Never. Psychoanalysis is one of those human extravagances which have always made him laugh.'

'He'll come round to it.'

'I doubt it.'

He seemed surprised. The flight for New York was announced over the public address. Serkinski clasped my hand and shook it energetically, as if he were trying to work up some courage.

'You know the thing that makes me most happy about this whole business? It's to see the look on my wife's face. She's a lovely lady, a bit on the fubsy side and maybe a bit wrapped up in her home and her kids. She lets me do what I want, but she's so happy when I go back to her that I get a thrill just thinking about the look on her face when I tell her I'm through with Mimi Bower. I know just what she'll do: she'll send the cook home for the evening and cook the tagliatelli herself. She makes the best tagliatelli in Beverly Hills, which is saying a hell of a lot. And in secret she'll light a candle to Mister Beren and pray for years of happiness for him and his new companion. Goodbye, my friend. . . .'

★

Shooting started a year later. Stanislas would probably have remained utterly uninterested in the screenplay and the adaptation generally, had Mimi not begged him to take an interest in it. Whenever he was interviewed on the subject, Stanislas repeated that having written a novel, he was perfectly satisfied with it as a novel, while Serkinski, once he was back in Hollywood, had assembled his screenwriters and told them to reconstruct the true puzzle of the lives of Vladimir and Nathalie. In short, the producer had decided to go beyond the fiction and find the facts that Stanislas had either glossed over or rewritten. This 'misunderstanding' was so total that there was talk of cancelling the contract and letting Serkinski and his writers tell whatever story they pleased; and the contract would have been cancelled but for Serkinski's sudden conviction that the title was a crucial element, perhaps the crucial element, in the film. According to his distributors *Singtime!* now stood a good chance of success on general release because sales of the book, which had only been modest for several years, had suddenly, thanks to a nostalgic revival, taken off. Faced with a stalemate, the producer gave way and Stanislas wrote a new screenplay which was, predictably, massacred during the shooting and, worse still, in the cutting room. However, there was something of it left in the final version, due largely to the acting of Mimi Bower, who was such a perfect Nathalie that those who remembered the real-life Nathalie were stunned by the likeness. The rest of the cast was of an almost equally high standard, for which Serkinski and the director, Joe Pressner, deserve all the credit. For the part of Vladimir they chose Ivan Eliner, a young Soviet actor who had recently defected to the West and for whom *Singtime!* became the start of a brilliant career. Serkinski's original idea had been to transpose the story to California, in breach of the contract which required the film to be shot in France. The weight of Stanislas' resistance sprang largely from the fact that he cared little whether the film was made or not. Mimi was almost constantly at his side and left him only to make frequent and rapid trips to Hollywood, where she finally persuaded Serkinski to change his mind. Thus the film was eventually made at Cap-Ferrat and, by an odd and unexpected chance, in the very house in which Nathalie and Vladimir had lived. It proved impossible to find a Duesenberg of the right type in any of the motor museums. Without hesitation the production team had a 'one-off' built which, in the final frames of the film, was driven into a tree by a stuntman. Yet another near-fatal snag struck the project when Stanislas found out that one of Serkinski's editors had sneaked in a scene which left no doubt about the incestuous nature of Nathalie's relationship with her brother. In the novel the reader is left to draw his own conclusions; indeed, he is free not to think about it at all. Serkinksi gave his word that the scene would not be used in the final cut, but at the world première, which took place in Sid Grauman's Chinese theatre in Hollywood, it was still intact. Stanislas had declined the invitation to attend and I was representing him in the producer's box, in the company of Mimi, the star of the evening. As if it were all a fairy story, she stared disbelievingly at the elegant and sparkling gathering which had already made up its mind, even before the screening, that the small blonde girl with forget-me-not eyes was to be its next darling. Sitting bolt upright on the edge of her chair, like a guest unsure of whether she will be admitted or not, Mimi masked her anxiety behind a dazzling smile. Dressed in white, with her neck and arms bare, she was being married to stardom. How many years would she be able to hold on to that charming candour which men find so attractive? In the film world where her future now lay, she was going to have to avoid the terrible traps and pitfalls which had caused the downfall of women as beautiful and talented as she; and Stanislas would not be there to guide her, to work through her scenes with her, to choose her perfumes and hairstyles, to teach her how to behave at table and to read Nabokov rather than Philip Roth, Faulkner rather than John dos Passos, Pynchon rather than Truman Capote. She had envisaged none of this, and in the wave of admiration which floated up to her from a roomful of people whose presence had been calculated by the mathematics of publicity, it was the one thing she must not be allowed to think about. She radiated such happiness that Serkinski and I were enveloped in it, along with a veiled and indefinable foreboding that some incident, some malicious quirk of life, was waiting in the wings to prick her bubble of joy.

When it came to the episode which presented her unequivocally in the arms of Ivan Eliner, I could say nothing. Perhaps Mimi had wanted the scene, and perhaps her hypocrisy was forgivable. The scene was cut in the version of the film distributed in France which was the only version Stanislas was likely to see. In fact he never saw the film at all, not out of any lack of curiosity, but because he could not bear the thought of seeing the screen bring to life Nathalie, and Mimi her double, at the same time.

Several times during shooting, in 1971 and 1972, I went to Cap-Ferrat to stay with Stanislas who, distracted by the atmosphere surrounding Mimi and the film crew, was fitfully writing the final stories for *L for London*,[1] whose publication was greeted by one critic with a venomous review entitled *F for Failure*. Félicité had sold La Désirade on their return from America and Stanislas was living in a room adjoining Mimi's in the Grand Hôtel du Cap. Mimi was woken by the hairdresser and make-up girl at six o'clock each morning so that she was ready for shooting to start at nine. She would knock on the partition wall, Stanislas would join her, and while she was being made ready for the cameras, they would go through her lines. Mimi's intensely serious attitude to her work was in stark contrast to the frivolous and volatile character of the girl-child that she embodied both on the set and off it. Stanislas refused to watch her during shooting, and when I was there we used to spend much of the time going for long walks along the coast road. He gave the impression of being happy, and anxious, at the same time; he was eager to talk to me to convince himself that everything he had been telling himself inside his head had some kind of reality. He badly needed a sympathetic interlocutor to help him believe in it all.

[1] *L comme Londres*, Editions Saeta, November 1972. The book was dedicated to Mimi Bower, who died two weeks after it was published.

'It can only turn out badly,' he would say. 'The difference in our ages is so great. But how can I deny myself Mimi? She nourishes me with her youth.'

'She says to me that she preys on you – did you know that she calls herself your vampire? – because of the multitude of things she can learn from you.'

'She is wrong. It is I who am the vampire. Oh, how will it end? It is intolerable to think that an external event, or a third party, might make the decision for her – or for me – and the premonition that she will leave me for another man is killing me by inches. So I shall have to leave her first. I have even fixed a date, you know: two weeks after the film is released.'

'Does she know?'

'No, not yet.'

'When will you tell her?'

'When the shooting is finished.'

In the end, he decided not to tell her until after the première in Hollywood so as not to mar her joy that day. During the screening at Grauman's, I could not help thinking how fragile was the happiness of this young and radiant woman, so blissfully unaware that her success and the parts she would soon be offered would part her from the man she loved and that he had already foreseen it. From the applause, from the departure in the sea of limousines ebbing slowly away, we went straight to the Beverly Hills Hotel where Mimi called Paris. With the eight hours' difference, we knew that Stanislas would be at the Saeta offices signing the review copies of *L for London*.

'Stani, the movie's wonderful. Everyone adored it.'

She motioned to the extension. I picked up the receiver.

'I am proud of you,' the distant voice replied.

Was he going to tell her of his decision? There was silence; he could not bring himself to dash the optimism audible in her excited, barely controlled voice.

'Stani, just about everyone is making me offers!'

'Accept them.'

'I'm going to turn them all down, because I want to be near you and I know you'd never live in Hollywood.

'Don't be silly. Accept.'

'I know you don't want to see the movie. It's because of Nathalie, isn't it?'

'I have forgotten Nathalie. I forgot her a long time ago. It is because of you that I did not want to see the film. It is you in flesh and blood that I love. You smell good and your skin is very pleasing on the tongue. Photographs do nothing for you.'

'Are you happy with your book?'

'As happy as I can be with anything. Actually, I am only happy about you. The book is dedicated to you.'

She turned towards me, looking lost, not knowing what this meant. With a gesture of my hand I tried to let her know this was his way of paying tribute to her.

'Are you pleased?' he asked anxiously.

'Of course I am. . . . M comes after L, doesn't it? So your next book will be called *M for Mimi*.'

'It's a promise.'

★

I flew back to Paris the following day. Mimi had to go on to Chicago, Philadelphia and New York with Serkinski, to be present at the gala screenings of the film. Between Philadelphia and New York, the film company's jet lost an engine and crash-landed on the freeway. Mimi Bower was the only casualty: the lovely girl who, three years earlier, had been photographed cycling down the avenues of a Japanese garden, floating languidly in a swimming pool and reading Freud on a zebra-skin sofa, the girl who had arrived for lunch at the Grand Véfour in a short skirt, an outsize sweater and a beret, and had left before the end of the meal with a man forty years older than her who had written a novel, long ignored by the public, but which she had fallen in love with. By some kind of dispensation, she had been spared the knowledge of Stanislas' decision. He learnt the news from the morning paper which the waiter at the Ritz had placed on his table with the breakfast tray.

'Have you heard?' he asked me on the 'phone.

'Yes.'

'How long ago?'

'Ten minutes.'

There followed a long silence. I guessed exactly what he was thinking. It had been he who had delivered the two-week reprieve. He had decided that they would part on the precise day that Mimi had died. Always the same obsession haunting him, that events might match what he had written.

'This time I wrote nothing down, and you are the only person to whom I said a word. Am I right?'

'Of course.'

'We had to stop seeing one another. I must just have thought about it too hard or too stubbornly.'

'But you were right. . . .'

There was a renewed silence.

'She was so different,' said Stanislas, 'from everything I have known. I cannot talk about love, because at my age the word ceases to have the same emotional charge it has in youth or maturity. What can I say about Mimi? She was like a fresh fruit within arm's reach; perhaps the last fruit on the fruit-stand. With something approaching reckless-ness I reached out and took her, satisfying one of those sudden desires that one knows will have to be paid for sooner or later. She disrupted my life, ruffled the surface of the tidy and wooden world I had retreated to. Now and again I was angry with her for intruding, but now that I have only silence left, I'm grateful to her for having reminded me of the emotion of meeting and the melancholy of departure, the fear of losing the person who revives the dead canvases of still lifes, and landscapes and souls rapt in cool evening breezes. . . .'

At the end of the morning, he was standing waiting for me in the Tuileries by his favourite Maillol statue, the smooth-skinned bronze of a young girl with an expression of purity on her face and a body of plump but gentle curves. The November day was so clear that had it not been for the bare flower-beds, the dull green of the lawns, the myopic blue of the cold sky and the passers-by hunched up in their overcoats, it could have been a day in summer.

'Maillol's ideal,' he said to me, 'is an infinitely soothing one. I can think of nothing that reassures me more than his pursuit of a beauty which, over the years, he amplified and simplified to the point of perfection. People were wrong to say that the faces of his girls were expressionless. Serenity is the noblest expression there is, nobler than anger or sadness or grief, which are transient moods of life and the easiest things in the world for the artist to portray. Although there is one exception, a little Pomona I saw once in a private collection, holding out a fruit in each hand. Maillol sculpted her in 1910, an early work that predates the serenity you can see in his Venuses and his Méditerranée in Perpignan. The little goddess's face has a kind of childish sorrow about it, a reflection of modesty dishonoured and left to brood in regret. . . . Enough. I hope you are free to lunch with me.'

'Of course.'

'I have booked a table at the Grand Véfour.'

I might have guessed. On the day Félicité had been buried at San Michele we had dined at the trattoria where, over the years, they had become increasingly regular customers. Stanislas had an idea that if one retraced one's footsteps one could somehow erase one's grief, deny it a foothold. So we walked down through the gardens of the Palais-Royal, between the rows of slender, denuded trees. There were the same old men with time on their hands as there had been two years before, sitting round-shouldered on the benches and warming their thin, blotchy hands in the sun. A small boy running past us suddenly sprawled headlong in the dust and lay there, arms outstretched. His mother grasped his collar with one hand and hauled him to his feet, dusting off his knees and front. There was anxiety written on the face of a girl coming towards us, then annoyance, then suddenly happiness: behind us a young man, bare-headed, was striding quickly towards her. We were not given Cocteau's table this time, but another, smaller one beneath the caryatid with the bunches of grapes in her hair, a downcast face, and a sidelong glance shaded by heavy eyelids. In a quick, self-conscious gesture, Stanislas stopped at the mirror and, with the palm of his hand, smoothed down the wisps of hair at his temples that had been ruffled by the breeze.

'I'm not only going grey, but bald too. Another year or two and I shall be able to strike just the right pose to impress all the friends and busybodies who come to pay their last respects. . . . You must not think that getting old is a dull business. It can actually be rather enjoyable if you can stop yourself thinking about the little wooden box and the decay that shares it with you. Did you know that when the Prince de Joinville went to fetch the Emperor's body from Saint Helena and the good doctor Guillard opened the coffin and folded back the shroud, Napoleon was still in extremely good shape? Admittedly his nose had deteriorated, but his chin and eyebrows were still intact and his teeth had scarcely gone yellow at all. They closed up the coffin and no one has thought to open it since, which is a shame. Then again, Napoleon was a quite exceptional man and there is every chance that I shall escape such morbid curiosity; unless they run out of room at San Michele one day and decide to get everybody to move up. Now I come to think of it, they were doing that the very day Félicité and I went there to choose a comfortable spot for ourselves. In the blink of an eye they emptied three coffins into one. The newly-dead are utterly ruthless, elbowing their elders out of the way with frightening brutality. Do you remember Arrigo Beyle, *il Milanese?* I thought I'd annoy him by ordering my headstone early. Stone, not marble; marble is much too cold. There is a craftsman I know in a tiny workshop in the Fondamente Nuove, a cheerful and charming man whose eyebrows are always white with dust from using the sander all day long, and he is at this moment carving the words "1908–19. . , Stanislas Beren, Parisian". The last two numbers will be your job. Stendhal was fond of Milan, but after a while he hardly ever went back, rather like me and Paris, except that nobody stops me in the street in Paris as they would have done Stendhal had he shown himself in Milan – being a diplomat, you see. In the end you always choose a city more for the friends you have there and the love affairs you've had than for its way of life or for its architecture. London is an unforgettable place, but I have very few friends there. Venice almost smothers you with its beauty. At least at San Michele, in Félicité's company, I shall be a little off the beaten track. People will not come and bother me quite so often. Perhaps you will, from time to time . . . and more and more rarely as the years go by; but we know one another well and we are both perfectly able to put up with each other's long silences. . . .'

On any other day I would have had no hesitation in cutting short such a garrulous and morbid speech. Today I could not. Behind the introspective contemplation of his own death lay the death of Mimi Bower, ever-present but not to be mentioned either now or in the future. After lunch we walked back to his hotel where the doorman warned him that there were journalists waiting to interview him and that the television people had been 'phoning non-stop to ask him to appear on the seven o'clock news. He sent a porter to collect his passport from the drawer in his bedside table. When it arrived he hailed a taxi and drove to Orly, where he boarded the first flight for London. The following day, and for a week afterwards, newspapers and magazines ran countless stories with photographs of him and Mimi together. Endless nonsense was written: that they had been about to marry; that following a bout of depression Stanislas was convalescing in a private clinic; and even that they had quarrelled because he had not been seen at the première. But in London he was safe. *Singtime!* was a runaway success in America, although under its French title *Les Temps heureux* it was much less enthusiastically received. The French, it seems, cannot bear to have 'their' stories told for them, nor – worse still – can they bear them filmed on their home ground.

I have almost overlooked one detail which is not without its place in the story. As we were walking back up the rue Saint-Honoré after lunch, just by the church of Saint-Roch, we were witness to an accident. An old man crossing the road at a green light was knocked down by a taxi. His lifeless body lay stretched out on the pavement. I can remember his grey raincoat, and his black trilby hat sitting in the gutter. Stanislas took my arm.

'You know what Stendhal said to his friend di Fiore one day? "There is nothing ridiculous in dying in the street, as long as it is an accident." He said that in 1841 and he died in 1842 – in the street. I don't know why that phrase keeps coming back to me.'

What can I say about the last five years? He was never where one expected him to be. Oh, he still spent time in Venice and London, but his comings and goings were erratic, no longer regulated by his fondness for Venice in summer and London in winter. He went to Venice for the christening of Adriana's first child, a boy she named Stanislas. Two years later she gave birth to a girl whom she christened Félicité. It was rumoured that Stanislas was the boy's father, and then perhaps also the little girl's father; which presupposed that he had continued to see Adriana after the death of Mimi Bower. Nothing is impossible. She spoke little and he had nothing to say to her. In a way, they were made for each other. Stanislas made flying visits to Paris. *L for London*, like all collections of short stories, had only moderate success. Two of the stories were adapted for French television, but he did not see them, just as he had declined to watch *Singtime!* Yet, strangely, his attitude towards his early books changed completely. He did not dismiss them exactly (or pretend to); but he had never re-read them, and now, quite suddenly, he picked them up one by one, correcting, cutting, rewriting and, in most cases, adding a preface for his new readers in which he tried to explain that the novel had to be read in the context of the viewpoint of its era. The gist of what he was saying was that the reader must be careful, because ways of life had changed so much and time had so accelerated that his novels had become historical novels and should be read as such, as one reads Balzac or Flaubert. He did not remove the far-fetched predictions like Jezero's lesson for the twentieth century embodied in his announcement to the sovereign that nations will crumble and that the coming of the European state will herald a golden age for its peoples. This, and similar instances of clumsiness, did not bother him. A novelist is no Pythian priestess, and in any case, the more glaring the error, the more enjoyable it is for the reader. What ages in a book is not the characters or their speech, but the author. Re-reading his books,

Stanislas perceived that in the course of two or three decades he had learned to tutor his prose, to be more economical with words, to make for the heart of the matter.

> If I were to rewrite my books entirely, I should restrict myself to a crisp ten-page summary in which everything that mattered would' be said. Even so, ten pages . . . ten pages is a lot.[1]

He would arrive in Paris unannounced, pay a short visit to Emeline Aureo who had had a stroke and was, unfortunately, vegetating in a clinic in Saint-Cloud, then come to my office and take me to lunch or dinner. We went to the places we had always been to, never mentioning – where was the need? – the fact that Félicité had often been there, or Audrey or Mimi. Now and again we would go down to the place de la Sorbonne and have a sandwich and a beer on the terrace of one of the cafés. Then I could sense Stanislas' gaze scanning the students coming out of the Sorbonne, seeking the silhouette of André Garrett, the man who had been his only friend.

Stanislas had not aged physically, but he confessed to some rather odd sensations. 'I thought I was one of those people who do not feel the cold. I know that if I had been susceptible to it when I was young I would definitely have died. Well, now I don't seem to be able to stop shivering. Wherever I go my feet feel as if they are on fire. In Paris I do not dare open the window. Yesterday in Lausanne, the lobby of the Beau-Rivage seemed so icy that I put my hand on one of the radiators, only to find that it was burning. I looked around at the other people in the room. They were all, without exception, old and yellow and wizened, sitting in enormous armchairs clutching either walking-sticks or crutches. I felt as if I were in one of those houses of the dead they used to have in China before Mao came along. You know, the old people used to arrive with a bundle of belongings, stretch out on a board and quietly give up the ghost. I could not get away fast enough. Did I tell you? I am leaving for Marrakesh tomorrow. Everybody has done their best to put me off going because it is so scorchingly hot there in June, but at least I shan't freeze. Have you ever read a more frightful story than *Master and Man*, with the death of Vassili Andreich, Nikita falling asleep and the bay horse standing frozen stiff between the shafts?'

'You must be ill.'

---

[1] Preface to *Cryptogram*, new ed., 1973.

'Not a bit. I am looking after myself like a good sixty-year-old, keeping an eye on my cholesterol, urea, albumen, and blood count. It's great fun. Every six months they send me a chart which I have taught myself to decipher. The diagnosis is quite clear: I am not suffering from anything. Except the cold. . . .'

'The reason you're cold is because you're not writing anything these days.'

'I once had stories to tell, and I told them. I haven't any more, so I shall keep my counsel.'

'I know you've given up the idea of doing *Bernis in Venice*, but there are other subjects. Why not *Stendhal in Milan*?'

'Because it's beyond me.'

'What makes you think that?'

'Because I know. My literary life is over. The only thing left to be published is *Where Are You Dying Tonight?* That will be your job.'

*

In those last five years I had very little news of him. Postcards announced his presence in Greece, then Turkey, then Spain, and in Portugal where he met Mario Mendosa again. After which he came back to London, or Venice, 'like a dog returning to its kennel,' as he said. In the course of these wanderings there were short-lived friendships, infatuations for other, sometimes eccentric, travellers he came across in hotels, bars, aeroplanes. Their charms were soon exhausted and he withdrew from these associations as quickly as he had formed them. Sometimes when the loneliness of an hotel weighed upon him, he would urge me to come and spend a couple of days with him. Thus I met him in Guéthary where he was re-reading Toulet, in Vichy where he was re-reading the whole of Larbaud, in Barbezieux where he went out for long walks with a copy of *Le Bonheur de Barbezieux* under his arm, imitating Chardonne's way of speaking; but it was in the house in Chelsea and the apartment on the Largo Fortunio that I joined him most frequently, spending long evenings with him after dinner at the Guinea Pig or the George and Dragon, or Simonetti's which he was particularly fond of.

'I stop feeling cold when you come.'

'Why don't you stay in Paris more often?'

'I've lost the habit. Paris frightens me. To tell the truth, everything frightens me.'

He used to open his drawers and take out fistfuls of photographs and letters and cuttings which Félicité had glued into albums of cartridge paper.

'Life is a lengthy business! So many things happen. Faces are uncovered, then fade into the distance, come back ravaged, and turn hazy with memory's neglect. By the end there is such a crush of people.'

So we opened fat envelopes stuffed with letters which he sniffed and threw on the fire.

'It would be better not to keep anything. I must have written too many letters too. Try and remember one day to get back the ones I sent to Eva Moore, will you? I shouldn't want them to be left lying around. The whole thing was a mistake. We all make them. Actually, I had a rather funny experience with her once. It was in 1956 or 1957, I can't remember which. For about three months I had had a wire-haired dachshund. We two got on extremely well together. Unfortunately I wasn't allowed to take him to London with me, and because of that I had not set foot there for quite some weeks. Eva was living in Sussex at the time – I think she still does – and so she came to visit me in Paris. But we felt uncomfortable in Paris, or rather she did, because she was scared stiff of bumping into somebody she knew. We decided to go and hide out in Biarritz. I put Günther – the dachshund – into kennels, and off we went in my car. Eva was tremendously excited, whereas I was a little bit sad. The funny thing was that several times on the way I caught myself stroking Eva's thigh, just where, normally, Günther used to lie asleep. Naturally Eva saw no harm in my stroking her thigh, but this unsettling case of mistaken identity became worse during the three days we spent at the Hôtel du Palais. All the time I was thinking of Günther's imploring eyes when I left him at the kennels. I shan't pretend that my feelings for Eva were of the highest order; and to my discredit, all through those three days that vision of my dachshund constantly came between us. One night I awoke with a start, thinking I had heard a dog barking, and I touched Eva's nose to see whether it was hot or cold. Another time, as we were walking down the avenue de la Chambre d'Amour – a name which was an absolute inspiration to my companion – I stopped listening to the utterly dull story she was telling, to speak to a lady being taken for a walk by a dachshund who was Günther's spit and image. Eva stormed off back to the hotel and packed her case, which I must say I didn't really mind at all. There are enormous numbers of women one can spend the most delightful evenings, and even nights, with, but who become a little too much twenty-four hours a day. Having said that, her jealousy of the dachshund was quite justified: he was much more engaging than she was. Given the choice, I didn't hesitate. We never saw each other again.'

'What about Günther?'

'I went to fetch him the minute I got back to Paris. He gave me such a look of reproach I thought he would never forgive me. As we came out of the kennels he suddenly dashed into the road. He was run over by a car. I've not had a dog since. . . . Ah, here's a photograph of Eva.'

A woman with short, curly hair, sitting on the lawn of an English country house, her long neck outstretched and her lips pursed, blowing smoke rings: her first and second fingers were brandishing a cigarette-holder. How old was she? Thirty at the most. So now she would be in her fifties. I jotted down the address. Stanislas seemed preoccupied by the idea that his letters might fall into the hands of a stranger.

The odd thing about Stanislas was that he sometimes went to great lengths to disguise his enjoyment of life. It was a natural reflex of his, to protect himself from himself, the ultimate reticence of a man who was still favoured by life and yet looked constantly and anxiously over his shoulder at his past.

'All my life I have refused to commit myself to causes, so people have jumped to the conclusion – wrongly – that somehow I lacked that dimension of commitment. Your father and I decided, when we were very young, to take the serious things in life as unseriously as we could. Everything that people assured us was of overriding importance seemed laughable to us, and by the same token everything that was fashionably regarded as trivial always seemed worth investigating. When André fell victim to the war, I vowed to myself that I would keep our promise to disregard the march of history which, in relation to the goal people claimed to be striving for, seemed more frivolous and criminal as time went on. I had already paid my price, in any case.'

'When?'

'Until I arrived in Paris, my childhood had been dreadful. I shan't ever tell you where or how, but I lived the life of a savage. Constantly on the watch for enemies, tensed for the slightest noise, rigid with cold and hunger and fear. I killed a man too, when I was sixteen. With a rifle, but at close enough range to see him die. . . .'

He broke off, as if he regretted his admission, disclosing something which had, I was now sure, been tormenting him in secret for most of his life. But he had said it, and in saying it had broken his pact with himself. After a moment he went on, 'When I was sure he had stopped moving, I went nearer. Picture a young soldier lying on his back, his eyes wide open and his face very pale. Take away his thick homespun greatcoat, his helmet and cartridge-belts and he would have looked almost as young as I did. I wanted to close his eyes, but somebody grabbed me by the leg and I fell on top of him. My mouth met his cheek and I planted a hasty kiss on his beardless and still warm skin. What happened afterwards is a little hazy. . . . I think they hid me in a grotto; I know I sobbed for hours. Of course it was either me or him, but then why, if I had really hated him, was he not mourning *me* lying there under a freezing sky, with a calm expression on my face which would always stay with him in his memory as a single, searing regret? . . . It was after this that they sent me to France. Perhaps they had some vague idea that they might salvage something for the future by sending me away. You can see how disappointed they must have been when I went back five years later. . . . I saw them in a new light too. They were just madmen whose dream had ended in banditry. They branded my arm and I left them. Félicité and your father had the tact not to ask me for any explanations. . . . Later, there were other fugues which I find harder to justify, but that first one was the flight of a man haunted by the face of a dead boy. . . . I steeled myself and waited for the reckoning. . . . It hasn't come, at least not yet. . . .'

We were sitting on the beach at the Lido. Every time we bathed there, his thoughts returned to the invisible Dalmatian coast beyond the horizon. He had admitted a great deal. He would not say any more. What must his feelings have been when he arrived in the fourth form at Janson-de-Sailly, among middle-class children who wrapped themselves in thick mufflers to go outside and play in the quad? The only gunshots they had heard were on shoots with their fathers. They got indigestion from eating too many of the chocolates they bought from the concierge. They were frightened of the dark when their parents left them alone in the apartment for an evening. They squirmed with anxiety when the master scanned the form for a victim to recite *Le Lac*. Stanislas could have, should have been contemptuous of them. Instead he had waited in silence, observing them, coming to an understanding of them. From this had come the parting of the ways, and Stanislas' second career.

I looked at him a half-century later. His torso and his muscular legs were thickening with age. His broad hands with their short fingers could crack a nut in their palm. The day before, in the middle of the riva degli Schiavoni, I had seen Stanislas grab the collar of a scruffily dressed young man who was beating up a girl and tearing her clothes in front of an apathetic crowd of passers-by. The man had fallen, then picked himself up and charged at Stanislas who had stopped him with a kick in the stomach. There was nothing wrong with his health. But he had given up writing and he talked more fondly about the thirties than about the seventies. Was he still seeing Adriana? From something he said, I suspect that his vigour was not what it had been, and that his pride prevented him from taking the field where once he had shone sufficiently for many a woman to court his favour; unless Adriana, now in full bloom but still dutiful and grateful to him, had a simple enough heart to accept him as he was, less distinguished perhaps, but more considerate.

At the end of the summer of 1977, prompted by some kind of prescience, Stanislas 'phoned me at the Saeta offices. I told him that Emeline Aureo was dying. He arrived the following day, and together we followed to Montparnasse cemetery the coffin of the woman whose devotion should surely have earned her a sainthood. On the way back Stanislas' eyes misted over.

'The last witnesses are disappearing. At least I've passed on one or two stories to you.'

He took the train for London the same evening. As he got out of the taxi in front of the house in Chelsea, a man running along the pavement collided with him. Whether he had the chance to see what was happening or not, we cannot tell. Most likely he did not. Two shots rang out, missing the fugitive but killing Stanislas outright.

The taxi driver, busy counting his fare, saw nothing. Two passersby claimed they saw a man in a green raincoat, another a man in a blue sweater and trousers. Both swarthy, of course. All street-killers are swarthy; it is one of those things, a cut-and-dried fact. When people do not know, they invent. It was said . . . it was said . . . it will still be said in ten years' time that Stanislas died from the bullets of a jealous husband's gun, that he was writing a novel on the London underworld and had to be silenced for fear of his indiscretions, that he was in close touch with a Serbian terrorist organization and had been gunned down by their Croatian enemies, or vice-versa. So it went on. . . . Stanislas had cuckolded no one; certainly he knew one or two bar-keepers in Soho but it had never occurred to him to write anything on London's criminal fraternity; and as for Croatian and Serbian terrorist organizations, he was totally ignorant of their activities and had the opportunity to enlist presented itself, his steps in the opposite direction would have been rapid and immediate. However much legend and the public's taste for mystery may suffer by it, Stanislas' death cannot be seen as anything other than an accident. Many others die the same way without any fuss being made beyond the appearance of a new statistic in the inside pages of the newspapers, but because of who he was, an accident caused by the most banal, the most everyday terrorist act inflamed the public's imagination. Theories multiplied, everyone claimed to have found the key to this intolerably futile murder. With the police's failure to trace either the fugitive or the killer, it seemed impossible for people to accept that Stanislas was the victim of one of those thousands of murders every year which are never explained. I remembered his premonition the day we were walking down the rue Saint-Honoré and saw an old man knocked down by a car: 'There is nothing wrong in dying in the street, as long as it is an accident.' He was right. Apart from the bloodstain on the pavement, which had been washed away almost immediately by the rain, it was a clean and painless death. He was already in his coffin when I arrived, but Harry Dawson, who had accompanied him on his exploration of the doors and door-knockers of London, assured me that, both bullets having penetrated his heart, the expression on his face was peaceful, even one of relief, like that of the young soldier Stanislas had shot fifty years before.

Three days later, on the long black gondola with the golden lions, Stanislas crossed the lagoon for the last time on his way to San Michele. The pink ochre walls cordoned with a lacework of white marble floated on the green waters, encircling the black cypresses. Stanislas would join Félicité beneath a sky flaked with small clouds whose projected shadows scudded across the waters. We had often come here, to visit Félicité and, dry-eyed, call to mind the times gone by; we had been enraptured by the profuse vegetation that protected the tombs from the rippling heat of the sun: steadfast, straight-backed cypresses, giant rose bushes, and acacias whose coral-coloured berries mingled with the gravel of the paths. Monks and nuns were consigned to the earth in a separate part of the cemetery, and there was a triangular patch of ground given over to the military who slept beneath crosses maintained with respectful devotion by the young recruits.

As the funeral gondola arrived the heavy wrought-iron gates opened; the pall-bearers stepped ashore with the coffin onto the seaweed-mantled steps and the cortège made its way slowly down the path to where the gravestone had been laid to one side and the hole opened up. As I went by I saluted, as we had always done when

Stanislas was alive, the martial bust of General Cadorin and the medallion of his much-loved wife, the Italian matron in all her horror. They would be neighbours to the Berens, although I doubted that any real intimacy would result, even when the cemetery had closed its gates to the mourners and the peace of a starry night descended on the dead souls who walked dreamily between the cypresses. The flat stone, long ready, was finally laid over the two coffins lying side by side: Félicité Beren, 1895–1968, Stanislas Beren, 1908–1977, Parisians.

On the return journey, quickly taking leave of the few friends present and not wanting to see Adriana's grief-swollen face, I jumped aboard the first vaporetto that came along, thinking it was going to Venice. Before long, however, I found myself at Torcello, where Stanislas had so liked to come and work in one of the rooms at Cipriani's Locanda. If we are to believe that the dead still exercise dominion over us in the days following the burial, then I cannot doubt that Stanislas compelled me to pay him the kind of tribute he preferred: to lunch in the garden among the pomegranate trees, and to order his usual choice of dishes: Parma ham with melon, langoustines from the Adriatic, Neapolitan ice-cream. At this very table he had one day read to me the *Lustful Sonnets of Messer Pietro Aretino*, 'called the scourge of princes, the magnificent, the divine'. His voice carried, and four Englishmen lunching at the next table had stopped talking to listen to the choice string of savoury Italian obscenities:

Fottiamci, anima mia, fottiamci presto,
Poiche tutti per fotter nati siamo . . .

At the next table a young woman in a leather blouson, her legs encased in a pair of tight-fitting, faded jeans, her blonde hair tied in a pony-tail, opened her bag, took out a book and, having removed her very dark sunglasses, began to read it. In Stanislas' works many such silhouettes come and go, poetic young women whose profiles he caught and set for an instant, shafts of light piercing a moment of tedium or lassitude. This woman would have pleased him with her air of independence, the way she drank her red wine without taking her eyes from the book and stabbed at the small artichokes – *carciofini* – on her plate, or occasionally stopped reading, replaced her sunglasses and watched, thoughtfully, as the waiters in white jackets moved between the tables, as if a phrase from the book corresponded to the animation of the open-air restaurant. She could have played Albina

Sansovino, heroine of *The Bee*, or even Redja Matchka in *The Countdown*, although she was not as provocative as that ginger-haired feline beauty; and she had something of Audrey's charm too, although one could see she was headstrong and sure of herself. When she picked up her book again after a moment's reflection, I caught sight of the title: *L for London* in the French paperback edition, with a photograph of the author on the cover. She was at the beginning and so was reading the first story, the account of John Mine and his love affair with Giorgione's *Tempest*.

I was filled with an intense feeling of joy, as if the last days had been only a bad dream. Stanislas had returned to my side with his sardonic, urbane sense of humour to extinguish all the traces of his horrible and gratuitous death and the moment when I had seen his coffin lowered to rest beside Félicité's in the vault at San Michele. This garden flooded with sunlight was his, this young woman sitting in profile was his: we had been reunited at Torcello. In a moment I would ask him to go and stand on the hump-backed bridge over the inland canal so that I could photograph him looking at his reflection in the glassy, greenish water; no, I already had that photograph, from the far bank: the subject was too small, the reflection invisible, the sky dirty.

The maître d'hôtel took the message I had scribbled on the back of a postcard and placed it on the young woman's table: 'Did you know that the author of the book you're reading was buried barely an hour ago at San Michele?' She turned her head and put down her book. The maître d'hôtel waited for the sign to move the covers together. I walked over to the young woman who was holding the postcard in her hand.

'I know,' she said. 'I was there.'

'I didn't see you.'

'You weren't looking at anybody. I am Sheila Moore. My mother's name is Eva. She was a very good friend of Stanislas Beren.'

'My turn to say I know.'

'Please sit down. We can finish lunch together.'

The perfect Venetian, with as much pleasure as Paolo Carlotto had taken in bringing together Stanislas and Sister Annunciata, the maître d'hôtel moved my cover to Sheila's table. She put her sunglasses back on, but not before I saw the colour of her eyes, which were a soft shade of green.

'I came to ask you a question,' she said. 'A very important question. Do you know if I am Stanislas Beren's daughter?'

'How old are you?'

'Twenty.'

'And who put this extraordinary idea into your head?'

'Mother did. Didn't they spend three days together in Biarritz, just over twenty years ago?'

'Yes. As the result of which, they quarrelled and never set eyes on each other again.'

I told her the story of Günther, the dachshund. She seemed disappointed.

'Mother must have dreamt it.'

'In any case,' I said, 'you don't look like him at all.'

'I don't look like Eva, either.'

'When did she tell you this fascinating piece of news?'

'Five years ago. We'd been to London for the première of *Singtime!* I'd enjoyed the film a lot and couldn't stop talking about it. Then Mother said that Stanislas Beren had been her lover, that she had about a hundred of his letters and that he was my father.'

'Well, to be perfectly honest, I don't know anything about it. It never occurred to Stanislas, I don't think.'

'It's very odd. Mother talks about him all the time these days. Did he ever talk to you about her?'

'Twice, and both times to ask me to get his letters back. I don't know why he was so preoccupied with them.'

She stretched out her hand to the large leather bag from which she had taken her copy of *L for London*.

'I've got the letters,' she said.

'Here?'

'Yes. Mother wanted to make a rather theatrical gesture. I was supposed to toss the letters into the grave, on top of his coffin. I don't know what stopped me.'

'Have you read them?'

'Of course I have.'

'So you must know why Stanislas didn't want them to be made public.'

'No, quite frankly I can't see why he should have minded. They're very nice letters. A bit overdone maybe, but I think he found Mother terribly attractive and he credited her with being more sensitive and more intelligent than she actually was. I should know, shouldn't I? I suppose he must have become disillusioned with her, come to his senses, and then regretted all his high-flown declarations.'

So after Audrey's death, he had tried to forget by inventing another love affair, only to see, as rationality returned, just how illusory and imaginary it all was. Once he was able to look at it coldly and dispassionately, the adventure – crowned by the comic events in Biarritz – had seemed an utterly unworthy successor to Audrey's memory.

'What will you do with the letters now?' I asked.

'Burn them.'

'That seems a very good idea to me.'

She laid a fat envelope on the table. A hundred letters? If there were a hundred of anything in it, they could not be more than those countless short notes he wrote when the mood took him during the day, and especially when he had sleepless nights. One of the notes had slipped out of the envelope and I reached for it.

'No,' she said quickly. 'You mustn't. Nobody must.'

'But you've read them.'

'I shouldn't have.'

She called the maître d'hôtel and asked him to burn the envelope on the charcoal grill in the corner of the garden.

The admirable thing about the Italians is that all extravagant behaviour on the part of foreigners – though only foreigners – is accepted as perfectly normal. There was one problem: the two crayfish at present occupying the grill for a table of Americans. But as soon as they were done, the letters would be thrown on the fire, he promised: *'Io giuro!'* A quarter of an hour later, nothing remained of Stanislas' mistake.

'Are you satisfied?' she asked.

'Me? No. But he ought to be.'

She shrugged her shoulders. There was nothing to be gained from thinking about it any more.

'Do you think his story about John Mine is true?' she asked.

'I shouldn't think so. He invented very freely and easily. He might have seen a couple like the Mines at the Accademia one day. You only have to add his own passion for Giorgione, and you have the recipe.'

We had finished drinking the *espressi* when she took off her dark glasses and offered me her face, bare and unadorned.

'Can't you see any traces of him in me?'

'No. Although he might well have imagined a girl like you. When I first saw you just now, I thought to myself how much you were the kind of woman he found attractive, and that there was even something of Albina Sansovino in *The Bee* about you.'

'I've read all Stanislas Beren's books, and I don't like the idea of being compared to Albina Sansovino.'

'I wasn't talking about her character, more her looks.'

'Perhaps I'm not so wide of the mark then. There is a sort of link between us if I look like the kind of woman he would have imagined.'

'No one can prove otherwise, can they?'

Had I annoyed her? She put her sunglasses back on and called the maître d'hôtel.

'No, let me pay for lunch,' I said.

'Yes, I think you owe me that. . . . There's a boat at three. I must be going.'

'As you like. I'm only sorry you've been disappointed about Stanislas Beren.'

'I'm not disappointed. My conviction is too strong.'

She stood up, putting the copy of *L for London* back in her bag.

'I wasn't going to tell you this . . . but after all, why not? One of the reasons for my interest in Stanislas Beren is because I am a writer too. . . .'

'Have you had anything published yet?'

'I've got a book coming out next month in London.'

'That may not prove a thing. There were no writers in Stanislas' family. His was a spontaneous generation.'

'I think talent's inherited far more often.'

Others had identified themselves with Stanislas Beren's characters. Now it was Sheila Moore's turn, and she had decided that she was the fruit of his labours in every sense of the word. But with his instinctive distrust of such things Stanislas had always denied claims to his paternity. Eva Moore's daughter was free to think whatever she liked, but her search added a dimension of pathos to a character ill at ease beneath her appearance of aloofness. As she walked away without a goodbye I had the fleeting impression – impossible to pin down because it disappeared immediately – that I had seen that silhouette and bearing before, that Stanislas had often turned his back on someone or something that had contradicted him or offended him with the same abruptness. The idea lasted a split-second, then vanished; yet it was strong enough to leave a trace in the memory, strong enough for a doubt to take root. A moment before, she had said the only thing that mattered when she said her mother must have dreamt it. But who had been dreaming, Eva Moore – or Stanislas Beren? The idea of walking out on a woman because one is haunted by the sad, reproachful eyes of one's pet dog is plainly a novelist's idea: one amusing enough perhaps for a man to sacrifice a night's 'machismo' for the sake of it.

I have not seen her again. Two months later the *Times Literary Supplement* published an interview with the young novelist I have called Sheila Moore. Her book seemed to do very well, perhaps rather more because she was young and photographed well than because of the (genuine) quality of her novel. Stanislas Beren's name was mentioned three times in the course of the interview.

Shortly after my return from Venice, I got hold of the key to the safe in the house in Chelsea. In it there was a green file, on which had been written, painstakingly and in capital letters:

WHERE ARE YOU DYING TONIGHT?
A NARRATIVE BY S. BEREN

The file was empty but for a note torn from a pad: 'My apologies, dear boy. There's no point in your looking for the manuscript. I have destroyed it. All things considered, Audrey's story belongs to me alone. The thought that were I to have an accident, these pages could be read by all and sundry, has suddenly become intolerable. S. B., 2nd June 1977.'